PRAISE FOR
THE WICKED COMETH

'Beguiling' *Stylist*

'Carlin can tell a good story' *Observer*

'Splendidly diverting' *Irish Times*

'Contains lovely lyrical writing . . .
and a heady romance at its heart' *Sunday Express*

'A sterling, historical, dark, twisty novel'
Kaite Welsh, Radio 4 Open Book

'This deliciously dark confection of a novel has as
many twists and turns as the London backstreets'
Ruth Hogan, author of *The Keeper of Lost Things*

'Charming and a delight to read' *Yorkshire Post*

'The darkest corners of Georgian London are gleefully
drawn in this brilliant story' *Emerald Street*

ABOUT THE AUTHOR

Laura Carlin left school at 16 to work in retail banking, and it was only after leaving her job to write full time that she discovered her passion for storytelling and exploring pockets of history through fiction. She lives in a book-filled house in beautiful rural Derbyshire with her family (and a very naughty cat). When she's not writing she enjoys walking in the surrounding Peak District. *The Wicked Cometh* is her first novel.

the
WICKED
COMETH

Laura Carlin

HODDER

First published in Great Britain in 2018 by Hodder & Stoughton
An Hachette UK company

This paperback edition published in 2019

3

Copyright © Laura Carlin 2018

A CIP catalogue record for this title is available from the British Library

Paperback ISBN 978 1 473 66139 4

Typeset in Fournier MT by Palimpsest Book Production Ltd, Falkirk,
Stirlingshire

Printed and bound in Great Britain by Clays Ltd, Elcograf S.p.A.

Hodder & Stoughton policy is to use papers that are natural, renewable and
recyclable products and made from wood grown in sustainable forests. The
logging and manufacturing processes are expected to conform to the
environmental regulations of the country of origin.

Hodder & Stoughton Ltd
Carmelite House
50 Victoria Embankment
London EC4Y 0DZ

www.hodder.co.uk

For Shirl,
with thanks and love

WHEN
THE
WICKED
COMETH,
THEN
COMETH
ALSO
CONTEMPT,
AND
WITH
IGNOMINY
REPROACH.

Proverbs XVIII, 3

The Morning Herald

SUPPOSED DISAPPEARANCE IN THE BELVEDERE ROAD

THIS NEWSPAPER HAS TAKEN NOTE THAT THE PAST MONTH HAS BEEN REMARKABLE FOR THE PREVALENCE OF CASES WHERE MEN, WOMEN AND CHILDREN ARE DECLARED MISSING. SCARCELY A WEEK PASSES WITHOUT THE OCCURRENCE OF AN INCIDENT OF THIS TYPE.

Such fears may indeed be well founded and made but too evident by the following account, the particulars of which we are about to lay before our readers.

We study the tale of an unfortunate, known familiarly by the name Johnnie Hogget.

On Tuesday afternoon of the 6th inst. between five and six o'clock, Johnnie Hogget, fourteen years of age, was making his way from his place of industry at Mr Sturtevant's, the soap boilers.

Master Hogget had been seen for some time loitering in the region of the Belvedere Road and it was in this quarter that the lad was last witnessed and then seen no more. Up to a late hour the following day, no one could be found who could add anything material to come at a reason for his disappearance.

The lad was in perfect health, of good repute and regular habits, and his respectable but unfortunate parents report that his absence is most out of character.

So, is Master Hogget another name to be added to the growing list of missing persons in the *Police Gazette*, or is his tale one of uncorrupted innocence?

Perhaps it is both erroneous and presumptuous of this journal to call out a parallel between these events. Yet, equally, an increasing degree of discontent prevails in the minds of the public and suspicion arises that a diabolical transaction may have taken place.

We have no intent to alarm our readers and it can only be hoped that Master Hogget, perhaps led astray by the inducement of good fortune or the promise of adventure, will soon be returned to the loving arms of his family.

CHAPTER ONE

Do you think you know London? They say it's the finest city in all of Europe. Perhaps you once stood and marvelled at the dome of St Paul's? Or took a ride on a passenger craft and wove your way past the wherries and steamers as the great Thames carried you to the heart of the city beneath the shadows of Blackfriars Bridge. And then, having paid your half-crown to the driver on the box, did you jounce along in a hackney carriage on your way to Vauxhall, humming a catchy little ditty? Or perhaps took a seat on Shillibeer's omnibus instead? Did you go from Paddington to the Bank, stopping at The Unicorn for beefsteak with oyster sauce?

Because that's all there is to know about London, isn't it? Well, that is what I once thought. No, more than that, it's the London I believed in, and its flavour and spices season my earliest memory.

I am sitting on my mother's lap in the parlour.

'Try not to fall asleep, Hester,' she whispers. 'You're too heavy for that now.' But her voice, with its warmth and softness, only serves to make me sleepier. The next memory is of my eyes snapping open, of my feet hitting cold flagstones as I am jolted awake by the sound of carriage wheels turning, then grinding to a halt outside. The evening air tingles against my skin and the rustle of Mama's skirts fills my ears; Papa has returned from London.

He lifts me off the ground and folds me in his arms. I breathe in the scents that rise from his cape: tobacco from the pipe he would have smoked; the spiced mutton he took for supper; the leather from the carriage seats and the cold night air. His whiskers brush my cheek as he kisses me and he lifts me high, higher. His hands are tucked under my arms as he raises me and swings me round and round, his deep-voiced mirth thrums a melody matched only by Mama's trilling laughter, and the music of their happiness is loud in my ears.

We return to the warmth of the parlour and Papa talks of London; of the great men he has met and the magnificent buildings he has seen. His eyes light up when he tells of the wondrous steamer that glided over the surface of the Thames: no oars, no sails, just the science of steam-power. How fascinated he was by the new exhibition of Greek sculptures at the British Museum. With his words he paints a picture of vitality and excitement and the splashes of colour cover the canvas of my dreams.

At three years old, I truly believed London was the most splendid city in all of Europe and that Mama and Papa's laughter would never be lost to me. But that was then, and fifteen years is a long time. Sometimes in life, incidents arise, quite unlooked for, and before you know it fate has changed the course of your destiny.

It is now the autumn of 1831 and my parents are both dead. Three babes lost at birth over the years: two brothers and a sister who I never held, never played games with. Three souls cut down in the springtime of their lives, to winter beneath the dust forever more. Mama passed away after giving birth to a fourth stillborn child, to be named Thomas, when I was eleven. Papa was taken by typhoid fever six months later. In less than a twelvemonth, death had snuffed out their lives like a wet candlewick, and I was without a family.

I left our parsonage in the Lincolnshire Wolds some six years ago. As the house was owned by the church, there was nothing to bequeath to me save a handful of mementos. Now I live in London with Papa's gardener, Jacob, and his wife, Meg. They encouraged me to call them Uncle and Aunt; they aren't blood relations but they took me in when no one else would. And my London isn't the one Papa visited, or the one you think you might know; of that I am certain.

Our district is to the north and to the east. Instead of the majesty of Westminster Abbey and the grandeur of the Banqueting House, here the houses spill over each other; dishevelled and ugly. A sickly, rotten stench rises from the streets and the rain-bloated gutters. Some thoroughfares bulge with black mud where pools of fetid water have collected, while others are narrow and meandering. All are swart with the lack of daylight and connected by alleyways and byways that seep over the scabbed ground.

Between Virginia Row and Austin Street there is a pile of dwellings to the right, a heap of dwellings to the left. It is a place where the houses are so close together that dawn is never satisfied and dusk is quick to come. To the right of the last wooden house, warped and stooping, there is a covered alleyway no wider than a whip thong. At the end of the alleyway there is a yard; small as a poke, never gladdened by the warmth of the sun. In the far corner of that yard, behind a door that hangs loose on its leather hinges, is a room. It is a small room with a brick and dirt floor. This room is the centre of my London. I cannot and will not call it home, but it is the place where I live.

It is in this room that I wake and stretch the stiffness from my limbs. The hemp mat and horse-rug have done little to protect me from the night air. We used to have mattresses and coverlets, but last year's frost necessitated their sacrifice as fuel. I take the boots I've been using as a pillow and pull them onto my feet. The leather is thin and they are down at heel, but my breath has at least left some warmth in them. I have no laces, so I use a twist of rag.

I am stupefied by the chilliness. It's not a biting cold but a clammy one; a wet washrag against my skin. A line of washing, gently dripping, is strung from corner to corner but there is not enough air to dry even a pocket-handkerchief. The wainscoting and plaster has long since rotted from the sagging walls and a breath of mist hovers midway between the ceiling and floor.

I yawn and my breath adds to this milky fog. The terrier in the corner, Missy, raises her head and sniffs the air. Her five pups wriggle, whimper and then take suck. Missy lowers her head then raises it again, her ears pricked towards the door. I listen too, but can't hear anything.

A breeze blows ash over the floor, carpeting the dirt with a veneer of grey velvet. The fire is down to its last cinder. I sit on the stool and prod the ashes, but can do no more than rattle the rust from the poker. The twins, asleep beneath the table where the iron washtub used to be, begin to stir. My belly gives a loud grumble, but the quartern loaf has all gone and there is no breakfast to be had.

'That you, Hester?'

It's Aunt Meg calling from outside.

'You awake, dearie?' she tries again.

I smooth my hair and tuck it behind my ears. It used to be thick and glossy, the colour of flax; locks that Mama used to brush for me a hundred times every evening. But with years and sorrows, the colour has dimmed to brown, and now I wear it short to reduce the appeal for vermin.

I tread carefully, reluctant to wake the day, and pull open the door. It has no latch, no lock. We have no need to protect ourselves from the bad sort, because we are the bad sort. Foglers, lifters and murderers surround us: everyone's on the dodge in some shape or form. Jews to the right, Gypsies to the left and Jacktars in the rooms above: all in all, a well of criminality. Besides all that, we own nothing: nothing to steal, nothing to sell and nothing to pop at the pawnbroker's.

A glimmer of daylight creeps out of the gloom. I close the door behind me and pull the shawl around my shoulders. Aunt Meg is in the corner of the yard, a rag in her hand and a pail of muddy water at her side. She works at Uncle Jacob's boots, but they are caked in earth and clay and the soft leather absorbs the dirt she is trying to remove. She casts the first boot to the floor, takes up a knife and begins to scrape the sole of the second boot. She uses her forearm to brush the stray hairs from her face as she works. I won't ask why the boots are this muddy when they were perfectly clean last evening. I know not to ask what Uncle Jacob does at night. I take a step forward and realise Aunt Meg is crying, almost inaudibly.

'Let me help you,' I say. She turns and in one movement wipes her sleeve across her face and sweeps a clump of hair over her right eye. But the bruise is already shining and her eyelid is swollen and dark.

'Oh no, dearie,' she says, her voice contrived, too cheerful for the circumstance. 'We must keep your hands ready for Mr Gaberdine's manuscript copying. Some folks say we treat you too soft, Hester, but there's no one hereabouts what can do what you do. You keep those hands like a lady's, there's a good girl, and leave these boots to me.'

I picture Mr Gaberdine's documents, shredded and only a little better than kindling, and the hours I spend piecing everything together and copying them out. I wish I could be more useful to Aunt Meg with the housework, but I also understand that the arrangement with Mr Gaberdine is how I earn my keep.

'Thank you, Aunt Meg,' I say, then add, 'Does it hurt?'

'This?' She points to her eye. 'It's nothing, dearie. It's not Jacob's fault. It's nobody's fault. It just is what it is. And we do all right by you, don't we? He don't hurt you, does he?'

'No,' I say. Yet I find I don't declare it emphatically.

Uncle Jacob was kindness itself after Mama and Papa died. With no relations who would own me and no means of subsistence, destitution seemed inevitable. It was decided I would stay temporarily with Jacob and Meg. It was hoped that the new parson would practise the benevolence he preached and take in a poor lamb of God to bring her up as his own. It transpired, however, that he was a bachelor whose sole interest was debating ecclesiastical matters with fellow bachelors in a haze of tobacco smoke. It was also assumed the new incumbent of the parsonage would still need a gardener, but he brought his own servants. Fortunately for us, Jacob's brother owned an errand-cart business in London and so, to the finest city in all of Europe, Jacob and Meg went. And with the innocence of a child and the blind perversity of a sheep, I went with them, for what else was I to do? The temporary arrangement became a permanent solution.

Initially, we lived in clean lodgings. I arrived in neat clothing with my meagre keepsakes, as few as they were: a silver comb, a gold locket and a prayer book. We had an old range to warm us and oil lamps for light. The kettle was always hot on the trivet and Aunt Meg cooked chitterlings twice a week and collared eels every Friday. The business thrived and so did we. Then Obadiah, the old dray horse, gently lay down in the street one day and never got up again. Jacob's brother followed his horse to the grave soon after and, with no horse or contacts, it wasn't long before the business died too. Jacob sold the carrier's cart together with his Dutch hoe, his rake, fork and shovel, and we moved to cheaper lodgings. Eventually, I was obliged to sell my locket and the comb. We moved a dozen times in as many months, each time to lodgings that were smaller, grimier, darker. And as a spider is washed down a spout by the force of water, so we were washed by the obstinacy of poverty into the corner of the yard at the end of the alley. Uncle Jacob sought solace in the gin shops, and a man soaked in geneva is hardly a man at all. He abandons propriety and loses control of his urges.

Uncle Jacob now spends his days odd-jobbing and devilling. He is known to pet and bundle with the eldest daughter of Mrs O'Rourke, the Irish gypsy. He is also frequently seen with Rabbity Sue, who makes a living from tuppenny uprights. Three months ago, he told me how lovely my blue eyes were and that I had looks that could win a man's heart. Of late he has started to pay me more unwanted attention: sometimes wordless stares; sometimes he brushes close by my breasts and I feel his sour breath on my neck. He uses more blasphemy than a bargeman and, with his sharp edge and his sharp words, some days he is a pair of scissors at me, clipping my spirits with his taunts.

'Jacob protects us all in his own way, don't he though?' Meg goes on. 'And providing scran's not as easy as it once were. You take Mrs O'Rourke in there.' She jabs her thumb over her shoulder at the dilapidated house behind her. 'She's been feeding her brood on potatoes and penny bran since Michaelmas. And we had meat just last Thursday, didn't we?'

I nod as I picture the greasy leg of mutton boiled to rags. And as much as Aunt Meg tries to hide it, I perceive the austerity of our lifestyle in her features, and hear the futility in her voice. The last vestiges of our respectability are being crushed by poverty. Yet she will not admit it. Perhaps she doesn't know it. But I do. We are in a most miserable condition and live on the lowest terms life has to offer. And the only incentive I have to counteract utter oblivion is to believe that hope will arrive at Smithfield today, in the form of my cousin Edward.

I've never met him but Aunt Meg fell in to talking with some of the Lincolnshire drovers last time they came to town, discovering the existence of a distant relation of mine, who would be joining the cattle-men on their next drove. She said she told them how I can write a pretty hand and add up lists of numbers, and in exchange for a home and board could make myself very useful. Edward has since become the embodiment of my desire to be free of London. He should have been at Smithfield three weeks since to meet with me but has yet to arrive. I won't give up. I will wait there every day, for I must leave London, I must escape this life.

'You're going there again, aren't you, dearie?'

'It's not that I'm ungrateful for all you've done for me, but—'

'I'm not blaming you, Hester. Your parents would have wanted a better life than this for you. God knows if I had the chance to go back to our little cottage in Lincolnshire and simply be the wife of a parson's gardener . . . but my place is here with Jacob, whether he knows it or appreciates it, well, I don't know. Don't get your hopes up, I suppose that's what I'm trying to say. You can't always rely on the word of a rustic, you know. Even if there is such a job, there's no guarantee it'll last for more than a few months. And being a dairymaid is as hard as any work, especially in winter. Just have a care for what you wish for, dearie. And . . . and . . .'

Her sentence trails away to nothing. She looks at me, her brow furrowed with worry. I raise my hand and find myself pulling her towards me. We embrace, and for the first time it feels as though she is smaller.

I make to leave, but then turn about.

'May I ask you a question, Aunt Meg?' I venture.

'Of course, Hester.'

'I've been reading the discarded newspapers at the market—'

'Yes?'

'Well, last week there was an article about a boy that had gone missing: a Master Hogget.'

'I've not heard o' that name, I'm sure. Did you know the lad, dearie?'

'Well, no. It's just that no one can explain what happened to him. And I was thinking about my cousin, Edward, and worrying if—'

'Hester, my girl. Let me offer you some advice where boys and men is concerned. Each and every one of them has a habit of being distracted. I think back over my life and I can call up the recollection of at least a dozen fellas what either went to sea, or joined Mr Astley's circus troupe, or simply sought adventure at the bottom of a bottle for a few days. Some are gone for weeks, some are gone for years, and some don't never come back, my love. But don't you go fretting. Your cousin will just be late; he'll have found some delight what he's not known before and once he's had his fill, he'll be back. It's what young men do, dearie. And Master Hogget; he'll be the same.'

'I was just concerned, that's all.'

'My advice is don't rely on a man to be on time and don't trust all what the newspapers write in their dailies.'

'Thank you, Aunt Meg.'

'You'd best get off, my love.' She digs in her apron pocket, produces a shilling and presses it into my hand.

'But,' I say, 'that's for Uncle Jacob's Blue Ruin.'

'Let me deal with that. Trust that you keep your own counsel about it, that's all. He can have porter instead of gin for once, I'm sure. And I can always take up that offer of work from dear Mrs Cohen, can't I? She always said if we was on our uppers, she would direct a penny or two in my direction. A good friend she's been over the years. So don't you worry. Just get yourself a bite to eat and some ale.' Her voice is brave, but her eyes betray her.

A whistle echoes in the covered alleyway and she shrinks back inside herself and resumes her cleaning. When Uncle Jacob enters the yard, I pull my wrapper over my head and make for the alley, almost tripping in my haste to be gone.

'Where d'you think you're going?' he calls after me.

'Oh, leave her alone, Jake,' Meg says.

'Don't you tell me what to do, woman! She thinks she's so special, that one. Well, I'm in charge and she'd do well to remember that. And she's not too old to be taught a lesson,' he adds, slurring his words.

I ignore him and push forward towards the road, worried that he might chase me and rip the shilling out of my hand. But I hear Aunt Meg instead, 'She's gone to fetch you a bottle of gin, Jake. I'm just on my way to borrow some coals for the fire and some eggs and flour, I'll make you some skimmer-cakes, shall I . . .?'

Then the fog, which settles in the dips and the hollows, absorbs her voice and I begin to make my way down grim alleys where the sun never reaches, my own hands lost to the enveloping fingers of mist. I might as well be walking through the murk of the Thames for all I can see.

All I hear is the tap of my heel as I go westwards then south, following a footpath where the mud and filth has been trampled into a firm crust. As I hurry down Old Street, past the Bunhill burying grounds, leaves spin in circles around the hem of my skirt. I cut through a by-path, regain the highroad at Goswell and scurry down Wilderness Row: a series of lodging houses with broken windowpanes repaired with rags and paper, caged songbirds behind every third sash. Most shutters remain closed, with few folks stirring and houses still asleep to the business of the day.

Through the mist, there is a shape. As we draw near, I recognise Annie Allsop.

'Well, strike me blind, if it ain't you, Hester! Chilly one, ain't it? A right piercer.'

She smiles. Her mouth is overcrowded with teeth and her breath is fragranced with gin. Her lank hair, which she usually wears down, is plaited up behind, baring a pale and narrow forehead. She is wearing her best linen collar, but it has grown yellow with age and the residue of snuff.

'Hello, Annie. You're up with the larks. Still cooking whelks?'

'No, I ain't done that in ages.'

'Thought we'd not seen you for a while.'

'I come round last week, you cheeky mare, selling pigs' trotters and plum puddings, but you wasn't there. Meg says you've set your heart on working at a dairy house.'

'Yes. It's in Lincolnshire; that's where I used to live.'

'When she said you wanted to be a dairymaid, at first I was struck all of a heap. I says to myself, that's a funny game, ain't it? They say the udders dry up something cruel in winter; it's like trying to squeeze milk out of a carrot.' She laughs, showing every tooth in her mouth. 'But I s'ppose if that's what you fancy . . . And I hear old Jake's rheumatics is back. You know, if I had a farthing for every ailment that had gin as a common father, well, I would never have to work again. Not that I need worry about that now!'

'Oh?'

'I've met a real good fella. He ain't your hearts and darts sort, but I don't mind that. Found him at the Fortune o' War, didn't I. He's quite the diamond in the dust heap, and in these dark times and with all them missing folks, I reckon it don't hurt to have a fella to look out for you.' She moves her head as she talks, her dull oval eyes and loose lids at once becoming bright, as if she can't quite believe her luck. 'He buys me a pot of half-and-half, he does. "Hear this," he says. "I've the very thing," he says. "I

13

knew straight away you was the woman for the job," he says. "And I should like a job well enough," says I.'

'What's the job?'

'It's what I'm best at, Hester. It's needlework, and for a proper lady too. He says she might give me some of her cast-off frocks in time. This day next month I'll be wearing a tufftaffety gown. Think of that! And boots that shine like a chimney-glass. I got all the stuff, look.'

She pulls out a blue pocket and opens it to reveal a little pewter pincushion in the shape of a pig, four needles, a dozen or so pins, and a bobbin of scarlet thread.

'He says he'll take me for some bite and sup today, too. I'm meeting him again at the Fortune o' War. I'll probably see you on your way back from Smithfield tonight, won't I? I could tell you all about it then. But here, Hester, you couldn't lend me sixpence, could you, dear heart? There's a hat I've asked Mrs Cohen to put aside for me at her shop. I should love to wear it when I meet up with him.'

'I've only got this shilling, Annie.'

'It's only borrowing though, ain't it? It's not as though I won't see you again. I'll be at this very spot tonight. And my new fella's quite free with his shillings and his crowns where the likes of me is concerned, that's for sure. I'll give it back to you later, I promise, with a penny for your trouble. Just you see as I don't. In fact, I've got tuppence in me pocket, look. Take it and I'll settle up the rest tonight. What do you say, dear heart?'

I hand over the warm coin and take the four cold ha'pennies from Annie.

'God bless you, Hester. Must cut along now. See you later eh?'

'Good luck, Annie.'

She walks away at a smart pace, singing to herself as merrily as a cricket, and as I slip through the groin of an archway, I'm suddenly in the belly of the town. I feel the rumble of the streets first, then the stir of activity reaches me. All is wide-awake here. Feet thump and carriage wheels churn. The fog has cleared, but now the air is brittle with cold as crowds of people jostle for space.

I turn out of the lane and direct my course down Liquorpond Street, where the gutters are swimming with offal from the violin-string manufactory. There are men selling bunches of firewood, and girls carrying milk pails and baskets of dried lavender. I pass the spoon-mender's shop on a busy corner and pause to look at the handbills that have been pasted to the wall outside.

The number of notices has grown over the last few months and the papers have conjoined to form a skin that covers the entire surface of brickwork. Some posters describe missing children or absent parents, some simply appeal for information. Most sheets have succumbed to the damp of the city and are now wrinkled or distorted and unreadable. I wonder if the parents of Master Hogget will have a notice pressed for him, and I pray that Edward is never reduced to pasteboard and printer's ink.

I buy a ha'penny pie and eat it, grateful for something hot to fill my belly, while watching The Dancing Doll Man as he sets up his pitch. He attaches two painted dolls to a peg and board with a length of cable and ties the other end around his knee. With his fipple-flute he squeaks out a shanty, accompanying himself with a drum, all the time moving his knee up and down to keep time with the music and making the dolls dance. Before I leave, I throw a ha'penny to him; he smiles and nods but his mouth still works at the flute and he doesn't drop a beat.

The crowds thin as I walk down St John's, and dark thoughts begin to trouble me. I cannot stop puzzling over those notices and wondering how and why a person might disappear. We rub along in this den of infamy and we can all tell a lurker from a dupe, a rogue from the down-on-his-luck, a sinner from a saint. But something else is here amongst us now. This new apprehension makes me shiver, and now any unexpected sound gives me a start; a slammed door, a heavy tread. I clench my teeth, press on and complete the final few rods to Smithfield.

When I arrive, the market place is already cluttered with waggons, some with beasts yoked to them, some with shafts in the air. As the bells of Shoreditch peal, I jump the puddles and weave in and out of carriages and barrows.

My attention is drawn to a single ribbon of beasts twisting and looping through the crowds. I rush to a man in his smock frock as he leads the cattle into a drove-ring, noses inwards, haunches to the outside of the circle.

'Mister?' I shout. But the panicking animals give voice and the drover doesn't hear me.

'Do you know Edward White?' I say. He doesn't even turn to look at me. 'I'm supposed to meet him here. As soon as he pastured his cattle in Islington, he was going to walk down with the London drovers and meet me. Have you seen him?'

The man finally deigns to face me and roughly shakes his head.

'Look,' he says. 'I don't know him. But the word on the street is that this place isn't as safe as it once was.'

'But why? What's changed?'

'I don't know. I don't want to know. You look out for yourself.' I am pushed aside as he smacks the rump of the next heifer and starts to form another drove-ring.

This is how I have spent the last three weeks. This is how I will likely spend today and tomorrow. Every dawn, when my senses are in that midpoint between sleeping and waking, I convince myself that when the earth has turned one more revolution, then my life will change. But then each day passes and the shadow of my fading dream draws long and dark and I begin to believe that my seeds of hope are sown where nothing will ever grow.

Hoping my cousin will be forced to materialise by my sheer force of will, and reluctant to return to Virginia Row for fear of Uncle Jacob's inebriated wrath, I spend the remainder of the day watching for drovers and asking fruitlessly after Edward. The brief pleasure of spending what I had left of the gin money has faded and I can only imagine how I'll be received when I return to the yard. Eventually, coloured by the glare of gas-lamps, I scuff my way through discarded meat wrappers and turnpike tickets; the street bordering the marketplace as grey as the fog above it.

Through my feet I suddenly feel dull vibrations and hear a clatter of hooves. I turn as a carriage appears from nowhere, thundering along the street towards me. It is being driven recklessly and, as I stand aside to let it pass, the horses with their wide nostrils and steaming flanks veer onto the footway. Gloved hands pull at traces and bits. The driver shouts. I let out a cry and, as my chest empties of air, I see the carriage bearing down on me.

It is at this moment I realise there is no hope. I send out a prayer for my salvation as the wheel-spokes spin and black specks dance in the air before me. There is a swimming sensation inside my head as my pulse becomes small and I cannot tell what is passing around me. At last my legs fail me.

I am trapped beneath the carriage and a dizzying throng of onlookers gathers in a knot around me: costermongers and hawkers in the main, all with faces and cuffs dripping with water. I cannot stop trembling as I hear the smack of a mallet and a crack of snapping wood. Someone tugs at the broken shaft while the coachman steadies the horses. Then, finally, I am pulled from beneath the wheels.

Someone cries, 'Is she hurt? I can't look.'

'No, she's just being theatrical,' another calls. 'Could earn her living at the penny gaffs, this one. A drop of gin-daffey's all she needs.'

'Do try to quieten down, miss,' the coachman says to me, and I realise that I have been wailing and promptly stop. 'Mr Brock. You might want to take a look, sir.'

I experience violent pain rushing up my right leg. It throbs and brings me out in a sudden fit of shivering, sufficient to banish all other thoughts. I snap my eyes closed for fear of what I might see. Perhaps my skin is torn and my flesh mashed beyond repair? A gentleman's footsteps approach and I peep from between my eyelashes. A hatted head is bent low, its owner searching my face. He squats and studies me, then flicks the cape of his grey surtout over his shoulder and presses the top of my thigh. I am numb with cold and feel nothing. He gently squeezes just below my right knee and I shriek. As a reflex, I look down at my leg and briefly note the point of collision. My skirts are ripped and my linen undergarments are blood-soaked.

'Her leg is probably broken, Jenkins. Get her in the carriage. And you there,' he points with his cane to a barrow boy, 'get some sacking to hold this shaft together. Here's a shilling for your trouble. Be quick about it.'

The coachman, with the assistance of a groom in his stable-jacket, lifts me up and I am placed inside the carriage. With the windows shut up against the cold night air, the coach moves off as soon as the steps have been put up, and we strike west towards the better part of town.

CHAPTER TWO

I'm placed with my back to the horses and my legs up on the
seat. My shin is burning hot and I am sensible to the slightest
jolt of the carriage. I daren't look at Mr Brock for more than a
moment and instead fix my stare on the dark bloodstain expanding
across the sacking in which my leg is wrapped. He sits back into
the recess of the coach, his face obscured by shadow; only his
gloved hands visible as they clutch his cane. I notice his neat cuffs
and bright buttons then look away.

Out of the window, lights from passing carriage lamps slide
along the ground, breaking the darkness. We pass an arcade of
trees along a road that is brightly lit with gas-lamps and the coach
begins to slow. We arrive at a row of scattered villas, bricked and
gabled, elegant and uniform, in a more sparsely inhabited region
of town. Gone are the roiling sounds of the city, replaced instead
by the occasional shouts from callboys for drivers.

Two male servants appear at the coach door and Mr Brock greets
them with orders then quits the carriage. Jenkins and the groom
lift me out onto the street and place me on a hurdle brought by
the others. I am bruised with pain and exhaustion and give a low
moan. It feels as though I am being carried like a corpse on a bier.
We approach a house that is set apart from neighbouring proper-
ties and at four storeys high, with pale golden bricks and a slope

of regular tiles, it is both grand and imposing. Bright light emanates from the many windows and the promise of warmth is enticing.

The furnishings are opulent; I am carried over a deep crimson rug, past elegant tables topped with marble busts and porcelain vases full of flowers. Ornaments and trinkets are on every highly polished surface. The walls are lined with red silk and hung with oils in gilt frames that must have cost a power of gold.

The family's ancestors stare down at me disapprovingly from their canvases as we ascend the stairs. The hurdle is jolted again but I bite my lip to stifle a cry; the ceiling is high and I fear any noise I make will echo loudly.

The footmen stop after reaching the top step and next we travel down a wide corridor, passing closed doors and servants in white aprons. Eventually we arrive at the last door and from behind us come the sound of footsteps and the rustling of skirts as two maids appear, dressed in black with white collars and caps. The first, who is small and can be no older than me, comes forward with a lively step. She tucks her red hair beneath her cap then straightens her cuffs, before she reaches for the door handle.

'I'll do the sconces and the fire, Sarah,' she says to the other girl. 'You can strip the covers from the furniture. Leave the one on the bed, mind you, until we've got her cleaned up a bit.'

After the first stiffness, the door springs open. The room is dark and has a breath of stale air about it. The two maids attend to their duties and, once I'm lowered onto the freshly made-up bed, the makeshift hurdle is dismantled and pulled from under me. One of the poles catches my leg and the pain is excruciating, but I grind my teeth to take the edge off it. Sarah, her face pock-marked and pale, approaches the bed, and gives a sidelong glance at me and a sharp sniff.

Over the next half-hour, I am alone with the two maids, and they peel the grimy clothes from my skin and wash me with a cloth, warm water and soapball. They are brisk, efficient, and move my arms as though I were strung to the knee of a Doll Man. When they have finished, my skin tingles and feels tight at my joints and I am shivering in my new linen smock. Eventually I begin to feel the benefit of the fire.

The sackcloth is taken from around my leg and releases a smell that is a mixture of my blood and the streets. The candlelight illumines a gash as long and broad as a taper, black at the edges and deep red in the centre. At the sight of the wound, Sarah throws me an odd stare that I am unable to read.

'Cor, it looks like minced mutton, don't it, Mary?'

'Sarah! Don't be so cruel,' Mary whispers. She quickly looks up at me with soft eyes, drawing a breath as though to speak. But whatever Mary is about to say is interrupted by a loud knock at the door. She smooths down her skirts as the door opens.

'Mr Brock.' She drops a curtsey.

'Now then!' Mr Brock enters the room dressed as fine as ever a man can be. He immediately turns his attention to my leg. 'Not been damaged further in any way, Mary?'

'No, sir. The menservants was careful and we've been very particular, sir.'

'That's good, Mary. Thank you. Sarah, I need you to bring me a pitcher of clean water. And tell Jenkins to fetch my bag; I left it in the carriage.'

I find his manner refreshingly straightforward but there is also a brightness to his voice, as though the whole affair brings him a degree of excitement. He moves his arms when he talks and each time he does, I catch the scent of tobacco rising from his coat sleeves.

'Yes, sir,' Sarah says. 'Will there be anything else?'

'No. You may leave us.'

Sarah turns towards the door, but the gentleman calls her back.

'I'll need some liquor . . . for the girl, Sarah. Tell Jenkins to fetch some of last night's negus or something.' His voice is more serious now. 'Tell him to fortify it, just as I've shown him. I'll need the girl to be brave.' Sarah nods and leaves.

I taste my heartbeat in my mouth. I can't think what Mr Brock will do to me. I imagine his bag containing chisels and saws and any number of torture instruments. I feel the blood drain from my face. Mr Brock must notice as he looks me in the eye and says, 'The Lord does not afflict us beyond the power of our endurance.' There is the faint aroma of tobacco and port wine on his breath.

I nod. But the novelty of my adventure has rubbed clean away. My nose drips as I quickly brush away my tears with the back of my hand. The room is no longer chill but I shiver uncontrollably. Mr Brock pulls a chair to my bedside. Hatless and gloveless, he looks younger than I first thought; he can be no more than five-and-twenty. And his eyes look younger still and seem interested in everything they look upon, lit up with an almost childlike wonder. His skin is smooth and unblemished, save for the little dark bristles that give his chin and top lip a tint of blue-black. He pushes a dark lock of hair back from his temple.

'Welcome to my home and allow me to introduce myself. My name is Calder Brock and I am a physician. Might you tell me where you were born?' he asks kindly, his voice gentle.

Fleetingly, I consider telling him the truth: that I am the daughter of educated parents; that I was schooled in Greek, and Latin; that I can cipher and write with a good hand. That all I desire is to drag myself out of the gutter into which I have fallen. I steal a glance at him as he waits for my answer. How fine his image would look in a painted portrait. I wish he would look me in the eye, but his gaze won't settle. I don't believe he wants me to be complicated. He rescued a waif and a waif I must be.

'I was born in a cockleshell at Honey Lane fish market, sir.' I steal the line from Annie Allsop. I've heard her quote it a thousand times. I even exaggerate the roundness of my vowels to sound more like her. And when it comes to it, perhaps I am more like Annie than I think after six years with Uncle Jacob.

'Well, I'm sure that is just a figure of speech—' he laughs.

'My name is Hester White,' I volunteer, in the broadest of London accents. 'I am eighteen years old and my mother and father lie underground, sir.'

He nods, but his attention is on my leg.

'Well then, Hester White of Honey Lane fish market. At first, I thought your leg was broken, but it is not. Nevertheless, you have a contused and lacerated wound and there will probably be a degree of suppuration before it heals, but when it has thrown off its sloughs, I believe you'll make a full recovery.'

'Why are you helping me, sir?'

He looks at me in surprise. But before he can answer, Jenkins arrives quite breathless.

'Your bag, sir. The water-pitcher. And the negus.'

'Thank you, Jenkins.'

'Will that be all, sir?'

'No. Stay. I might need you to hold the girl. Mary, could you bring that lantern closer?'

Mary edges forward, holds the lantern in the air with the beam directed towards my leg.

The thought of what procedures Mr Brock will undertake fills me with dread and I catch my breath. I take the cup and drain it. The spices are keen. It has a sharp taste and leaves my throat with a gritty feeling, as though I have swallowed hot cinders. It is a stronger drink than I imagined. Within a few moments, warmth radiates through my chest and there is a strange ringing noise in my ears. I lose interest in both Mr Brock and my leg as he gently pushes me back down, his hand warm on my shoulder. I recline without resistance, my head feeling soft on the goose-feather pillow.

'How much laudanum did you use, Jenkins?'

Jenkins stiffens. 'Three minims, as you directed, sir.'

'Perhaps it should have been two. The girl is slight and likely has an empty belly too. It'll wear off tomorrow, though.'

In spite of the pull from the spiked drink, I shake my head awake. 'Will you cut my leg off?' I sob. I think I speak these words, but can no longer be sure. I am torpid, my head and faculties heavy. Then muteness surrounds me and at last, overpowered by laudanum and fatigue, I surrender to the draw of sleep.

As soon as I wake, I gingerly pull the bedclothes from my leg. I squint through the greyness, the only source of light coming from the daylight at the edges of the curtains. My leg is bound in court-plasters and, true to Mr Brock's prediction, it is suppurating. I cover it over and listen to the tick of the clock.

I am cocooned in softness and warmth. The sheets are laundered, pressed and scented with lavender water. I inhale their clean perfume until my head becomes light, and realise that I have not known such comfort since the days at the parsonage. Years of darkness and roughness spent in poor lodgings have intensified my appreciation of the soft mattress, the soft bedding. I cherish the sensation, saving it for when the dark times return, and the hairs on my head shiver with the bliss of it.

I begin to think about Edward waiting for me out there on the cheerless streets while I am comfortable in this warm bed. Now unable to fulfil my obligation to meet him, my thoughts wander from guilt to blamelessness, from agitation to indifference, concluding that, after all, he never arrived at the agreed time or place and there is nothing I can do to change that fact.

I drift back to sleep until the twelve chimes of noon wake me. Soon after, the boards outside my room creak and the door opens. The maids from the night before enter, one carrying a tray. As soon as the curtains are opened, a flood of daylight spills over the floor and I blink at the smart of it. The breeze has changed its temper and brought with it clear skies and a warm sun.

Mary has entered the room with a smile, but Sarah approaches me with caution, looks me up and down and then attends to her business in silence. Mary turns her attention to the fire and sconces; new coals and fresh candles. She hums a quiet melody as she works and twice enquires if I am comfortable. Sarah places her tray on a tea table and brings me food served on a blue and white China plate. I eat the kidneys and buttered toast as though I have never eaten before, and next comes a bowl of pot-liquor followed by oat cracknels and milk. I thank Sarah but she gives me no more than a nod in response.

Over the next two days, I am visited by Sarah and Mary four times a day. Initially Sarah seems to view me as an exotic creature to be treated with caution, and she never turns her back to me. Once she realises I don't bite, she looks upon me as just another chore. Mary is the opposite. She always wears a smile; not simply on her lips, but also in her eyes. Every picture that she dusts or fire she mends, she does so with the utmost care, as though she is quite pleased with life and seeks to share this pleasure with everyone and everything in it. And she never leaves my room without plumping up my pillows and straightening the blankets on my bed.

On the second morning, I ask if the girls are well. This simple enquiry into their soundness of health produces a pleasing effect on Mary. At first, we go on to exchange a brisk click-clack of rehearsed pleasantries, but soon we are on common ground: we discuss parts of town we both know; familiar street-characters and friendly shopkeepers. Our dialogue flows smoothly and rapidly until eventually, Sarah, too, is drawn into it. When they visit me after lunch, I offer to help them with their chores; ask if they might bring a little mending that I may do to while away the hours.

'Well, that's a fine and proper thing to offer, Hester,' Mary says. 'I'd be most obliged if you'd do that.'

She returns with a small workbox, a pair of stockings and a pillowcase, and I set about the task. The light in the room is good, the needles are fine and sharp, and compared to copying out Mr Gaberdine's documents, the occupation gives me a sense of well-being and a domestic cosiness I have not known for years. I had quite forgotten the pleasantness of honest industry.

On the third day, however, when the girls enter my room, I notice a marked change in Sarah's demeanour. Where before she had been brisk in her work and, albeit with diffidence, undertaken all possible duties to aid with my recovery, today she appears sulkier than ever, clumsy to the point of negligence in her tasks. She heaves a sigh and sits in a chair by the window, lost in her own thoughts, with her feather duster lying dormant across her knees.

'Is everything all right?' I ask, looking from Mary to Sarah. There's a brief moment of pause, before Mary replies:

'She's all right, aren't you, Sarah?'

'Mmm,' is all that Sarah says, and she turns about to look out of the window.

'We've heard from Jenkins,' Mary goes on, taking up the story as she sits on the edge of my bed, 'that we're all going to the country.'

'To where?' I ask.

'To Waterford Hall. It's the Brocks' country house, two days away from here, on the Stratford road.'

'You know what that means, don't you?' Sarah chimes in. 'It means I won't see as much of my Archie as I might wish; the stables are miles away from the garrets at Waterford. And it ain't just Archie I'm worried about. It's either you or me, Mary, what's got to do for Miss Rebekah. Well, I shan't stand for it. I'm not being her maid, not for nothing. I'm not ending up like poor Agnes.'

'Come now, Sarah,' Mary says, her tones gentle, calming. 'Nobody knows for sure what happened with Agnes.' Mary turns to me and, in response to my questioning eyes, she says, 'Agnes was a maid, Hester, like me and Sarah. She left one day, that's all. She up and left Waterford to go to London. Then she was never heard of since, like she disappeared.'

'It ain't right, if you ask me,' Sarah adds sourly.

'We don't know that, Sarah. She's probably wed to a sailor and heavy with child by now. She'll be as happy as ever she was and won't care to visit the likes of us, and who can blame her?' Mary laughs as she speaks, but Sarah will not be mollified.

'I don't think she ended up like that at all,' she says.

'And how do you reckon she ended up, then?' Mary asks.

'Well, I can't say. I can only say what I seen. Miss Rebekah Brock was too close to poor Agnes. It ain't right. I seen her following her about, whispering to her in corners. I caught 'em in an embrace, I swear, like they was a couple of turtle doves. And such a blush come to my cheeks, as I can't tell yer.'

I want them to continue with their tale, as I'd like to collect another little dab of colour for the portrait I am already beginning to paint of the infamous Miss Rebekah. But both girls now sit in silence, until I say to Mary:

'And does Miss Rebekah live alone at Waterford?'

'Oh, no. Her uncle, Septimus Brock, is there most of the time. He owns Waterford and this place. Miss Rebekah and Mr Calder – they're orphans, see. When Septimus's brother and his wife died, he took them in and brought them up.'

'And you'd have thought,' Sarah says, 'that she'd be off his hands and married by now. You'd think she could be introduced to some of her brother's friends at the very least, although I doubt any of young Mr Brock's acquaintances could ever be half so very handsome as he is!'

'You're being a bit harsh to her there, Sarah. I mean, you can't blame Rebekah for what happened to her intended.'

'Why? What happened to him?' I say to Mary.

She pauses, looks down at her hands, before saying quietly, 'Sir Humphrey died . . . the night before their wedding.'

'How awful,' I say.

'He was old though, to be fair,' Mary adds. 'Still, it's marked her out as a bad one as far as taking her up the aisle goes, that's for sure.'

'It ain't Miss Rebekah we should be sorry for,' Sarah declares, 'it's poor Agnes. To have to put up with all that unwanted attention and then just up and disappear. It ain't natural. None of it's natural. Here, what time is it?'

'Nearly eleven,' Mary says. 'Why?'

'Oh, I got to fold some linen. You'll give us a hand, won't you, ducks? Come on.'

Sarah sweeps out of the room in an instant and is gone. Mary tarries and, standing at the doorway, she turns to me and says, 'I'm afraid Sarah's a bit one-sided. And she don't always have the sweetest temper. I reckon Miss Rebekah only gave her the job 'cos Sarah's aunt is one of the laundry maids here. But she's all right once you get to know her. Anything I can get you before I go?'

'No. Thank you, Mary. You've been very kind.'

She leaves, closing the door behind her, and I am left alone with my thoughts. I picture Mr Brock's sister as old beyond her years, grown peevish with the failed promise of matrimony, now apt to spend her days succumbing to a deficient and narrow life of railing against her inferiors, sour with the potency of privilege. Agnes I see as small, fragile as a bird, susceptible to her mistress's excessive attentions, and I am troubled by her disappearance.

Over the next two days either Sarah or Mary attends me, but never together and there is little time for chatter. The plaster on my leg is changed and the stiffness diminishes. Mr Brock makes time to visit me several times a day. He has a face that always smiles and he never fails to cheer the room with the light of his eyes. He knocks before he enters the room and always bows his head to me, as though I were a countess.

Once, he calls to see me just as Sarah is leaving. She drops a pitcher from her tray and the handle breaks. I look up, worried Calder will berate her for her clumsiness and dismiss her instantly. But instead he stoops with an obliging smile, retrieves the jug, hands it to Sarah and proceeds to open the door for her. She blushes as she leaves and it appears that no person or event seems to hold the power to dislodge Calder Brock from his merry moods.

The household is preparing for its move to the country and, on the sixth day of my convalescence, just as Mary is stoking the fire and Sarah is taking a feather duster to the ornaments, there is a knock at the door. Calder enters, but he is not alone. Three gentlemen, all dressed in black and sporting bosky grey whiskers, follow him in. Mary brings chairs and the three visitors take their seats at the bottom of my bed.

'It is assumed, gentlemen,' Mr Brock begins, standing at the side of my bed, 'from Hester's clothes and appearance when she arrived, that she comes from one of those less salubrious regions in the north-east of our city. As painful as it is to acknowledge, we must all understand that the residents of that quarter are born of low breeding and have no access to education. And through no fault of their own, the problem is compounded with each generation. They are surrounded with unimaginable squalor in which to raise their children and are forced to swallow their pride and accept the gift of alms to facilitate their survival. And this girl, gentlemen, is testament to such a lamentable social structure.'

The men shake their heads and mumble through their whiskers as Mr Brock uncovers my leg, peels back the plaster and shows his handiwork. They stoop and inspect me before returning to their chairs. As I push my head into the pillow, the gentlemen talk in a whisper and Sarah moves closer to them in order to eavesdrop. Finally, the guests rise and leave the room. Mr Brock sees them to the door, but does not leave with them. Instead, he returns to my bedside and seats himself upon a chair. He looks at me kindly, but doesn't speak. The fire crackles in its grate, the clock ticks and I begin to wonder if he is waiting for me to say something.

'Thank you, sir. I don't know how I'll ever repay your kindness—'

'Nonsense! You owe me nothing, Hester. I have the knowledge of both surgical procedures and physic. It's as natural to me as breathing air. And, above all, I revere the luxury of doing good.'

'But, why would you help me, sir? Folks like me ain't worth a rush.'

'Now that is a very good point. And I am here to explain, as simply as I can. Hester, have you ever heard of The London Society for the Suppression of Mendicity?'

Until now, as a guest in Mr Brock's house, I had felt there was less chance of any harm coming to me here than living in the yard with Uncle Jacob. But with the final three syllables of Mr Brock's sentence, fright cuts through to my marrow and I shiver at the sound of them: di-ci-ty.

The inhabitants of my part of London do not call this society by its full and proper name; we simply refer to it as 'the Dicity'. Its name is spoken in hushed tones, draped in shame and swathed in fear. And it is that fear of accepting the poisoned chalice of parochial relief that drives men to gin and women to tuppenny uprights. Just when you fall as low as you can; when labouring is scarce and food even scarcer; when you can only gain your bread by sweeping or thieving, that's when the Dicity comes for you. Just as your grimy fingertips curl themselves around the last tussock on the cliff face of survival, the Dicity prises them off one by one and down you tumble to the very bottom. And they have their own particular way of holding a foot on your chest as off they take you to number thirteen, Red Lion Square, Holborn – an unlucky number if ever there was one. There, you are perhaps charged with vagrancy and sent to the hulks. If it is the first time you've been caught, then you are put to work in the yard, but from there you slip ever downward into the poorhouse, until you throw off your mortal coil. And the word they use to excuse their brutality is 'help'. Yes, the Dicity 'helps' those unfortunate vagrants, like me, who litter the city streets like so many piles of filth. Many a time I've had to run as fast as the wind to escape a Dicity constable. And lying in a feather bed with an injured leg is not the way I will escape this gentlemanly representative. I am cornered.

'Yes, sir. I know the Dicity.'

'Well, I'm to join the board of this great charitable cause. The gentlemen that came to see you today are also on the board of patrons. What differs, Hester, is that I intend to approach the matter of poverty in a different manner. I intend to use you as an experiment. I am certain that you know that the Society would normally have you breaking rocks in their yard by now. I would also hazard that – without my intervention last Saturday – you would either have slept under the pig-boards at Smithfield or would have bedded down with the rest of the vagrants at Covent Garden. However, my charity to you is not yet done.

'I am leaving for the country tomorrow and you are to accompany me, subject to your endurance against fatigue. Not only do I intend to build up your physical strength through diet and exercise and provide the proper medical care to make your leg as good as new, but I also wish to prove that even those from the gutter can be educated. When I am finished with you, Hester, the Society will see a model citizen of this new era of King William. And who better than my dear sister to teach you? Mendicants should not be suppressed; they should be educated! Do you have any objection to my scheme, Hester?'

I pause to gather the sense of his words and think quickly. Abused by Uncle Jacob, pitied by Aunt Meg and abandoned by my cousin; anyone with breath in his lungs could see that I have only one choice.

'I'd consider it an honour, Mr Brock. Of all things in my life, I love to learn. I shall work as hard as ever a girl could work. And if I could better myself, sir, then I'd be grateful ever more.'

'There. That settles everything. Mary, please arrange to have a tisane mixed for the journey and make sure Jenkins and Pelham get the girl into the carriage without breaking open the wound.'

With that, Mr Brock rises from his chair, throws open the door and leaves us.

Mary straightens my bedclothes and smiles at me. Then, with a touch of humour in her eyes, she says, 'I'd wager you didn't expect all this to happen to you when you woke up last Saturday morning. You settle down now. Get yourself some sleep, eh?'

Sarah and Mary leave the room, but not many minutes pass before the door opens again. Sarah enters alone, eyes me and pads around my bed.

'Don't get me wrong, Hester,' she begins. 'But I wouldn't get too settled with the Brocks if I was you. I don't know what's going off. All I do know is that it weren't just Agnes what disappeared; there was a girl called Martha Briggs, too. Summat's not right. Just look out for yourself with Miss Rebekah, that's all. And don't say I didn't warn you.'

CHAPTER THREE

Sarah's words are wormwood and gall to me for the rest of the day and well into the night. I cannot decide if she has my best interests at heart or whether she is just fond of gossip and too ready to be vindictive towards her employers. I vacillate between innocent explanations and then darker thoughts, but ultimately I recall the cellar in the yard and the darkness that gathers there, rotting and decaying. Despite everything, I am grateful to be somewhere different.

The following morning at six, Mary and Sarah enter the room. Mary leaves breakfast on the oval table at my bedside and Sarah drapes an assortment of clothing on the bed, before she says, 'You can dress yourself well enough, if you plan on travelling to Waterford Hall.' It is clear that in her opinion I am an additional burden to her and also the reason for the sudden removal of the household to the country. She leaves the room as sharply as she delivers her words, but Mary lingers.

'Don't mind her,' she says. 'We're all a bit cheerless today.'

'Anything you can share with me?'

'It's a girl we all know; works as a scullery maid at a house around the corner. Slip of a thing she is – only twelve or thirteen years, I reckon. She's gone missing. Four days since.'

'I wonder what happened to her?' I ask, pausing. 'There have been so many disappearances in the city of late.'

'I know, it's a mystery,' Mary agrees, 'and not like her at all. She's not one of them flighty sorts. Her mother's beside herself. It's shook us all up, especially with all the rumours going about.'

'The city has never been a safe place to wander at night,' I say, 'but it seems as though the days are now just as dangerous. I wish I knew what was happening.'

'Yeah, me too. But I'm sure the girl will turn up; they always do. And don't you go fretting yourself about it; we'll be skimming past woods and hills soon, on our way to Waterford Hall; we'll all be out of London in no time at all.'

When Mary has left, I start to think. The news of another young woman joining the growing list of missing persons leaves me deeply saddened. I worry for the girl's safety; more than that, I fear the shadows of the night are indeed crossing over to the days and exposing every one of us to boundless risk. Despite these concerns, in my weakened state of health I can only surrender to what destiny dictates and be thankful that I am leaving London at last. Eventually, I rise and, in between mouthfuls of breakfast, dress myself in the laundered gown and polished boots that have been left for me. Simple as the dress may be, an age has passed since I have worn a frock made of soft fabric, and I can only offer thanks to Providence for bringing me to this place of safety and to this brief moment of respite.

A few minutes later, there is a knock at the door, then Jenkins and Pelham enter the room with an old wicker chair and tell me I am to be carried in the makeshift litter to avoid any injury to my leg. They manoeuvre me into the seat and raise me off the ground to take me down to the carriage. The doors of the coach are thrown open and the pavement is cluttered with bags and cases. As trunks and bandboxes are heaved onto the back, so I am loaded and packed inside.

The morning is cold and the sky is blanching, reaching a hue that suggests the day will be bright and clear. I am so excited at the prospect of leaving London, of relinquishing this feverous town and the misery of the last few years, that I can think of nothing but hills and vales, of sheep-cropped pasture and rough heaths, of hedgerows gay with hips and haws, of ripeness and a time of plenty. Notwithstanding the disappointment of my cousin's absence, I am ever hopeful of a fresh start.

Loading and packing continues until distant church bells ring out eight chimes. At the end of the final cadence, Mr Calder Brock appears from inside the house dressed in a jacket of pale blue velvet, a buff-coloured silk waistcoat, nankeen trousers and black boots. He jumps into the seat opposite me, causing the carriage to tremble a little. We are joined by two others, one of whom I assume is Mr Brock's valet, the other is Mary.

'Ah, Mary!' Mr Brock says as Mary seats herself, a grin upon his lips and a smile in his eyes. 'I hope you don't mind travelling in my carriage. Perhaps it's a little unconventional, but I thought you would be better able to look after Hester. I trust you've no objection?'

Mary blushes and allows the smallest of giggles to escape her lips. 'No, sir. I've no objection.' She turns and smiles at me, her eyes aglow with excitement.

With two grooms on their saddle horses, an old phaeton behind us with a handful of servants and their baggage, and with our four carriage horses pawing the ground, Jenkins flourishes the whip and we set off.

Mr Brock settles himself into the corner and partitions himself off with a broad journal. Every so often he addresses me; asks if Jenkins and Pelham knocked my leg during my descent from the upper chambers of the villa, or later if I need a rug over my knees. When he has finished reading his newspaper, he offers it to his valet and twice asks after Mary's family; her mother's rheumatics and her father's lumbago.

We head northwards, leaving the shrinking town further behind us with every turn of the wheels. The journey is long, and more uncomfortable than I expect. We thread through a market town, prosperous and thriving, and we rumble over the cobbled high street lined with an inn, a gingerbread stall, a shoemaker's shop and a woman selling cheeses and new-laid eggs. Later we pass a series of quiet hamlets where low cottages are strung alongside the village greens. We trot past churches, cart sheds and gardens, until the towns and villages become sparser, finally giving way to acres of pastureland dotted with lonely farmsteads. My eyes become heavy until the scenery is merely a blur of verges and trees, bouncing up and down to the rhythm of the horses' trot.

Our first stop is just before noon, when Jenkins pulls rein at The Rose Inn. Mary takes my arm and helps me out of the carriage. As we enter the inn together, she waves to Sarah and calls out salutations to one or two of the other servants, but stays with me as we find somewhere to make ourselves comfortable.

'Thank you for sitting with me, Mary,' I say as we take up our places on a bench by the fire.

'No need for that, Hester. There's no reason why we can't be friends, is there?'

'No reason at all.' I smile.

'That's settled then. And don't worry if some of the other girls aren't quite so chummy.' She flicks her eyes towards Sarah at the other end of the room, before continuing, 'She's like an out-of-tune fiddle that one; always at discord with someone!'

I smile at Mary's words and she grins back at me.

'I really do appreciate how obliging you have been to me, Mary.'

'Think nothing of it. My mother came from Bethnal. I know it can be hard up there, Hester. You want to make the most of this opportunity. Because Mr Calder – well, he ain't like other toffs; he's a true gent, really he is.'

'How so?'

'Well, he's so kind to everyone, of course.'

'And what of his sister?'

Where before her eyes had been bright and merry, with her friendliness making me feel at ease, this reference to Mr Brock's sister clouds Mary's features.

'It's best if you ignore the tittle-tattle, Hester. Remember, gossip is just other folks' opinions, it's not proper facts. Best to wait till you meet Miss Rebekah yourself. That'd be my advice.'

I nod my understanding to Mary. I know she respects the hardships I have suffered and in turn I trust her advice. In light of her recommendation, I try to dismiss Sarah's words, but a certain discomfort endures.

We stop once more during daylight hours and sleep one night at a tavern. Mary and I tentatively develop our friendship; I with tales from our cellar in the corner of the yard, and Mary with stories from below stairs at Waterford and the London house. It is late on the second day, as the sun dips on the western horizon, that we approach a steep ascent. As the road levels, we turn in past a lodge. The driveway curves before it cuts between two lines of yew trees and reveals the large country house to which it has been leading.

We alight from the carriage and I am relieved to be quit of it; both my legs are as stiff as sugar-tongs. A cuff of wind bends the trees and hampers the men with their unpacking. I wait for Mary on the driveway, my skirts stirring in the wind about me, until she joins me, gives me her arm and helps me round to the back of the hall to the servants' entrance.

She guides me along a passageway and directs me towards a wooden seat.

'I'd best be off now, Hester. All that unpacking to do!'

Mary leaves me, but I am not alone. Bells ring and every once in a while servants criss-cross the network of passageways. Some pass by alone; others are in pairs, deep in conversation. Soon I realise that every sentence contains Rebekah Brock's name: 'Miss Brock has requested this or that', or, 'Miss Brock would very much like such-and-such'. After twenty minutes or so of over-hearing her demands and instructions, I don't doubt there is a roof tile or shoe latchet within a mile of me that has not been influenced by her in some manner or other.

Just as I am pondering this, Mary appears, carrying a small cup.

'I brought you this; it's hot milk.' She hands me the steaming cup and then produces a small package from her apron. 'Couple of biscuits for you. It's not much, but it will keep you going.' She hands the biscuits to me and tucks the napkin back in her apron pocket.

'Thank you,' I say.

'I've just been airing your room; it's the one the old governess used to have. It's a bit sparse, because it's not been used for years. But it's all right. And at least it's not up in the garrets where me and Sarah are. Sometimes feels as though the wind might whip the roof right off those garret rooms.'

'And are the garrets far from my room?'

'No, not at all. I could pop down and see if you're all right, if you like? Explain the house routines and who people are.'

'Yes, I'd like that very much, thank you.'

'Well, I've got to go now. Just put the cup on the chair when you're done, I'll clear it away later.'

Mary leaves and the brisk motion of below-stairs activity continues. Eventually, a man hurries along the corridor and pauses before me. He illumines my face with his lantern and clears his throat then says, 'Right, young miss. My name is George Rudd, head footman. I've been asked to accompany you to the library.'

'Oh, of course,' I say, feeling drowsy and stiff. 'Pleased to meet you, Mr Rudd. My name is Hester. Hester White.'

The man nods, smiles and hands me a walking cane. Designed for a gentleman, it is too tall for me to use comfortably but it eases the weight from my leg as I lean on it and I am glad of its support.

'Thank you,' I say, and smile at him gratefully.

'You're welcome. It's quite a walk to the library, I'm afraid. We're down below stairs of course, so there's a few steps to climb before we're up on the ground floor.'

We begin walking, Mr Rudd always several strides ahead of me, his silhouette marked by the light he holds out before him. My leg tingles and I wonder how much farther we have to travel. At the top of the servants' stairs, we walk along a short corridor, then Mr Rudd stops and turns to face me.

'Hester, the owner of this house might be in one of these next rooms. His name is Septimus Brock, uncle to Mr Calder and Miss Rebekah. He might be a bit abrupt; that's just his way. If he asks you a question, answer him clear and simple. Don't stand with your chops open. He won't like it.'

'Yes, Mr Rudd. Thank you for the warning.'

'Come on then.'

We push through a baize-covered door and enter a room with an ornately carved ceiling. The warm air hits me, a stark contrast to the chilly corridors we have just walked through. The roaring fire gives an orange glow to the room, its reflected lustre showing on the table tops and screen. We weave through rosewood armchairs and ornamental tables and then come to a panelled door. Mr Rudd places his lantern on a table and knocks. He twists the doorknob and I follow him over the threshold.

We enter a smaller room. Thick velvet drapes hang at the windows, blood red and immobile, and sconces project from the walls. As we continue towards a door at the far side of the room, a gentleman rises from one of the high-backed chairs. When Mr Rudd sees the gentleman, he stops and gives a low bow.

'Mr Brock. We're just on our way to see Mr Calder—'

'Is this the girl from the Society, Rudd?'

'Yes, sir. I have been ordered to present her to—'

'Yes, I know what Calder's up to.'

The gentleman looks at me narrowly, then holds a quizzing glass to his right eye and inspects me more thoroughly. He bites the tip of his pipe as he studies me and puffs three jets of blue smoke through compressed lips. Although his skin is paler and his hair is grey, it is as though I am looking at Calder Brock through a sheet of ice; the features are recognisable but somehow flatter and colder than the younger man's. The man resumes his seat and disappears from view. I shiver in spite of the flames in the fireplace and turn and follow Mr Rudd through the door.

We enter the library and he leads me past book-lined walls into the centre of the room. Calder is leaning against a bookshelf, ruffling his hair and apparently deep in thought.

As Mr Rudd departs I notice a woman standing to the left of a fire screen. The gift of delicate, feminine beauty has not been bestowed upon her, but she is handsome in quite another way. As Calder features Septimus, this woman's looks echo them both. She is tall with high cheekbones and penetrating eyes, and her features are in full harmony. Men may not describe her as enchanting, but to my mind she is a remarkable-looking woman; so this is Rebekah Brock.

She turns and stares into the fire, one foot raised on the fender in a masculine way. She wears her dark hair in curls, tucked at the back with a tortoiseshell comb, and her long, pale fingers distractedly play with a loose lock. She heaves a sigh; as she swishes the thick, madder-brown skirts of her gown, I catch the subtle fragrance of gillyflower water.

Although time seems to have slowed since I entered the library, the minutes begin to jostle forward again. Calder snaps out of his reverie and strides towards me.

'Hester, here you are. Leg not giving you any trouble, I hope?'

'No, sir.' I lie. It throbs. I am tired and lean heavily on the walking cane and wish for nothing but the chance to sit.

Calder notices my strained expression. 'Take a seat. Here,' he says. He draws an armchair towards me over the thick carpet.

'You don't have to minister to my comfort, sir,' I say, politely. 'But I am most grateful for the opportunity to rest my leg, sir.' My London vowels are rounder than ever. I sink into the chair and prop the cane up beside me. Several uneasy moments follow as Calder paces up and down. Eventually, Rebekah breaks the silence.

'So this is the girl,' she says, surveying me with distaste, as though I were the sort of person to have brown hair on purpose. She throws herself into a chair and takes up a book, thumbing the pages.

'Come on, Becky,' Calder begins, at last facing her. 'It would do you good to educate her and have a little more companionship around here.'

'I admire your benevolence, Calder, but caulking one small hole in a riddled hull does not stop the ship from foundering. You cannot end poverty in this country by demonstrating that one young woman can be educated.'

She begins again in a softer tone. 'As ever, Calder, your morals are sound, but your reasoning is out of all proportion. Give the girl a handful of silver and send her back home. I'll wager the shillings will be in the pocket of the pot-boy at The Birdcage before Jenkins has time to bait the horses.'

'Indeed, sister, I fear you are mistaken.'

'I'm not some sort of governess, Calder. Perhaps, ten years

ago, I might have been more willing. By rights I should now be mistress of my own home, and if you believe that my teaching this . . . girl is in any way a substitute for the life I might have had, then—'

I consider speaking up for myself, confessing to my formative years at the parsonage and convincing her I am worthy of her time. But I am no fool. I realise how matters will play out: I must exaggerate my ignorance and demonstrate my enthusiasm to learn. In short, the more I can convince Calder and Rebekah I am uneducated but compliant and agreeable, the longer I will stay. The longer I am away from London, the greater my chance of escaping poverty. All I have to do is hold my tongue and impress Rebekah with my obedience and usefulness. Perhaps, at the end of all this, I could even get a job in service at a country house like this one. Just as I have played the part of an ignorant slum-dweller for Calder, so I must do the same with Rebekah. If I have learned one thing from my life in London, it is that sometimes it is necessary to descend to deceit, and that those who survive have the wit to know that.

In time, I look at Calder; he sits now with his head in his hands. I steal a glance at Rebekah: she stares into the fire; it reflects in her eyes, and throws streaks of yellow and red light upon her face. She stands as if to leave the room and Calder turns to me.

'Hester. Before my sister leaves us, is there anything you might wish to say?'

'Me, sir? Well, yes, if I might be permitted.' I rise to my feet and move slowly towards Rebekah, but her eyes remain fixed on the fire. 'By a chip of chance, I've found my way here, Miss. I've waited a lifetime for an opportunity such as this. I shan't be any trouble to you and I'm so very keen to learn from you. I'll work hard, I promise, and I can do any mending that's needed here to earn my keep.'

My words fail to stimulate any response from Rebekah, and the atmosphere is awkward, until Calder strikes in with:

'See, Rebekah? Hester has demonstrated more than sufficient willingness to apply herself. She'll be an excellent pupil.' His enticement only induces further silence from her, so with a wink to me, he says to her, 'Will a Turkish sweetmeat take the edge off your tartness, Rebekah?'

With that she leaves the room. The fire is dying and Calder takes the poker and rattles the cinders, eliciting a handful of sparks. But the flames will not be reignited.

'My sister,' he eventually says, 'my sister and I are at variance, Hester. It's not unusual; she's always out of temper with me these days. But I am still convinced she will come around to my way of thinking. The gentlemen of the Society have already received my proposals with great éclat. I shall engage the help of my uncle Septimus, and I am certain we shall change her mind.'

Calder's words are hopeful, as is his voice. He takes up a decanter, splashes brandy into a glass, then pulls at the bell cord. In an instant Mr Rudd enters the room.

'Ah, Rudd. Take Hester to her room.'

Mr Rudd nods and I follow him. I am led up two flights of stairs until we arrive at a passageway lined with doors. He stops at one of them, swings it open and beckons me to enter a small room, which is plainly but elegantly furnished, from what I can see through the darkness. He hovers in the doorway and eventually says, 'Don't you want a light?'

'Oh, yes. Please.'

'Pass it here then, Hester.'

I search through the shadows and see a rush-light on a table at the side of the bed. I stumble across the boards and take it up, offering it to Mr Rudd. He lights it and returns the dip to me before wishing me goodnight and leaving, his footsteps diminishing until they are nothing but faint echoes.

A breath of cool air bends the yellow flame, throwing shadows across the walls before it settles. The fire must have been lit some time before we arrived and is now burning low, so I prepare for bed quickly, putting on the nightdress left for my use on the small bed. Beneath the sheet and blanket I am soon warm. The pillow, once plumped, is soft and dense when compared to my old pair of boots, and it feels as though that distant, cold cellar was the home of another girl entirely.

I snuff out my rush-light and wait for sleep to catch up with me, but the past few days replay in my mind. Here I am on a bench at the tavern speaking with Mary. There the countryside jogs past from the window of the carriage. Faces come and go. Then a strong sense of irritation arrives in my consciousness alongside the image of Rebekah. Endlessly I find my mind revolving that same obstinate image: Rebekah, with her angular build, her white and regular teeth, her dark hair as shiny as paint. I wonder why she has remained unwed. I wonder if there have been other suitors. I wonder why she's so abrupt. But aside from these riddles, I consider the strange turn of events that have led me to this moment and I wonder how my own life will progress beneath the eaves of Waterford Hall. It is on these thoughts that at last the exhaustion from the long journey takes mastery of my body and draws me into a deep sleep.

I am awoken at first light by voices. Their conversation is incoherent at first, dull and muffled. I roll my head along the pillow and realise that they must be standing outside my bedroom door.

'Well, George Rudd does sometimes add a bit of a flourish to his stories, don't he though, Sarah?' It's Mary's voice, I'm certain.

'I'm just telling you what he said, Mary; that Miss Rebekah was so set against tutoring Hester, he thought she was going to ask Mr Calder to send her to Botany Bay.'

'Oh, Sarah. That's horrible. I'm sure she wouldn't say such a thing. I mean, I know she can be a bit sour sometimes, but—'

'Sour? Too right. I just feel sorry for Hester. Having all this happen to her, then if Miss Rebekah's going to make it rough for her. And what if Hester's in danger? What if she ends up like Agnes or—'

'Stop it now, Sarah.'

'I just wish Miss Rebekah could be more like her brother, that's all. But there's more chance of the Thames drying up!'

A set of footsteps departs and there is a rustle of material and a knock. A hinge creaks, a narrow strip of light appears on the threshold of my room and Mary enters. I lift my head and face her. She sets down a lighted candle and places a pitcher of water beside the washstand.

'Morning, Hester. Did you get much sleep? I expect not in this big house. You're to breakfast in the scullery at seven then report to George Rudd. They run that poor man ragged, they do.'

'Why?'

'Well, they let half the servants go last year, so we all do twice the work as ever we did.'

'Why would they do that?'

'The old housekeeper told us it was for the sake of economy. But George told me that Septimus had a big loss at cards.'

'He gambles?'

'So George says: cards, dice, horses; even cockfights and dogs. He never entered a profession, see, Septimus. He lived off the fortune his father made in India. George reckons they used to own half the county and had land overseas. Of course, most of it has been lost now on the turn of a card or the throw of a dice. But Septimus still likes to keep up the appearance of grandeur and there's probably still some gold left in the coffers; well, you'd hope so, what with Mr Calder to inherit when he reaches five-and-twenty next year.'

'So Septimus has been looking after the family fortunes for Calder?'

'Yes. What did George call it? Trust. Yes, that was it. Septimus has held it in trust.'

'Isn't Mr Calder worried about how it has been managed for him?'

'Well, I suppose he might be, but he sees Septimus as a father in many ways, and won't hear a word said against him. He's so set on his medical learning, he doesn't seem to think about anything else. It's a pity Mr Calder didn't choose to work for a bank or the East India, but I suppose if medicine is his calling, then follow his heart he must. George says it's all happened gradual like; if Septimus loses at cards, he just sells another ten acres and if he wins, all is well and there's a fancy dinner. But there's only Waterford and the villa left now. And fewer domestics to run even those places as each year goes by. Anyway, I've got my work cut out today, but I'll try to find you later.'

She withdraws from the room. Although I am heartened by her visit, the unfamiliar surroundings and the question around what today will bring leaves me feeling anxious. I lift the candle and pass the light around the room. In addition to the bed, table and washstand, there is a chamber pot and a small armchair. A crucifix adorns one of the walls and a watercolour scene of country life hangs on another. I open the curtains to reveal a view of the dawn sky. I guess from the hue, which grows paler by the minute, that it must be after six. A single chime from a distant bell tower suggests it is half past. As soon as I have washed, dressed, and tidied my hair, I set out for the kitchens.

I share a table in the scullery with four others, none of whom can be more than twelve years old: a scullery maid, garden apprentice, boot-boy and under-groom. The upper servants and elders are in the servants' hall, where knives chink and pots rattle above a swell of loud conversation that cuts through a strong smell of bacon. The scullery table, however, is breakfasting on gruel with bread and butter, and the conversation is not so hearty.

When the pots have been cleared, the servants walk past me to begin the business of the day. They don't even notice me, and I feel awkward and out of place. Then Mary passes by, calls out my name and smiles, genuine and broad. This public endorsement acts as a key in a lock and the remaining three domestics smile as they pass, one even bidding me good morning.

When they have all dispersed for the day's work, Mr Rudd explains that he has been left with instructions from Mr Calder. I am to walk in the gardens for an hour and then sit and rest for twenty minutes, then repeat until lunch. In the afternoons, I am to help with sewing and mending and must continue in that same regimen for three consecutive days, after which time Mr Calder will give further orders. Rebekah has not yet had a change of heart and I am keenly aware of the precariousness of my situation.

So, with Rebekah's caprice hanging above me, I venture out into the gardens of Waterford Hall. Mr Rudd provides me with an old pair of pattens and a thick cape made out of an old pea jacket that keeps the chill autumn air at bay. I keep to the gravel walkways, lined with clipped privet hedges that frame the gardens and run parallel to the walls that protect both the plants and me from the northerly breeze.

That first day, I find the fresh air exhilarating and the views compelling. There is a fountain-pool, from which grass paths lead outwards to a rose garden and herbaceous border. Beyond that there are glades and paths weaving between hedges of hornbeam and yew, which stretch out to the woodland and parkland beyond.

Heat from the sun barely materialises, but the light cast down from it throws a cheerful yellow patina over every tree and shrub. One or two gardeners clear dead foliage and trim hedges and they nod as I pass. The rumble of their wheelbarrows and the smell of wood smoke are comforting. The whole garden has a feel of order about it, as though it has been tamed into submission and is waiting, waiting for spring to come.

On the second day, the gardeners have moved into the glass-house. I'm grateful for the quiet – so unlike London where all was noise and dirt. It provokes happy memories of my days at the parsonage. I stand still, close my eyes, and in my mind I can almost hear the voices of my mother and father. I begin to recall past images of my home in Lincolnshire: the meadow, our garden gate, the parlour, a church pew. Certain scenes still hang on my memory after all these years: bonnets and caresses, roses and smiles. How glad my parents would be that I have left London at last. How strange they would consider my journey through life; I am so altered, I doubt their ghosts would even know me.

By the third day I amble through the grounds with my cane and I am alone except for the sparrows and blackbirds. I tire of the same circular route I have tramped and my leg is feeling stronger. Curiosity leads me to deviate from the walled garden and scuff my way around the outer walls of the hall, along the gravel walk beneath the library windows.

I stop before I reach the low window and the glass-panelled doors that open out onto the lawn. I realise suddenly that I am hoping for a glimpse of Rebekah and I edge closer to the library window, peering cautiously in.

She is there, in a crimson gown with long, close-fitting sleeves. She is sitting at a table working at a notebook. She lifts her face and I am sure she will see me, so I back away swiftly; stiff and silent.

I brave it again and peer in. She doesn't notice me; perhaps the fire reflecting on the windowpanes disguises me. She pauses, taps the pen end against her teeth, writes a sentence or two more then finishes with a flourish and takes up an old pounce-box to sand it. Whatever she has written seems to please her. For a moment her eyes soften and she looks kinder and lovelier than I had first perceived. I find I am smiling in response and I wonder at myself.

There is a lick of rain on the window and her image is obscured. I am about to turn away and take cover from the impending shower when footsteps approach. I hear the crunching of gravel before I see the shape of Mr Rudd rushing towards me.

'Hester!' he shouts, coat-tails flapping wildly. 'I've been looking for you everywhere! You're wanted in the library.'

At once I am both hot and cold with fear and anticipation. He takes my arm and marches me swiftly back around the building. Out of the corner of my eye I catch a movement at the window, a toss of dark curls and the sweep of crimson skirts. Whether she has seen me, I don't know. Whether I am to see her again after today, I shall soon discover.

CHAPTER FOUR

It is nearly three o'clock and the sky is already darkening. As I shake the pattens from my feet, Mr Rudd pulls the cape from my shoulders and hangs it on a peg. The cane slips from my hand and hits the flagstone with a smack. I fumble to retrieve it; out of the corner of my eye I see Mary looking at me with a worried expression. I inhale deeply and follow Mr Rudd to the library where he knocks and opens the door but doesn't enter. I must run the gauntlet between the bookshelves alone.

Rebekah is seated with her back to me, staring out through the window, the same window behind which I covertly watched her only moments ago. Before I can take another step, Calder rises from his chair at the side of the hearth and his uncle, Septimus, appears from behind a book-lined alcove.

'Ah, Hester,' Calder begins amiably. He glances over his shoulder at his uncle. The older man nods, and Calder continues. 'As you know, Hester, you have been brought here to convalesce after your unfortunate accident. In addition, you are to be offered a rudimentary education, the finer details of which have now been resolved. The work will be different from any you have known before and you must be willing to apply your utmost concentration.'

'Yes sir, I shall.'

'Your tutor is to be my sister, Miss Rebekah Brock. You shall be a distraction for her during these long winter months, but this is also a wonderful opportunity for you to improve yourself. I hope you will make the most of it.'

I steal a glance at Rebekah. She has turned away from the window and is looking towards me but not at me. Her pocket book and pen are on her lap. The room is silent; although I feel a squirming in my belly, I straighten my spine to give an outward impression of confidence.

Finally, Rebekah glances at me. Her eyes are darker than velvet, and deep with intelligence, but they hold me at a distance. I hold her gaze, but as she looks at me with an air of disapproval, I flush and feel entirely wrong.

'I have exacting standards, Hester, and will expect you not to waste my time,' she says to me.

'What my niece is trying to say,' Septimus strikes in, 'is that she has considered Calder's proposal carefully and decided that she is willing to give you her time and attention in the hope of inculcating in you a basic schooling. You are to stay at Waterford until spring, when Calder will present both you and his findings to the committee of the Society.' Septimus turns to Rebekah. 'The girl looks to be a promising student, don't you think?'

'Yes, Uncle,' she says compliantly. 'I dare say she might soon strike her name in round-hand.'

'Oh, I'm sure you can achieve more than that, Rebekah,' Septimus concludes. Rebekah gives a swift nod but says nothing more, her eyes blank.

So, I am to stay in the country for the best part of half a year. It is such a relief, I almost weep. It will give me time and opportunity to learn about the neighbourhood. There may be work to be found somewhere nearby when spring comes. In time, I might even persuade Calder to give me a reference, perhaps help to find me work as a maid in a local house. Or better yet, facilitate a reunion with my Lincolnshire kinsfolk. Once I am settled in a new life, I will send word to Aunt Meg and tell her that I managed to escape from London after all. How proud she will be, how happy at my good fortune.

I wonder what has been said to persuade Rebekah. Calder gives a dash at the bell-pull for Mr Rudd, and I am dismissed. As I close the doors behind me, I overhear Rebekah saying to Calder, 'If she chooses to go, I refuse to be the person to discourage her.'

As I make my way back to my room, I wonder why Rebekah thinks I might want to leave. I repeat the words out loud to myself in a whisper, 'If she chooses to go, I refuse to be the person to discourage her.' Do they sound like a threat? Or are they a defence? Such words might conjure fear in any other, but I can only think about the suffering which masks the rhetoric. It is in this perplexed state of mind that I begin to drift into slumber, but where fear should be present, instead curiosity prevails.

The following morning, at breakfast, Mr Rudd tells me to report to Rebekah in the library at ten o'clock, the hours before to be spent exercising my leg in the gardens. At five minutes to ten, I arrive at the library. The door is open and Rebekah is at her needle. She is sitting in an armchair with her workbox open, searching the contents. I stand on the threshold, silent as a ghost, and I'm certain she doesn't hear my arrival, so I am able to watch her covertly. There is an indefinable sense of vitality about her and I suspect the day has suddenly become interesting.

I clear my throat and take a step forward.

'Well, come in and close the doors behind you,' she says, without even raising her eyes to me.

'Yes, Miss.'

'Sit down over there, please. We shall be working together every day except for Sunday. I trust you know the days of the week?'

I have to stop myself from raising my eyebrows in disbelief. She must think I have no more brains than a boot-boy.

'Yes, Miss.'

'And can you tell the time?'

The circumstances in which Calder found me must lead her to believe I am quite the imbecile.

'Yes, Miss. My uncle taught me to count the chimes. You don't need no dial or hands or ticking, if you can count the chimes, Miss. That's what he says.'

'Perhaps you are not as ignorant as I first thought,' she says.

'You flatter me, Miss,' I say dryly. She looks at me sharply and I fear I have exceeded propriety, but she says nothing.

'I wonder,' she continues, 'if you have been listening to gossip from clacking tongues. Some of the servants are wont to make mischief from their ignorance. For the most part it is harmless, but I do worry for them sometimes.' She is lost in her own thoughts for a moment and then says, more quietly, 'Are you afraid of me, Hester?'

'No, Miss.'

I say the words gently because I truly mean what I say. Once again, she looks surprised but then rapidly looks away. She rises, walks to the window and throws up the sash and, with her countenance settled, returns to the chair.

The morning continues with Rebekah writing the letters of the alphabet on a folio of manuscript and speaking the names and sounds of each character. After each group of four letters, she tests my writing and pronunciation. I take care to give sufficient correct answers to encourage her, but throw in the odd mistake here and there in an appropriate impression of ignorance. Whenever she studies the manuscript, I take the opportunity to steal a glance at her and, as the morning wears on, her frown begins to soften.

The following day, I arrive early and stand at the side of the desk. Rebekah appears on the stroke of ten and sets me to copying out alphabetical letters. As I work, I perceive she is observing me and this sharpens my mental faculties. I take pleasure from her attention and so work studiously. When one task is complete, she lays out another. At one point she even brings herself to say, 'Good, Hester!' and I feel a thrill of excitement at pleasing her.

Initially there is cautious brevity to her speech, but by the end of the second week she is divulging tales of her ancestors, and of Waterford Hall. She tells me the story of the Puritans who took away most of the hall's furniture, and of her Royalist forebear who was too young to take sides, thus saving Waterford from Cromwell. She tells me of secret passages and hidden rooms, but she never talks of herself. In turn, I ask her questions, and am ever inquisitive for more stories of the Brock family.

Each day, as I detect a tempering in Rebekah's haughtiness, I feel increasingly comfortable in her presence. I am playing a part, I know that, but I feel our enjoyment of each other's company is real, even if our tentative friendship is built on my lies.

It is Friday afternoon of the third week and I am sitting in the stillroom with Mary darning stockings. Mary's conversation gently simmers as we sew, but sometimes my unbridled inner thoughts simply rise like steam: I wonder where Rebekah is and what she does to fill her afternoons. Does she ever think of me when we are not in lessons? It is in this state of gentle, distracted industry that a cry, loud and shrill, is heard coming from the kitchen. Mary and I stare wide-eyed at each other, before running towards the source of the sound.

We arrive as Lottie, the kitchen girl, is helping the scullery maid into a chair. There is a pan and a broken basin on the floor and the scullery maid is badly scalded. The skin is red and already puckering; the uppermost layer beginning to separate. Lottie draws a fresh bowl of cold water and proceeds to submerge the girl's arm. This stimulates a piercing scream from the scullery maid. Mary takes her right hand, saying, 'You'll be all right, Susan.'

But Susan is trembling violently from the shock. The colour drains from her and sweat breaks out across her face before she folds limply in the chair, the bowl knocked to the floor. At this Lottie wears an expression of panic, tears welling in her eyes, and her face pale.

'Is she dead, Mary?' she asks.

'No, of course not. You don't die of scalds like that,' Mary says briskly, but the colour is blanching from her own face. She thinks for a moment, then says, 'Where's Mrs Jacques?'

'It's Cook's afternoon off. Whatever shall we do?' Lottie sobs.

I take one further look at Susan and the swollen, raw flesh of her arm, and then say to Mary, 'I'm going to fetch Miss Rebekah; she'll know what to do.'

I run up the back stairs, tear across the hallway and first try the library, then the ante-room, and finally the smaller drawing room, where I find Rebekah, bending over a table top scattered with springs, cogs, and ratchet-wheels. Absorbed in her task, I am only two feet away from her when she looks up and greets me with eyebrows raised. Before she can ask the reason for my intrusion, I say, 'Miss. There's been an accident in the kitchen and the girl has fainted.'

Immediately she removes her apron and takes up a small bottle and a decanter of spirits from the tray on the sideboard. She walks briskly beside me asking questions which I answer as best I can: Who is injured? How is she afflicted?

When we arrive in the kitchen, four or five other servants have joined Mary and Lottie, surrounding Susan, some raising their voices to be heard above the rest with advice, while others shrug their shoulders and shake their heads. Rebekah's presence in the noisy room is noticed swiftly, however, and within seconds of her arrival, the hubbub diminishes to nothing and a sense of order and relief finally prevails.

Rebekah first wafts the tiny bottle of smelling salts under

Susan's nose and the girl wakes with a start. While reassuring her with quiet words, Rebekah mixes vinegar with water and cleans the injury from top to bottom. She asks me to dilute some brandy from the decanter and give it to Susan to sip at while Mary is instructed to slice a potato thinly. Once the scald has been bathed, she places the slivers of potato over the wound and binds it with linseed-oil-soaked linen, then has Mary take Susan upstairs to rest. Like Eros organising Chaos, so Rebekah restores order and peace to the confusion below stairs.

'Was it your idea to fetch me, Hester?' she asks as she washes her hands.

I hesitate and before I can make any sort of reply, she says:

'I'm glad you did. It was a wise decision. Thank you.' Then she leaves as quietly as a sunset, gilding the landscape of my day.

Over the course of the next few weeks our daily routine in the library is rarely broken. Winter is approaching, with each day becoming chillier until the air prickles with cold and the trees are silvered with frost. The days are shorter and the nights come all too soon but, in the library, we sit before the roaring fire, as warm as a hayfield. My mind is animated with learning again, but it is my conversations with Rebekah that make me feel so very alive. Each day my contentment grows and I feel closer to my lost life at the parsonage than ever before. In the comfort of my bed at night, I am filled with wonder at the extraordinary change in my fortunes and am grateful for the circumstances that brought me to Waterford, and to Rebekah.

My lessons with Rebekah start precisely at ten o'clock and end at one. After luncheon, I work alone in a corner of the library for an hour, followed by exercise for my leg outside, and then sewing with Mary, where we chatter happily together. With Mary's gift of lively conversation, she steers from childhood memories to tales of Calder as an adolescent; and from her hoard of stories,

I'm often rewarded with pearls of information about Rebekah, which I treasure above all others.

I do not know exactly how Rebekah occupies herself later in the day and we rarely cross paths in the house. Eventually I ask Mary, as indifferently as I am able, about Rebekah's whereabouts, and discover she is visiting an old gentleman in the village to gain knowledge in the science of bee-keeping.

After that, I ask Mary more frequently about Rebekah's afternoon occupations and I learn of her varied and active schedule. Eventually, it becomes a customary point of amusement between us that I ask, 'And what activity do you suppose the dynamic Miss Brock will undertake today?'

One day Rebekah might inspect the household accounts, direct Cook on a complicated menu and hold a meeting with the head gardener. The next, she might rebind old books, take an inventory of the wine cellar and repair a clock. Sometimes she thrashes away at her piano, or takes two or more hot-blooded horses out one at a time to put them through their paces.

Mr Rudd tells me that some weeks ago, a local farmer's prize plough-horse, worth thirty guineas, came down with colic. The horse doctor declared that the animal could not be saved and must be shot. On hearing this, Rebekah prepared an admixture to her own recipe, which she fed to the horse while nursing it through the night. The following day, the farmer proclaimed the horse was a better beast than before; Rebekah declined all offers of recompense and begged that word of the deed should not be broadcast.

Twice, Rebekah passes me as I walk in the grounds, first with an injured lurcher in the back of her dogcart, the dog mournfully licking at its wound. Three days later, she drives her trap past me in the opposite direction, heading towards the park gates, the dog sitting beside her, bright-eyed and wagging its tail. She passes me with a wave and I smile as I return it. I notice how the fresh air has brought a rosy colour to her complexion and I take pleasure in the ripeness of the tint. I am more surprised at this than I am willing to confess.

Only twice does Rebekah vary our morning routine. Once, she has me accompany her on a tour of the hall's many rooms. The house is grand and unlike any place I have ever been before, but it is Rebekah's stories of the rooms that harness my interest most. The second occasion is when Rebekah reads aloud to me from one of her books. It is poetry, and I have never before heard such a harmonious unity of words and tones. The composite result stirs a feeling I cannot name, a glow beneath my ribs. I can only stare raptly as I listen and hope that Rebekah believes I understand little of it.

Apart from these events, the routine of my lessons continues. Rebekah's commitment to order and details is unquestionable. She is vigorous and efficient, of seemingly limitless energy. Septimus, inversely, reads a little, smokes a little, strolls a little. He does nothing definite but, sometimes, when I pass the drawing room before dinner, he can be heard upbraiding Rebekah for her lack of femininity and paucity of potential suitors. I can only sympathise from afar, wishing I could stand up for her against him and explain how productively she fills her long hours of solitude.

Rebekah herself gives no obvious clues to her opinion of me. She talks only of facts and never of feelings, but this makes me all the keener to gain her esteem. I notice she has taken the brittle edge off her countenance when she talks to me, her tone now much warmer than when we first met, but overall I am hardly any closer to understanding her than when I first came to Waterford.

CHAPTER FIVE

It is eight weeks since my arrival at Waterford Hall. My room is cold, and through the dawn's pale tint my breath forms little plumes of mist as I lie facing the ceiling. The servants are awake in the rooms above me. A water pitcher is clunked on its stand and heels tread the boards overhead. But I am barely disturbed by their activity as I smile at the thought of how soon ten o'clock will arrive, and how close I am to entering the library, with its fire and deep-piled rugs, its smell of books interlaced with a subtle fragrance of gillyflower.

Mary appearing at my door with a lighted candle interrupts my thoughts.

'Can I come in?' she whispers.

'Of course.'

She deposits the candle on my bedside table, briefly disappears before returning with three parcels of varying sizes. I slip out from beneath the bedcovers to help her and take up the top one, following Mary's lead and placing it on the floor at the side of the bed.

'I'd get back under the covers if I was you, Hester. You'll catch your death.'

I sit upright against the pillows and draw the blankets around me. Mary perches on the end of the bed and looks at me with kind eyes.

'These are from Miss Rebekah, Hester.'

'What are they? Why has she sent them?'

'I reckon it's a new outfit for you. I wasn't going to say nothing, but Sarah thinks . . . I don't know what she thinks. I just want you to look after yourself, that's all. Miss Rebekah can be a bit up and down, you know. Sarah calls her a regular seesaw Sally! Keep your feet on the ground, that's all. Anyway, I'll leave you to it. See you later.'

She rises, giving one more glance at the delivery as she leaves.

Troubled by Mary's words, I perch on the end of my bed and examine the parcels. I take up the largest one and fumble until I find the end of the string that binds it. Once loosened, the paper falls away to reveal a dress made of deep blue muslin and calico. The various frocks and undergarments provided for me thus far have been plain, smart and suitable to the purpose. But this gown from Rebekah, wrapped in thin paper, is the finest I have ever had. I lift it and hold it against me. She has managed to estimate my measurements well and I am flattered at this attention and experience a delightful fluttering in the pit of my stomach as I imagine her scrutinising me. From the next package, a petticoat falls to the floor and, as I unravel it, a pair of leather slippers tumbles out from the folds. As I dress myself I consider seeking out Rebekah immediately to thank her, but instead decide to wait until our lessons later.

After my morning walk, I make my way towards the library. As I near the open doorway of the drawing room, out of the silence comes Rebekah's voice: 'Hester? Is that you?' The room is yellow from the wide beam of sunlight that pushes its way in through the window. Rebekah is at the piano, a folio of music open on the bracket. She picks out a selection of chords and I am familiar with them. She goes on to play a phrase from the *Moonlight Sonata* and, being one of my childhood favourites, my heart quite melts at the recollection of it. As the final chord fades, she rests her hands on her lap and looks up at me.

'Mary delivered the outfit to you then?'

'Yes, Miss.'

'It looks very well on you,' she smiles.

'Thank you for your kindness. And for your kind words.' For the first time, I forget to use exaggerated round vowels and no longer sound like Annie Allsop, and in response she looks thoughtful, almost pleased with herself as she says, 'Hester, I need to visit some of our neighbours and I don't like travelling alone, so I thought I could drive myself and you could accompany me. I've asked Rudd to arrange for a few provisions to be packed and for the trap to be ready at ten.'

The clock in the hallway is already chiming the hour.

'Come along then!' she says cheerfully, taking up her bonnet and gloves. I follow her out into the hallway where Mary hands me a broadcloth cape and a new coal-scuttle bonnet, a concerned look in her eye. Rebekah is already on the steps when I catch up with her. Mr Rudd is there with the dogcart, its green-spoked wheels glinting in the sunlight. Rebekah takes up the reins of the grey pony as Mr Rudd helps me into the seat beside her.

'Leave your cane with Rudd, Hester. There's hardly any walking to be done.'

I do as she instructs and I realise my leg is now strong enough to bear my weight without the aid of the stick and that I have been using the cane more out of habit than necessity. Rebekah clucks to the pony, snaps the reins and off we trot.

Although it is cold, the sun is out and the sky is clear and blue. There is a light frost and the carriage ruts are coated in thin ice so there is a satisfying sound as the wheels turn. Steam rises from the pony's flanks as we trundle along through the shimmering haze of the December morning.

'We have an apple orchard and a nuttery over there,' Rebekah says, pointing to the left between a series of tree-clothed banks. 'Cobnuts, hazelnuts, and they say the finest walnuts in all England. Have you had any yet?'

'No,' I answer. 'Not yet.' I think of the gruel and stews served to us below stairs by Mrs Jacques, the cook, and I can't help but smile at Rebekah's belief that we are provided with an assortment of nuts to round off our meals.

'The fishponds over there,' she goes on, this time nodding to the right, 'were originally dug as fire-fighting reservoirs over a hundred years ago.'

'How interesting,' I murmur as our arms briefly touch with the bounce of the trap. I forget my accent again, but she doesn't seem to notice and continues pointing out local landmarks and explaining their history.

Eventually, she pulls up beneath a naked elm where the grass has been rubbed bald. She drops the reins and says, 'Sweetie needs a rest. She's rather long in the tooth now, aren't you old girl?' The pony gives a snort as though in direct response, and Rebekah and I both laugh at the timing. 'I've had her since I was a child. I used to ride her everywhere. We even used to run with the hounds. Do you ride, Hester?'

The image of Father teaching me to trot on our old sorrel saddle horse is suddenly strong in my mind; I recall the softness of the reins and Father's proud face and I want so much to tell Rebekah who I really am, but some deep-rooted instinct warns me not to.

'No, Miss. I don't ride. There's only Shanks's pony where I live.'

I say it with a gentle smile, but the false words leave me feeling awkward. Rebekah says nothing, but toys with the button on her glove. She reaches for the reins, but before I can think what to do, I move my eyes first and then turn to face her. Our knees touch, as gentle as a doubt. She looks back at me and holds my gaze for longer than a moment. Unsettled, I eventually look away and move back in my seat, but surely the damage is done? I wait for a reprimand at my impertinence, but it doesn't come. Time itself slows, as if to draw still more attention to the moment. As the seconds stagger forward, I raise my eyes again to fix them on Rebekah and find she is still looking at me. There is a sudden glow to her expression, and with it pleasure and thrill radiates from her to me; the pleasure surging in my belly, the thrill at the top of my thighs. She takes my arm, threading it through the crook of her own, and there we sit, hooked together.

'Tell me, Hester,' she says eventually. 'Where you live in London, is it really as terrible as they say?'

Hoping that she cannot sense the hammering of my heart I say, 'It is in some ways; in most ways I suppose.' For the first time, I consciously speak in my own voice, dropping the mimicry of Annie. Perhaps it is rash to do so, but I want so much to show Rebekah a portion of my true self.

So, I tell her of the cramped quarters and our neighbours, of the cold and the damp and the hunger. She listens and nods and has me describe the exact location of the accident, and the circumstances that occasioned my meeting with Calder. I tell her of the dismal day I had spent at Smithfield looking for my cousin, and of the moment, just before colliding with Calder's carriage, when my hopes were at their lowest ebb and I sent out a prayer for salvation. Her eyes are thoughtful.

'And do you spend every day at the meat market?'

'Oh, no. I was supposed to meet my cousin there, you see, but he never arrived. My aunt arranged the meeting and from then on my thoughts were filled with dreams of how my cousin would come for me and take me away from the misery of London; take me back to Lincolnshire where I am from. I wanted to work as a dairymaid and even dreamed of saving enough shillings to buy my own Alderney. I could make butter and cheese, build my own dairy business.'

'Where in Lincolnshire is your family from?'

'You won't have heard of it, I am sure. It's a tiny village called Welton.'

'In the Wolds?'

'Why yes!'

'We have some relatives from Louth. Lord and Lady Appleton. Lady Appleton is a maternal great-aunt; Great-Aunt Eleanor. I was always one of her favourites. She's suffered a great deal from ill health over the years; the death of her only daughter left her rather frail, but her mind's as sharp as a pin. I write to her frequently, but it's been a good while since we visited. I can't call an image of the village to mind, but I know its name. And what is the name of your relation?'

'Edward White.'

'And when was he to come for you?'

'Well, Aunt Meg said she'd told the drovers what an asset I might be, and that they should be very glad to have me return with them after the autumn drove. So, I believed Edward had good reason to meet me. It seemed there was a real chance of bettering myself, but Edward was late. Aunt Meg said he may have been distracted by temptation, and that I mustn't worry. But, in the end, he was more than three weeks overdue by the time of my accident with your brother.'

'That sounds odd. And no word from him?'

'No, nothing.'

'As though he simply disappeared—'

'But people don't just disappear into thin air, do they?'

As I speak the words, I remember Rebekah's missing servants,

Martha and Agnes. Rebekah must be thinking the very same; she pauses before saying, 'No, Hester. People do not simply disappear into thin air. Though the newspapers I get sent up from London suggest that they can do, and with increasing frequency. It is very troubling.'

There is no defensiveness in her voice. She seems as mystified as I am.

'Does the lad drink, Hester? Might he have gone to a tavern and—'

'I don't know. I don't know what to make of it.'

After a thoughtful pause, Rebekah gathers the reins and pulls Sweetie's head up. She touches Sweetie with the whip and we jog-trot in silence to a square house at the end of a lane where Rebekah alights from the dogcart. She hands me the satchel of food.

'I won't be long, Hester. Please eat whatever you fancy.'

True to her word, she is gone briefly, and I am nibbling a piece of game pie when I hear her heels on the gravel.

'I told you I wouldn't be long. Is the pie good?'

I nod my reply and reach into the bag for another slice for her.

'Oh, no thank you, I'll eat later. Calder's due up from town today, so Uncle Sep will want us all to dine together.' She pauses before taking up the reins and says thoughtfully, 'There's a house just over that hill where I attended my first ball. I was barely fifteen. They say that dancing is like poetry of the feet, but I'm afraid my feet didn't rhyme very well. I was rather nervous, and clumsy. But the music was very beautiful.' She looks wistfully towards the horizon, then turns to me and says, 'But Hester; you must be freezing! How selfish of me to prattle on. Come, sit closer, keep warm.'

Rebekah drives us around the village, down lanes and cart tracks, which in summer would be bordered with meadowsweet and scented with the heady fragrance of elderflowers. Today the vegetation is sparser, but berries beam out every once in a while through twining bracts of ivy.

We meet no other vehicles, just the occasional walker and rider, all of whom greet Rebekah with a smile and a nod. She leaves me briefly to call at a white cottage with a hipped roof and returns just as the church clock is striking twelve. We continue on our journey and she announces that she no longer wishes to call on the vicar, the last intended beneficiary of the day's visiting.

'He's an old busybody, anyway,' she says with a laugh. 'I'll tell my uncle he wasn't at home.'

With that we begin to make our way back, past a row of cottages on the village green and the glowing blacksmith's forge on the hill, until we retrace our steps and join the road to Waterford. Conversation flows easily, but we are at peace when the words end too. We travel on, the silence only occasionally broken by Rebekah pointing out where the violets will bloom in April, or the trees where chaffinches will nest.

We re-enter the grounds of Waterford and, as we reach the house, Rebekah leans towards me and remarks, 'There's something unique about you, Hester White, you have the depth of quiet water.' She speaks the words softly, like footsteps in a church; and her voice is softer than the low notes of a cello.

I quit the dogcart and, as I make my way to the servants' entrance, I take one last look at Rebekah. She pauses at the top of the steps, bold against the sky. Then she is gone and I am left with a mixture of feelings I can barely contain.

That night I am restless. I relive the moment when I saw the look in her eye, and each time there is a pinching in my belly, acute and delicious. Oh! How I long to be near her.

I rise before dawn and find myself pacing the room with impatience, trying to control the rolling tautness in my stomach. Each time I think of Rebekah, I feel shy of her. I wonder how the first moments of my lessons will go. I wonder if she will wish to teach me at all; perhaps she will want to go out in the dogcart again. Perhaps yesterday can be repeated in all its wonderful glory.

I descend the stairs to the kitchen with a heightened feeling of expectation. Lost in my thoughts, I don't immediately realise that it is quieter than normal at breakfast and that I have not seen either Mary or Sarah. I walk through the hushed underbelly of the house and decide to visit the library before my morning's exercise.

A little snow has fallen in the night, and outside the window ledges are coated with an inch of white powder while the panes are glazed with fingers of frost. The room is dull, the candles unlit, and the fire not laid. I take the opportunity to tidy Rebekah's books and pencils, arrange her pens and bottles of ink.

I stroll along the bookshelves, cast my eyes around the room, and notice a small stack of papers, neatly bound with a scarlet ribbon, placed on an occasional table. Rebekah has sometimes worked on these during my lessons and must have left them here last night. I ignore them at first, but as the minutes pass, curiosity gets the better of me. I quickly loosen the binding and glance at the first sheet. It is some sort of report. I scan the text and realise it is an assessment of the circumstances surrounding Martha Briggs's disappearance, written in Rebekah's hand. Other sheets record transcripts of conversations Rebekah has had with Martha's mother, her village acquaintances, and every servant at both Waterford and the villa. I leaf through the papers and realise there is a similar account relating to Agnes. They recount Rebekah's efforts; either to find the maids, or to discover their fates. There are also newspaper clippings from London journals detailing other cases of missing people.

With each page, my belief in Rebekah is strengthened. Where

before a degree of suspicion had persisted in my mind, a glowing coal fanned by gossip and Mary's concerns, now a reassuring breeze of truth blows cool and quenching, banishing my uncertainty. My instincts about Rebekah are right and the discovery is a tremendous relief to me. When I see Rebekah today, I am now determined to give her an honest account of my life and to offer my help in her investigation.

I leave the library for my morning walk in the garden, imagining how the conversation will go. As the clock strikes ten, I return and take my usual seat next to Rebekah's. I wait for the tap of her heels, for the rustle of her skirts. I straighten the folds of my dress and smooth my hair. The house is still quiet. Too quiet.

By half past ten I am filled with foreboding and begin pacing the room. I go to the window and rub a small circle on the frosted windowpane with the heel of my hand so that I might peer through. At first the snowfall seems undisturbed, but staring at the quilted driveway, I suddenly realise I can see wheel ruts and footprints. My heart sinks as panic begins to cloud all my thinking. Running from the room without any idea of where I am heading, or to whom I might appeal, I collide headlong with Mr Rudd.

'Slow down Hester, whatever's the matter with you?' He takes my shoulders and looks down at my face, 'Are you ill?'

'No, Mr Rudd. I just don't know where Miss Rebekah is this morning. I waited in the library and—'

'Surely she told you?'

I look up at him, a question in my eyes.

'Mr Calder changed his mind,' he continues. 'He was supposed to spend Yuletide here, but sent word last night that he has decided to stay in town. Mr Septimus and Miss Rebekah set off this morning before dawn to join him at the London house.'

'I see.' I take a deep breath and try to calm myself. 'When will they be back?'

'I imagine they'll be back just after Christmas. They always spend Twelfth Night at Waterford. Miss Rebekah has written a list of lessons and tasks you can do while she's away.'

And so, like the last rose of the summer, Rebekah is suddenly gone from the hall and I feel her departure keenly over the next few days. I follow her instructions and continue to spend mornings in the library, but without Rebekah the atmosphere is gloomy, and my work is wearisome.

Despite many of the servants departing with Septimus and Rebekah for the London house, there are several who remain at Waterford with me, including Mary. With Sarah gone to London and no roommate to listen to her chatter, Mary seeks me out more frequently for company, and I am glad of it. At first, sensitive to my demeanour, she avoids the subject of Rebekah. But in time, with kind eyes and caution, she reintroduces her to our conversations and I find it comforting.

As the days pass, I withstand Rebekah's absence better, not because my feelings towards her are tempered but because I feel so close to her here; in her house and library; at her desk. My thoughts of her grow more tender each day, and my recollection of our happy acquaintance becomes more precious. As much as I value the friendship and easy intimacy I've developed with Mary, my feelings towards Rebekah are different to any I've known before: more potent, fragile and complex.

The house is quiet, and above stairs dustsheets are placed on chairs, tables and Rebekah's piano. Rooms are closed up, hearths left empty, and winter is as present as an unwanted guest throughout the upper reaches of the old hall. But below stairs is a different world, as all the little jobs that have been laid to one side while the Brocks are in residence are now attended to. Sheets are mended, silver is polished and Mrs Jacques's kitchen is a bustle of industry as she re-stocks the pantry. As Christmas day approaches, the activity only increases, and suddenly evergreens and mistletoe are brought inside, with ivy leaves to dress the doorframes and holly to adorn the newel posts. Suddenly, the twenty-fifth is upon us.

Mrs Jacques has had a flitch of bacon smoking at the side of the fire and is carving thick rashers and throwing them on the griddle as we file in for breakfast. We sit together in the servants' hall as the bacon, with eggs, is brought to the table. Then Mr Rudd hands out gifts from Septimus: new caps with long ribbons and an orange for the girls; neck-cloths and a twist of tobacco for the men.

'Old Septimus must have been at the dice-box again,' he whispers to Mary as he passes.

After breakfast, we walk as a group to the village church for the morning service. The nativity is told and a sermon is read, before we return to Waterford through a flurry of snowflakes. We pass two groups of walkers, merry with the season and calling out glad tidings to us. We wish them God's speed in return, our voices clear and bright through the cold, our sentiments cloaked in warmth.

Back at the hall, Mrs Jacques and her kitchen girls busy themselves preparing the roast duck. Our meal is taken much later than usual and finished with mince pies and hot spiced mead. Normally everyone leaves as soon as the eating is done, but today all remain seated and the hum of conversation continues uninterrupted. Then, with tongues loosened by mead, and time relaxed by absent masters, the telling of stories begins. Some tales are short and disordered, the mere relating of a special moment in time. Some are sad, some very funny, but my favourites are those about love: the yearning and the winning and the losing. With the shutters closed fast against the snowstorm outside, we sit on our benches, our faces glowing before the blazing fire, and we sip cups of warm, spiced ale from the wassail-bowl.

As darkness falls, Mr Rudd reminds us that the carol singers are due to walk past the hall at six o'clock on their way to the widow Benton's house. Mary and I volunteer to take a lantern and watch for them. The air is biting, the snow a foot deep, and I begin to doubt if they're coming. Mary and I are shivering after only a few minutes of standing in the night air. But then, just as the wind has dropped to no more than the stroke of an angel's wing, a host of tiny, blinking lights appears in the distance, like a lost constellation.

The choir approaches, the snow lending their feet a velvet tread, and their lanterns lighting up tree branches that sparkle with frost. Mary rushes back inside to rally the others and, as we all huddle together on the house steps, the singers begin. Accompanied by a fiddle, they serenade us with songs of shepherds and angels and the most precious child born this night. The music is sweet to the ear as they sing 'Adeste Fideles', and together we carry the chorus with them, our breath frost-white against the sky. Perhaps Rebekah once stood on this very spot, the music kindling warmth in her heart, just as it has in mine. When it is over, I stare out across the quilted landscape, so near yet so distant from Rebekah, and I think how lucky I am to be here. I recall Christmases in the cellar room, waking up to a meagre fire in the grate, and Uncle Jacob sleeping off the gin and violent commotion of the night before. And I do not underestimate how fortunate I am to be here at Waterford, able to chase away the cold with warm thoughts of future tomorrows.

We return to the kitchen, teeth chattering, hands burning with cold. The chorister with the fiddle joins us and is soon plied with plum cake and spiced wine to encourage him to strike up a jig for us. One dance leads to another and soon there is a frantic crossing of hands and shuffling of feet as we pair up and dance a four-handed reel. Elbows are knocked, toes are stepped upon and I find myself laughing as heartily as ever I have.

At the close of the day, George Rudd has supped enough liquor to make a cat speak and sleeps soundly with his head on the table. The younger maids and apprentice boys have ambled away to the garrets and Mary, Mrs Jacques and I are the last to retire. As I lie in my bed I thank Providence for the cherished Christmases of my early childhood, for the new year yet to come, for the season and the song; but most of all for sending me to Waterford and to Rebekah Brock.

When Christmas has passed and the New Year has been welcomed in, I can think only of Twelfth Night and the Brocks' return. Twelfth Cake is mixed and the dried bean carefully hidden in it, but Rebekah is not here to find it. And when the last crumbs have been eaten, still the Brocks do not come.

Mary and I labour daily together now as maids of all work. With a Turk's head broom, we sweep curtain poles. We wipe grates and dust rooms, wash paintwork and polish glass decanters. But mostly we spend our afternoons sitting in the scullery, polishing great copper pans with a leather rag and a jar of oil and rottenstone. My hands are either red with the work or white with cold, but nothing hurts as much as the longing in my heart.

It is the second week in January and a letter arrives for George Rudd. It is from Rebekah and she makes a particular point of asking after me. She hopes I continue to learn and that I have been keeping myself busy. I ask him if I may see the letter. He laughs at first, believing I am still illiterate, but I plead that it will help with my learning. He gives up the missive and when he is gone I stare at Rebekah's handwriting, touch my fingertips to the ink. Is there a small blot against the aitch of my name, where perhaps the nib paused? Are the words in my paragraph written with a thicker flow of ink, where the author wrote more slowly, more thoughtfully? I conjure these delusions out of nothing and feast upon the hope they provide, but still the day passes long and slow.

Each morning when I enter the library, I stand at the open doorway and stare at her chair. The room is no longer welcoming. With her absence, it feels as though a dense cloud has passed over the face of the sun. I find myself always listening for her, watching for her dogcart and pony. New Year passes to Hilary Day and beyond to Candlemas, and Waterford Hall remains cold and empty.

CHAPTER SIX

J ust as a deer lifts her nose in the air to smell a change in the wind, so I feel a shift in the atmosphere at Waterford Hall on 7 February. No sooner do I rise and dress, than the silence is broken by voices and clattering hooves outside. Winged by the possibility of Rebekah's return, I attend to my toilet in all possible haste and run to the kitchen.

The room is astir with activity. Mrs Jacques's hands are powdered with flour as she works at a dough while inspecting lists of produce and directing three kitchen maids on how she wishes the root vegetables to be prepared.

George Rudd, meanwhile, is flushed. A small group of men and boys hovers at the doorway, listening to his instructions. He divides them, telling some to unload the waggon packed with rout seats and hired candelabra, while others are to unhinge the dancing-room doors and replace them with muslin hangings. The final two are to carry plate and glassware from the basement to the dining room. Through the confusion, I snatch a heel of bread and a hunk of cheese, eating it on the hoof as I head to the grounds.

As I walk, the day blooms through the treetops, unfolding its petals of light to me one by one. The pond water, frozen into silence for so long, has stretched and thrown off its icy veneer. Rooks wheel through the blushing skies and the grass wilts underfoot. The wind itself is milder and it feels as though it is breathing the words that are on the tip of my tongue: she's coming home.

Throughout the morning the relentless busyness continues, and every few minutes George Rudd appears on the portico steps to receive provisions that arrive by the waggon-load. From sides of salt pork and iced barrels of fish to boxes of sweetmeats and cases of wine, he waves his arms to orchestrate their movements.

Later, I catch up with Mary and help her make up the beds in the west wing. As we unfold sheets and plump pillows, Mary says:

'Exciting, don't you think?'

'What? Making beds?'

She snorts and rolls her eyes. 'Very droll, Hester. No, you know; the Brocks finally coming back from town.'

'The whole world seems like it's upside down to me, Mary. I don't quite know what to make of it.'

'Well, last year they came back with some "society friends" as George calls 'em. Sir This, Lord That and Lady Somewhere-or-Other. George even reckons there might be a great theatrical actor with them this time and a maharaja from Bengal!'

I imagine the gentry arriving in their carriages: the ladies and the lords, the players and the Indian princes. But, at the heart of everything, I see Rebekah.

'You all right, Hester? There's such a flush come to your cheeks. If you weren't smiling so wide, I'd think you was having a turn.'

'I'm fine, Mary. Don't worry. But you're right. It is exciting, isn't it?'

When the chores are finished and supper has been served, there is nothing for me to do except wait. At twilight, the entourage is yet to arrive. By half past six, I have tired of the bustle inside the house, so I take a shawl and walk outside to the front of the hall. The windows are a-glow with candles and the flickering fires within. Twice I hear horsemen in the distance and twice I am disappointed as the noise fades.

Then, at last, just before seven o'clock, a rider enters the park. Three men with flambeaux run down the driveway to greet him and then continue towards the gates. Within minutes, three more horsemen come into view, leading a snaking line of five or more closed carriages. One by one the horses are reined up and the occupants alight from their coaches.

Immediately an infectious giddiness charges the atmosphere; footsteps, laughter and chatter drifts from the medley of sweeping skirts and feather-decked hats. I take myself away to the far side of the steps and watch the Brocks' carriage. Eventually, the door is thrown open and Calder jumps out, his mood as cheerful as ever. He strides towards a gentleman dismounting a horse, claps the man on the back and bids him a hearty welcome. He greets another man with a vigorous handshake as he weaves through the crowd, spreading jollity as he goes and leaving several guests in fits of laughter.

I turn my eye back to the carriage. Finally Rebekah descends the carriage steps, waving her gloved left hand dismissively, eschewing help from both Jenkins and Sarah. Rebekah seems altered in both complexion and demeanour. She is sallow, deflated and more abrupt with the servants than I have yet known her.

I move towards her, threading my way through the crowd. Without seeing me she bows her head, covers it with her hood and proceeds into the hall. I follow at a discreet distance and, as she makes her way between the pillars, I find myself wanting to reach out and touch her shadow as it glides over the cold stone.

I know she must be fatigued after the journey, exhausted at being amongst society so much, but doubts needle me, and I wonder if during our lengthy separation she has forgotten about our conversations in the library or the moment that meant so much to me when we drove round the village.

As more visitors emerge from the carriages, the crowds thicken and the chatter increases. Yet, as quickly as the tempest arrives, so it passes. Grooms lead the horses to the stables; maids scurry to the servants' entrance; valets make their way to the servants' hall. I swallow back my disappointment at not gaining Rebekah's attention and hasten to the back door.

I return to my room and, as soon as I close the door, tears come, uninvited. As I cry quietly into my pillow, the corridors come alive with footsteps and voices as guests are shown to their bedchambers and servants are directed to the attic rooms above. Later on, faint sounds from the dining room waft up the stairs and beneath the slit at the base of my door. The distant thrum of footsteps is accompanied by the dim chink of glasses and cutlery. Occasional raucous laughter resounds and there is always the low murmur of conversation.

As the tears slowly subside, I lie on my side upon my mattress with my knees tucked under my chin. The pillow is damp with my tears so I turn it over; but still sleep will not come.

By midnight, there is a lull in the noise from downstairs. All is quiet for a while, before a piano and fiddle strike up in the main drawing room. Not long after, there is a gentle tap on my door.

'Hester? It's Mary.'

I feign sleep, remain perfectly silent, but she persists.

'Me and Sarah and Sue from the scullery, we're having a little dance in our room. Mrs Jacques has given us a drop of sherry and some pastries. Please join us, it'll be a lark.'

I wipe my eyes and approach the door, but don't open it.

'I'm sorry, Mary. I have a dreadful headache. You go and enjoy yourself, I think I'll just stay here.'

'Sure you're all right?'

'Yes, please don't worry.'

'Well, come along if you have a change of heart.'

The music grows louder, the girls spend the next half-hour thumping around their room in time to the rhythm, and in my mind I imagine them mimicking the ladies in a Roger de Coverley. By the time the clocks strike one, the girls are silent. By three o'clock, the whole house is finally quiet and I submit to the pull of sleep.

The following morning, I am woken early by the new noises of the house. In recent weeks, I have become accustomed to the comforting annoyances of creaking floorboards stretching away the cold night air, and doors opening and shutting as the day's duties begin. This morning, however, a gentleman's voice rises from the room below mine and footfalls sound from the bedchamber adjacent to my own. The servant quarters hum with conversation, and hooves clatter outside in the courtyard.

I dress briskly and hurry down the back stairs to the kitchen. With the library out of bounds to me, and the servants' hall heaving with new faces, I am relieved when after breakfast Mary beckons me to her.

'Never seen the place so busy,' she says and heaves a sigh. 'Too much to do and not enough time to do it. We're all going to need your help today, Hester.'

Mary's prediction proves accurate and my day is spent mending petticoats, sewing on buttons, ironing napkins and undertaking a whole host of sundry chores endless in their monotony. But as busy as my body might be, my mind is set to wandering. I think only of the activity above stairs; of the discussions Rebekah is having with the ladies in the drawing room; of the gentlemen with whom Rebekah converses in the library. And so the day passes, until just before I am about to climb the stairs to my bedchamber, George Rudd sends for me. He is waiting outside the butler's pantry and says:

'I have a message from Miss Rebekah.'

In my heart, I always knew she would send for me eventually. With her time taken up with guests and entertaining, I understand how difficult it must have been for her to arrange. But she has found a way.

'What does she say, Mr Rudd? Where am I to meet with her?'

'She simply says that lessons are cancelled while the guests are at Waterford, Hester.'

'I see,' I say quietly, 'and she said nothing else?'

'No. That was all.'

'Thank you, Mr Rudd.'

I retire to my room and, through the music and merriment of Rebekah's society guests downstairs, I have a weary and fitful night's sleep and am awash with disillusion.

The next morning passes slowly; the atmosphere below stairs is busy and fractious. I spend my time polishing plate in the scullery until I am called upon to clear away a broken decanter from the drawing room. With a basin for the shards and a cloth for the spilled liquor, I weave my way past ladies with fans and trilling laughs, and past gentlemen with sherry glasses and ruddy complexions. There was a time when a housemaid's duties seemed favourable, but since Rebekah has expanded my mind and elevated my aspirations, the work no longer holds any appeal for me.

As I return to the back stairs, I cross the hallway and there is a sudden gust of air. I wonder if the doors have blown open and I look towards them. There, with the glow of outdoor freshness on her skin, and wearing a velvet cloak as dark as her eyes, stands Rebekah. I move towards her. She doesn't see me at first; she is pulling at hatpins and removing her bonnet. Then, suddenly, as though she feels my gaze upon her, her eyes meet mine. Her lips curl into a smile but in less than a moment she collects herself, the welcome in her eyes rapidly dissolving. She glances quickly over her shoulder then calls out to me:

'Lessons are cancelled. I sent a message with Rudd.'

She doesn't use my name. She doesn't look me in the eye while she speaks and her voice is flat. She doesn't deliver the words cruelly, but nevertheless they bruise me. She sweeps past as Septimus and a woman in a feathered hat follow her in from outside. I stand rigid for several seconds, then reluctantly leave with a heavy heart.

Just as yesterday, monotony and menial tasks fill the rest of the day's waking hours. Mary attempts to bring heartfelt cheer, and arrives at my room with a flask of Mrs Jacques's damson wine. The wine is warm with the fruit of autumn and Mary's words are warm with the fruit of wisdom; she assures me that matters will right themselves once the visitors leave. I tell her all is well and that I am just a little out of sorts.

When Mary has left and it is long after midnight, I am wide awake. My candle is burning low but I will not extinguish it. Unable to sleep and unwilling to close my eyes to the uncertainty of my future, I think of nothing but Rebekah and how changed she is upon her return, and over and over again I replay her warm smile turning to ashes before me.

My powerlessness increases as I toss and turn. One moment, I resolve to go to her, to enter her rooms. The next, I shrink from the prospect with abject fear of how I might explain myself. I wrestle with sense and reason until I determine that I must see it through while the possibility of success still remains. Buoyed by optimism and fortified by Mary's wine, I take up the candle and open the door.

I pad along the corridor in my stockinged feet, the shell of my hand curved protectively around the trembling flame. Steady to my purpose, now I have made the decision, I do not waver. Grunts and snores, whispers and sneezes all emanate through doors as I make my way to her. The secret noises of the house are disconcerting, but I am not afraid.

Rebekah's bedroom is at the end of the west gallery. Over time I have learned the layout of the house from Mary and can see a map of the route in my mind's eye as clear as quire and quill.

My eye marks her door and my pulse races as I near it. I listen, but can hear nothing from inside. The thought that she is on the other side of the oak panel makes my heart skip a beat and I am almost dizzy from the blood rushing in my ears. As I place my palm on the skin of the door, my hair prickles on my scalp.

'Have courage,' I whisper to myself. I twist the door handle and enter. The light is weak, coming only from the glowing logs in the grate. The sight of her bonnet on a hook and her gloves on a table gives me a thrill and I press on, moving around on velvet paws, until I reach the door to her bedroom.

I curl my fingers around the handle and relish the feel of it. I lean against the door and listen: nothing. Insensate to the risk I am running and the consequences that may befall me, I twist my wrist and feel the latch biting. Retaining my grasp of the handle for support I push the door open; my legs are weak and my bladder feels full. I catch the scent of Rebekah's rose-petal pomander lingering in the air. I lift my candle and let its beam fall on the furnishings, but the bed-hangings are tied back and the counterpane is smooth; she is not here.

Suddenly everything feels flat. I stand irresolute, stunned by my disappointment. I aimlessly cast my eyes about the room and am drawn to a small oil painting on the table at the side of Rebekah's bed. The portrait is of a man and a woman, perhaps in their twenties. The man is unmistakably a Brock; although his features are gentler than Septimus's, he has the same shape of face and his thick, dark hair is just like Calder's. And Rebekah, in her own unique way, features them all. The recurring family resemblance is so strong that I wonder if I passed a Brock in the street, in any town or city in England, I would instantly know from which family they originated. The woman in the portrait is nothing less than beautiful, with raven hair and persuasive eyes, and I suppose that these people must be Rebekah's parents. I meditate on the picture for some moments, but am suddenly roused by passing voices from outside in the corridor. I draw a sharp breath and in my haste to retreat, I knock a book from the table. I retrieve it from the floor with shaking hands and inspect it, realising that it is her diary, the vessel for her most intimate thoughts.

At once, temptation enters my mind: what if I were to open the pages and read? What if Rebekah's opinion of me were laid bare in black and white on these pages? In the silence, I tempt the devil to me, show him the opportunity and challenge him to watch me do his bidding. But it is one thing to feel temptation, and quite another to succumb to it. Eventually, the allurement passes and I restore the book to its place on the table, snatching away my fingers as though it is white hot.

Crestfallen, I begin the journey back to the east wing. My mind is in a flux and I cannot think rationally. I conjure explanations for Rebekah's absence at this time of night. I imagine her ill on the chaise-longue in the drawing room, her face contorted with agony. Next I visualise her talking intimately with the Bengali prince, brushing his hand with her own, using the purring tones of her voice to seduce him. I swing from jealousy to contempt, from fear to ardour, all in the space of a heartbeat. I'm only disturbed from my wild imaginings when distant voices rise from downstairs, from the library.

Through the quiet of the night, Rebekah's voice rings out and lingers in the air. With no thought of how I might explain myself, I hurry towards the sound and find the doors to the room are slightly ajar. With my heart in my mouth I approach one of the doors and push it so I might peep through the crack.

The candles are still aflame and the fire has been fed. The air is thick with the odour of tobacco and breath laced with spirits, the faintest fragrance of gillyflower hovering between the two. Rebekah is seated to the right of the fire screen, her face flushed. Calder and Septimus also have ruddy, shiny faces. There is another gentleman too, short of stature, wide of girth and partially obscured. His hair is fashioned just as Calder's but lacks body and sheen, and his clothes are of a cruder cut. Ash falls from the tip of his fat cigar onto his scarlet waistcoat, then he lifts his dimpled fingers and runs them between his shirt collar and the flesh of his neck. Whether distant cousin or family friend, he slouches in his chair and is perfectly at ease.

I have arrived at a break in the conversation and I fear that Calder will ring for a servant and I will be discovered. However, as soon as he has refreshed the gentlemen's tumblers he says, 'So, Blister, how's business?'

'Well, you know, Brock old fellow, many fingers in many pies. Don't like to go into too much detail in front of ladies.' He has the confident swagger of one who is not confident at all.

'Don't mind Rebekah, Freddie; she knows how to hold her tongue.'

'I'm sure she does.' Blister throws a cold look at Calder and his heavy-lidded eyes tell tales of guile and concealment.

'Always the secretive one, weren't you?'

'Always the sensible one, as I remember it, Calder.'

'Are you riding out with the others tomorrow, Frederick?' Septimus asks, slicing the atmosphere. 'Calder's got his eye on a spirited filly over at Popplewell Grange.'

'Spirited fillies,' Blister says, 'go either one of two ways, Septimus; they either drive you to distraction with their untamed spirit or disappoint you with the lack of it.'

'Nonsense, Frederick,' Septimus parries. 'They simply need a firm hand. There's nothing that a sharp pair of rowels and a stiff whip can't remedy, even in the most wilful of creatures. Spirit, character, defiance: call it what you may, they will always bend to the will of a firm master.'

I glance at Rebekah. Her features are expressionless and her eyes blank, as though she is wearing a mask. The man they call Blister turns his bulk to face her.

'So, Rebekah,' his voice condescending, 'what do you do all day in this fine house to amuse yourself?'

'I am never at a loss for occupation, Mr Blister. I frequently visit our local acquaintances, but equally I am more than content in my own society. I enjoy sketching and riding. I work at my needle, and take a great deal of pleasure from playing the piano. There are plenty of books at Waterford, of course, and in the evenings, when I may lack convivial company, I commit my thoughts to my journal.'

'And what,' Calder interrupts, 'of your latest venture, Rebekah?'

'I don't know to what you refer,' she stutters.

'Come now!' Calder goes on. 'Our little experiment. How is she coming along?'

'What's all this, Calder?' Blister chuckles.

Rebekah breaks her silence. 'The experiment has not worked, Calder. The girl's intellectual faculties are as deficient as her attitude. I will not waste my time or risk your reputation any further. I have arranged to dismiss her.' Her voice is low, as though she is talking of the dead, and I stare at her with unblinking eyes as she toys idly with her necklace. Her words pass through me and render me immobile; such is the potency of her rejection. For the first time in my life, I truly wish I were grassed down in the churchyard along with my parents, able at last to stop the relentless ache of this life.

Rebekah moves to stand before the men, her lips firmly compressed, making them paler than they are naturally. She drops her eyes before saying quietly, 'I have made preparations to return her to The London Society for the Suppression of Mendicity.'

The name of the Dicity can cause any heart to contract, but spoken in Rebekah's voice it petrifies me with shock. I am trembling with fury and fright; clenching my fists until my fingertips tingle.

'I have arranged for her to be admitted to the Society in—'

I hear no more of her arrangements as I turn on my heel, lift up my skirts and flee. My candle flame flickers at the speed of my departure. Twice I stumble up steps, but I do not stop, cannot stop. I must retrieve my boots and cloak from my room and then make my escape. As I reach the top of the second flight of stairs, I stop. No one has heard me and no one has followed. My face is damp with tears. I wipe my hand from brow to chin as though I have been caught in a rain shower. The action does not serve to cool my temper and suddenly I am overwhelmed with a desire for revenge.

I turn and head towards Rebekah's apartments. I don't pause to think; I just run to her door. Once inside, I feel my way through the shadows and then I find it: her diary. I tuck it under my arm. I can use it against her. I'll ruin her. All these thoughts and more crowd my mind as I return to the top of the main stairs and eventually find my way back to my room.

Breathless and bitter, I gather a bundle of linens and wrap them in my shawl. With boots laced and a cloak about my shoulders, I press my bonnet onto my head and force the bonnet-pins close to my scalp. They scratch the skin and draw blood, but I take grim satisfaction in the pain. Briefly, the thought of my perilous situation stops me cold, but the night's revelation that Rebekah never cared a snap about me surpasses everything.

There will be time to nurse my rage against her later, but for now I must move. I turn to leave and on the floor beneath my door there is a note; a wafer of paper sealed with a drop of wax. I can't recall if it was there when I entered or whether it has been slipped across the threshold while I gathered together my belongings. I stoop to retrieve it, noting the scrawl addressing it to 'Hester' as I break the seal and read:

You should never have got in the carriage. You should never have gone to Waterford Hall. Take heed and profit. If you value your life, get out before you hear the fatal bellman give the sternest goodnight.

The note is unsigned, the writing careless, as though written in haste. Who has sent me this warning? I read it twice more, but gain no more intelligence and instead am filled with a profound feeling of danger. I tuck the note into Rebekah's diary, gather my meagre possessions and leave; leave my room, leave Waterford Hall, and above all, leave my hopes.

My candle is almost burned away as I hurry through the kitchen doorway. With swiftness and silence, I take up a leather satchel left on the back of a chair by one of the gardener's boys. I replace the contents with an offcut of ham from the larder, a small loaf of bread, some apples and a parcel of cheese. I feel no remorse for my thieving, for I owe nothing to the Brocks. My hand doesn't even waver as I snatch the purse of coins used to pay tradesmen from a drawer in Mrs Jacques's stillroom.

In the grounds, I creep along the base of the hedging and beneath the trees, my thoughts darker than the shadows beneath which I stoop. The ground is already wet with drizzle, but a more intense downpour begins as I reach the trees. I shelter beneath the matted boughs and, as I take refuge from the storm, I glance back at the hall, and I see no fireside pleasures, for all homely comforts are now lost.

In time the force of the storm subsides, until only intermittent sobs are wrung from the clouds. Before I surrender my place of shelter, the moon slides across the skies. Where moments before the hall was shrouded in black, it now glistens and regains its shape.

On the steps a shadow moves. The skirts of a dark wraith blow wildly before the hood is drawn back to reveal Rebekah's face. I press myself harder against the tree trunk. Rebekah, hair loose in the breeze, stares out across the grounds. She turns towards my place of seclusion and the expression on her face penetrates my heart and makes my stomach turn over. She gives one more look into the night before she lowers her head and retreats.

CHAPTER SEVEN

Many score miles I have to travel before I reach the suburbs of London. My stolen purse of coins permits me passage on the overnight mail coach, and when my fare runs out at the village of Chalfont St Giles, I rely on the generosity of waggoners. Not once do I dare to look at Rebekah's diary for fear that someone will recognise the Brocks' insignia embossed on its cover; that someone will guess I am a thief, or a fugitive from the Dicity. Though, in truth, if an opportunity did arise to allow me to read it freely, the discomfort of trespassing upon Rebekah's private deliberations does give me pause for thought; hidden in my satchel as it is, I still feel its potency and fear the secrets that it may hold.

With my bonnet exchanged for bread and ale along the way, I arrive at the outskirts of London besmeared with road-dirt and without so much as a cantle of pie to my name. I am as dishevelled and poor as an apple-woman, and walk with eyes cast downwards. Beneath my cloak, pressed close to my body in its tattered satchel, is my only valuable possession in the world: Rebekah's journal.

I smell the city before I see it, its poisonous vapours and stagnant scent heavy on the air and concentrated further as the fog wets the ground and releases the smell of horse-dirt. I bend my steps towards Virginia Row.

Familiar steeples and chimneys appear on the horizon, their image growing harder as the mist recedes. That unforgettable wan light surrounds me, that eternal dusk. With each step, I feel the stricture of the alleys and the oppression of the streets. Warped buildings, dark and impersonal, leer above me, and I find that I too am stooped with the dejection of the place.

But in many ways, the dismal streets are also a comfort to me. There is a feeling of normality about the place, and it is only when I come to the spoon-mender's shop that the atmosphere changes and I see the fresh body of handbills pasted to the wall; myriad paper fingers blowing in the breeze. I am back in the thick of it all.

I arrive at Austin Street. I'm hesitant about seeing Uncle Jacob and suddenly feeling guilty for the difficult position in which I left Aunt Meg all those weeks ago. I stop, leaning against the spears of a fence, and I begin to fret. Mrs O'Rourke's eldest daughter Kitty passes by. I meet her gaze and there is a fraction of a second when I know she recognises me. She seems to take my measure for a moment, but she throws her stare to the ground as she nears, drawing her tattered shawl over her head and crossing to the other side of the street.

What stories has Uncle Jacob broadcast to explain my sudden disappearance? Has he damaged my reputation, or instead could he have been suspected of foul play? I turn about, intent on catching up with Kitty O'Rourke, but she has already been swallowed by the tracery of pathways.

I can delay no longer and advance to Virginia Row, entering the passageway that leads to our yard, a little heartened by the silence that means Uncle Jacob must be out devilling. Then I realise it is unnaturally quiet and I am unnerved by it. Before Aunt Meg comes out to greet me, I could turn about and leave. Kitty O'Rourke can never be certain it was me she saw. I could stay with Annie for a few days to regain my strength, then strike out for the country again. As I ponder on this, a voice snaps the thread of my reverie.

'Mary, Mother of God, it can't be—'

I look up to see Mrs O'Rourke approaching out of the shadows. Her eyes are wide and her skin pallid.

'Mrs O'Rourke. I've been away—'

'Sweet lamb of the world, we'd got you down for a dead 'un, we had.'

'What can you mean?' Her expression makes me feel faint as I imagine Uncle Jacob being carted away, visualise Aunt Meg weeping, drawing the twins close to her.

'Oh, child,' she breathes, and drops her shawl over her elbows. She draws near to me and in spite of her frown she carries a welcome in her eyes. She throws her arms about me in an act that renders me ill at ease.

She leads me to the mouth of our cellar, where the door flaps open but reveals no sign of life within. I break free from Mrs O'Rourke as she makes to catch at my arm and I push my way through. The gloom makes it hard to discern shapes, but the room is definitely unoccupied. The dirt floor is unencumbered by any furniture, with only a single child's boot in the corner and a pile of rags before the empty fire-grate. I turn to Mrs O'Rourke who is dabbing her eyes with the corner of her shawl.

'Come, my lamb. There's much to tell you.'

She shepherds me out of the yard and into her own parlour. The room is warm with the smell of stewed oats, a row of enamelled plates glints above the fire and various articles of leather horse tack are nailed to the walls. The room is far larger than our cellar, and after my long journey it feels welcoming.

Mrs O'Rourke takes up a slender pipe from the fender and nods for me to sit in a wooden armchair by the fire.

'Bridget, Padraig, be outside with you, now. I've some jawing to do with the missy here.'

Two street-coloured children appear from beneath a rug.

'Aw, Mammy, do we have to?'

'Now you do what I say, do you hear now?' She fumbles in a pocket beneath her shawl. 'Take this ha'penny and tell Mrs Flannigan I sent you. She'll let you sit by her fire and feed her finches. And don't talk to no one. Away with you.' The two infants, with no more than four years behind them, skip away down the alleyway.

Their departure serves to increase the sense of secrecy and silence. Mrs O'Rourke bends over a copper on the fire, stirring the contents.

'God bless them and spare them to me. They're good kids,' she says. Then, 'I'm sorry, my love. But they're dead. Jacob and Meg, and the twins too.'

I give a slow nod. My heart is beating fast, my hands clammy. I experience a slow, sinking sensation and, for an instant, the room begins to sway. I don't want to faint, so I clench my teeth.

'They had such a hard time before God let them go. Jacob died just as he lived, you know, with trouble surrounding him all the way till the end. And the same bad air rose up to the sailor-men above. Three Jacktars lost in as many days. To hear those grown men crying out for their mammies . . . I'm sorry, my lamb. I shouldn't tell it all to you, should I?'

'You must, Mrs O'Rourke.'

She stirs the pot of oats vigorously and draws on her pipe before settling back down.

'It was Jacob who went down with the fever first. Meg said he'd met up with some swain from afar. Your man Jacob did some devilling for him and was paid handsomely, not that Meg saw more than a shilling or two. He got himself filled with Blue Ruin and staggered home three days later. He was taking his time over sobering and I expect Meg was relieved at first, glad he was out o' trouble. Then he started moaning about his belly, saying his knees hurt and that the calves of his legs wouldn't stop twitching. Well, Meg up and told him it was God telling him to lay off the gin. I think she'd about convinced him too, by the look of remorse he carried from then on.

'Then the sickness came. The man couldn't keep nothing down, not even milk. All the time he'd be holding his belly and purging every ounce of water in his body. I told Meg it wasn't safe to stay, that "the devil was in the air". She wouldn't leave him, though. I offered to take the twins in, but she wouldn't have it. The last time I saw him, his pulse was softer than a sparrow's, his face blue and his eyes were sunken. I touched his hands. They were washerwoman's hands; wrinkled and wet and—'

She shivers and draws her shawl tighter.

'I went to stay with Mrs Flannigan; took my little ones and Kitty and Michael. When I came back three weeks later, the family were all dead, my lamb. The two babes snuffed like candles and Meg . . . I should have stayed, I should have helped her more, but you know when you have young ones to think about and . . .

'Meg was convinced you'd found happiness though, Hester. She was sure you'd met up with your cousin, just like you wanted. It gave her comfort to believe it and that's the truth of it. But I thought maybe Jacob had done for you and that's the holy truth too . . .

'We all heard him y'see, on that last morning before you were gone. "She's not too old to be taught a lesson." I heard it with my own ears! Kitty heard, too. Of course, we all know Jacob can be a rash man when under the screw of liquor – same as all of them; quick to do hurt or ill. But at heart he was just an old josser and we thought it was the gin talking, so I didn't know what to make of it as the days passed. Meg said you must have found your cousin and gone to the country, but I could never be sure, never be certain—'

'When did they pass away, Mrs O'Rourke?'

'Well, it'd not be long after Yuletide.'

'And has no one taken the room since?'

'They've been slow to take their chance with it. I think they're all a-feared of the devil coming back, but there's an old fella with his daughter moving in tonight or tomorrow, I hear. I know all this is sudden for you and you'd be expecting to—'

'I . . . I'm not staying, Mrs O'Rourke.'

'Of course, I'm forgetting myself. Your fella there, your drover-cousin, he'll be waiting for you.'

'No. He never arrived so I've been working as a maid to a lady.'

'Well, I'm sorry about your lad and all. But that's lovely to hear you got work, it is. One of us breaking out and doing a bit better. You always had that look in your eye, like you could be better. Kitty was always saying you had that look about you. Was it a nice house, and was the mistress good?'

'Yes, Mrs O'Rourke. It was very pretty and my mistress was . . .' Suddenly a sob escapes from inside me.

'There now, Hester. I know Jacob and Meg weren't your real family, but you were with them for many a year, so you let those tears come. If tears don't come then nothing can prevail. That's what they say.'

She offers me a grey rag. I politely shake my head and use the heel of my hand to dry my eyes, but the tears still come full and fast. I'm not so sorry that Jacob is gone, but I do miss Meg and the twins. And though I have just cause to hate Rebekah, the favourable image of her I have formed in my mind will not be laid to rest. It pains me to confess it to myself, but I'm certain I feel more bereaved at Rebekah's betrayal than at any of the subsequent sorrows.

'That's better now, isn't it, dear?'

I nod, the tears having dried up.

'And you were saying that you'll be moving on?'

'Yes, I'll be calling on Annie and staying with her for a while and—'

'Annie Allsop?'

'Yes.'

Mrs O'Rourke looks pensive. She fidgets, uncrosses her legs and scratches her head.

'Have you not seen Annie lately?' I ask.

'That's the thing, you see. People keep . . . moving on—'

'People are always moving on. Annie had met someone and—'

'People like Annie don't move on and never keep in touch. She couldn't hold a hap'orth of news inside her head without having to tell someone about it. You know what she was like. She wouldn't just leave in silence, not Annie.' Mrs O'Rourke's voice drops to barely a whisper. She leans forwards. Taking my arm, she says, 'And take one o' them Jacktars. The Captain, they called him. I don't think he was a proper captain, but that's what we all called him. Good-looking fella, he was. Fine shock of hair. Well, I took to talking to him. Reminded me of one of my brothers, he did. He was waiting to go to sea, looking forward to warmer climes, had a girl somewhere or other. I had him in by the fire, just as you are now. Cheerful as anything, he was.' She picks at her teeth with the nail of her forefinger and dislodges a flake of tobacco.

'When he left, he said he'd come back and take Padraig to see the ships at the dock. But I never saw him again. I thought he was up to some foolery at first. I thought he'd come back tomorrow and tomorrow, but he never came. And he never came back for any of his chattels either. Belongings he brought from overseas and from home. You know, precious goods. It didn't feel right. There's others too.'

'I know. I've seen the handbills at the spoon-mender's shop.'

'And I was talking, just yesterday, to your Aunt Meg's friend, Mrs Cohen; you know, the one with the shop. She asked if I'd heard from you and I'm sure she'll be glad when I tell her you're back. Anyway, she says there's a new name in the *Gazette* every Tuesday, as well as those handbills they keep pasting up. She says folks are getting in a spin about it, and in her experience fear and crime are often bedfellows. And folks keep talking about a murder.'

'What murder?'

'Oh, you don't want to know, my lamb. It was pitiful. Such a wicked deed. If what they're saying is to be credited, it was a terrible mess they made of him. Broke him up and put him in a sack, they reckon. Makes you shiver, doesn't it? Even I'm wary of going about my own business now. I can feel the fear of it all.'

'Was it a drover?'

'No, no. Just one of those beggar boys.'

'What was his name?'

'Oh, now then, you're asking. Er . . . I think they said it was Tulley: Matthew Tulley, or something like that. He was one of those Dancing Doll men.'

'I think I know him. I saw him on the day I left.'

'Well, don't go roughing yourself with more sorrow. It's a common enough act they perform. There must be a dozen or more youths in the city peddling the same tricks. It might not have been the lad you knew.'

'And what of Annie?'

'I fear for her, I do. It's been a while since even her sister has seen her. It was ages ago, she said. Annie had brought her a white straw hat to dye. You know how Annie loved her hats. But she'd bought a white one and then changed her mind; got her sister to dye it black. And off she went to meet some fella at the Fortune o' War. Never seen her since. Oh, look at me rambling on at you, getting off the strait of the tale and all. Will you take a bite and a sup, now? You've had quite a shock.'

Her eyes express benevolence and I accept. She serves me stewed gags and oatmeal and pours a cup of ale from a jug. The ale is warm and has a smack of ginger about it.

'I'd love to be able to offer you a bed, my lamb. But with Kitty and Bridget and Padraig and . . . Michael with his new girl and—'

'Oh, I couldn't impose on you, Mrs O'Rourke. You've been too kind already.'

'Perhaps you could go to Mrs Ingham's, Annie's sister? She's a kind woman, you know. I'm certain she'll put you up. She lives on Great Chart Street, you know?'

'I've never met her, I couldn't—'

'Nonsense! I'll send Kitty with you. She knows her.'

'I'd rather not. I'm very weary. I just . . .'

The tiredness I've staved off for so long begins to consume me. I don't fight it; I have such little fight left within me. I can sit upright no longer and begin to recline into the chair, feel the warmth of the fire on my skin. I close my eyes, just for a moment, but they are heavy. I fall asleep and my dreams are haunted by shadows of the past. I imagine I am in the cellar room with Aunt Meg and the twins; detaching themselves from the world little by little and fading away from life. Then I dream of dogcarts and sunsets, soothe myself with the memory of laughter in the library at Waterford. Suddenly, I wake. Mrs O'Rourke is watching me from her chair.

'Well, Hester, you've certainly been out for the count!'

'How long?' I mumble, stretching and sitting upright.

'You went out like a light, two hours since. I thought it best to let you sleep. Look, why don't you have a proper rest in the cellar room, just for now? The new folks won't be here for hours, perhaps not until tomorrow. I've a couple of spare tallows and a scuttle of coal for you. There's no one that'll bother you for a good while.'

'Thank you. I think I will.' I nod as I speak and look Mrs O'Rourke full in the eyes, but can't help noticing that, behind her, one of Aunt Meg's shawls is on the back of a chair. Mrs O'Rourke follows my eyes and says:

'I couldn't think of lifters coming and making off with all Meg's stuff. It would have pained me to see her robbed. I took it in case you came back, my lamb. It's all yours, not that there's much to be had, just the pots and spoons and—'

'You did the right thing to take it, Mrs O'Rourke. Aunt Meg would have wanted you to have them.'

'But they're yours, my lamb.'

'Perhaps I'll come back for them one day, when I'm settled. You could look after them for me till then.'

'You're a good one, Hester, that's for sure. But at least take the shawl; it's good cloth, well made, you know. Now come on, let's get you settled over there.'

Mrs O'Rourke rises and disappears to a back room. She reappears with the candles, an old jacket and a folded square of cambric holding a lumpy cargo.

'It's the coal, my lamb,' she says, passing the makeshift sack to me and handing me the shawl. I take them from her and follow her out into the yard. We cross the patch of dirt and enter the cellar, the old familiar smell of damp and decay meeting my nostrils.

'It'll be cheerier when we get the fire going,' she says. She kneels, draws a tinderbox and kindling from her pocket and sets to work on the fire. There is a streak of white as the tinder flares and darkness is pushed back into the shadows. But the coal is reluctant and, when flames finally splutter forth, they are pale and sickly and tremble at the slightest breath of air. I light the tallows from the fire and the odour of rancid fat fills the room.

'There now, my lamb. That's more cheery, just like I told you.'

Mrs O'Rourke makes her excuses and leaves. Grateful for her hospitality and relieved at last to find some solitude, I lift the satchel's strap over my head, place the bag on the floor at my side and curl up on the old jacket, with Aunt Meg's shawl drawn over me. I shiver and touch my fingers to the leather pouch, its contents both precious and contemptible. I stare blindly at the satchel for some moments. Then, unable to be steadfast any longer and relieved at last to succumb to temptation, I open the bag and ease the diary out.

The cover is cinnabar leather, tooled with a gilt pattern in each corner. A hint of gillyflower hovers then fades, consumed by the rank smell of the cellar. Small dots of dark leather begin to form on the cover, in a haphazard spotted pattern at first, and then bleeding into one large and expanding patch. I touch the leather; it's damp. I touch my face and feel tears.

I open up the first page. I run my fingers over the flyleaf and the paper is stiff and exudes quality. I turn another page and see her writing. My anger is no longer hot against her and I find myself holding the journal to my breast, as close as a mother holds a newborn babe.

I try to resist, but I can no longer stop myself. I know it to be wrong, but it doesn't matter any more; I will never see her again. Sitting here in this cellar that I thought I had escaped forever, I realise I have nothing. No means of subsistence, no future to look forward to. There is now nothing left to lose.

I sit upright, draw the tallow nearer and begin to read.

CHAPTER EIGHT

Initially, I don't read the words; I merely stare at Rebekah's script. I see the point where she must have placed the nib on the page and I trace the loops of ink with my eye, as an apprentice examines his master's work. I know her hand well; I have seen her write dozens of times. But the words before me now are different. They are not passages for me to copy; not perfunctory and detached. These words are the heart of Rebekah, her very essence captured on these pages.

Mrs O'Rourke's coals give a wheeze and the flames rising from them tremble. I blow gently at the coals and one catches and flares. It sends out a finger of yellow light and I shuffle myself round to harness the arc, and to the throb of its glow, I begin to read:

11th March 1831
It has been a full five years since I have kept a journal. I believe it will be cathartic to discharge my opinions with pen and ink and I suppose I do need some entity with which to share my thoughts, and through a diary I am at liberty to write the truth; for no other shall read it.

12th March 1831
Another one of Uncle Sep's dinners. Two old gents up from his club, Mr and Mrs Hartwright, Parson Ashton, Squire Benton's

widow. Conversation was dull. Tried to discuss the Reform Bill as I have been reading of it with great interest, but you'd have thought it had never been drafted. How can whole cities of people remain unrepresented in Parliament, when a single owner of a rotten borough, inhabited by a washerwoman and a donkey, can swagger into the Commons and change the laws of the land? No one at dinner seemed the least bit interested. Parson Ashton simply smiled and the widow Benton talked absolute nonsense.

Yet an un-married, dependent woman approaching her twenty-eighth year has no just cause to rail others. With each frown from Uncle Sep, I feel him chiding me for the drain I am to him. Each time I mention scientific conundrums or politics, I feel the breath of his sigh that tells me I should be tempering my views and instead developing solely the traits of a pleaser of menfolk, a giggling goose who lives only to serve and compliment.

I didn't remain long over my wine and retired early.

17th March 1831

After breakfast, I took Uncle Sep's hunter, Star, and put her to the canter. The air was cold, but the ground was forgiving and she was on the bit from the very start.

We returned through the village where I chanced upon Mr and Mrs Hartwright and a young lady, introduced to me as Jane, their niece.

Mr Hartwright was desirous for Jane to make my acquaintance, keen for me to familiarise her with the notable features of the parish.

21st March 1831

Such little time to write today. Jane and I have spent the last four days in each other's company. She does seem a little distracted at times, but makes up for it with her strength of character and formidable sense of fun. I believe we shall grow to be great friends.

22nd March 1831

Calder has written and his letter brightened my day. Even through the medium of paper and ink, Calder always seems able to enthuse about some enterprise or other. He gains so much enjoyment from all that he does and one cannot help but be infected by his zeal. He is to come to Waterford the day after tomorrow and I cannot wait until he is here. He will arrive after lunch, along with a gentleman called Frederick Blister, and his old friend Arthur Talbot. I will petition Uncle Sep to invite Jane Hartwright to dinner when the gentlemen arrive and I shall supervise all aspects of the occasion to make it the best Waterford has yet seen.

23rd March 1831

The dinner went well. Calder presented himself in very fine attire and was in excellent humour. Jane talked at length with him, then spent the evening playing chequers with Arthur Talbot. In the drawing room, I was left for some time to make idle talk with Mr Blister. His clothes were loud as was his voice. He took my hand when we were introduced and it was like holding a ball of dough. There were crumbs in his moustache and I didn't warm to the man. And encouraged by Mr Blister, Calder has begun to relax his abstemious efforts and repeatedly petitioned for more bottles of claret.

10th April 1831

Over the last two weeks, my notes to Jane have been left unanswered and there were countless times we managed to miss each other. Calder, Mr Blister and Arthur Talbot spent their time riding and hunting, so my suspicions were not aroused until poor Mr and Mrs Hartwright called upon Uncle Sep with the sad intelligence that Jane had eloped with Arthur Talbot.

Apparently, Jane had met Arthur in London, which was the reason her father sent her to the country. It appears Jane's sole purpose in befriending me was to secure a place and time to meet with Arthur again.

Calder denies any knowledge of the matter and pleads that Arthur used him just as sorely as Jane used me. The Hartwrights and Uncle Sep appear less convinced and seem to believe I must have been in collusion with the couple. Only now do I realise how easily I strayed into the shadow of deception. I feel such a fool. And the benevolence I bestowed upon the ungrateful girl!

Mem.: Write essay on the abjuration of kindness!

The affair has left a sombre pall over Waterford and the whole village. As with all scandal, servants are the first to disperse the seeds of malice, and where facts are unknown, they are invented. I overheard Mrs Jacques talking to the new girl, Sarah, and speculating on my involvement in the elopement. Of course, they both denied it when I challenged them. To the deuce with servants! Their imputations against me are without foundation and yet I wager that the gossip will persist and spread like bindweed around the community. I no longer feel inclined to take Sweetie and the dogcart into the village, such is my discomfort.

11th April 1831

Spent the morning directing Martha in the reorganisation of my gloves. I seem to receive at least four pairs every Christmas; most from Uncle Sep. Perhaps it is his way of inducing me to feminise and subjugate my restless hands! Still, classifying gloves is a convenient distraction for me when both the outdoors and even my own home are peopled with dwellers quick to censure and malign.

Martha was cheerful company and, thinking back, I have never once had cause to suspect her of idle talk. It is a pity about the facial tic that blights her appearance. Martha seems quite oblivious to its effects and I suppose she must be quite used to it. Out of politeness, I have never raised the subject with her.

12th April 1831

Managed to avoid my uncle at breakfast, but was informed by Rudd that Martha was feeling unwell. To reciprocate her geniality of yesterday and to bring her some cheer, I thought I would gift her a pair of gloves; she had admired a pair of lavender cheverels which never did fit me well. Informed that she was sitting in the kitchens, I fetched the gloves and descended the back stairs. However, as I was navigating the kitchen corridor, I came across Frederick Blister. He had his back to me and appeared unaware of my approach. I moved forward with stealth then slipped into the doorway of the butler's pantry. Being within earshot of Mr Blister, it became apparent he was talking to Martha; he seemed to be asking about her facial palsy. The man has no manners, no sense of propriety.

When he left, I gave the gloves to Martha and asked if Mr Blister had offended her in any way. She assured me that he had acted like a gentleman and had said she mustn't worry about her affliction. He was concerned whether the condition hurt Martha at all and remarked to her that it is a very mild case and that she bears it very calmly.

Martha seemed unaware of Mr Blister's indelicacy; quite ignorant of the fact that he has no formal medical training or surgical knowledge; he is merely a dilettante who hangs on Calder's coat-tails. But I sensed it profoundly. The man always renders me aggrieved at his presence, and relieved at his absence.

13th April 1831

After breakfast, I was summoned by Uncle Sep. I supposed it was to be further interrogation over the Hartwright business, but I was mistaken. He received me irritably, ignoring me at first and continuing to turn the pages of his periodical. With a strategy of pre-emption, I declared that I had no reason to reproach myself regarding the Hartwright affair. But Uncle Sep interrupted me and announced that he had no interest in that matter either; except his regret that Arthur Talbot had not 'carted' me off instead.

He then proceeded to speak disparagingly about my age, repeating the words 'seven-and-twenty' twice over, as though the numbers might reduce themselves by repetition.

He was rather critical of my work and pastimes, suggesting that I was less feminine than I might be and that if I could make half as good a wife as I did a scholar, then he would be mightily relieved.

Before I could think of a retort, his expression softened and he informed me that he had established contact with Sir Humphrey Babbitt. The man's wife died some years ago and he recently confided in Uncle Sep that he is considering a second alliance to give him solace in his twilight years. I was tempted to ask if the man required assistance in finding a nurse, but I could guess what scheme the two men had conceived together.

Uncle Sep went on to confirm he thought I would be perfect

for Sir Humphrey's requirements. He made me sound as though I were a suit of clothes or a carriage horse!

He assured me that Sir Humphrey was a very learned man and the prospect of such an alliance should be a palatable diet for an intellectual mind such as mine. I suppose I should have voiced my gratitude, but the whole matter lacked in dignity. If Sir Humphrey does not approve of me, what next? Will I be invited to Uncle Sep's club dressed as a painted peacock and paraded before the gentlemen?

Uncle Sep noticed my reluctance and reminded me that I was in no position to object. All I could do was stand there, mute as a stick. He informed me that he would be holding further counsel with Sir Humphrey. I lowered my head and refused to respond. His last word on the matter was that he assumed I was clear on all points and then he dismissed me.

Caught in that perpetual circle of respectability and respect, and my life about to be destroyed by avuncular dictates of lineage and lucre, the contract was apparently struck by my tacit agreement. I knew at that moment I was duty bound to act in accordance with his wishes.

I collected my diary from the breakfast room and ran to my boudoir. Martha was there, tidying my dressing table and, when I entered, I threw my journal down with such force that a perfume bottle was knocked to the floor and smashed into a thousand shards. Martha bent down to clear away the fragments, reassuring me that no harm had been done and that she would have it all swept away in no time. But her comforting words only served to stoke the furnace of rage that was already burning within me. I couldn't find it in myself to be cordial towards her. I said much that was discourteous. More than that, I said something disagreeable with an impulsive spark of fury in my tone before I dismissed her from my rooms.

Devil take Uncle Septimus! Devil take Martha! Devil take them all!

14th April 1831
I barely slept last night; I couldn't stop worrying over Uncle Sep's words. I'm dreading the prospect of meeting Sir Humphrey and wish I had the financial means, and the strength of character, to escape Uncle Sep.

I confess too that poor Martha has been in my thoughts. A better servant could not be had and I deeply regret subjecting her to the keenness of my tongue. I will find her out after breakfast and make an apology.

～

Breakfast was disagreeable. The only words Uncle Sep saw fit to direct to me were that Calder and Blister had left early for London. I was sorry not to have seen Calder before he left, although judging by the amount of wine he took last evening, I wonder whether his mood might have been compromised. It takes only the slightest indulgence in brandy or claret and Calder's weaknesses are fetched out. If only he would stay his habits at the third cup, but Frederick Blister finds great mirth in the intemperance of his friend and is always set on inciting Calder to excess. I wish Calder would set him adrift.

The rest of breakfast was taken in silence, with Uncle Sep occasionally lowering his newspaper to glare at me over his spectacles.

I didn't tarry long over my coffee and went to find Martha Briggs. But before I could descend the back stairs, I bumped into Mary and learned that Martha has not been seen since the previous night. I must wait to deliver my apology until she returns tomorrow.

15th April 1831

Still no word from Martha. It is highly unusual and no one seems able to come at an explanation for her disappearance.

17th April 1831

It has been established that Martha must have left Waterford without any personal belongings. All of her outerwear and her personal effects remain in her garret room. I have interviewed the servants, but obtained very little information. I shall take the dogcart and make my way to Martha's parents' cottage tomorrow and hope that all ends well.

18th April 1831

The Briggs's homestead stands some ten miles from Waterford. Mrs Briggs hesitated to invite me in after I announced myself, even before the contentious elements of our dialogue had been reached.

I told her about the moment of discord I had effected against her daughter. I asked her about Martha's acquaintances; enquired if there might be any reasons why Martha would leave Waterford so suddenly and without word to another living soul. There must be a simple explanation as to her whereabouts. People with jobs and families cannot just disappear without explanation.

Mrs Briggs was prickly, her demeanour suggesting she was ready to take offence at the slightest provocation. The only intelligence she let slip was that Martha had spoken of a man she had met in London, but I could gain no other details.

19th April 1831

Rained all day, making me feel peevish. Didn't dress or go down to eat, just stayed in my peignoir and ignored every knock at the door. Toilsome day. Enjoyed nothing. Endured much.

2nd May 1831

Sir Humphrey has written. With Uncle Sep's permission, he seeks a meeting with me and has suggested that he calls at Waterford next week.

I have begun to wonder what changes matrimony might impose upon me. It is surely an opportunity for me to relinquish the confusion of the past, the uncongenial servants, the gossip, the loneliness, and become head of my own household. I can acquaint myself with new tenant farmers, new domestics, new churchmen, new friends; and all without the duress of Uncle Sep's perpetual critique. And once I am wed, I shall no longer be impelled to search endlessly for a suitor. The chance of freedom is so alluring, but do I truly know Sir Humphrey's character? My wishes are only temporal; reality will last the whole of my life.

9th May 1831

Sir Humphrey is come. He is older than I thought; late fifties inclining to threescore. But his virtues indemnify him against his advancing years and I am certain I will become accustomed to his head, which is as bald and pale as a duck's egg.

We dined together and Sir Humphrey made a good impression upon me with his intelligence and kindness. I began to wonder about the pathways along which he may lead me and the doors he may open.

The day was a success. Yes, there is certainly flatness to his manner, but I must become used to it. And is his voice a little grating at times? I am reluctant to consider improper thoughts, but I do wonder what expectations Sir Humphrey might have regarding the physical aspect of our relationship. How I might disguise my indifference (my repugnance, if truth be known) may be quite challenging, and I have a strong disinclination to encourage such a thing altogether.

11th May 1831

Sir Humphrey has returned to London to settle his affairs, and a provisional wedding date has been set for 4th July. He has promised to write with his proposals for our honeymoon.

News of my forthcoming betrothal has reached both the servants' hall and the village, and in both quarters I believe there has been a softening of attitude towards me. The atmosphere in the hall has changed to bustle and excitement. I shall confer with Uncle Sep to see if we can offer the servants a day off to celebrate. Perhaps the merriment of a wedding is what everyone needs. I know many things will be missing in my marriage to Sir Humphrey, but I also know my life can only improve greatly after 4th July.

12th May 1831

Two letters in the bag: one from Sir Humphrey suggesting a tour of Europe following the wedding and listing cities and countries I have only read about. How thrilling to explore them in reality! How wonderful to know I will finally be free of my uncle, and able to see a world outside Waterford.

The other letter was from Calder, expressing delight at my forthcoming alliance. Calder also added a note about a man I asked him to employ in finding more information about Martha Briggs. The man came recommended by Frederick Blister and has a great deal of experience in finding debtors for the Marshalsea. As yet he has been unable to discover any intelligence on Martha, who has been missing for almost a month now, and her disappearance remains a mystery.

Perpetually, a sense of fear dominates all my thoughts on Martha, and I am frustrated that not a scrap of discovery is to be fetched from any quarter.

I must take it upon myself to search further afield; order up broadsheets and journals from the city, just in case, as her mother disclosed, Martha was indeed meeting up with a gentleman friend in London, and, Heaven forbid, met with misfortune instead. I could also draw up a list of her acquaintances and habitual movements to see if logic and patience can unravel what mere conjecture cannot. There must be an answer to this conundrum.

Uncle Sep is pressing me to interview for a new lady's maid. I am reluctant; because, by so doing, we are all accepting Martha will never return. I have resisted the motion for a number of weeks, but admit I cannot continue to put upon Mary and Sarah. I shall place an advertisement tomorrow and then begin work on my investigation.

19th May 1831
I was presented with a respondent to my public notice for a lady's maid. The girl's name is Agnes and she was both attentive and neatly turned out. Though reluctant to accept Martha's disappearance as a permanent state of affairs, I kept the interview brief and provisionally accepted her for the role.

20th May 1831
A letter from Sir Humphrey. The date of the wedding is confirmed as 4th July; there is much to do to prepare for it and for my long-awaited departure from Waterford.

Meanwhile, my portfolio of documentation concerning poor Martha continues to grow, yet will not yield up resolution, and in some respects perhaps embodies my heartfelt regret over the whole mysterious episode.

Agnes has settled in well, seems to have a kindly disposition, and provides a much-needed spirit of cordiality to daily life here.

21st May 1831

Another missive from Sir Humphrey. His letter, as usual, is well composed, but there's a whiff of Parson Ashton's sermon about it. In truth, Sir Humphrey has a habit of making everything just a little bit tedious.

Before retiring, Agnes was brushing my hair and had the audacity to ask if I loved Sir Humphrey. I ought to have chastised her for such impudence, but I thought of Martha and the terrible guilt I still harbour and didn't have the heart to upbraid Agnes. I overlooked the presumption and, going further, I determined to show a greater awareness of Agnes's feelings, in the spirit of self-improvement. Or perhaps to salve my own conscience?

In spite of this, I answered her more haughtily than I intended and said that, in my opinion, there were many and varied aspects of love. I went on to propound that young love or passion can be thought of as transient and shallow, whereas the truest and most enduring love is born of mutual respect; an affection for like-minded intellectual capability. I concluded to her that I did love Sir Humphrey, but in a different way than that with which she might be familiar.

Seeing her crestfallen features, I realised that in my words I was only trying to persuade myself; the passionate love I have read about in Byron and Shakespeare will always be missing from my life with Sir Humphrey. But I have no choice, and in reality there are scant other options for unwed women of my age. Better this than stay on at Waterford alone: better the plague than hell.

28th May 1831

Sir Humphrey has arrived at Waterford. We walked the grounds and discussed botany and modern agricultural practices. He spoke at length about Linacre House, his country seat near Warwick, where we shall spend most of our time, and to where we shall retreat post-honeymoon. The house was built in 1598 and designed by Robert Smythson. Sir Humphrey described the rooms and the décor, and for the first time I began to imagine living there; began truly to see myself as mistress of my own domain. The day and evening passed well and I am beginning to feel a sense of resolution and contentment.

30th May 1831

Sir Humphrey has returned to London and must spend the following fortnight in Paris. I shall next see him on 3rd July, the day before we are wed.

Agnes was less ebullient today and, when asked why, she replied that the prospect of her own marriage was beginning to falter because her intended cannot earn enough to rent a workshop or lodgings. Agnes, red-eyed and hoarse with the sorrow of it, confided to me that to see her man brought so low was beyond her endurance.

After retiring to my boudoir, and long after nightfall, I sat at my dressing table pondering on Agnes's plight.

2nd June 1831

I slept soundly last night and woke determined to help Agnes in her present situation.

I have written to Mr Staidly at the bank, to request the release of twenty guineas. I have created a diversion to explain away the transaction by alluding to my forthcoming marriage and have requested that the matter be conducted under the strictest confidence. Uncle Sep takes great pleasure in reminding me every day of the escalating costs which he must defray; from my bridal gown to the wedding breakfast, from bouquets to silver-corded cards. So frequently do the bills come in, that a further few guineas will hardly be noticed at all.

5th June 1831

This morning I sought Agnes out and handed her the gift. I whispered to her that the wallet contained twenty guineas and that they were to set her and Joe up in clean lodgings and pay rent on a workshop. I informed her that there was no need to repay and that I would be deeply offended if she ever made any attempt to make restitution. Her hand grew warm, she wiped tears from her eyes and then, without warning, she threw her arms about me while exclaiming her gratitude! She was uncomfortably close to me, and in the tail of my eye I caught sight of one of the servants. I extricated myself and, using an elevated tone to reaffirm my authority, I instructed her to come to the drawing room twenty minutes later to conclude the transaction.

I informed Agnes that I would expect her to contact me to confirm her safe arrival in London and that all was going to plan. Once married to Joe, I would be under the assumption Agnes would resign from my employ and, of course, I would supply a suitable character reference to aid her in her future endeavours.

10th June 1831

Agnes has left for London. Such fervency and excitement I have not witnessed before and her joy will remain long with me. I need never tell a living soul what I have done, but will be comforted whenever I think of her happiness and my part in it.

25th June 1831

So many days have passed and I have received no word from Agnes. Neither is there mention of her alliance in the public journals. I am sure there is no cause to worry yet, but my experience with Martha has left me nervous and with a tendency towards pessimism and suspicion.

27th June 1831

I slept poorly last night. I have written to Agnes's parents, a curt epistle demanding nothing more than resolution.

In the same spirit of banishing my demons, I confessed all to Uncle Sep. I braced myself for his usual acerbic retort, but he was strangely restrained and vaguely indifferent; he quoted a line from Shakespeare and then recommended I talk to Sir Humphrey. I believe he is reconciled to cutting me adrift.

My only chance of happiness is to leave Waterford. The next week cannot pass soon enough.

2nd July 1831

A letter from Sir Humphrey. He will arrive tomorrow and has (apparently reluctantly) agreed for Calder and Frederick Blister to join him and Uncle Sep for claret and cheroots tomorrow evening. I expected Calder to be present, but why that awful Blister should be invited, I cannot wonder.

For my part, I have been invited to spend my last night of maidenhood at the widow Benton's Jacobean pile, meaning I shall not see Sir Humphrey until the pageant of our ceremony begins.

3rd July 1831

For most of today, I sat alone in my rooms in the north-east corner of the widow Benton's house. Not through dint of nerves or apprehension or even unsociable feelings towards my hostess; but more as a means of creating a tranquil pathway to divide my past and my future.

I am so glad to be escaping my suffocating life at Waterford. I will be content to live within the limits Sir Humphrey imposes and bear his wants and needs as best I can. He may not be a proper mate in every way, but this is my proper time to marry.

This time tomorrow, it will all be done and I will be a married woman.

4th July 1831

How do I muster the strength to hold the pen, let alone push its nib to the page? What point to writing? That I might review this journal as my hair blanches and my skin sags away from my bones? This shall be my last entry.

I am not married. I write again, in larger script: I am not married.

The boy knocked on the door just after three o'clock this morning and roused the Benton household. I was asked to dress quickly and return to Waterford. The carriage ride was swift and torches had been flamed on the approach to the hall.

I found my way to the drawing room. Uncle Sep was sitting at a card table and, when I entered, he said simply: 'Sir Humphrey is dead.'

I could say nothing.

He went on in a pragmatic manner to explain that Sir Humphrey, according to Calder, must have been suffering from an entrenched disease of the heart. He assured me that when Sir Humphrey took ill after dinner, nothing more could have been done for him and that he had not suffered.

Uncle Sep was stoic, but Calder was standing in the shadows

looking less composed. He took a step closer to me, then stood, his hands worrying a thread on his breeches. He said that I must bear up, that I must be strong, have courage.

Frederick Blister was standing just behind him. Having wormed his way to Waterford on the promise of free claret, he must have supposed he was now accepted in the Brock inner circle, privy to intimate family matters. How presumptuous! Insupportable man. He offered no words of solace.

I cannot recall what happened next. I remember retiring to bed and, as dawn broke, I watched the clouds from my bedroom window; low clouds, tattered: defeated flags in battle.

There I stayed as the day bled away, until the lamps were lighted, the curtains closed and my bridal gown, trunks and trinkets returned from Mrs Benton's. I must resign myself to characterless days, which will stretch into forgettable weeks, months that will contort into seasons, years that will ebb away and leave as little a mark as raindrops in a puddle.

The diary ends. I sense tightness around my throat at the situation in which Rebekah found herself. I recall my initial feelings towards her and now regret the lack of empathy I might have afforded her. If only I had known, I would have understood. But still, she had no justifiable reason to betray me in the manner she chose, to deceive me as she did. Why did she not learn compassion from the hurt of life? And, for my part, if only I had spoken more boldly to her; given her better reason to trust me. Why was Agnes afforded her support and affection while I was to be cast out with nothing? Had I only imagined the growing warmth between us?

I push tears from my eyes and sit with the journal in my lap. I am disappointed that the entries finish before I arrived at Waterford and that Rebekah's opinions of me are not recorded. Even with her documented thoughts held in my hands, I am no closer to Rebekah than I ever was. I pass my fingers softly over the leather cover, across her embossed initials and down the tooled spine. I open it again and turn to that final entry, stare at that last page.

There is a nauseous contraction in my belly and it rises to constrict my lungs, and weeping builds in my throat. I press my palm onto that final page then I stop. The next page feels thicker beneath my fingertips. I try to turn the next leaf, but the sheet is double thickness and there is a line of glue around the edge. I use my thumbnail and pick at the corner, teasing the paper apart and revealing two separate sheets. Written on the pages, in smaller, fainter script, is a continuation of Rebekah's diary, and halfway down the page I see my own name. My skin tingles with anticipation as I read on:

18th October 1831
I find I am greatly depressed by the turn of events. My energies and interests have deserted me and I tire of my uncle's endless suggestions of yet more benevolent projects and charitable visits, to aid somehow in my suppression of these fits of despair. I believe Calder has also been corrupted by my uncle's infinite desire to see me more gainfully occupied as he has written to me about some charity girl.

I know in truth Calder has my best interests at heart; I acknowledge that he is the only one to voice his support of me, and that usually his letters reassure me, but this is too much! He wishes for me to educate her as part of some project, but in light of recent events, I can't help but wonder whether Waterford itself is imbued with a fatal hex. I shall resist the motion to school her, in the interests of both her preservation and my own.

22nd October 1831

Calder is come with the girl. I stood my ground, as planned, and hid my vulnerabilities beneath a shell of obstinacy, convinced that the waif would run back to the borough of her nativity; and be all the safer for it.

At times, my look alone seemed to stimulate her like an icy gust. She looked pinched. I think she even shivered. Yet how well she withstood my indifference and how strongly she pleaded her case to stay. Her tolerance against my coldness made me rather ashamed of myself.

26th October 1831

My recalcitrance has been in vain. Uncle Sep has resorted to an underhand stratagem. His words were veiled and subtle, yet I received the message with absolute lucidity: if I do not occupy my hours with educating Calder's peasant girl, I may find myself 'subject to an enforced period of reflection at a convent, to support the recovery of my recent bereavement'.

Could he really stoop so low as to forcibly incarcerate his own niece in a religious institution? A year ago, I would have been inclined to ignore him. But after all that has happened, I can't take the risk.

27th October 1831

The girl's name is Hester. I suppose I shall take her through Murray's English Grammar. I have to confess; she is quick to learn and has some wit. I found I almost began to take pleasure from giving the lesson, and from her company.

28th October 1831

Hester is brighter than I had first thought, and I am intrigued as to how a girl with her background can be so articulate. This morning she was confident and attentive, and she was unafraid to answer questions. Odd as it may be, I seem to recognise my own shortcomings more when in her presence. She certainly manages to lift my mood and I look forward each morning to our time in the library. Is it the science of teaching? The discipline and routine of developing another?

4th November 1831

The rain and sleet has been relentless these last two days. I haven't been able to get outside at all and am becoming troubled with unrest. As warm and inviting as the library is, I was unable to be still, and so I asked Hester if she might wish me to give her a tour of Waterford; she was most receptive.

I took her through the ante-room, the stag parlour and on to the drawing rooms. The saloon, with its curios and paintings, is as impressive as ever it was. But I believe even Hester noticed the moth damage to the tapestries in the old state bedroom, and the crumbling plasterwork and frayed rugs in the long gallery. How cold those upper chambers on the north corridor were; yet how warm I felt with Hester by my side.

18th November 1831

There was a pleasant diversion in the library this morning. Not long after I began the lesson, I noticed that Hester was momentarily distracted. I'd left one of the large books of maps open on the lectern and her eye was drawn to it. I invited her to satisfy her curiosity by looking at it, and this led to further questions about the other books in the collection. I showed her the scientific commentaries, the atlases and books of history, and finally some volumes of poetry. It was this last that interested her most. She looked over Coleridge and Wordsworth with a great deal of interest, holding the leather covers reverentially in her hand. She turned the pages as though she understood the words before her, and more importantly understood the sentiment.

I took down a volume of Keats and read aloud to her The Eve of St Agnes. Throughout, Hester was spellbound, and never once removed her gaze from my mouth for the duration of the reading. Afterwards, I felt strangely euphoric, as though I had taken more wine than I should have.

7th December 1831

I set Hester to copying out script this morning. And with my sketchbook on my lap, I began discreetly to make a drawing of her as she worked. I recalled my old drawing-master's words: confident touch, patience and a good eye. But I was incapable of capturing the look I was after. I couldn't preserve those fleeting moments when Hester's eyes express that gentle serenity.

The longer I studied her, the greater the paucity of my artistic skill affected me until, unable to record her likeness to my satisfaction, I was forced to lay down my pen and accept that some things are too complex to be reduced to ink and paper.

19th December 1831

I took Hester around the village in the dogcart this morning. The attire I had sent to her room suited her just as well as I had imagined. Oddly, her London vowels were far less noticeable than usual. I've noticed this irregularity before and wonder if in the past she knew a better life than the one in which she was discovered by Calder, or if it is only my influence. The girl intrigues me; she learns so quickly. Can it be she has improved swiftly out of a desire to impress me? Or do I flatter myself and is the improvement solely to keep her place with us? Do I grasp at the nearest piece of flotsam as I drown in the ever-quickening current of my life? Do I search too readily for the dawn in order to end the despondency of my cheerless night?

She seems to trust me, though, and confided in me that she has concerns over a cousin of hers, an Edward White. I have resolved to review the newspapers I have been collecting for clues concerning Agnes and Martha; perhaps one of Hester's relations has placed a notice in the Police Gazette publication, appealing for the boy. I shall also write to Great-Aunt Eleanor with enquiries to see if one of her tenant farmers has heard of the lad.

21st December 1831
I feel wretched! Calder has changed our plans for Christmas and we have hastened to town instead of remaining at Waterford. What point to spending Yuletide in the city? Calder is out all the time with that awful Blister at the theatre or his club. And the city presents a greater temptation for Uncle Sep to gamble away yet more of Calder's inheritance. I, on the other hand, will spend my time wishing I were back at Waterford.

So, here I sit in my room at the villa and my separation from Hester is affecting me more deeply than I would have expected. I wish there had been time to talk to her before we left, but hope she adheres to my list of written instructions to maintain her progress and development. I'm also disappointed that Uncle Sep and Calder both wish Hester to experience a break from my tuition in order to prove that her mind retains the information it has been taught. They both feel it is a critical part of Calder's experiment, and talk of her as if she were a laboratory specimen.

23rd December 1831

I have received a reply from Great-Aunt Eleanor, confirming the boy Edward White is indeed a local cattle drover, whose parents are tenant farmers on the Appleton estate. Just after the autumn drove arrived at Smithfield market, the boy was seen drinking with three men at a public house called The Fortune of War. The boy's disappearance was reported in the Morning Herald and the Police Gazette. Other enquiries were also made, but all to no avail.

Great-Aunt Eleanor has also invited me to stay with her in the new year, and she draws reference to an unhealed rift between Lord Appleton and my uncle, of which I had only suspicions; this explains the interval since our last visit. With Uncle Sep's current humour, I am inclined to take up her offer, certain he will not be welcomed and thus relieving me of his ever-present disappointment in me. It also raises the possibility of another plan, which I shall think about overnight.

24th December 1831

I failed to sleep last night. My thoughts have a single theme: vulnerability. Martha Briggs, according to servants' gossip, harboured a weak mind and even carried with it the possibility of self-murder. Agnes, carrying with her twenty guineas, could have been, and probably was, robbed and has been too upset to come back to Waterford or face her family. Hester, as soon as she has proved Calder's point, will be returned to her borough or placed in the hands of a benevolent society which will transport her to the far side of the globe.

And am I any different? Would it not be simple for Uncle Sep to facilitate my incarceration in a convent at the snap of his fingers? It could be so easily explained away, leaving me to rot in oblivion.

I must be captain of my own destiny and navigate the vessel of my own fortunes to brighter horizons. I have determined to help Hester; it is my duty. I will never again be the subject of rumours of ill-treatment. I will protect her and find her absent cousin. I refuse to tolerate life's uncertainties.

~

I have written to Great-Aunt Eleanor to apply to her about a position for Hester and also to accept her kind invitation for me to be her guest in the new year. I shall not name a date for my visit until I have received her reply regarding Hester. This time, I shall tell no other of my plans for Hester and leave no evidence of my involvement. Some servants' clacking tongues are like birdcalls; they have no care as to whom their twittering reaches. How do I know to what extent I can trust Sarah or Mrs Jacques or even Mr Staidly's clerk? No, this time I will not mention a word of Hester's future employment to another living soul. I shall weave a thread of deceit to obscure my plans and endeavour to devise a stratagem to explain away Hester's absence from Waterford.

27th December 1831
Yuletide passed unremarkably, yet my spirits have been lifted by the prospect of my sojourn in Lincolnshire. Uncle Sep and Calder appear pleased with the change in my demeanour. However, I am dismayed at deceiving Calder. He has always been my confidant, my dearest friend. How foolish he will look when he next reports to his Society board when Hester is long gone from Waterford. I am reluctant to humiliate him, but I must be resolute and do what is best for her.

30th December 1831

Great-Aunt Eleanor has written; she will provide a situation for Hester! I am to arrange a hired fly for Hester for 10th February. I shall request that it arrives well before dawn and that the driver understands the transaction to be covert; I will pay him well for his discretion.

In similarity with Uncle Sep's vague threats, I shall tell the world that Hester has left Waterford to be committed to an institution. I will tell Calder and Uncle Sep that I have written to The London Society for the Suppression of Mendicity to inform them that Hester was unsuitable to be educated after all. When she has left for Lady A's, I must convince the world that Hester has pre-empted her dismissal and run away. No one will care to pursue her and it will reduce the embarrassment for Calder and his Society fellows to believe the girl's desire for self-improvement could not be fulfilled.

I shall arrange my own transportation to Great-Aunt Eleanor's for the day after Hester has begun her journey to Lincolnshire, where we will then be reunited.

6th January 1832

Sent a letter to Waterford this morning, for the attention of George Rudd. Its pretext was to ensure that the servants are all adhering to their duties and that Rudd is aware we are delayed in London for longer than usual. However, in truth I wanted to send word to Hester so included a paragraph about her; asked Rudd to make sure she knew I had written of her in my missive. Of course, the words were concise: simply hoping that she has been able to continue her studies per my previous instructions. But I wish I'd been able to write to her directly. I wish she were able to read fluently. I might have described my time in London or reminisced fondly of our weeks in the library. I might even have confessed that I sorely miss our time together.

13th January 1832

I strolled through central London today. At a bookshop, I found an exquisite copy of Mr Keats's Lamia and Other Poems. I bought it and shall present it to Hester when we are safely in Lincolnshire.

22nd January 1832

I prepared a letter of introduction for Hester this morning. I shall leave it unsealed and read it aloud to her, before I send her off to Lincolnshire, so she may know how highly I esteem her.

I am thrown by the complexity of my emotions regarding Hester. A change has come over my mind and my spirit during the time here, and I am much the better for it. Yet I cannot determine if I have changed myself, or been amended by Hester's presence in my life.

23rd January 1832

The hackney carriage is booked for Hester.

Uncle Sep confirms he will be detained in London until the first week of February. I am counting down the days; pray God that all will be well.

25th January 1832

Read a letter in The Times newspaper today. It was from a gentleman with grave concerns over the whereabouts of two missing children. The gentleman felt obliged to engage the newspaper's assistance, as the children's parents were too poor and uneducated to elicit publicity themselves.

It put me in mind of Agnes, Martha, and of Hester's cousin.

More than that, it provoked a meditation on Hester's current vulnerable position, together with the precarious nature of my plan to have her moved safely to Lincolnshire and out of harm's way.

27th January 1832
Received a letter from Parson Ashton. Mrs Briggs has been taken ill and Parson Ashton suspects it is the result of mental anguish over Martha's disappearance. I have responded to offer my sympathy and have proposed to pay a visit to Martha's mother when next I am at Waterford.

28th January 1832
I spent much time today considering the various strands of my scheme to facilitate Hester's safety. I realise I must give the impression to Calder, Uncle Sep and the servants that I believe she is a hopeless case. Of course, I will be busy with the guests when we return to Waterford, but still I must take every opportunity to demonstrate outwardly that I have cut her adrift.

I suspect Hester will perceive that matters are not as they seem, but I believe she trusts me. And I have faith in her. On the night she is to leave, I will explain everything.

31st January 1832
Today I was inclined to record my feelings about Hester, but found my confusion too profound for syntax. With the benefit of perspective, did I spend my time at Waterford indulging myself in watching her? Did I begin to avoid her eyes, fearful she might understand my thoughts, vague and muddled as they were?

1st February 1832

Dare I confess that my world seemed deeper and wider with Hester in it? Or was my lonely existence easier to bear with company and occupation?

But Hester . . .

Why do my fingers tremble when I write her name; why do I write in an unknown hand? I cannot rationalise this feeling.

7th February 1832

The journey back to Waterford was more tiresome than expected, and it was chaos when we arrived. Calder has invited more guests than ever before and I harboured a profound fear that Hester had gone; I couldn't see her anywhere. I summoned Rudd as soon as I was in my rooms and he assured me she was safe and well and had been working under the set of directions I had left.

It was a full hour before all the visitors had been conducted to their sleeping apartments and an age before they came down to dinner. This day has been long and exhausting. Yet my mind is so active with worry that I surely will not sleep. But I must try. I have faith in the plan and I have faith in Hester. I must rest and be ready for tomorrow.

8th February 1832

The day passed better than I hoped. The weather, although cold, was bright and allowed the guests to enjoy the park and gardens in the afternoon. I walked the grounds with Lady Rowsley's daughter, Euphemia. I sent a message to Hester with Rudd saying that our lessons would be cancelled, but didn't see her in person at all today; which serves my purpose well and, I hope, demonstrates the withdrawal of my patronage.

9th February 1832

This morning has been very difficult. I had hoped that I would be able to show my outward detachment from Hester without having to meet her directly. If only our paths had not crossed in the hallway! If only I had been alone instead of with Uncle Sep and Euphemia. I kept the moment to a minimum, but could not fail to notice the hurt and troubled look in Hester's eye.

The day is passing too quickly. I had hoped to find time, when the ladies were resting after lunch, to seek Hester out and apprise her of the plan, but such an opportunity never arose. I was late returning to my rooms and now I am called to the drawing room.

~

I paced my room this last hour, hardly able to dress for dinner. I have an awful foreboding all will be thwarted. I thought there would be more time to make Hester aware of my plans, yet the day is far behind schedule and I dare not be late for dinner.

The dinner bell has been rung. I must wait until the evening is over before I see Hester. When the house has retired, I shall have to go to her room.

Dear God, I pray my nerves will be strong enough. I must have faith; I will see this through.

CHAPTER NINE

On reading Rebekah's words, I feel as though I am dying; not a death that renders flesh chill and eyes black; but one that marks the sudden end of a life that might have been and substitutes it with a dark and bruising future. With one faithless action I have changed the direction of both our destinies and unwittingly discarded my chance of future happiness.

I let the journal slip from my hands as I stare into the dying coals. I don't look at them, but through them, to the room inside my head where memories linger, shimmering like a lattice of spider-webs.

How long I stay in this torpor, I cannot say, but it is broken by Mrs O'Rourke. She arrives at the doorway breathless and says, 'Hester, my lamb. It's our Kitty. She's come home with tales of men asking questions about you.'

'What men?' I ask. I push myself to my knees and look up at her.

'They've been asking at The Birdcage and the King o' Denmark. We can't protect you, my lamb. If Jacob and Meg hadn't . . .' She stumbles over her words. 'If you'd stayed, maybe. It's just . . . you're . . . not one of us.'

With those final short words, Mrs O'Rourke writes a treatise that I understand in the blink of an eye. It doesn't matter if the men are Dicity constables or from the New Police; whether they are seraphs or serpents. They could be princes from a far-off land throwing handfuls of gold coins from their saddlebags. The point Mrs O'Rourke is making is that I am no longer afforded the protection I had as a destitute orphan. The feeble, the immoral, the sly and the poor, all weak threads and easily snapped, but stitch them together and, however garish the fabric, they say all colours agree in the dark. But now I am no longer amongst them, I must fear them. Where once I was given sanctuary by the lifters and foglers and men who cut throats in the night, now I am tainted and cast out of the fold.

There is no pleasure in Mrs O'Rourke's eyes, only concern, so I nod as I take up Rebekah's diary and tuck it into the satchel. One wafer of paper escapes: the letter pushed beneath my garret door. Mrs O'Rourke bends to retrieve it, hands it to me. I take it from her and hurriedly tuck it down the front of my bodice as I push open the door and see Kitty running across the yard towards us.

'You've no more than two minutes, I threw them off the scent as much as I could,' she says, half hoarse with the cold evening air. She has detained the men where she might easily have profited from surrendering me. I hand her Aunt Meg's shawl by way of gratitude and she smiles to gesture to me that the debt is repaid.

'Goodbye, Mrs O'Rourke,' I say. 'And thank you, Kitty.' Then I turn and exit the yard.

Instinct compels me to run, and at first this is what I do, clutching the satchel close to my body. But artifice learned from Uncle Jacob reminds me that I must be cunning and so, once I cross to Austin Street, I slow my pace. I walk quietly, casually acknowledging an idler and a vagrant who pass me by at intervals. I must blend inconspicuously with my surroundings and play the part of a denizen of the borough. I listen through the darkness as the bells of Shoreditch peal the hour with six chimes and, although the moon has already risen, its beams are weak and I walk through the shadows, concealed and indistinct.

Down the long, straight byway of Old Street Road I am less confident. The moon waxes brighter here and there are fewer passageways down which I might dart. I dare not look back and I find myself listening intently to my own footsteps on the pavement. Behind, I hear an echo to my footfalls, where before there was none. I press forward with a faster stride and the echo matches the rhythm. I should be reassured, but I am not, and with my heart throbbing in my head, I stop. I stand stock still in an instant and the echo continues for three or four more beats. I turn and glance back down the road; in the distance there are two irregular shapes pressed against a wall. I turn about and, to give the impression that my pursuers remain undetected, I walk on casually until I reach Goswell Road and once round the corner, I run faster than I have ever run before.

At first I believe I give them the dodge. The streets are busier here: weavers with no more daylight have come down from their attic rooms to smoke pipes; girls from the manufactory, hatless and hot, have come outside to cool their faces. I thread my way around them, searching the horizon with my eyes. My inquisitiveness is my downfall, and my gaze is at once met with an equally inquiring expression from a man in a felt hat. He appears to recognise the look of his prey at the exact same time I recognise the look of my hunter and once again the chase is afoot.

This time, I cannot afford complacency. I employ all the energy and physical cunning I can muster; I slip through palings, crawl beneath low-slung footbridges, and squeeze between pillars, as though I were born a true native of the streets, reaping the knowledge of my years here.

I find myself entering a labyrinth of covered alleyways, winding my way ever deeper, until I emerge on a street where the fog has gathered and there is no breeze to spin the wreaths of smoke-laden vapours away.

Breathless, I sprint along a row of low buildings broken by the entrance to a courtyard, and I fling myself into the recess. I listen, holding the stale air inside my labouring lungs. Sounds are only half-distinct but footfalls still advance. I turn and creep, furtive and silent, hoping my pursuers are deceived into passing the threshold to the byway where I now find myself.

With my legs tiring and my throat raw, I sense panic rising. I am running blind now, the map in my head obscured by a blanket of fear. On I stumble, past lines of blackened bricks, groping at each street door in hope of sanctuary, but they are either latched or stiff and none opens up to me. Finally, one gives way, opening into a corridor that is no more than a fissure between gabled ends.

I hasten along the path, the earth slippery beneath my feet. As the passageway narrows, I fear I have run myself into a dead-end. I push on, desperate now, and at the end of the passage a short flight of steps descends into an underground compartment. I slither down into the basement, the air bitter with the smell of decomposition.

Beneath my feet is bare earth and above, rafters rib the ceiling that supports the floor of the chambers overhead. I have heard of such caverns from Uncle Jacob and know they are cavities built to allow the flow of travellers from one set of rooms to the next by the most direct artery, yet in reality are used solely by rogues and rascals. But as they are known only to the souls unfortunate enough to have been dragged up here, I am certain the men at my heels will not think to descend into what appears to be a closed vault.

But no. Footsteps approach the stairway and I scurry with renewed energy towards the other stairs that I know are at the opposite end of the cellar. It is not until my searching hands touch the damp wall and my squinting eyes see the open doorway some six feet above me that I realise there are no stairs with which to reach it. Perhaps the steps have been withdrawn to stay the movement of criminals, or perhaps they were just eroded by rot. Whatever the reason, I am caught at last.

The men's voices grow stronger. I push my back against the sweating wall, my eyes straining with fear. There is a broken washstand in the corner of the room with a bucket where the basin should be, and into the misshapen pail a pulse of water beats down from above; one drip after another in quick succession, the sound short and smart, like a clack. And it feels for all the world as though I am in the decaying chambers of London's blackest heart.

In these final moments, my mind begins to wonder who these men are. At first I supposed them to be Dicity constables, perhaps having learned from Calder that I absconded from his care. But these men seem coarser and more determined than Dicity men. Then a thought strikes me that they may be Uncle Jacob's associates, perhaps suspicious that I am a free-tongued niece who knows too much? Whomsoever these men are, they are persistent, and I am soon to face them.

The first man calls for a lantern, his boot on the top step. I move along the wall, away from his voice. My foot touches something hard. I stoop, the blood emptying from my chest into my skull, throbbing loud in my ears. My fingers find damp wood, soft with moss. A ladder! I heave it upright and lean it towards the doorway.

The men rush towards me, groping in the half-light, but I am smaller and faster and already on the top rung. Once through the doorway, I turn, heave the ladder up behind me, and dash it to the ground as far away from the mouth of the cellar as my strength will allow. As I take to my heels, the men's shouts and foul oaths are hot upon the chill evening air, but they will not scald me this night.

Long after I have taken flight from the men, I avoid main thoroughfares; keeping to the passages that stretch between lodging houses and courtyards. I skitter down narrow steps over broken tiles and push through the gloom, all the time heading towards the river.

An hour or more since I ran from the yard, I arrive at the Thames, that noble waterway and bringer of fortunes. I stare at the twisting blade of rusty water that cuts into the bank beneath my feet and wonder what will become of me now. I have neither the means nor the physical energy to make my way back to Waterford, and no reason to believe the Brocks will take me in if I did. I stare at the undulating water and the wind-waves that ruffle its surface, and I move back from the edge. I dare not look downstream at the new London Bridge, or upstream towards Blackfriars. I dare not look at bridges, for all my bridges are burnt. Instead I listen to the shouts across the water, and feel as listless as the waves that rub along the embankment.

Overhead, the clouds narrow into rags and, as the moon skims over the surface of the water, I see my own reflection. My shape, although obscure, is definite. The water below me might be anonymous and powerless against the motion of the tide, but I am not. I am Hester White. I cannot give up. I touch my hand to the satchel, take heart from the sight of my reflection and am buoyed by the reminder that while ever I am alive, I have hope.

I turn and, with a great sense of urgency, I ply my way west. However arduous it might be, I must find my way to the Brocks' villa. I shall not be dragged downstream any longer. I will find Calder and tell him the truth; that I am educated and have fallen on hard times; that I only deceived the Brocks out of desperation; that I can offer more to the world than breaking rocks for the Dicity. And I will speak up for Rebekah.

I constantly shuffle the thoughts around my mind as I tramp the streets, dealing myself a fair future one moment and a foul one the next as I search for landmarks to guide me. I recall flashes of yellow paving flags, and stuccoed walls chequered with windows and street doors. After hours of dead-ends and false hopes, I am rewarded with a familiar street, and find myself following two servants, one of whom I am certain is Sarah.

The women have linked arms, each holding a wicker basket in the other hand. I am able to follow snatches of their conversation as they approach the gate in the villa's wall, through which the servants' entrance is situated. They talk of mercers' prices, their cap-strings fluttering in the breeze. They stop at the gatepost ahead of me and, as I continue past, I listen.

'They say it might be a case of never recovering this time,' Sarah says, bold and loud as ever. The scullery maid is more cautious, her voice hushed:

'You mean dying?'

'For all we know the funeral might be as soon as a week on Wednesday.'

I dare not linger and draw attention to myself, so cross the road and hurry away, then pause and watch as they near the Brock residence.

When their forms have been swallowed by a closing gate, I return to the house, but stay on the opposite side of the thorough-fare, hidden beneath shadows thrown down by a fretwork of branches overhanging the pavement. Who is ill? Could my flight from Waterford have weakened Rebekah's constitution? Pray God it's not her. I cannot stop the flow of such dreadful thoughts and the sensation of guilt is at once overwhelming and sickening.

I blow on my fingers as I stare at the villa, watching as blinds are dropped and curtains are drawn over the lamplight. At this moment, movement from inside the house provokes a feeling of hope within me; the flicker of candles, the promise of warmth. I gaze back at the villa's yellow eyes and I wonder how I might be received. Distracted by my thoughts, I fail to hear the approach of a carriage to my left. The rhythm of the hooves and the grinding of wheels evades my senses until the coach draws up squarely between the villa and me.

The horse throws back its head, sending two jets of vapour through the arc of the carriage lamps. I turn to examine the carriage, to observe the visitor yet to alight, but no one climbs out. Instead the driver jumps down and opens the door, not to deliver, but to receive. Then, suddenly, through the misty lamplight, I see Rebekah. To my relief she looks well and I am lightheaded with the surprise of seeing her.

The image is fleeting. She climbs inside the carriage and is away before I can reach the other side of the street. I am faint with hunger and my legs are stiff with exertion; but I must follow her. I hurry after the coach and twice I clash elbows with passers-by in my endeavour to keep up with the driver, as the carriage cuts through the night.

Finally, the carriage stops at a house on Arlington Street, and Rebekah is out of the coach and through the front door before I can catch up. The tree-lined street is quiet and I note that the house is considerably less grand than the Brock residence; a double-gabled, red-brick town house. I suppose Rebekah is visiting, but as much as good sense suggests waiting to approach her when the carriage returns, my heart's throbs compel me to seek her attention without further delay.

Conscious of my bedraggled appearance, I stand before the row of iron palings that abut the pavement and attempt to brush smuts and mud spatters from my face, smooth down my hair and scrape the black road-grease from my boots. But, despite my best efforts, I know I must still look like a sloven.

I press forward through the gate and close it behind me. I make my way to the top of the front steps, and after a tug at the bell chain I wait. Making one last futile attempt to tidy myself, it is in the attitude of fussing over my boots that the door is opened to me. I straighten and meet the stare of a middle-aged woman, wearing an apron, a mobcap and an expression of discomfiture.

'Get away with you. The likes of you shouldn't be—'

She starts to swing the door closed and I am momentarily lost for words, unable to explain myself. The woman pauses and glances over her shoulder before standing aside. I am left with a clear aspect of the entrance hall and, at the far end, Rebekah walks into view, splitting the light as she enters.

Suddenly, nothing exists for me but her presence. Since I last beheld her face, I have sculpted and shaped her image to my own fancy to such an extent that I had begun to wonder if she were like that at all. But my memory has not lied. She walks towards me and her eyes exude more kindness than I might have wished for. I stand shivering, wet skirts clinging to my legs, and the sight of her sublimes me. As she smiles at me it radiates warmth, more warmth than the sun on a wheat field, more warmth than I have yet felt in my life.

'That'll be all, Peggy,' she says, moving past the woman and fronting me. 'I'll take care of this.'

Peggy glances at Rebekah, then moves away with a gentle shake of her head.

Now we are alone, I can do no more than sink slowly to my knees, at last overcome with both exhaustion and relief. Rebekah rushes to me and puts out her hand. I fear it for the passion it ignites in me. I take her fingers in mine and the resultant delightful tug inside my belly cannot be described; I am tranquillised by her touch. I regain my sensibilities and, with Rebekah's help, rise to my feet. I realise that suddenly my world is divided; there is Rebekah and there is everyone else.

My tongue sticks to my teeth, my mouth drier than a lime basket. Then I say hurriedly, 'I am so sorry I left.'

The ensuing silence is deafening, endless. Rebekah simply holds my hand and looks at me. I try again with, 'Can you find it in your heart to forgive me?'

'Hester. You have nothing with which to reproach yourself. I cannot . . .' Her cheeks change colour and she fingers her brooch. 'I thought . . . I was convinced . . . what with Martha and Agnes . . .' Still holding my hand, she closes the front door and leads me into the entrance hall. With her long fingers, she closes her hand around mine and emits a sort of laugh or a sob, I cannot tell. Then, with sudden gravity, she looks at me and asks, 'Have you been hurt?' I shake my head, ready to start to explain, but she interrupts with, 'Were you taken by force?'

'No, Miss,' is all I can muster.

'I don't quite understand. But . . . no matter, for now. It is such a blessing and a grace that you are here. You are safe.'

She lets my hand fall and at once her expression implies she is deep in thought. She puts her hand to her face and dashes away a tear.

'Hester. Hester White. You are clear of the danger I feared you were in.' She smiles and shakes her head. 'I conjured all manner of wild explanations for your vanishing. I was worried about what had become of you. But you are here and you are well and I am so very pleased to see you.' She pauses for a moment then, touching my shoulder, she says, 'But you must be cold. And hungry.' She steps away and calls, 'Peggy. Peggy!'

At Peggy's arrival, Rebekah formally introduces me as 'Miss White', as though Peggy had never opened the door to me, as though I were an old acquaintance, a friend. Rebekah announces that I have been entreated to stay as a guest. I am to be taken to the green room, provided with soap, hot water and a clean set of garments. Peggy eyes me with curiosity and says, 'This way, Miss White.'

She leads me up a stairway as a further instruction is shouted up from Rebekah: 'And please ask Tilly to prepare a supper for Miss White. The veal pie perhaps, some fruit and cheese, served in the breakfast room. Oh, and, Peggy? Make certain the fire is stoked so the room is warm enough. Thank you.'

When I enter the bedchamber, I am glowing with relief and

happiness. I quite forget my damp clothes and mud-spattered legs. Then I sense the weight of the wet leather bag on my shoulder and my heart tightens at the remembrance of my deception. Taking the diary from the satchel, I push both it, and my deceit, beneath the mattress on the bed. By the time Peggy returns to my room, the diary is hidden beneath bedsprings, goose-down and blankets.

Within the hour, I am sitting on a chair that has been placed on the hearthrug in front of a crackling fire in the breakfast room. My skin is tight and tingling and the freshly laundered day-dress, which I assume to be one of Rebekah's, hangs loosely on my frame. I am tired from my journey and weak with hunger, so graze from one dish to the next, taking a moment to relax and enjoy the warmth, while I wait for Rebekah to send for me.

Soon Peggy knocks and enters, saying, 'Miss Brock will see you in the dining room. Please follow me this way.'

When we enter, Rebekah is hunched over an easel. At first I believe she is painting, but the canvas is in fact a large square of slate, upon which she is furiously scratching numbers and letters. Before Peggy can announce me, Rebekah turns to face me, smiling as she says, 'Come in, Hester. Come, be seated.'

I obey and, as Peggy tugs the door shut behind her, Rebekah pulls a chair close to mine and sits down. Suddenly she is standing again and shuffling the great many papers that strew the surface of the dining table. She absent-mindedly scratches her head then resumes her seat.

'There must be some logic to this, Hester,' she begins. 'There's always a way through these enigmas. Always a solution, but I . . .' She looks at me intensely, as though appealing for inspiration, but I cannot continue without confessing how I have misled her.

'Miss. I am not who you believe me to be,' I venture, sudden, daring. Rebekah sits back in her chair and says, 'Go on.'

'I was wrong to use you; to use Mr Calder. Wrong to repay

your kindness with concealment, but my family was subject to a series of misfortunes and life had pressed me so firmly to the bottom of the heap that when the chance of salvation presented itself . . . I'm afraid I embraced it with both hands. I saw it as a way out; the only way out.'

With Rebekah's encouragement, I describe my father's naval heritage and the abandonment of his appointed career; how he chose the church and was disinherited as a result. I explain how my mother was also ostracised by her family for marrying against her own father's wishes and below her station, and that after Mama and Papa died, no family came to claim me and no one advised me what to do. I tell Rebekah of how Jacob, our gardener at the parsonage in Lincolnshire and his wife, Meg, took me in and how we were washed ever downwards to the cesspool that is at the end of the alley, in the corner of the yard.

'I'm so sorry,' Rebekah whispers at the close of my oration. 'You must have suffered terribly.' She touches her index finger to her pursed lips, tapping them as though in deep thought, before asking, 'And how well were you educated, Hester?'

'Well enough, until my father died, Miss. He taught me how to read and write and tutored me well in English grammar. I also learned a little ciphering, some Greek and Latin.'

'Yet how well you mastered the vernacular of the London native,' she says, with a wry smile. 'You were very convincing at first, though less so as time went on!'

'I am sorry,' I say in earnest.

'I understand why it was necessary, of course.'

She rises, gathers a handful of papers from the table top and says, 'I have experienced a minor conflict with my uncle, Hester. Consequently, we have mutually agreed that I should accept dear Lady Appleton's generosity: this is her house, Hester, and I have been given liberty to stay here for a month, together with the use of her carriage and her driver, Bostock. Originally, I was scheduled to visit her home in Lincolnshire, but of course my plans changed when . . . Anyway, Lady Appleton believes it will do me good to spend time away from our town house and Waterford. And Uncle Sep says it will provide a peaceful environment in which I might learn to temper some of my natural traits, to modify my opinions.' Her eyes are downcast as she delivers this last confidence to me and I can almost sense Uncle Sep's presence in the room with us, feel the weight of his authority over her. Then she lifts her head and declares, 'However, I have different plans.' She excitedly hands a bundle of papers to me and asks that I read them.

I scan the first, which is written by a Jack Radnor, Agent to the Marshalsea. It comprises both physical and biographical depictions of Martha Briggs and Agnes; their build and eye colour, their last place of abode, their father's professions and sundry other facts, all neatly recorded. As I read, Rebekah says, 'They were both my maidservants, before you arrived.' I nod, at once finding it difficult to conceal my knowledge of her diary, her private thoughts. I think about telling her the truth, but I can't do it, not yet. She seems to detect my discomfort and asks, 'I wonder, were you aware of their existence?'

'Yes,' I reply. 'Mary and Sarah did confide in me about them; they viewed it as quite a mystery.'

Rebekah nods and presents me with another paper. It is the letter from Lady Appleton, the details of which were recorded in Rebekah's journal. As I pass my eyes over the script, I note the detailed description of the clothes Edward was last wearing, which Rebekah did not chronicle: black breeches, fustian jacket, seal-skin cap.

'Thank you for taking the trouble to write to Lady Appleton, Miss,' I say.

'Nonsense, Hester. Don't you see? It's all part of the same narrative, I am certain.' She rises and looks again at the slate easel.

'I started to catalogue names and details of missing persons soon after Martha went missing from Waterford, you see, and the list keeps expanding; what with Martha, Agnes, then your cousin. In all honesty, Hester, as much as it troubles me even to say it, I thought that I might have to add your name to the portfolio until today. It seems so sinister and perplexing. I've asked Calder, but he's so busy with his work and hasn't time to look into it.' She shakes her head, sorts through another handful of papers and places a bundle of clippings into my hands. 'There are others, too. Look here.' She jabs the uppermost sheet and steps back.

I read the first paragraph. It is a newspaper excerpt from *The Times*:

> On the night of Wednesday the 5th inst., a further missing person case has arisen in the district of Islington. Mrs Green, a widow of good character, has suffered a great deal of mental distress since the disappearance of her little boy. He was missing when she returned home in the evening and has not been heard of since. He was eight years old. The police have commented on the peculiarity of the case and appealed for information regarding the lad's whereabouts.

I turn the slip of paper and set about reading the article beneath, this time from the *Weekly Despatch*:

> Information has been received that on Thursday 27th October last, a young man named Harris, aged 16, with dark complexion and thick brown hair, left his house in Camden Town. He failed to return home that night as was his habit and has not been seen since. The police are keen to engage the assistance of any witnesses to this matter and to establish the fate of Mr Harris, with the hope of ruling out any suspicion of foul play.

There are a dozen or so similar articles detailing the disappearances of youths, children, women and men. I look at Rebekah and say, 'There are more to add to this list, Miss: there are countless hand-bills pasted to walls about town appealing for lost people, and since returning to the borough this last week, I have learned of others who appear to have experienced the same fate as these poor souls. There is a woman named Annie, Annie Allsop. And a seaman, but I don't know his name. And a beggar, a Doll Man called Tulley. And some months ago there was an article about a missing boy called Master Hogget, in the *Morning Herald*.'

Rebekah takes up a pen and records their names and the brief details I am able to impart. Then the room is cloaked in silence as the gravity and scale of the situation becomes apparent, before Rebekah says, 'I have written to the Home Office, of course. And the Commissioners of the New Metropolitan Police, but they have not replied. If only Calder were able to help us . . .' This last sentence she speaks more to herself than to me. Then she looks at me and says, 'Calder is not well, Hester.'

I immediately think back to Sarah's foreboding words outside the villa and I realise that they were not speaking about Rebekah, but Calder. I ask her, 'Is it serious, Miss?'

'Yes, well; no. I don't know, Hester. He works so hard. His practice has grown and he won't take on a partner. His patients take advantage of his kindness, I'm sure. I'm afraid this over-work has compromised his health, enfeebled his spirit and prompted him to seek sustenance from wine and laudanum. I have pleaded with him to make an attempt to reform, but he denies there is any reason to. He becomes so subjugated by the effects of his intake that he finds it necessary to repeat the dosage to restore his former vitality, and so the wheel turns.'

Rebekah blushes, as though she has spoken out of turn. All this time, she paces in front of the fireplace, worrying the collar of her gown. Now she sits and says, 'Hester. I have been selfish. I'm sorry, but these riddles rush around my head with such a clamour that I cannot think of any other subject until they are all ordered. Forgive me. Tell me do, what happened at Waterford? Why exactly did you have to return to London in such a secretive manner? Did you not realise how concerned I would be at your departure, at your leaving without anything to your name?'

I am winded by the change in Rebekah's direction; flattered by her concern, but ill-prepared to explain myself, and I cannot confess to stealing and reading her private journal. I think back to the night I left, relive the moments before my escape, and remember the note that was pushed under my door.

'There was a note, Miss. Someone slipped it under my bedroom door. I didn't see who.'

'And what did it say?'

'It was a warning.'

'About what?'

'It said that I should never have entered Mr Calder's carriage and I should fear for my life.'

'And how did you dispose of this note?'

I colour at my own stupidity and say, 'I didn't. I believe it is still tucked in the folds of my dress upstairs.'

Rebekah stands and gives a sharp dash at the bell-pull. She turns to face me and simply says, 'But where have you been these past days? I assumed you would return to London and I hired two men from the Marshalsea agency to search for you. They came highly recommended and, when I met them, they seemed most respectable. They assured me that if you could be found, then you would be found. I couldn't think how else to trace you.'

At Rebekah's disclosure of her reputable hirelings, I am perplexed. I recall my pursuers' appearance and persistence, and wonder if Rebekah would have hired such men had she known how brutish they could be. But in the haste of the situation, hire someone she did; and for this I am grateful. I consider her words and conclude that it is discourteous to mention my concerns to her and so refrain from doing so. But a certain discontentment endures as I call to mind the men's hard faces, their dogged perseverance.

'I went back to Virginia Row,' I begin, 'where I lived before Mr Calder took me in. I learned that my aunt, uncle and two cousins had all died while I was away. I was alone, unprotected, and when I found myself being chased across the city by two men, I panicked. I couldn't know that you had hired them and I believed . . . they were going to harm me . . . and . . .'

My tears begin and I am too exhausted to stop them. I hide my face in my cupped hands. Through the gaps in my fingers, I sense Rebekah is moving towards me. She is as close to me as that day in the dogcart. I feel the folds of her skirts brush against me, and inhale the fragrance of gillyflower rising from her.

I part my hands and she is before me. A charge courses through me: a shiver, a swell, a rush. My neck and cheeks grow warm as the moment quietly advances, hesitant in its progress, nervous in its steps. There is a twist in my heart and a throb deep inside. All I can wish for is that she will reach for me, embrace me, and hold me close.

But my hope is quashed. Peggy's footsteps grow louder as she approaches the dining room door, breaking the thread of intensity within the room as surely and cleanly as a blade. Rebekah is distracted; she steps backwards, unsteadily. She takes a moment to compose herself, to touch the comb in the back of her hair, to straighten the bodice of her gown.

Peggy knocks, and at Rebekah's invitation she enters, and looks from me to her mistress quizzically before receiving orders from Rebekah to search for the note. Peggy leaves, returns within five minutes and places a soiled shred of paper on the table.

'Will that be all, Miss?' she asks.

'No,' Rebekah chimes. 'Please could you bring me some wine and cold savouries. And have Ned bring a comfortable chair from the drawing room. With a blanket, too. And have the fire trimmed and fresh coals put to it. I want a steady blaze that will last until morning. And bring more candles, I need light.'

With no further explanation, Rebekah sits, unfolds the note, studies it hard then begins furiously to scratch nib against paper. Her verbal instructions are executed with efficiency, and within twenty minutes the fire is obediently giving off heat, the newly recruited candles stand erect and in line, wine is decanted, the repast is plated and I have been seated in the padded chair with a blanket draped over my knees. When in turn Ned, Tilly and Peggy have all exited, Rebekah turns to me and says, 'I felt so sure of you, Hester. I am so happy not to be disappointed.'

I observe her face without speaking, and there is a ripple of change in her demeanour; the relics of sadness are less obvious in her eyes. Perhaps sometimes we allow life to suppress us, let our pride be eroded. Perhaps it is a state of our own consciousness, not truly driven by circumstances at all, simply a gradual shifting of the sands as life's sorrows swell and break over us. Then something changes – the meeting of a kindred spirit, the potency of mutual trust – and the tender graces of self-belief once more visit themselves upon us and we are as complete as ever we may be.

All I can do is watch and admire. She works away at her papers, but every so often she looks at me and smiles. I don't question her; I sit patiently, sometimes answering questions she poses about small details. In this manner we continue, and gradually Rebekah gathers and records all the information I can impart on Edward, Master Hogget, Annie, Matthew Tulley and the sea-captain, from the original date of Edward's anticipated arrival at Smithfield, to Annie's tryst with a man at the Fortune of War, from Matthew Tulley's dolls, flute and drum, to the sea-captain's fine shock of hair. Every particle I can remember is catalogued and ordered.

Eventually I fall into a deep sleep and I remain undisturbed until the clock on the mantel rouses itself to speak four clear chimes. I sit upright, eyes still a little heavy with fatigue. The shaded candles are burning low, the fire is subdued and an empty wine glass is stacked on a China plate of crumbs. Rebekah hears me shifting in the seat and turns to me.

'Ah, Hester!' she exclaims, as though I have been physically absent, not just asleep. Without any soft words to ease me from my stupor, she begins, 'I know how I can resolve all these matters.' She nods at the disordered papers before her. 'Ciphering and logic feed from the same trough, Hester. Don't you see?' I shake my head. 'It's about the level of minutiae; if there is sufficient detail, then a pattern will emerge.' All the while she is talking, she addresses the papers rather than me. Then she presents me with a neat bundle, nods for me to read and I begin.

In her neat, uniform hand, Rebekah has recorded details of Martha, Agnes, Edward, Annie, Matthew Tulley and the captain. But they also include the names of the missing, chronicled in newspapers and broadsheets. Where facts are known, they are recorded in meticulous detail: eye colour, hair, complexion, height, build, description of gait and other such physical attributes. The remaining leaves of notebook describe articles of apparel and accoutrements, coinage about the person and respective denomination, maps with last known journeys plotted, places habitually visited, family, acquaintances, and endless diagrams of direct and indirect links. I am confounded by the quantity and complexity of the intelligence and begin to wonder if it is all a bigger muddle than before Rebekah began.

I wear an apologetic expression in which she reads my confusion and breaks in with, 'There is no connection, no solution . . . yet. But, Hester, I am determined to discover exactly what wickedness has been let loose upon us, as well as who has loosed it! I believe we have enough here to guide us to the answer, wherever that may lead us. We will be in a degree of danger, for the prospect before us carries great risk. But who else but us will do it? And . . .' She hesitates, as though fearful of choosing the wrong words, of saying too much or too little, before she finishes with, '. . . I believe we are better able to climb the steep together.' With a nod of my head and a smile from Rebekah, we have struck a bargain of complicity. We have found a common purpose, a calling.

For the remainder of the dark hours, Rebekah reads aloud from her lists and has me write down any issues of commonality. She seems to be ahead of everything; declaring that the recurrent reference to inns around Smithfield, particularly the Fortune of War, must be more than coincidence. She says that many of the missing appeared to have a relationship with an unknown other. At this point, she has me make a note to write to the close associates of the missing, to request a detailed description of the respective friend, fiancé, lover with whom the victim was last seen. And she builds a plan for us; we must confirm the information we already have while gathering more facts. In short, she believes we should go to the Fortune of War ourselves and elicit what intelligence we can.

'Yet I imagine,' she says lightly, 'if I enter such an establishment in my present garb, I will either be ostracised or hit over the head with a liquor pot.'

'These inns are dangerous places, Miss.' My tone is serious, cautious. 'But perhaps we might sell our gowns to Mrs Cohen, and have her dress us in cheaper clothes. She owns a shop on Thieving Lane – well, Field Lane, to give it its proper name.'

'That's a wise idea. You could say that you work as my maid, but I've fallen upon hardship and must sell the garments we wear to raise a little capital. I shall have Peggy unpack some of my finest gowns; it will help secure the transaction if the outfits are of the best quality. Once we are incognito, we will be able to move more freely about the area and extract the information we desire. Well done, Hester! What a team we make!'

I give a half-smile, but I wonder if Rebekah can quite grasp the level of squalor and lawlessness we will be subjecting ourselves to. I feel a pang of foreboding in my breast, a disappointment in having to return to the backstreets from where I thought I had finally escaped. But destiny has thrown us together, and if I am to face danger and death and finally be overcome by a world I have tried so hard to escape, then what better ally than Rebekah?

She responds to my ambivalence by studying my face for a moment and then she remarks:

'You look anxious, Hester.'

'Yes, I am a little.'

'I too have been experiencing a period of uneasiness. Yet . . .' There is a break in the conversation as she seems to consider her next phrase. '. . . less so now you are here with me.'

She raises her eyes to meet mine with bold frankness, apparently keen to gauge my reaction. Unable to reply, I smile shyly at her. She seems buoyed by this and wades in a little deeper.

'Waterford was not the same without you. I didn't know what had become of you, and I . . . didn't know what might become of me without you.' She pauses here, turns away from me and brushes a stray hair from her face, saying, 'I found that you had become every third thought.'

These words she mumbles and I feel a tingle of excitement; but, though gratified, I still wish for more. However, Rebekah it seems must be out of her depth, and she retreats to the shallows.

'So I hired two men to search for you,' she adds.

Seemingly on firmer footing, she delivers these words in her usual, easy tones; gone is the uncertainty of a moment before. Then, from an apparent place of safety and assuredness: 'You see, as I came to know you better, I believed you had a mind I could respect.'

A day since, this statement from Rebekah would have satisfied my most ardent cravings. But instead there is a twinge of disappointment at this new choice of language. I don't simply want to be a mind she respects. I don't want to sit beside her at one of Uncle Sep's dinners as Sir Humphrey used to, discussing intellectual matters. I want more. I believe there is hope of more. I know there is.

At this moment, lost in the intricacies of thought, doubt appears before me; that ever-present shadow of truth. I wonder if there is any affection between us, after all. Do I project something unspoken onto her and conjure false reciprocation to satisfy my yearning? At last, I understand how so much dubiety surrounds the calling out of emotions: one wrong step, one misplaced word, and the quicksand of foolhardiness holds you fast. I determine to say something but, as I look at Rebekah, I realise I have been silent for too long; the moment of note, if indeed it did exist, is over, leaving an air of flatness in its wake. And each of us steps back into ourselves.

Rebekah retreats to the mounds of papers on the table. She seems safer there, laying a series of newspaper cuttings on her lap and saying, 'Others appear content with contriving innocent explanations or denying the gravity of these absences. And yet, all these names! Is it just we two holding our trembling candles into the darkness, Hester? Or are some too blind to want to see?'

With this we begin our discourse again, practical and pragmatic, revisiting our schemes and designs, determining to unravel what mysteries are set before us. In my mind, I can neither rank nor separate one riddle from another: the enigma of love, the inscrutable Rebekah Brock, the unaccountable vanishings; and I wish with all my heart that I might solve every one of them.

When finally our plans are drawn and the fire is burnt out, Rebekah entreats me to retire to the green room, to rest before we commence our journey later this morning. I accept her suggestion and leave her writing letters.

Sleep takes me as soon as my head touches the pillow, and I am only awoken when the clocks strike nine. My room is bathed in morning light, bringing with it the persistence of reality and the checking of hopes and dreams.

I descend the stairs and enter the dining room. There is just enough daylight permitted by the drapes to show me the room. Rebekah is asleep in her chair, hunched over the table with her head on one side. Her breath is gentle. I don't wake her, I just watch her, and part of me wishes that our quest could be delayed just for a little while longer. But time has a different plan and, as the servants go about their business, Rebekah stirs.

'I'm sorry, Miss,' I say. 'I hope I didn't wake you.'

'Oh, that's all right. I was only nodding.'

Rebekah stands and casts her eyes over the papers on the table top, at the cuttings and letters, at her pens and ink. 'Well, I must freshen up before breakfast, Hester,' she says. 'Please excuse me.' She offers up a confident smile, but there is a hint of nervousness behind her eyes.

From the safety of speculation and theory, Rebekah is intent on transporting us imperceptibly into a realm of menacing reality. Time will not pause for our journey; we can but brace ourselves and make shift to begin it.

CHAPTER TEN

At ten o'clock we take breakfast, and by eleven we are dressed in our finery for the journey east. I move awkwardly; the gown's material is heavy, the undergarments layered and unlike anything I have ever worn. We step outside and the pallor of the morning is virtually no different from the dusk of the night before. It is what I would refer to as a true London Particular; it tastes of coddled eggs and coal-smoke, smells of quenched fires and horse-dirt. It catches the back of my throat as I climb into the carriage and, as Rebekah follows me in, she gives a little splutter. Snapping the door closed behind her, she signals to Bostock, the driver, to set off.

'They say the cholera is in London, again,' Rebekah remarks casually to me. 'Surely this noxious air will kill it off in an instant!' She gives a light laugh, but when she turns to face me, her eyes show increasing anxiety, and I wonder if the gravity of our task is dawning on her. She takes my gloved hand in hers, presses her fingers around mine and says, 'Climb the steep together, Hester. We'll climb the steep together.' She releases my hand and we travel along in silence for several moments, before she says, 'So, Mrs Cohen's shop was Annie Allsop's destination on the morning you met her?'

'Yes.'

'Annie might have mentioned the name of the man she intended to meet at the Fortune of War, assuming he wasn't a figment of her creative faculties.'

I sense that tug of alarm in my chest again and wonder if Rebekah has a similar trepidation inside her. The theoretical work she completes is safe and contained; she controls it. But this reality, this raw world we are entering, will not bend to the will of her logic; it will throw up danger and surprise instead, and all I can do is hope we are strong enough to withstand it.

Bostock pulls rein on the far side of Holborn Bridge, and we step out onto unpaved paths strewn with corrupting vegetables and all manner of filth. In spite of discouragement from the sunless skies, the mounds of rubbish still manage to give off a steaming stench. Rebekah claps her hand to her mouth, closes her eyes and gives a little retch. She stops, takes my arm and leans her weight against me.

'I shall be all right in a moment,' she whispers. 'I shall become accustomed to it.' She takes her hand from her lips, breathes in two or three times, then nods to me. 'There,' she says, 'I am well again.'

We walk over the bridge, the Fleet ditch below black and suffocating. The bridge itself is made of bricks and mortar but trembles beneath each step, and the rotten palings that fringe it lean this way and that as we move.

I guide Rebekah to the right and turn onto Thieving Lane. Every so often people appear out of the mist. Everyone jostles for the centre of the road, as though they are fearful the whole street might collapse if the fog were ever to clear and no longer shore up the bricks and plaster. Continually Rebekah is bumped by shoulders as we trail along and all she can say as we walk is, 'It's so dark.' She repeats a little later, 'It's all so dark.'

Her literal observation is obvious; the light is scant and weak.

But I know that even if the sun were to illumine the whole borough, it would still be dark. Dark with the business of the people who live here. Dark with the deeds that are done. As we press forward, a group of men seep from a scab of low shop-fronts, and for once I am glad the fog is always here to shroud the streets; I am glad each footstep we take is obscured.

We arrive at the shop and Mrs Cohen is pegging her wares in rows across the shop-front. Her sleeves are pushed to her elbows in spite of the February air, and she stands beneath her board, which reads: *Elizabeth Cohen, sells you the best & most fashionable frocks and sutes of Fustian, Ticken and Holland, stript Dimmity, flannel and canvas waistcoats, by Wholesale, or Retale at Reasonable Rates.*

Before I can speak, Mrs Cohen offers a curtsey and bids us good morning. I am certain she cannot recognise me, and so loosen my bonnet strings to pull it from my head and at once her expression changes. Her dark eyes widen, she blinks in close succession.

'Well, saints alive! Hester White of all people. Heard you'd gone away, I did, my love. Sad affair about dear Meg and old Jacob.'

'It was a pretty smart shock, I should say,' I reply, my consonants clipped, my vowels round, London-round. I slip back into the vernacular as if I have never been away.

'And the twins,' she goes on. 'Never saw a blade of grass, I'd wager. Fragile and jaundiced as two buttercups, they was. Still, you're looking well-fed, my love.'

'I've been gone for months, Mrs Cohen.'

'What you been jobbing at, my love?'

'I been a maid, see. This is my mistress. We come to talk business with you.'

Without looking up, Mrs Cohen leads us deep into the folds of the little shop. Jackets, caps, breeches, frocks, aprons and stockings all hang from the walls, the staleness of their previous owners still ripe in the air. Mrs Cohen stops, draws three stools into a tiny space in front of the counter, bids us be seated, picks up a cold tallow candle and shouts, 'Rosina! Rosina. Bring us a glim, my love.'

To my left, through the shadows, a black frock moves seemingly of its own accord. It is hanging limply at floor level one moment, then springs to life the next. I jump up from my stool in a sort of horrified reflex, catching Rebekah about the neck as I do so. The apparition moves towards us. Rebekah stands and, speaking with the assuredness of one who intends to be understood and is certain of success, she says, 'What is the meaning of this?'

'Why, no devilry intended at all, Miss,' Mrs Cohen says. 'This is my daughter, Rosina.' She turns to me, 'You remember, Hester? Didn't Meg tell you I had a child?'

I shake my head and say, 'No, Mrs Cohen. Aunt Meg never told me. I'd be certain to remember such a thing, I'm sure.'

Rosina noiselessly moves around us, is swallowed in the shadows briefly, and returns with a lantern. She hovers in front of her mother for a moment, her shoulder standing three inches higher than mine. I guess that she is older than me, and suppose her build was once the same as Rebekah's, but is now atrophied and gaunt. But I cannot see her face, even when Mrs Cohen places the lantern on the counter-top, because Rosina, as well as being dressed head to toe in black, is also wearing a veil. I am disconcerted by her presence, whether it is the initial fright she has subjected me to, or because her face is obscured, I cannot tell. I hope we may soon transact the business we have come here for and be gone. But I underestimate Rebekah's inquisitiveness, and I deflate a little as she asks Mrs Cohen without ceremony, 'Why is Rosina in mourning weeds?'

'Well, that's a tidy tale to tell. You can ask her, Miss. But she won't say. And the reason she won't say, is that she don't know. See, she always done it. Right from being a scrap of a thing. She watched a funeral procession when she was little, saw all them dark frocks, all them veils. Set about dressing herself in the same manner, like she was grieving. Saddest child you'd see in your life, she was.'

Rosina leaves the lantern, leaves us, and is at once entombed in the blackness of a back room. But a certain gloom has settled in her wake, and we take our stools again and sit in silence.

Until now, Mrs Cohen is cheerful and polite, as always. She is the Mrs Cohen I remember when Aunt Meg and I would call for apparel for the twins: composed, regular, unexcitable. But when Rebekah removes her bonnet, and just as the arc of the lantern-light catches Rebekah's face, Mrs Cohen becomes someone I don't recognise. The colour spills out of her face and her lips tremble.

'Mrs Cohen?' I say. She appears not to hear me. I try again with, 'Are you ill, Mrs Cohen? Shall I fetch Rosina?' She ignores me. More than that, she raises her hand, as if to bid me let her be. Her hand hovers mid-air before, with an apparent will of its own, it touches Rebekah's face. Mrs Cohen lets the back of her fingers stroke Rebekah's cheekbone before she slowly lets her arm fall. All the time, Rebekah and I are perfectly still. And Mrs Cohen looks so deeply into Rebekah's eyes that the whole scene becomes unnerving. Mrs Cohen seems to collect herself by shaking her head. I cannot bear the silence, so I say, heartily, 'Mrs Cohen. This is my mistress, Miss Rebekah Brock.'

Mrs Cohen repeats the name deliberately, 'Miss . . . Rebekah . . . Brock, you say? Well, bless my soul; I thought you was someone else for a moment!' Then she is herself again, as if the last few minutes have never passed. 'Miss Brock. Delighted to make your acquaintance, I am. What sort of business are we to discuss today, Miss? Have you want for servants' raiment? I'm sure to have such garments that will answer to the purpose. You'll not find a better price and quality in all of London.'

'Mrs Cohen,' Rebekah begins. She checks herself, gives a little cough and then continues, 'I trust I can rely on your discretion?'

'If honour is a sin, Miss, then I am the most offending soul alive.'

'Thank you, Mrs Cohen. As you might have guessed, I have fallen prey to ill circumstances, which have resulted in a reduction in my income. Poverty is an ill bedfellow, Mrs Cohen, and a wretched inconvenience. I must have liquidity and I must have it today.'

'And what asset, Miss Brock, to grease the palm of liquidity?'

'Every particle of raiment I am currently wearing. The same for my maid.'

Mrs Cohen stands, leans one way and the other, her lips puckered, her eyes narrow. She brushes her fingers over Rebekah's shoulder, catches hold of her sleeve and raises it to the lantern. 'Damassin?' she asks.

'Yes, Mrs Cohen. And Hester's is bombazine.'

'Very fine. Very fine indeed.' As she speaks, she takes up a pen from the counter, dips it in an ink-splashed pot and scribbles on a wafer of paper. 'And you'll be needing an exchange of garments today?'

'Yes. If your price is fair.'

Mrs Cohen finishes her list of fabrics and prices, and slides the paper towards Rebekah, who in turn inspects the figures and gives a nod of approval.

We are then led by Mrs Cohen between racks of jackets and frocks into a closet, the walls of which are lined with flannel petticoats and woollen stockings, the odour damp and fetid. There is barely enough room to turn and, although Mrs Cohen leaves us with the lantern swinging on a nail, the dank air and the soft wall-lining absorbs the light and we are left to feel our way through the shadows.

We help each other to undress and Rebekah's skin is chill, her fingers ice-cold. As the layers of undergarments are peeled away, we both emit audible shivers; teeth chattering while we replace our gowns with poor imitations: fine cotton with linen, best silk with wool. The clothes scratch my skin; a skin supposedly grown resilient with the rub of poverty. I can only wonder at the discomfort Rebekah is experiencing, yet she says nothing as we retrace our steps into the main body of the shop. Mrs Cohen is waiting behind the counter and steps forward to take the clothes draped over Rebekah's arms.

'Mmm. Essence of gillyflower,' Mrs Cohen says, taking the gown from Rebekah and placing it on the counter-top. She straightens the creases in the skirt and stares at the material. 'I used to know a lady who had the same aroma about her,' she begins, her tone wistful. 'Of course, this would be five-and-twenty years since. And when I say lady, I mean a real lady. Tall and strong as you, Miss Brock. But she was fragile at the end, poor dear. Cut off in full bloom she was. And death lay on her like frost on a flower.'

Silence ensues and although Mrs Cohen's words are a lamentation, her tone is superficial and I distrust the woman. I believe Rebekah harbours the same doubts, for she takes up the receipt and stack of coins from the counter with such speed that some drop to the floor. I rootle on bended knee among the dirt and sawdust, and when I return the coins to Rebekah, her fingers are trembling.

Despite the oddness of the atmosphere and the quiver of her hand, Rebekah's voice is as calm and imperious as ever as she says, 'I may return with other garments and—'

'Well, you know where I am. Always a deal to be struck, my

love. Always barter to be had.' Mrs Cohen interrupts Rebekah without an apology for doing so. Gone are the fine gowns, and gone is the respect. Suddenly her manners are blunt, unvarnished. A flash of irritation glows in Rebekah's eyes, before she smiles, apparently already wise to the terms upon which Mrs Cohen's acquaintanceship must now proceed.

'One more matter, Mrs Cohen,' Rebekah begins.

'Yes, my love?'

'Hester has a friend in these parts whom she wishes to locate.'

'What friend is that then, Hester?' Mrs Cohen turns to me, her eyes squinting, her stare hard.

'It's Annie, Mrs Cohen. Annie Allsop.'

'Why should I know the whereabouts of Annie Allsop?'

'When I last saw her,' I say, my voice weak, 'she said she was coming here, to buy a hat.'

'Was she then?'

'She appears to have gone missing, Mrs Cohen,' Rebekah strikes in, sounding weary of Mrs Cohen's evasiveness. 'Of course, we don't expect you to know where she is, but it is possible you know the name of the man she was intending to meet later that day.'

'Well, this all sounds a bit mysterious, don't it?' Mrs Cohen says, rubbing the back of her ear, then lightly pinching the creased skin of her throat, drawing out her words, leaving wider gaps.

'Will you name him to us?' Rebekah presses again, her tone impatient now.

'Well, if I ever can lay my tongue to it, I'm sure I shall let you—'

'A shilling.'

'Two, my love.'

'Name him.' Rebekah skims the coins onto the counter with a rap and a scrape.

'Jack Morton.'

With that, the ceremony, the game, is concluded, and Mrs Cohen turns her back on us and is at once absorbed by the cloth phantoms that haunt the walls. Rebekah wastes no time in heading for the door, stopping only once when a black gown moves in the shadows. Rebekah turns her head and stares at Rosina's veiled face. I can hear Rosina's breathing as they exchange glances, and the moment lingers until Rebekah turns away and I follow her out.

Where previously the street air had been choking and sour, it is at once cool and quenching when compared to the inside of Mrs Cohen's shop. Rebekah walks quickly and I trot every couple of paces to keep up with her. I don't believe she has a care for the direction she chooses, she just seems to have a desire to be gone from the peculiar shop and the oppression of the street.

At the top of the lane Rebekah begins to slow, but before I can draw level with her, she tumbles neck and crop to the floor. The bucket which upends her is sent flying and gives a clang as it catches another hard surface. I bend down to help her to her feet and we are both caked in street dirt, to the apparent amusement of a crowd of passers-by.

Rebekah's expression is one of horror; I believe she has not yet reconciled her thoughts to those of a street-peasant. She most likely expects to be accosted, to be robbed of her fine silk handkerchiefs, her sovereigns and jewels, but as she looks down at her woollen cloak and her clogs, she gives a grin and pulls us both up as the last onlookers wander off. For she is no longer a spectacle to behold. She is not a lady in the wrong part of town to be jostled or robbed; with her skirts daggled with street mire, she has become invisible. But even stripped of her finery and indistinguishable from the denizens of the borough, she is still remarkable to me.

On we press, duly stamped with the seal of impoverished circumstances, and make our way towards Smithfield, towards Giltspur Street and the Fortune of War.

'What did you make of Mrs Cohen, Hester?' Rebekah asks as we walk, pausing and turning to face me.

'Before today, she was just an acquaintance of Aunt Meg's. Always keen to discuss business and nothing else. I can't imagine what came over her. I'm sure she must have traded with ladies before. Perhaps none so grand as you though.'

'And what of this Rosina?'

'I can't say, Miss. I truly didn't know she existed. What a strange thing to hide.'

'Yes. We must record all these events, Hester. When we return home tonight, we must be meticulous. Any piece of intelligence, however small, might help us. And the fellow, Morton, do you know of him?'

'No, Miss. But the truth is lots of folks from around these parts use different names at will. Uncle Jacob would call himself Jacob or Jake, but then sometimes he would say his name was Tom or James. I suppose it confuses the Charlies and the Dicity constables.'

'I see.'

'Miss?'

'Yes?'

'What do you suppose we'll find at the Fortune?'

'I don't know, Hester. But we must be discreet and we must listen carefully. We have come this far and we must see it through to the end, for the sake of those who are missing and for our own futures.'

I am gazing back at Rebekah as I see them out of the corner of my eye; two men leaning against a lamp-post. They have their backs to us but slowly one of them turns. He reaches down and toys with the fastening of his high-lows before scratching his groin through his smock frock. Without his felt hat I don't recognise him at first.

'Miss,' I whisper. 'The men you hired from the Marshalsea, they're behind you.'

Rebekah screws round slowly, then fronts me again and simply says, 'They're not the men I hired.'

I look at them again and, with a growing feeling of agitation, I know they are the same men who pursued me. In the space of a heartbeat, I realise that Rebekah's men did not find me; that I was sought by these other men, and am still wanted.

Discreetly, I look towards them, hoping they have not yet seen us, praying they have gone away. But it is too late and they are already strolling towards us. Alone, I would bolt, I would slip through the alleyways like an eel through the Thames. But now I am not alone and not driven solely by self-preservation. I have a care for another; I must preserve Rebekah, at whatever cost. I dare not take my eyes from the advancing men, so without looking directly at Rebekah, I whisper to her, 'I believe we can outrun them, Miss. But there will be danger.'

'Danger is never overcome without danger,' she whispers in reply.

I lay hold of Rebekah's un-gloved hand and, with the skin of our palms pressed together and fingers curled one against another, we turn about and dart into the mist. Down steps and over mounds of waste, I lead her. We squeeze down an underground corridor, slipping down the throat of an abandoned building, and are at once swallowed by a honeycomb of covered alleyways. Eventually we stop in a doorway to catch breath and listen for the sound of our pursuers.

We stand, bodies thrust together by the narrowness of the space, and I breathe the air Rebekah exhales as I look up at her. I sense the shape of her through the thinness of our dresses, feeling soft-ness and bone. Still we hold hands; the grip looser now we are no longer running, but the slackness has a more sensual feel and

I cannot resist moving my thumb in gentle, tiny circles. In the dimness and the silence, as we strain for the sound of footsteps, there is nowhere to look except into each other's faces. I am only a breath away from Rebekah's lips. I could simply lift myself onto my tiptoes, she could bend her head and we could push the air between us away. As this thought fills my mind, it ignites heat beneath my skin and the warmth quickens my heartbeat, quickens the pulse between my legs and sends a thrill to the inside of my thigh. I feel a terrible yet exciting lack of control, as intense and frightening as the moment I watched helplessly as the Brock carriage swept me under its wheels.

I press myself closer to Rebekah and the action throws up incongruous recollections of the time I caught Uncle Jacob bundling with Rabbity Sue. Back then, I tried to turn away, tried to close my eyes against their rubbing and grunting, but there was some power which I could not subdue, some entity outside of my head that forced me to watch them until their cries and moans subsided, until they dropped loose and steaming with perspiration into a conjoined heap. Despite the incident being so long ago, I still recall that I was upset. I was angry, confused. I was frustrated. As though a splinter dwelt beneath my skin and the pain of it could not be released.

Looking up at Rebekah I feel the splinter now, in my belly. From her stare and short breaths, I wonder if she feels it too. I am in a high state of excitement and I feel the pain of it, a pain that is somehow also giving me pleasure. I realise it is not pain at all; it is physical want; desire. With passions and propriety at war within me, I am relieved when the descent of my thoughts is checked by the cursing of a man. Instantly I am stiller than a draper's figure, all passion quenched, all fervour chased out of my heart and leaving only fear in its place.

'She can't have given us the dodge again,' he spits out, angry, impatient. There is a pause before a reply comes. 'I swear they come down here.' This voice is louder, closer. They are on to us, I'm certain. I slip past Rebekah, tighten my grip on her hand and pull her along the covered alleyway, slowly at first and then faster, more urgently, as we emerge into the daylight and drizzle.

The maze of footpaths which hitherto had been sticky underfoot is now inches deep in grey sludge and our progress falters. The wooden walkways over which we hurry are perilous with wet moss and rainwater. Our mud-caked clogs are without traction and the more we hurry, the more we slip and stumble. We pass an old set of stocks and enter Hangman's Warren, where families of gallows-fodder exist in the most meagre terms and where sin turns the very bricks themselves black.

We shuffle with heads bent, past vagrants whose sole occupation it is to loiter with hope to plunder, and all the time we are losing ground. Breathless and shivering, I lead us towards the relative safety of the brick-fields. Gradually, Rebekah's hand becomes heavier as she seems to resist my pull. I slow to a walk. There is one more tangle of footpaths to navigate, then we will be close to Old Street, where there will be a chanter sending out wreaths of breath as he sings of Maria Marten from his broadsheet; where there will be the hurdy-gurdy man with a boy rattling his salt-box; where there will be enough of a crowd into which we can melt.

'Hester,' Rebekah says, pulling hard on my arm and then letting loose her hand. 'I have to stop, just for a moment.' She is breathing fast and deep. She coughs and drops her hands to her hips, lets her body fold in half so she is staring at the ground.

'There's a safer place, just up here.' I point behind. 'Just one more courtyard to cross, Miss. I can't see the men. I think we've lost them.' Rebekah twists her head round to view the path we have trodden, nods, but says nothing. 'It's not too far now,' I add.

She catches her breath and we start again, walking side by side, hands no longer linked. The rain abates, but the wind takes swipes at us every few paces, and the few remaining raindrops are sharp and cold against my skin.

Assured we have finally outsmarted our pursuers, our pace is moderate, but our conversation is non-existent. I am unable to speak as I think back to the proximity of our bodies as we stood in the covered alleyway. Was I improper? Were my thoughts obvious to Rebekah? Could she know how tenderly I esteem her, the depth of my passion? I dare not look at her, nor let her see into my eyes.

'Are you all right, Miss?' I eventually ask in a voice that is artificially light. 'This world of mud and murk is so different from your own; I wonder you can have even imagined it existed?'

There is a gap before Rebekah replies stiffly, 'I don't suppose anyone not acquainted with it in person could imagine how spare life can be. I shall certainly have a new perspective when Parson Ashton and the Widow Benton bring talk of poverty to the dinner table.'

We appear to have stepped back from each other. Politeness replaces sensitivity, propriety supersedes intimacy. So we walk on together, as closely as before, yet apart. I squirm at the thought of my foolishness and wonder whether Rebekah will ever forgive me. So occupied am I with feelings of dread and regret that I lead us straight into a trap so obvious it might as well be marked with bright coloured flags and trumpets.

We are beyond the brink of the courtyard before I notice our path is blocked by him, his head bent over a pipe as his hands shield the igniting tobacco. He draws from the tip, long and slow, then exhales a cloud of blue smoke. I don't have to turn about to know the other is now behind us, obstructing the rear exit.

All the while I suppress a foreboding as to how the matter will play out. I imagine Annie Allsop standing in the same courtyard, faced by the same men, her heart racing as fast as mine, her breath coming thick and uneven. With our backs against damp plaster and warped wood, the two men come together, advancing until they stand before us.

I stare at the ground, at their mud-spattered boots. Then I raise my eyes to the dirt-flecked moleskin trousers of one and the leather breeches of the other, to the smock frock of one and the shirt-lap of the other, to the missing buttons and the shabby cuffs, until I finally examine their faces.

One man is angular and slightly built. The other is barely taller than his companion in height, shorter than Rebekah, with broad shoulders and quick eyes. He lifts his pipe to his mouth and the slender clay tube appears fragile in his stubby fingers as he widens his lipless mouth into a grin, winking at his companion.

'Hester, ain't it?' he asks, lowering his pipe.

'What's it to you?' I speak in my East End voice, dispatching the words with ostensible confidence, though I am a fake, a fraud. I am no more confident than I am born within the sound of Bow bells, and at this moment I feel nothing but the will to survive.

'I knew you was back the minute you set foot in Bethnal. There's plenty of spies on my patch. But you're a slippery one to lay hold of, ain't you?' he says.

'Depends if I'm running from you or for you, don't it?'

'You dodged me twice.' His eyes narrow, small and black, no bigger than shirt studs. 'A woman dodges me once,' he goes on, 'shame on her. A woman dodges me twice, shame on me.' At this, he nudges his companion, and they both laugh, until my interrogator's mirth subsides into a wet cough, which he deals with by spitting a gob of phlegm to the ground.

'Hester,' he begins again, solemn, pragmatic. 'I knew Jacob. And Meg. They was good people.'

'And who might you be then?' I venture, my voice thinner than before, my faux-bravado on the wane. 'I don't know your face.'

'Morton. Jack Morton.'

There is a stony silence as I feel Rebekah give the barest of starts next to me. It is all I can do to stare at his face, rock-grey, pebble-hard.

'Still don't know you,' is the best I can muster.

'That's good,' he says, his voice measured and calm. 'It means Meg and Jake knew how to hold their tongues. But you know how it scores: the name don't matter; we all got plenty of names for plenty of people. It's the deed what counts. I like it, Hester, that you can dodge a man like me. I like your sauce, too.' He pauses at that and looks long and hard at my face, before continuing, 'Reckon you can do what Meg used to do, then?'

This question confounds me. I think back to the days in the yard and try to fasten ill deeds to Aunt Meg, try to recall possible incidents which might have involved the likes of Morton, but in my panic am unable to do so. I can only brazen it out, so I say, 'Why? What do you think she used to do?'

Morton's demeanour is dark but, although his eyes remain expressionless, his lips surrender to a simper and he says to his companion, 'She's a staunch one, all right, Bill.' He turns to me, still smiling and says, 'I reckon Meg used to take a pot of stewed gags and go and sit with someone who was on their way to the Land o' the Leal.'

He pauses and I nod. I cannot count how many times Aunt Meg received word that an old friend, a distant relation, perhaps just a passing acquaintance, had grown ill with a fever. So many times she went out, at any hour of the day or night, to nurse and comfort them, to be there at their dying breath.

I remember once it was so cold that a blackbird dropped out of the tree at the end of Austin Street and lay frozen like a stone.

The air was choking with fog that day, the ground hard with frost. Even Uncle Jacob left off his devilling to stay by the embers of the fire. Yet, in the dead of night, Aunt Meg pulled her shawl over her head, took a parcel of bread and cheese, and went out into the desolate darkness to sit with a dying neighbour, so keen was her desire to give succour. I respected her all the more for her gentle way of trying to displace Uncle Jacob's wickedness with these acts of kindness. So I nod at the words of Jack Morton with a sense of pride.

'I reckon she used to sit and watch for the death-sweats,' he says.

I nod again.

'And listen out for the death-rattle,' he adds, his voice far too bright for the subject matter, as though the conversation is a game to him, where he holds the cards and I am to guess his hand.

I close my eyes for a moment and picture Aunt Meg's lot, her stoicism, the way she never came home and wept in front of us. I feel the tears building within my own eyes at the recollection and, when I open them, Morton is grinning again.

'I reckon,' he says, 'she used to pour a glass of water. But she never put it to their lips, did she?'

His words pull me up sharp and then lie thick upon me.

'I reckon,' he begins again, 'she served up the gags, but she didn't spoon 'em into their dry mouths. I reckon she done her best to hurry them along, in fact. Then, as soon as they'd passed, she'd come for us at the Fortune o' War, she'd take her shillings and she'd not say nothing to no one.' He finishes his words with an air of triumph, as though I have set him a riddle and he has solved it.

Just as the sun's rays can burn away a winter fog, so Morton's revelations begin to make lucid what before I could not see. Aunt Meg could only suffer Jacob's world of improbity if she belonged to that world herself. Countless times she defended him. Endlessly she lied for him. She wasn't reproving; she was acting in concert. More than that: she was toiling in a realm too dark for even Jacob to tread.

She was not, after all, infected by the diseased malevolence of our surroundings. Aunt Meg was not a symptom; she was a cause. Would she creep out in the dead of night, arriving with a smile on her face before dropping her mask? Then what? A knee pressed against ribs as Aunt Meg's shadow drew long and dark over pleading eyes? An unyielding palm covering withered lips to speed them to their last breath? Plundering their final peace and stealing away the most precious thing they owned: life itself? She acted as a merchant of the darkest order, as a pedlar of death. And for what, a shilling or two? Perhaps less? So that Morton, Bill and Jacob can strip the tepid corpse of what few riches it harbours, taking the soiled clothes to sell on to that witch Cohen?

My knees tremble beneath my skirts as I realise what mortal peril Rebekah and I are now in. For the present time, I must swallow up my anger, repress my thoughts of Meg and try to play Morton for the fool.

'Well, I must say, Mr Morton,' I begin, injecting a hint of arrogance to my tone. 'You got most of it right, except one thing you said at the end.'

'What's that then?'

'Meg didn't tell no one nothing. She told me, though. She told me stuff I ain't telling no one, not even you. She told me how she moved them on as quick as you like, no marks on the body, no suspicion. Turned their lips blue whenever she fancied. I know how it's done. And I reckon it's worth more than two shillings.' I purse my lips tight together and breathe hard through my nostrils to calm the nerves which might break into my voice. Morton seems to think it is all part of my spirited character and the joyless grin returns to his lop-sided mouth.

'Here, Bill,' he laughs, turning to his friend. 'Jacob and Meg said they'd make good money out of this one someday, and I can see why.' He addresses me, but is now staring at Rebekah. 'And who's this one then, Hester? Is she as sharp as you?'

'This is Rosie, Mr Morton,' I mutter, desperately thinking up a story and clutching hopelessly at Rosina's name as the last I heard spoken, to inspire a hasty appellation for Rebekah.

'Rosie, eh?' He pushes me to the side, takes Rebekah's arm and pulls her out from behind me.

'Well, it's Daft Rosie, actually,' I venture. 'On account of her idiocy.' It's the best I can do to prevent the need for Rebekah to have to speak.

'Hideous? She don't look hideous to me!' Morton laughs and nudges the man, Bill.

'No, I mean she's a simpleton, Mr Morton.'

'How's that, then?' he asks, still laughing.

'She was dropped on her head when she was a baby. She ain't got no intellectual faculties and . . .' I make an attempt to elaborate, but both Morton and Bill appear to find the story hilarious and the words are silenced by their raucous laughter. They point at Rebekah and I turn towards her to see that she is playing her part to the best of her capability. She is wide-eyed and grinning, a tiny dribble of saliva worming its way down the side of her mouth, the suggestion of humour playing in her eyes. The men seem to find the whole scene irrepressibly funny. And, as incongruous as it feels, I begin to laugh with them. It is a release of tension I am unable to resist and, at the point in my life where danger looms largest, I find myself embracing the opportunity to shield myself with laughter; to give vent to the vile deception of Aunt Meg by shaking with mirth instead of horror. Instantly, my unshed tears are dried, my unspent anger is quenched and my immediate fears allayed.

As the laughter diminishes, Morton takes up Rebekah's hand

and says, 'Your hands is soft, Rosie.' Rebekah pulls her hand free and lowers her head shyly. She plucks at my sleeve and gives a little whimper, mimicking the sound of an imbecile.

'Don't mind her, Mr Morton,' I explain. 'She don't like being touched, that's all. She cut a man last month, in Derby. That's why she come to me. No one else in the family would have her. He touched her, y'see, and she wanted to stop him. She's an idiot, so she don't get that you got to be smart about stuff. It's only if you touch her, that's all. She just don't like it.'

Morton backs away and, for a moment, I believe he is tired of his fun and might leave us. But instead he is calculating how he might exploit Rebekah.

'I've the very thing,' he begins, looking directly at her. 'If you could use them little hands for needlework, Rosie, I might yet find you some employment. I knew straight away you was the woman for the job. You might even get some cast-off frocks in time, like you was a lady. How about that?' Morton's tone is gentle, conciliatory, yet as he talks there is a glow in his eyes. Not a warm glow, but a sickly flame, such as that in a fire-grate when something rancid is burnt.

I shudder and picture poor Annie with her bobbin of thread and her pincushion, and wonder if Morton might pull the very same items, stripped from Annie's body, and present them to Rebekah as an act of good faith, as he did with Annie and goodness knows how many others. The gravity of the scene fixes itself upon me again and I feel desperate to move away from the oppression of the courtyard.

'Looks like we might have some business to talk about then, Mr Morton,' I propose, my tone tempting, cunning; hopeful that by moving, a chance will present itself for Rebekah and me to run from these despicable men. 'What say we find a public and you buy us girls a gin?'

Morton assents without further persuasion and we find ourselves sauntering along as a cosy little group, with him leading the way, Rebekah and I trailing like cap-strings behind him and Bill bringing up the rear. No longer requiring a covert route, we take the main thoroughfares and, to my relief, the rain has stopped and the streets are busier, safer. With clearer air and brighter skies, we make good ground. But all the while, Morton and his companion watch us closely and, as hard as I search, there is no opportunity to extricate ourselves.

As I suspect, Morton walks past The Bell, The George and The Three Tuns, until we break out onto Giltspur Street, and on Pye Corner we are confronted by a narrow façade. The doors and fascia are fashioned from soot-coloured wood, above which are three storeys. A begrimed plaster cherub is mortared to the grey stucco, its cadaverous arms folded across its chest as though shivering. And in the gloom, there is a scar of wood above the door which reads simply: The Fortune of War.

CHAPTER ELEVEN

We follow Morton through the door and across the sanded floor until we reach a low table. With the door shut behind us, the outside noise of passing carts and barrows is subdued, as though spoken in hushed tones. Although the parlour room is small, there are at least nine or ten men sitting on mismatched stools, clustered around tables in a rough semi-circle before the counter. Yellow dice are still and playing cards are immobile. I take care to avoid the men's eyes as faces approach me through the folds of smoke. We have intruded and silence has walked in with us, holding all conversation at bay until we are settled and then gradually the voices begin again.

The stools, as well as the table top, are greasy to the touch, and through the smell of smoke the air is laced with the odour of damp earth. From the floor to the ceiling, the entire hostelry seems soiled with the dark thoughts and deeds of generations. And behind all the secret conversations is the tick of a clock, exuding an air of furtiveness each time its hands jab forward.

As Morton reaches into his breeches and brings out a handful of coins, a man appears behind the counter, his apron smeared with streaks of brown. He eyes us from in front of a rack of pigeonholes holding bottles, and then makes his way over to our table, flattening the froth of thinning hair on his head with the palm of his hand.

'Here, Morton,' he begins. 'Not more bitches! You'll give us all the Covent Garden Gout,' he says, his mind in keeping with his apparel.

'They ain't bitches,' Morton replies. 'It's Hester White and her cousin. You know, Jake and Meg's girl.'

The landlord is unapologetic but mollified, hovering vacantly until Morton growls an order and sends him away. He returns with four rum-hots and places them on the table.

Before we take sup, Morton drags his stool nearer to me and says, 'So, Hester. Two concerns I got about you. One I can explain away; them two men what was looking for you, the ones I took care to divert. Bill Corby here thinks there's bad odour about it, but I says if I took a shilling for every time agency men set about searching for the likes of us, I'd live in a villa and drive a chariot.' He sniffs at this point, throws a cursory glance at Corby, then goes on, 'Second thing; well, that's quite another pair of breeches, ain't it? It looks like you know more than Meg thought you did. Yet she swore to me on her life you wasn't involved.'

'True,' I say, my voice narrow, my lips dry. 'I didn't know nothing when I was young, and greener. But I'm all grown up now, ain't I? And just like what Uncle Jacob used to say, I'm worth a shilling or two of anybody's money. I'm talking on the square, Mr Morton. I mean it.' I expect Morton to smile his vacuous smile and the conversation to move on, but his eyes just stare into mine and his features remain unlit.

'Certain you know what Jacob used to do?' There is a goading tone to his questions now.

I roll my eyes and glance at Rebekah, in an exaggerated attempt to efface any suspicion of my ignorance and fear, then say, 'Course I do. Want me to spell it out for you? Want me to tell the business of it all to these men here?' I laugh, but Morton appears to be done with mirth.

'We're all in the same business, ain't we lads?' he says, loud enough for the whole room to hear, his eyes glancing from man to man. There is a pause, before he adds, 'We all use the same tools for the same trade. We all got wooden spades and ropes with billhooks. Now,' he adds, turning his eyes on me again, 'if you know so much, you tell me what's in your head, here and now, or I'll let you know better.'

We are silent and the atmosphere grows thicker for it, and I cannot think what to say or do. The air tastes tense and I wish at this moment that I might run away and touch something smooth, hold something warm in my hands. I have gagged Rebekah with my foolish story and ravelled my own words into a knot. And the longer I am silent, the more impatient and suspicious Morton will become; already the veins in his neck are beginning to swell.

The weight of it is heavy on me, pushing me downward, all fortitude deserting me, until I feel gentle pressure on my leg, just above the knee. Warm fingers squeeze and release, squeeze and release. I shift my gaze to Rebekah's and she is looking at me, yet somehow beyond me and into my heart. Again comes the warmth of her touch to my thigh, again the flash in her eyes, prompting a glow of defiance within me.

I stand, toppling the stool from which I rise with the skirts of my dress. I take a sharp breath inwards and, looking Morton full in the face, I spit the words, 'Oh, all right then. I'll just open the door and holler every ruddy secret I've got kept in my noddle, shall I?'

My voice is perhaps not as loud as I would wish, but the sentiments of annoyance and sarcasm are captured sufficiently to needle him; for he stands and, as any man in ire, thumps his fist on the table top. We seem to reach an impasse, and I believe the only way forward will be for Morton to subjugate me with the back of his hand. As I wait for the blow, attention is diverted from our altercation by the opening of the front door.

At once there is a wave of street-sounds and, through the billow of noise, a small boy trickles in, his cap clutched in his hands. He stands motionless, only his eyes moving, until he fixes his gaze on Morton, approaches our table and, in a piping voice, says, 'Mr Morton. There's a gentleman come to see you.' The boy turns as he speaks and points to the dust-coloured window next to the doors and, through the murk, there is a glimpse of an old, green-painted sulky, drawn by a cob. The carriage slows and slides out of sight. It makes an instant impression on Morton; he appears to forget our cross words, swallows his rum-hot in one and turns to leave, mumbling something like, 'C'mon, Corby. This is the business we need.' With that, both men hurry from the bar and tumble out into the street.

Our fellow customers appear unconcerned; their discourse continues to ascend and fall, just as the beer-pulls rise and sink, spewing froth into empty vessels. With the absence of Morton and Corby and the insouciance of the inn's clientele, I take it as an opportune moment to prepare to slip out and away to Arlington Street. I shuffle my stool closer to Rebekah's and touch her arm to gain her attention, but she is distracted. She is leaning forward, apparently to gain an advantageous view of Morton, Corby and the driver of the carriage. Eventually she fronts me, her cheeks flushed and her lips compressed.

'I believe I know the gentleman in that carriage,' she whispers.

'Who is he?' I say, my speech barely above a breath. Without replying, Rebekah stands and strides over to the windowpane. I fear that Morton's acquaintances will think Rebekah's behaviour suspicious. I cast a secret eye around the room, at the rough faces and hard eyes, but no one appears to take notice of either Rebekah or me. Even the landlord seems content to wipe empty tankards with the corner of his apron and pay no heed to any other matter. I look back at Rebekah and she has wiped a circle of grime away from the window and is cupping her hand to the glass. Still dissatisfied with her view from the window, she moves to the door, eases it open and is out on the street in an instant, and this time her action does stimulate the attention of the landlord, for he shouts to me, 'You ain't running out on Morton, is you?'

His voice cuts through the hubbub and clips the conversations, trims the atmosphere.

'Oh, no,' I say lightly. 'It's my cousin, Rosie. She's from the country and only sees waggons and carts from one year to the next. Loves a proper carriage, does Rosie. Loves them shiny spokes and that green paint.' However unconvincing my yarn is, there is no mileage in doubting me, and the landlord says nothing more on the subject, returning to his task with the vaguest suggestion of a sneer on his face. But his eyes are restless, and suddenly the air is primed and cocked, with one move enough to set the whole room upon me, I am certain.

Frightened to leave, yet fearful of staying, with my heart in my throat, I find I have no alternative but to take Rebekah's place at the window and, through the gauze of grease, I watch helplessly as she pulls her wrapper over her head and takes bold steps across the street. She hurries along until she is behind Morton and Corby. Lifting and tilting her head, she observes the gentleman seated high in his open carriage who is deep in conversation with Morton. She steps nearer and, for a moment, I wonder whether she might take hold of the gentleman's coat sleeve and accost him there and then. But, apparently satisfied with the man's identity, she retraces her steps and returns through the inn's doors.

It is a sallow, drawn face that meets me and accompanies me back to our table. Rebekah's expression is unintelligible. I wait until she finally lets loose the name: 'It is a man called Frederick Blister.' She snatches her fingers to her lips, looking pale and afraid.

Subsumed by the revelation, I am struck silent, as my thoughts scatter themselves in all directions; firstly, I must maintain the appearance that the name of Frederick Blister is unknown to me and therefore of no significance, unless I am to confess to Rebekah that I stole her journal and eavesdropped on her private conversations. Secondly, disparate strands are already knitting together in my mind, the pattern connecting Morton to Blister, impossible until a moment ago. And, from that foundation, spidery threads are thrown outwards and suddenly a link is supplied between Waterford and The Fortune of War, between Rebekah's world and mine.

For Rebekah's part, she holds her glass of rum-hot as if it might be the Eucharist and, raising it to her pale lips, she sips at the liquid, her breathing unsteady. Once the glass is drunk dry, she presses the palms of her hands together and lifts her index fingers to her mouth, then drops her hands to the table.

'Hester,' she says, barely above a whisper, 'the fellow Blister is a rogue. I have always had my suspicions. And the times he has strutted about Waterford . . .' She stops herself and brings her right hand to her lips. I fear she is about to sob, but she checks herself. Her eyes express terror and when she resumes her speech, her voice is withered. 'And how he holds sway over Calder; I cannot understand it. And Uncle Sep will hear no ill said against the man.'

Her words are curtailed when Corby and Morton burst in through the doors. Corby is grinning and Morton has an air of smugness about him as he swaggers first to the counter and then to our table. He slides four glasses onto the table top with one hand and pours gin from a bottle with the other, more being spilled than fills the vessels. Our words from before are forgotten. He proceeds to chink glasses with Corby and they both swallow the contents in a single gulp. Their merriment continues as Morton refills, the suggestion of a frown only returning as his eyes rest on the two untouched drinking-glasses.

'Come on, girls. Why, we must celebrate the good fortune life bestows on us. We've just received welcome news; as good as sugar in your grog. A business associate,' he continues in a faux gentleman's voice, 'has this very moment secured the services of both myself and Mr Corby here.' He claps Corby on the back, before adding, back in his Cockney cant, 'And I have a little task for you ladies that will earn you a crown apiece by the end of today.'

I am stupefied by this offer, not least for the threat it presents of having to stay with these soulless wretches for a moment longer. I am weary and frightened and the nightmare through which Rebekah and I are living seems to know no depths. The chance of returning safely to the fireside at Arlington Street grows dimmer with every lurch of the clock. I flick my eyes towards Morton. He is studying me, and I wonder if he may guess how I revile him, how I wish for nothing better than to be away from him and never to cast my eyes on him again. He misreads me, thinking I wish to barter for more and says, 'Fair price for a fair day's work. And you'll be doing a favour, it ain't nothing bad, nor hard.'

I wonder at how easily and smoothly the lies issue from his peeling lips. Two crowns will pay a hackney-cab fare from Old Bailey to Shoreditch, every day for a week. A week! Two crowns will buy bread, cheese and potatoes for a whole month. Two crowns is the weekly wage for an East End silk weaver, who works with failing eyes and bleeding fingertips for twelve hours a day. Two crowns are not paid to two unskilled doxies for an afternoon's soft and honest industry.

As I ponder a ploy to excuse us from accompanying the men any further this day, I sense a tug to my sleeve. Rebekah pulls it again and she is wearing the façade of Daft Rosie. She is grinning and nodding, apparently to compel my agreement, and I realise we are too far in to stop now. She is right, of course. We only suspect and dislike Morton; we must find out more about him. Yes, tenuous connections are indeed growing between Annie Allsop and Morton, Morton and Aunt Meg, Morton and Blister;

but many keys and many doors do not an open passage make. We have so few links and little stratagem for the game, and can only identify one move ahead of us. For all the preparation we have completed, we are still at the very beginning, and I wish we could just walk away and leave the horror of it all behind us.

'See?' Morton observes, 'Rosie wants to make shift for jobbing. She knows a benevolent offer when she sees one.'

'Why, it's your generosity, Mr Morton, that's what stupefies me,' I say. I cup the gin glass with my hand, drink it off in one and Rebekah does the same. All the false jollity from an hour before returns and, once Morton settles the score with the land-lord, we leave the Fortune of War and head to the north and to the east.

Corby and Morton are in good spirits, laughing at private witti-cisms, maintaining an unbroken stream of humorous chaff. Morton tells Rebekah and me that we are to walk to his cottage: number three, Midden Street. I know the area, it being an unsavoury district, even by the standards of the residents of Virginia Row.

At intervals, Morton discloses details as to the nature of the task we are being employed for, and it eventually transpires that Morton's sister, Bessie, is to leave off sharing a house with her family, and take up her own lodgings instead. All we must do is carry her chattels to the new rooms.

The plan sounds innocuous enough, but such thoughts are soon trod underfoot as we approach the isolated cottage, by way of a narrow garden. We enter through a gateway and Morton bids us wait; he alone walks the remaining few yards before entering the doorway beneath the shadow of a sloping roof, cut like a mouse hole into the side of the house.

Corby strikes a match on a brick he finds in the soil and lights his pipe. The glow from his tobacco is blood-red against the dark relief of the cottage, which throws its silhouette up into the skyline, its squinting windows staring back at us, the curtains only half-lidded over the dim lights within.

After ten minutes, Morton pokes his head out of the doorway and shouts, 'Come on then. We ain't got all day.'

Corby takes a long pull on his pipe, knocks out the burnt tobacco against the heel of his boot and tucks the stem in his belt before heading for the house. Rebekah and I follow, sinking in the soft, uneven topsoil.

'Oy, Hester!' Morton shouts, just as my left clog sinks deep in the mire. 'You mind how you go,' he goes on. 'There's an old well thereabouts. We don't want you tumbling neck and crop into it, do we? And stay away from that privy; it needs some attention, that's all.' He laughs, and his voice is carried like the caw of a crow.

I glance to my left and see the top of what appears to be a barrel sunk into the earth. I take care to avoid it and arrive at the back door just as Morton is carrying out a selection of baggage. Between us, we are to carry a sack, a wicker hamper, a small trunk and a bandbox.

Morton spits, wipes his mouth and directs his voice through the open door. 'Daisy, Bessie! We're off!'

With that, Corby takes up the wicker hamper. Morton places his hands about the neck of the sack, squeezes it tight and then knots a length of rope around it and hands it to Rebekah. I am given the bandbox and Morton takes up the weight of the trunk on his left shoulder.

'See?' observes Morton. 'You're servants and we're porters. Told you it weren't hard or nothing.'

But the errand is both hard and dangerous, for the weight of the baggage belies its true contents and I have seen this ruse before; stolen wares are transported from one rogue to the next by way of disguise such as this. Judging by the groans that issue from Corby, and the number of times Morton has to change shoulders, my guess is that we are transporting stolen plate and tableware, wrapped in plundered fine fabrics, across the city.

We trudge along familiar streets, with occasional small talk between Morton and Corby. But as the boroughs change, there is also a shift in the two men's demeanour. Their eyes become narrow and restless, their gait soft and sly. Like stray dogs lowering their tails and dropping their ears as they are forced to roam in another cur's patch, so Morton and Corby are noticeably quieter when the streets become wider and cleaner and the pedestrians more upright and honest.

We finally set down our load, a full two hours since setting off from the cottage, at an address at the top end of Little Windmill Street. Corby wheezes and kneels over the hamper, his breathing sonorous and hard. Morton wipes sweat from his forehead, before saying, 'That's it, girls. We'll take it from here.' He pulls a leather pouch from his belt, fishes inside, hooks two crowns and presses them in my hand. 'You done good, Hester. Now hear me well. I want you to return to my cottage on the Friday of this week. Today is Monday and I want you to do some night-sitting on Friday. You clear on that?'

'Yes, Mr Morton,' I say.

'You can bring Rosie along too, if you've a mind. It won't do no harm.'

'Thank you, Mr Morton.'

'Come after nightfall and ask for Bessie; she'll accompany you this time. You understand?'

'Yes.'

'And if you can work as good as your aunt and keep your mouth sealed – well, we shall have good business ahead of us, shan't we? For if we don't make good business, we might as well plait straw for a farthing to sell to the Luton hatters! Friday, Hester, remember; so we don't have to come looking for you again.'

I nod, but my desire to talk to this trickster has long since expired, and I believe Morton himself is weary of the day's turns, and is keen to return to the murk of his familiar habitat, for he turns his back to us as soon as we make to depart.

As the dying sun crimsons the pavement and our shadows stretch long and deep, we walk until we are many streets away from Morton and Corby. As incongruous as we appear, and however much the waterman eyes us with suspicion, he returns to his pails and his pump, and Rebekah is able to call a hackney from the stand, her voice and a fare of five shillings enough to engage the driver to take us to Arlington Street without any interrogation.

The journey is brief; when we return to the house at last, we are both tainted by the odours of the boroughs we have traversed, and the shock we are feeling is an inaudible resonance radiating out from us, as though we are bells lately struck by clappers. Conversation is dreamlike and subdued as we file into the drawing room and drop heavily into the two fireside armchairs. The lamps are lit and Tilly has made up the fire, but Rebekah still looks pinched by coldness, her skin sallow. Hunched in the chair, her clothes ill fitting, she appears frailer than I have yet seen her.

Through the silence I scrutinise the air between us, try to hear her thoughts, study her mind. Eventually, I break in with, 'We have gathered much intelligence today.' She nods, as though she agrees, but her thoughts are elsewhere. 'If we are methodical,' I begin again, 'we will surely turn something up. Why, the information we already have is enough to convince the New Police, I am certain. If we can record it and present it to a superintendent, then we can evade further danger to ourselves. All this uncertainty can end.'

I understand that really we have nothing better than suspicions and conjecture, but the more depressed I am by fears, the more I talk of hopes. I am not sure if Rebekah responds to the thought of a night's cataloguing or to the fanciful prospect of transferring risk to the Bow Street Runners, but there is a flicker of concord behind her eyes, and I can but hope she receives my words as they are intended; as a balm to chase fear and anguish from our hearts by presenting a wishful alternative to the path on which we are fixed.

'We are climbing the steep together,' I add, heartfelt, bold. Rebekah smiles and I take heart from the warmth in her eyes. This seems to stir her and she rises and rings for Tilly, who arrives to take orders for a copper of water to be heated, for fresh gowns and linen to be laid out and for dinner to be prepared for eight o'clock. At that, I part company with Rebekah and retire to my bedchamber.

Within an hour I am washed and Tilly has helped me to dress, but hunger and the exertions of the day have left me weary. I sit at the dresser and run my fingers over the enamelled brushes, the ivory combs, the gilt perfume bottles and the ceramic pots. I sit on the bed and push my fingers into the goose-down bedding and watch as my hands sink in to the wrist. I nod a little. But it is not until the dinner bell rings that I realise I must have fallen into a dreamless sleep, and it is with an apology for tardiness that I present myself to Rebekah in the dining room.

The table is dressed with apples and sugared plums and, as I enter, Ned is bringing in a tureen of what smells like mutton soup. We are each poured a glass of claret that has been warming on the mantelpiece and then we are left alone. I scour my eyes over the table top, at the knives and spoons, at the wafers of chinaware and the crystal glasses and decanter. It feels as though it should be some great occasion, some celebration; but only two places are set and Rebekah sits at one end of the table and I sit at the other, and the atmosphere is sombre, the conversation polite but stilted, Rebekah reluctant to discuss the events of the day.

I find myself reimagining the evening without the trammels of new sorrows and unresolved riddles. I conjure a world where only goodness prevails. Rebekah, relieved of her furrowed brow, would chatter on to me about a poem she had read, or a theatre performance she had seen. We would laugh at private jokes born of close acquaintance and discuss the worth of all things simply for the happiness they might bring; and our hearts would be unafraid, content in their own felicity. How I wish it could be so. But the awkwardness continues as the oyster-stuffed woodcock and greens are brought to table. A subdued course of cheese follows, and it is not until we are eating dessert of creams and jellies that Rebekah dabs at her lips with her napkin and says, 'Hester. My mind is not easy over the intelligence we have discovered today.' She toys with the napkin, then lays it gently on the tablecloth before continuing with moist eyes and with tears in her voice, 'It is Calder. I am most anxious about his friendship with Frederick Blister. The man seems so drawn to iniquity and Calder can sometimes be naïve. It makes him vulnerable. In the past, I have been . . . short with him sometimes. Lately, he is so distant, I feel I am no more than an encumbrance to him. I have been selfish and . . .'

Suddenly, there is a change in Rebekah. She casts her eyes about the room, to search or to be evasive I cannot discern, until eventually she settles them on me and a teardrop falls from one eye then the other, until her face is wet and her shoulders are convulsing.

I slip from my chair and run to her, encircling her with my arms and gently pulling her to me, until her face is pressed tenderly against my bosom. I feel her grow warm against me and she sobs, long and deep, as though the tears of a thousand hurts have finally undone her. I too find my eyes misting with the honour of her trust in me and the pity for her pain. I cannot measure the time we stay in this union, and only when she is perfectly steady do I take a step back, releasing my embrace, kneeling by her side as though she is a deity. She looks at me, smiles, and dries her eyes and cheeks. There is a pause and then we both speak simultaneously, our single words blending together. I say, 'Miss,' just as Rebekah says, 'Hester.' We stop and smile.

Rebekah begins again, 'Hester. You must stop calling me "Miss". I owe you a great deal and believe we have become . . .' She searches for the word but, frowning, appears only partially content to settle for '. . . friends. You must call me Rebekah from now on.' I nod with tacit understanding and say nothing, because I know by her look and her touch that we are indeed friends. True friends. And I am already affected deeply by the concerns Rebekah has regarding Calder. I am even beginning to sense a closer bond with Calder himself, by virtue of the high esteem in which his sister holds him.

'You must go to Calder, Rebekah. You must see him tonight. You have to warn him.'

'Warn him? Of what, Hester? What intelligence do we truly have?'

'That Frederick Blister is of dubious character. His proven association with Morton is surely enough to convince both Calder and your uncle that Blister should not be welcomed into the house of Brock. You saw him with your own eyes, Rebekah. And if Calder is sometimes apt to be misled, is it not our duty to show him what dangers might lurk on his chosen path?'

Rebekah meditates, takes a sip of wine then stands.

'You're right, Hester,' she declares. 'If Calder had not been made weak with laudanum, and if I had not seen Blister and Morton with my own eyes, then we might have waited until tomorrow. But we cannot waste any more time. I shall call for the carriage.' I believe she is going to list the actions we must take, imperious as ever, but then she picks up again with, 'But what of you, Hester? I cannot abide the prospect of leaving you alone, not after today.'

'I could come with you and wait in the carriage?'

'No. I would still worry. You must accompany me into the house; I insist. But how we—'

'I could come in some sort of disguise,' I suggest vaguely.

'Yes. With a veil, or a shawl, or something like that. I could say that you're a nurse or someone who helps men see the folly of their dependence on stimulants. Yes, that will have to do.'

The recollection of Calder's intemperance again casts a shadow over Rebekah, and I wonder exactly how he will receive the news we intend to communicate to him. It is with unease that I pin an old black mourning bonnet and veil to my hair and join Rebekah in the carriage that will take us to the villa and to Calder.

Tonight the streets seem quieter than usual, and as the carriage trundles along, grey drizzle forms a curtain of opacity. Whereas the city's night-time complexion is generally spotted with hawkers, theatre-goers and cabmen, tonight the pavements seem empty. The eeriness magnifies the unease I feel as we near our journey's end.

It is eleven o'clock when we pull up outside the villa. The lights inside are indistinct; the brickwork damp with clusters of water droplets. Whereas before I was struck by the opulence of the interior, tonight the entrance hall is chill and dim. The man to whom Rebekah surrenders her travelling cloak, bonnet and gloves is George Rudd, but he pays little attention to me, disguised as I am in my bonnet and veil. Rebekah says curtly, 'Please announce my arrival to my brother immediately.'

'But Miss Brock . . . I thought you were aware,' he begins, his words slowing.

'Aware of what, Rudd?' Rebekah snaps. 'Oh, never mind. Is he in his rooms?'

'Yes, but—'

Rebekah pushes past him, takes up his lantern from the sideboard and ascends the staircase, splashing light and shadow as she goes. I step after her into the half-light, somewhat disadvantaged by my veil, occasionally brushing ornamental tables with my skirts. Rebekah pushes on through the dark corridors, both fearful and fearless in her quest to reach Calder.

She stops at a particular doorway, her palm hesitant and flat against the finger-plate. I wonder if the room is locked against her, for she hesitates. She regulates her breathing, twists her hand around the handle and there is a faint click when the door opens.

It is the stale warm air that I notice first; air infused with brandy and tobacco, but also tasting of something more exotic and dangerous. Rebekah must sense it too, for she hovers on the threshold, as though making the transition between one world and another. She finally enters and is swallowed in a haze of smoke and refracted candlelight. I follow and, once used to the lack of light and air, search the room with my eyes.

The room is a gentleman's study; a velvet-pile carpet, bookcases all about, easy chairs before the fireplace, a desk and papers. The apartment is quiet, but not well ordered. Books lie open on the seats of chairs, some with torn pages, some splayed on the floor. Ink is spilled across the desk, and newspapers mingle with discarded clothes on the rug before the fire. But it is the number of phials, wine glasses, empty bottles and dry decanters that causes me most concern. On an occasional table there is a dish containing a liquid that looks like honey, together with a wrapper revealing a solid substance that is tawny in colour.

As the room is unoccupied, save for Rebekah and me, I pull the veil from my face and, touching Rebekah's arm, I draw breath to speak. Rebekah seems to anticipate my question and, without turning to face me, she says flatly, 'I didn't tell you everything, Hester. I told you that Calder takes wine and laudanum. But some months ago, he found that even these habits had become insufficient to sustain him. Calder is an opium-eater, now. He takes the boiled residue, some twenty grains a day, I believe.'

I am about to respond to this disclosure when from under the crumpled blankets on the sofa, there is a groan. I replace my veil and stand behind Rebekah as she crouches and gently peels the covers away from the form beneath. Calder claps his hand across his eyes, even though they are closed against the dim candlelight, as though a great conflagration is burning before him. His shirt sticks to his flesh and, although I am standing a full arm's length from him, I can feel the feverish heat radiating from his body.

Momentarily he snaps his eyelids open, delirium playing in his pupils, and yet it appears he is still asleep. He raises his arms before him, his frail upturned hands searching the air; as though he is not seeing either us, or any object in the room; as though he is stranded on a bridge between his dreams and reality.

At length he labours and wakes, crying faintly, 'Do not let me dream.' Rebekah takes up his colourless hand, presses it to her lips and fleetingly Calder's eyes take focus on her.

'Becky? Becky, is that you?' he whispers. He trembles and a strained expression distorts his features, before he lets out a long, slow sigh and relaxes the muscles of his face. Then he lies perfectly still and I believe he must be dead.

CHAPTER TWELVE

Rebekah releases his hand and touches instead his dark curls, now damp and slick upon his temples. A ripple of light breaks out from the fire-grate and sends a wave of orange across the room, illuminating Calder's features; the dark circles around his eyes as though he has rubbed at his face with a sooty finger; the hollows dug beneath his cheekbones; his lips oyster-pale.

Never such a sorrowful sight have I seen. I lift my veil, but cannot speak; what is the use of words? Words hold no value in comparison with the potency of silence, and it lies over us like a poultice, trying to soothe, trying to heal.

It is my heart which speaks first by giving off a sigh, such as you might for love; but this sigh is for loss and at the unutterable scene before me. At length words I learned from my father issue from my lips.

'They whom God loves die young,' I whisper.

Rebekah wears a troubled expression but taking my hand says, 'Calder is not dead, Hester. It is the opium. He is tranquillised by its effects and will remain in a state of quiescence for the next hour or so, at which moment he will wake and require a further dose to return his vitality.'

So, my sight has played me false and I cannot tell if it is the shock of his death, the relief of his resurrection, or the embarrassment of my own ignorance, but I find myself in a state of agitation. Tears well hot and stinging behind my eyes, and my skin prickles with perspiration.

'I'm sorry, Rebekah,' I mumble. I don't make it clear exactly what I'm sorry for; it's a universal apology, a general atonement. I rue that such an innocent-appearing substance could change Calder so drastically. Why, three months since, his constitution was vital, his health robust, his looks handsome enough to turn every maid's head at Waterford. Now he is pale and sickly, the gleam of youth already fading.

'You mustn't grieve yourself over this, Hester. We cannot change the past. But what we can do is to try and reason with Calder, get him to recognise his folly and reduce the amount of opiate he imbibes; at the very least demand he ceases all contact with Frederick Blister.' Rebekah compresses her lips and gives a little nasal snort at the bitter taste of Blister's name in her mouth. 'Dreadful man,' she goes on, 'I cannot tolerate him, with his pouter-pigeon chest all puffed out. His tongue may be adroit, but his mind is not.'

Rebekah walks towards a cabinet.

'Will you take a glass of wine?' she asks, already pulling the head of the decanter away from its body.

'No, thank you,' I say, suddenly aware that the exotic odour about the room has, in my mind, at once become associated with great bodily harm and great suffering. I wonder if the fumes might infuse the wine and induce its drinker to crave a dose of the tawny substance in the paper wrapper that for all the world looks like a bonbon you might feed an infant. I wonder if Rebekah has the same doubts, for she pours her glass of blood-red wine, but she does not sip from it; she leaves the glass, contents and all, on the sideboard, and instead takes up a seat by the fire.

'Come,' she says, her voice sounding tired, her spirit subdued. 'Sit with me, Hester.'

I clear the books and papers from an armchair and sit opposite Rebekah, the firelight gentle on her face, the flames steady and warm.

'"It lies not in our power",' she begins, as though quoting from a book, '"to love or hate, for will in us is overruled by Fate". Do you suppose Mr Marlowe has it right, Hester? Does it make any difference if we try or if we don't? Does Fate have full command of us after all?'

'Oh, no,' I say, certain of myself. 'Mr Marlowe cannot have it right, not at all. Surely the only concern we do have in life is to try. I've heard tell that a newborn infant, before it has even had any chance at learning, puts all its effort into breathing. It somehow knows it must try, that to stop trying will surely bring about the end. It already knows you cannot achieve anything by doing nothing. No, I do not agree with Mr Marlowe at all.'

'Neither do I, Hester. Neither do I.' Rebekah sits back in her chair, her face contemplative.

'But . . .' I begin again, hesitant, '. . . sometimes it does appear that Fate is working against you and, however hard you try, sadness still prevails.'

'And how do you overcome such times, Hester?'

'I dream of goodness yet to come. I dream . . . I dream of friendship, and a warm fire, and a mind free of all vexations.'

'Perhaps we are more alike than I first believed,' she says, her voice soft and warm, her brow smooth, her lips curving upward.

'And I wish,' I add, grateful for the moment, glad of Rebekah's attention, 'I wish we could perhaps unlearn what we know of bad things, discard the recollections of life that have been so very hard to bear.'

'Do you mean about your parents? And your aunt and uncle?'

'Well, yes. And I wish we hadn't met Morton. I wish I didn't know what Aunt Meg used to do. I still don't fully understand what Uncle Jacob did, with his ropes and billhooks. I suppose Morton put him under duress and they started to become impatient, waiting for the dying to expire. I suspected dark deeds were being done when Jacob went out at night, and I realise he might have excused his action on account of his desperation, but to hurry along a soul's demise to such a degree – well, it's unforgiveable.'

'Yet, what is arresting,' Rebekah replies, 'is that Jacob and Meg did not act alone; they were in collusion with Morton, and in turn, Morton is in connivance with Blister. And according to Morton's boasts, half the clientele at the Fortune of War subscribe to this dark confederacy in some degree. It seems that evil spreads readily from root to stock and from limb to leaf; and with so many tormentors, then how many victims? The whole business is far greater than we first suspected. Granted, the pickings must be lean from the poor, but once you move up to mercers and tradesmen, to professional men and beyond, well I suppose both the market and the profit are virtually limitless. I believe I can think of at least five or six young bucks, heirs to vast estates, who have already gambled and drunk their way into debt, and would be sorely tempted to speed the death of their fathers, in order to inherit their family fortune.'

'And could Mr Blister orchestrate such a thing?'

'Mr Blister, Mr Blister,' Rebekah repeats with obvious distaste. 'All I know about Frederick Blister is that he once worked in India, in a province called Bengal. He worked for the East India Company and should have returned to England lauded as a nabob, marriageable and with a fortune to his name. But there was some trouble with a married lady in India; I think she was the wife of an old army officer. He came back virtually penniless and relies on the provision of funds from a distant aunt, according to Calder. Spends most of his days, or so I thought, moping around that new club in Hanover Square, The Oriental. That's where he met Calder. So, in

193

answer to your question; I believe Blister is desperate enough to stoop so low, but as to whether he possesses the brains in his head to effect such a business and evade discovery, I could not say.'

'I just wish we could put a stop to it. And do you realise we aided a crime when we carried the baggage today?'

'I guessed as much. Do you suppose it was stolen silver?'

'Yes.'

'I regret the deceit. But don't forget we were in a position of boundless risk. Tomorrow, we will examine all the intelligence we have gathered and present it to the superintendent of the police. We already have good reason to doubt Blister's character, for I know of no other gentleman who would conduct transactions with the likes of Morton, and as Blister was visiting Waterford when Martha went missing, then the doubtfulness is surely more compelling. And if he discovered that Agnes . . .' She stops, perhaps resistant to the recollection of the past, then says, 'Well, it's nearly over, Hester, I'm certain. We are almost there.'

I heed Rebekah's words and they give me comfort. But I worry if, once the information is communicated to the Runners, Rebekah and I will have no common cause and will be forced to part. By taking up my position with Lady Appleton, the intimacies Rebekah and I have developed may be prised asunder by the variance of our social standing. How the doubts swarm about me. Beneath the cobwebs and dust of my life, a spider is always lurking.

As the fire burns down, I glance at Rebekah; her eyes are fixed on an uncertain point in the middle distance. The floorboards beneath the rugs creak at the receding heat and the wall clock ticks louder against the thicker silence. I suddenly feel as though I must prepare to tell Rebekah the truth about the night I ran from Waterford; about the betrayal I believed she was plotting and the diary I stole from her room. But there are such doubts in my mind that I find myself unable to think beyond the potential consequences: the disappointment in Rebekah's eyes and the possible withdrawal of hard-won intimacies. The words stall on my tongue and I dither to such a pitch that I abstain from all prospect of it and sit defeated.

In a welcome act of armistice, the clock intrudes its voice on the room with twelve clear chimes, and the noise yields a wakefulness that laps over me, flows about Rebekah and finally breaks over the motionless form of Calder. He raises his arm to his face and rubs his eyes with the heel of his hand. With a childlike innocence he yawns, then exhales breath that is thick with brandy and tobacco.

Rebekah is at once alert to him. She rises and whispers to me, 'Draw down your veil and wait in the shadows.' She points to a chair in a gloomy recess, between two low bookcases. 'He is sometimes . . . unpredictable,' she adds, 'when recovering from his intake.' Her eyes make signs of apology and I step away as commanded.

Calder appears to have no realisation I am in the room and I am uncertain if he is yet aware of Rebekah, for he pushes himself into a seated position and mumbles to himself.

'Calder?' she tries. He appears not to hear her and, with his head bent low, he continues to grumble to himself.

'Calder? It is Becky,' she says, more firmly.

Without looking up, he says, 'I need laudanum. If I eat the opium, it's too slow. The laudanum is quicker. There.' He points with a quivering finger and Rebekah takes up a dark green bottle. She uncorks it, pours a glassful and resignedly hands it to Calder. He swallows it, gives a cough, and holds the empty glass out. Rebekah refills it and he drinks it off again.

'Now brandy. I have a terrible thirst.'

Rebekah decants a tumbler and takes it to him. He reaches for it and, as his fingers encircle it, he blinks twice and stares at

Rebekah, as though only now realising she is in the room. He puts the glass to his lips, throws his head back and takes a mouthful. His eyes then return to Rebekah, his expression troubled.

'Calder,' she begins patiently. 'I have come to talk to you about a serious matter, but perhaps I should return another time. You seem . . . fatigued.'

'You mean intoxicated, do you not?'

'I don't know the right words. I just know you need help. I want to help you, Calder.'

'I am not intoxicated by opium, Becky, only by the impurity which carries it; the brandy or the port that makes up the laudanum. I am better if I eat it. And the best way you can help me is to fetch me more from the druggist's shop.' He ends his little monologue with a chuckle, as though they are both children again and he has won a minor disagreement.

Rebekah ignores his badinage and, with authority, says, 'You say you are better when you eat it. But, the truth is, you are better when you leave off it all together. It makes you ill, Calder. Can you not see?'

'It is not an illness,' he contests. 'It is a remedy, Becky. I am afflicted with a nervous irritation on account of my work and I become weary. Yet with opium in my veins, it sharpens my intellect, strengthens my mind. And it would aid me more if it were not loaded with impurity.' Here, he breaks off, reaches for a crumpled jacket and slides his arms one at a time into the sleeves. He appears to be perfectly steady and the transformation from an hour since is startling. He cups his glass of brandy, sips it smoothly and continues, 'Am I inarticulate? Am I bewildered? No. More than that, I have become an industrious visionary. And it is an anodyne, Becky. Would you have me live in pain?'

'No, of course not, but—'

'Would you have me abandon my work?'

'Oh, Calder, you know how I am in awe of all that you do to help people, but I worry so much.'

'But, Becky, my dear Becky, there's nothing for you to worry about. It's not a problem, it is a solution.'

Calder stands and approaches Rebekah. He brushes an errant hair behind her ear and then takes her hands in his. 'I am approaching a great moment in my career,' he begins. 'I will soon be able to publish papers and my name, our name, will be known the world over. You won't have to find a husband, for I shall provide for you. We won't need Uncle Sep or anyone else.'

'What of Frederick Blister?' Rebekah has chosen her moment and the question is ice on coals, hissing and spitting long after it has been asked. Calder releases Rebekah's hands and looks into her eyes.

'What about him?' he says, a perplexed expression on his face.

Rebekah draws a breath. I cannot guess her thoughts, but my own mind is analysing the subject. If only Calder could harbour the same suspicions about Frederick Blister. If only the burden of our secrets could be discharged to Calder and everything bad could end. I lean forward in the shadows and move to the edge of my seat, the future hanging on the thread of Calder's next word.

'You can't mean,' he says slowly, 'that you want to marry the fellow?'

At first Calder's answer quite astounds me. I believe it is the least likely response I could have imagined. But, as I think upon his reasoning: why else, in his mind, might an unmarried sister, especially one under duress to temper her traits and modify her opinions, visit her brother in the dead of night to discuss his closest friend, if not for the prospects of matrimony? Or is the absurdity of such a match suggested by Calder simply to ridicule Rebekah, to take the wind from her sails before she has chance to set her course on reprimands and admonitions? I steal a glance at Rebekah.

'Good God, no,' she says, looking aghast.

'My Lord!' Calder cries. 'I . . . I thought . . . I mean he's a capital fellow and a good friend but . . .' Then mirth consumes him and he shrieks with the fun of it until tears wet his face. He sits and takes a gulp of brandy, but starts to choke. He waves Rebekah away playfully and the giggles continue for some minutes. Rebekah can only smile at him and I see the love between them.

'Oh, Calder,' she begins again, tender, reproachful. 'It is the very opposite of that; I cannot abide Frederick Blister, to such a degree as I would have you part ways with him for good.'

'Nonsense! He's harmless enough,' Calder dismisses. 'The only complaint I have about Blister is that he insists on bringing me East India opium when I am prepared to pay seven guineas a pound for Turkish. *Madjoon* is what I want, Becky, by God! So tell the Turks to work harder and make it in more abundance.'

There is a glibness to Calder's tone, which in normal circumstances would be amiable and endearing, but is instead a sharp contrast to the obvious and painful reality of the situation. Even though Rebekah shows no outward sign of reaction, I know we are defeated and we will not recruit Calder to our cause this night.

'Perhaps you might pledge to stay away from Blister until your constitution improves?' Rebekah's voice is different; it is superficial and dejected.

'For you, Becky, of course,' he says in the same light tone. 'Besides, I have a great deal of work to attend to.'

'Tonight?'

'Yes. But I shan't go out. I'll sort all these papers and work here. I can't sleep, Becky. I'm too awake for that. If Blister shows his face, I'll send him away. I'm tired of him, anyway.'

With that, Calder kisses Rebekah on the cheek and leaves through a concealed door at the far end of the room, into what I assume is his bedchamber.

'Come, Hester,' Rebekah whispers, already at the door to the corridor. 'We must leave. Calder may ring for a maid and if it is Sarah she may recognise you.'

We make haste through the dimly lit passageways until we meet George Rudd in the entrance hall. Rebekah says nothing to him as she takes her cloak and bonnet but stops after pushing her fingers into one of her gloves and says, 'Rudd, Mr Calder has informed me that he does not wish Mr Frederick Blister to be invited into this house.'

'Yes, Miss.'

'And it is better for Mr Calder's constitution that he leaves off visiting The Oriental. Perhaps you will remind him of this if he forgets. And Rudd?'

'Yes, Miss?'

'Send a boy round to let me know if his condition deteriorates. Whatever time of day or night.'

He nods in a solemn way, unlatches the front door, and we step out into a wall of cold air. The gas-lamps are hissing and the carriage horses give out snorts of impatience, but apart from these noises there are no other sounds to pollute the night. The moon hangs silent and silver and the stars flash mute and white above us. Just as the brittle air follows us into the carriage, so the hush creeps into the creases of our cloaks and renders us silent. I don't suppose it is necessary for Rebekah to speak the words, but at length she does so anyway.

'I did not believe Calder was well enough to withstand the revelations we planned to disclose to him tonight, Hester. As you saw, he is consumed by the work he undertakes and his craving for opium has caused him to lose his way. And so . . .' She pauses and shivers, from the cold or from the prospect of what she must say, I cannot tell. 'And so, we have no alternative but to seek out Blister and confront him.'

'But what of presenting our papers to the superintendent?' I ask, already in full comprehension of the answer Rebekah will give. For all along I suppose I have willed myself to be deceived by our lack of evidence, driven by an enduring desire to escape whatever it is that is dragging us down into this vortex.

'Hester, we have papers and we have thoughts, but we don't have any verification. A superintendent will politely relieve us of our letters and our lists and he will ponder over them at leisure, as he smokes out his pipe and eats the mutton pie his wife has made for his lunch. As he devours his meat and pastry, he will also consume time itself. And time is what we do not have in plentiful supply. *Tempus edax rerum.*'

Echoing Rebekah's Latin and the prospect of dangers coming all too quickly, the carriage speeds along and we arrive at Arlington Street. Ned must have been waiting just inside the front door, for it opens as soon as the carriage steps are thrown down, and the arc of his lantern illumines the pathway. I follow on Rebekah's heels, partially absorbed by her shadow.

Despite the lateness of the hour, Peggy presents herself in her mobcap and shawl and insists we take either hot chocolate or spiced wine. But Rebekah declines the offer and I, too, refuse; perhaps because such comforts will only serve to bring into sharp relief the hostility we will surely soon face, or perhaps simply because we cannot afford the time.

When I am undressed and warm beneath the blankets of my bed, my thoughts, of course, turn to Rebekah. She is only a wall's thickness away from me after all and, in my head, I fancy I can hear her breathing. Just as a single snowflake can join with its brothers and sisters to quilt the ground for mile upon mile, so my fancies meld into a blanket of dreams. It is through this hazy fantasising that I hear the clocks chime two, then three. I lie on my right, then on my left arm. Then I lie flat on my back, my eyes closed, drifting in and out of my half-dreams and yet never wholly able to sleep. Finally, I rise and pull on my night-rail and slippers.

The room is dark but the definition between objects is still discernible by means of moonlight tiptoeing in through the gap between the curtains and window. I rise, gently sweep the curtains apart and invite a wide, white moonbeam into the room. The night outside is bright with a quilting of snow, and some flakes still drift downwards, carrying fragments of moonlight with them as they descend. I sit on the windowsill and watch, hypnotised by the flakes swimming and darting through pools of night, until a noise from Rebekah's room startles me.

The fire, although low, is still glowing in the grate, so I take up a taper and light a candle. The flame dips and trembles as I push the candle forward to transpose the colour of the night. I find myself opening my door, opening Rebekah's door, and standing inside her room.

The blankets are ruffled and one of her pillows is on the floor, but Rebekah is perfectly still, lying on her back with one arm beneath the sheet and one resting on it. Just as I have been rendered spellbound by the snowflakes moments before, so I am now entranced by Rebekah. In the half-light and in her state of peaceful slumber, the creases of angst are quite smoothed away from her brow and she is younger in her countenance. And I am glad she is blessed with the ignorance sleep brings her; glad she takes respite from the woes of the day, from Calder's opium, from Morton and from Blister. Then she gives a little gasp and clenches her hand, as though daytime demons are crossing into her dreams. She turns her head from right to left, her breathing coming short and fast, until a sigh checks her and, once emitted, leaves her at peace again. I watch her for some moments more, but I dare not advance further for fear of waking her. All I can do is send her a look of deep affection and longing.

At length I withdraw from the room and pull the door to. But with wakefulness flowing at full spate through my veins, I do not return to my room. Instead, I descend the stairway and go to the dining room. The latch clicks as I push the door, but rouses no sleepers. I take my candle and sit it on the mantelshelf; with the solitary flame the room is a homely dusk with a mellow sun.

I set to work immediately. I open Rebekah's escritoire, and I take out the lists and letters she showed me before. In the course of sorting them into ordered piles, I discover three letters which are new to me; one is a reply to Rebekah from Mrs Green in Islington. Written in crude script, yet honest and endearing, it reads that her neighbour believes her missing boy had been talking to two men prior to his disappearance, one wearing a smock frock and leather breeches. The second epistle, written in a similar manner from a Mr Harris (senior), quotes that his son had lately been in with a crowd of men from the Smithfield area. The third is a polite and apologetic missive from a Mrs Larkin to advise that, since her daughter was reported missing in the *Gazette*, the girl has returned home safe and well and that she, Mrs Larkin, is very sorry to put a lady to so much trouble on account of an ungrateful yet repentant child.

I shuffle the letters, re-read them, and place them with a stack of other papers at the back of the desk. As neatly as Rebekah and I have ordered these deeds, the solution is still vague and nagging questions linger. Why risk a hanging, for the threadbare clothes of Mrs Green's little boy? What wealth did Annie hold worth the taking of a life? The questions accumulate and I can find no certain answer until the frustration of it pulses thick within my skull.

I draw my hands to my forehead and press the pain away, my eyes screwed tight and my mouth compressed. It is not until I exhale, drop my hands and open my eyes that I notice the candle flame dip and shiver. I, too, feel the movement of air. I turn, perhaps catching sight of a phantom shape, perhaps sensing the ghost of gillyflower water; and Rebekah is here. How long she has been standing framed by the doorway, I cannot know. With her hair loose about her neck and her velvet night-rail about her, her edges are soft against the scant light; to the point where I cannot be certain if she is indeed here, or just conjured by my fancy. With the candle flame only just enough to delineate her from her surroundings, it is her face which captures most of the light. Her expression is obscure, but her eyes are clear as she moves forward and says, 'We lift the veil, but behind it is always another veil. Don't you agree?'

'Yes,' I say, almost startled to hear her speak after projecting so many silent thoughts upon her.

'You look troubled. Have you discovered something new?'

'No. Well, it's just a feeling.'

'What sort of feeling?'

'A sense of . . . incompleteness. A sense of something we are missing.'

'Go on,' Rebekah says, encouraging me, drawing a chair and seating herself beside me.

I tell her my thoughts on the Green boy and Annie; their poverty and the risk out-ranking any possible financial gain for Morton, Corby and Blister. She nods and says that Matthew Tulley's crudely made dolls and musical instruments were surely of insufficient value to justify his demise. We continue to talk and it feels as though the Fates are indeed pressing us in a certain direction and against hope we are bound to confront the head of the monster: Blister.

'We must go to his rooms,' Rebekah concludes. 'We might have to fight fire with fire,' she adds.

'What do you mean?'

'Resort to deceit, if necessary. We might tell him more than we know; suggest the New Police are already aware of his business with Morton, that Uncle Sep has arranged for lawyers to prosecute him, those sorts of things.'

I nod my understanding, but cannot conceal a yawn brought on by sudden fatigue, and Rebekah seeing it says, 'Come. We must try to get a little more sleep.' We turn to depart and she produces a crumpled paper, placing it on the table.

I take up the candle and am about to lead Rebekah from the room, when a yellow finger of light falls on the paper: Mrs Cohen's receipt. The ink grows dark on the page and at once becomes bold and clear, not only on the page but also in my mind. At once, I recognise the hand.

'The writing, Rebekah!' I say, animated. 'I know it.'

'Perhaps you do,' Rebekah replies. 'Your aunt might have been in possession of similar—'

I don't hear the end of Rebekah's sentence, for I am already busy sifting through the heaps of papers. It eludes me at first and then I find it. I hold it out to Rebekah, triumphant: it is the note that was pushed beneath my door, the night I left Waterford.

Rebekah approaches the table and stands so close to me that I feel the shape of her against me, feel her breath on my skin. I hold both papers up to the candlelight to examine the script closer, but my hand shakes, distorting the writing. Rebekah lifts her arm and gently places her hand over mine and she is perfectly steady. We look from one note to the other. She points her finger to the repetition of a slant here and the style of a loop there, and we scrutinise it, awed into silence. The writing is not just similar; it is the very same.

'But how did Mrs Cohen get the note to me at Waterford? And why did she think me in mortal danger?' I ask the questions rapidly, only to make the point of their existence, not to elicit any answers, for what answers could there be? Rebekah stares at the notes, still standing impossibly close to me, as though protecting me from the prospect of an answer, or perhaps even the discomfort of another question. Eventually, she says:

'How well do you know Mrs Cohen, Hester?'

'Hardly at all, I'm sure. Aunt Meg would buy from her, but she went mostly on her own. I went with her fewer than half a dozen times and she never really spoke to me. She was just one of those people you might see about town and nod a salutation to, maybe comment on the weather, but no more than that.'

'The one thing we can be sure of,' Rebekah replies, 'is that Mrs Cohen knows more than she was willing to let on. And this is good news, Hester,' she says, but her tone is cautious.

I wait for her to elaborate, but she must be turning the matter over in her mind and, with childish impatience, I break in with, 'What will be our next move, Rebekah?'

'We might yet avoid any confrontation with Blister, if only we can talk with Mrs Cohen and, more importantly, press her to confide in us. Whatever her reasons for warning you, warn you she did; which suggests she cares. If she cares, she will surely wish to help us further, once she comprehends the gravity of the situation.'

'So shall we go to her?'

'No. I think it will be better, for her and for us, if I send Ned. I shall request he brings her back here, where we are all safer. And I shall send a boy with a letter to summon a superintendent and we will present him with our papers and with Mrs Cohen's information.' She sighs at this point and I feel her arm slip softly about my waist. 'It's nearly over, Hester,' she says, and although I do not turn around, I can hear in her voice that she must be smiling. 'So, come. Let us rest easy in our sleep and see what the day brings.'

It is with these gentle tones still orbiting my mind that I enter my bedchamber, extinguish my candle, bid goodnight to wakefulness and for once sleep deeply and peacefully.

I wake at first light, having left the curtains open, and am presented with a cloudless sky, the sun climbing the facades of the buildings opposite, hauling its yellow light to the gables that rise at intervals, and to the iridescent frost on the fluted roofs. I rise and inspect the street outside, clean and fresh with its carpet of snow, drifts baled here and there against the skirts of the buildings. Against the pale background, the bare tree branches are beginning to show a suggestion of green, their buds pushing out into the daylight.

It is with a feeling of resolution and new beginnings that I enter the breakfast room, to the aroma of toasted muffins and to the sight of Rebekah. She is wiping a crumb from the corner of her mouth with her napkin, and simultaneously reading a letter which she has opened out in front of her.

'Good morning, Hester,' she says, her eyes remaining on the note. 'It's from Rudd,' she adds.

'Oh dear,' I say. 'Is everything well with Calder?'

'Yes; Rudd says he's no worse. Apparently, Blister did call around last night, but Rudd sent him away; ruffled the fellow's feathers by the sound of it. I wonder if the tide is beginning to turn in our favour, Hester. Blister's wings have been clipped for now and, although we cannot be certain of Mrs Cohen's allegiance, if we tread with caution, she may yet furnish us with useful information.'

'Has Ned left yet, for Mrs Cohen's?'

'Yes. He went about twenty minutes ago. I expect them back by ten thirty. I haven't sent for a superintendent yet. We'll talk to Mrs Cohen first; I don't wish to frighten the woman out of her wits.'

After breakfast, Rebekah writes her letters and I sit by the fire with a book. The company and comfort brings me great gladness. I wish the moment would stretch to infinity. Rebekah must have been observing me, for she says:

'Hester. If you could be reconciled with your father's family, would that please you?'

'Oh, there's no possibility of that,' I say. 'If they had any concern over me, someone surely would have found me by now.'

'And do you have any plan at all, to gain your advantage in life? When this is all over?'

I almost weep at the asking of this question and, for an instant, I feel a rage building within me; not of wrathfulness, but of passion. If only Rebekah could know what tenderness I harbour for her; if only our stations in life could be less divided. But even then, how would Rebekah react to my declared adoration, and what point if she does not reciprocate? All I can do is look at her. She returns my gaze and it is as though we are both held in check, and do not yet have the courage to call Love by its name.

A few seconds later Ned's voice is heard in the hallway, helping me to evade Rebekah's question, and then there is an energetic knock on the breakfast-room door. Peggy enters first to say that Ned has returned and, once his snow-caked boots have been exchanged for shoes, he enters.

'Miss Brock,' he begins, an apologetic tone already present in his voice. 'The lady, Mrs Cohen, is nowhere to be found.'

'How have you come at this conclusion, Ned?' Rebekah asks.

'Well, Miss. I did as you instructed. I went to her place of business, but the shop is all shut up with a notice saying it's closed for good. So I asked some of the traders thereabouts, and they were all in unity; the woman has simply disappeared, along with her daughter. A Mr Butcher at the chandler's says Mrs Cohen has opened up her shop every day for nigh on five-and-twenty years and she gave no word of closing down. It's all a mystery, Miss Brock. And a dark mystery at that, if you were asking for my opinion.'

Ned and Peggy quit the room, and Rebekah and I are left alone. This time I can read Rebekah's expression as clearly as the printed word on a page, and it tells of nothing but foreboding and danger.

CHAPTER THIRTEEN

J ust as a fire is banked up with fuel, the coals stacked high and thick, the kindling dry and brittle, so we take our accusations and admonitions, trim them, stoke them, and prepare to repel the darkness that is Frederick Blister. Whether the rush of heat will scorch him into submission, or the flames will be turned on us at the whim of the wind, I cannot tell.

We take to the road and make our way to Blister's chambers in Lincoln's Inn. The streets are still cloaked in a mantle of snow, with few people yet astir, the scant figures that do choose to brave the cold hopping and flapping like so many rooks and daws. But, as we leave the villas and town houses behind and enter the business districts, the carriage wheels begin to make a squelching noise, and what was white and iridescent in the rays of the dawn sunshine is now grey and oblique in the stark daylight. Hackney carriages and pedestrians abound and, by the time we cut down Chancery Lane, the snow is trodden away. Rebekah has Bostock pull up while she checks her pocket book. She searches the edifices with her eyes, before she points with her forefinger and says to me, 'That must be Blister's. There.'

It is a shabby street door, wearing a coat of black paint that has become dull and worn, and is now only pretending to be what it once aspired to. It must lead to several lodging rooms, for a number of lean young men dressed in black coats enter and exit during the five minutes or so we sit in the carriage. There is a lull in the traffic, Rebekah hands her calling card to Bostock and tells him where he must deliver it.

Just as he is consumed by the building, a carriage passes us from behind and brushes so close that our horse labours against the brake and attempts to rear up. Rebekah is out in an instant, taking hold of the bridle and steadying the horse, calming it with her velvet voice. I push my head out of the window to enquire if all is well. But instead of looking at Rebekah, my eyes are drawn to the passing carriage. Rebekah is staring too as the familiar green-painted sulky judders away from us.

Rebekah boards our carriage just as Bostock is returning, and she orders him to follow the sulky on the road to High Holborn. We follow Blister to the top of Gray's Inn Road.

'He's heading north, perhaps out of the city,' she observes. 'He seems to be going towards Hampstead.'

I turn to her, but before I can ask what we are to do, she says, 'We must follow him, Hester.'

'But he may travel for miles, and to where? And what about the weather?'

'I know. But surely there is greater peril if we do nothing. We can do this together, Hester.' She touches her hand to my knee, leaves it there for a moment, and this gentleness is her firmness, to which I readily submit.

We head north, and gradually the city and its inhabitants melt away and are reduced to one distant identity. Rebekah has Bostock pull rein for a moment or two, at which time she explains to him our endeavour of tracking the green sulky by dint of unobtrusive passage. He has the carriage fall back and we continue some way behind Blister, who in turn is reduced to a quarter of his size on the horizon. Fleetingly, I feel relief that our hostilities with Blister are at a greater distance, even by such a minute degree. This concession to immediate danger also seems to have a liberating effect on Rebekah, for she begins to talk.

'There is a village at the end of this road,' she begins, her eyes penetrating, 'close to the house where St John, my father, grew up as a boy.'

'He didn't live at Waterford, then?' I enquire.

'No. Not as a boy or a young man. It was before my grand-father inherited it.' She pauses, and I know I must wait for Rebekah to unfurl her words to me at her own time of choosing. She recommences with, 'I was just two when St John Brock died; the week after his wife, Charlotte, my mother, passed away during the birth of Calder.'

I note that her language is flat, as though she reads from a page, long since written, taken from a book where an age ago the covers were gently closed on that chapter of her life.

'St John,' she continues, her voice narrow at the apparent remem-brance of long-buried feelings, 'was the eldest son, and what one might call a bon viveur, who died as he lived: in debt, drunk, and in the company of rascals.' She worries her bonnet strings, straightens her collar and fidgets in her seat, as though she can neither understand how her father died in such circumstances, nor indeed how he could have become such a man. 'So, with my parents sodded and grieved within a week of one another, Uncle Sep was forced to surrender his bachelor life and adopt a child in leading-strings and a swaddling infant.' Rebekah issues the words and names carelessly, and I mark that she seems uncomfortable referring to her parents as 'Mother' or 'Father', as though the unfulfilled promise of parenthood negates the privilege of tender epithets. Yet her face betrays the impassivity of her voice, for it colours and blanches in quick succession, and her eye must catch a mote of dust, for it sheds a teardrop, which she is swift to blot.

Once outside the city, the roads are hard with frost, the ruts deep. Our going is slow, and unremitting clouds gather and threaten snow and sleet. The north wind rises, the increasing cold stultifies our conversation and I find myself hypnotised by the subtle interchange of hues the day produces. By the time we pass the Regent's Park, heavy snow begins to descend, layering the ground and consolidating shapes. Our horse toils against clogged wheels, and soon the road is quilted with powder. Through the haze of this weather, Blister's carriage slows and draws up outside a cluster of shops.

In turn we halt and watch. Blister, his topcoat and hat white with the elements, descends from his seat. Once grounded, he dusts his shoulders, removes his hat and shakes it, then scrutinises the vicinity. Momentarily he faces us and, although I know we are obscured by a curtain of snow and our carriage is too distant for him to know us, I recoil from his gaze and pull back from the carriage window. By the time I have courage to look again, Blister is entering a shop doorway and disappearing from sight, but I continue to stare at the spot he was last visible to me and the ghost of a shiver touches the small of my back.

'I suppose we must sit and be patient until he moves on,' I remark.

'Patience, Hester, was invented to exempt people from decisiveness. We must be ardent and active,' Rebekah says with encouragement.

Rebekah now calls to Bostock and instructs him to drive on. We draw up behind Blister's carriage, outside the general draper's shop into which he has entered. There are also two workshops on this side of the street: a cobbler's and a saddle and harness maker's. On the opposite side there is a confectioner's, an inn and a china shop. Rebekah has Bostock put down the steps and it is towards this last that she leads me. She offers me her hand, I take it, and we forge a path together through the snow.

On entering the shop, a bell suspended above the door rings and a woman appears from a back room in response. She engages us in conversation about what particular ceramics we might be looking for, but, all the time, Rebekah is watching through the large street windows and I realise she has chosen the perfect site from which to examine Blister's business. I watch the draper's too, and through whirls of snow blown down from the rooftops, I observe a pair of gentleman's gloves being fetched from the window display. But again I underestimate Rebekah's resolve and daring, for her sights are not apparently limited to observations.

Instead, the moment Blister leaves the outfitter's, she is away into the blizzard; as I follow in her tread, fears fall thick and fast about me. She crosses the road on the diagonal and meets Blister head on, her head tilted forward against the wind's truculence, her left hand anchoring her bonnet. He must recognise her instantly.

'Miss Brock!' he booms; no manners, his large head seated low in his collar.

'Ah! Mr Blister,' Rebekah says. 'What are you doing in this part of town on such a day?' The same question is no doubt on the tip of Blister's forked tongue, but Rebekah is quicker and he is at a disadvantage. He looks up at the changing skies, then cups his hand beneath Rebekah's elbow and guides her to an arched passageway. Once sheltered from the snowstorm and, having cleared a path towards his next choice of words, Blister ignores Rebekah's question and says:

'Miss Brock.' He pauses then repeats, 'Dear Miss Brock,' this time purring her name, obsequious and smooth, 'what a happy surprise to find you here, "Oh, happiness! Our being's end and aim. Good, pleasure, ease, content! whate'er thy name". I cannot recall the next lines, or the fellow who wrote it, for that matter.' He laughs and a melting snowflake worms its way down the side of his right temple.

Rebekah does not laugh, but says, '"That something still which prompts the eternal sigh, For which we bear to live, or dare to die". From Pope's *Essay on Man*, Mr Blister.'

'Yes,' he agrees, but the mirth has left his voice. 'Yes, that's the fellow. Fine words from a fine fellow, I'm sure . . .' His voice tapers and there is an awkward moment, but Rebekah does nothing to end it, does nothing to aid Blister. Then he seems to trespass upon another thought and says, 'And to whom do I have the honour of addressing my attentions, dear lady?'

He turns to face me and, without invitation, he lifts my gloved hand and touches it to his moustache, which grows unchecked, broad and unkempt over his cheeks, concealing his lips. This is the closest I have been to Blister and an innate distrust presses on my heart. His face is soured by ill habits, with no trace of kindness in his countenance to temper the acerbity. If ever I doubted it before, now I am certain; there can be no sympathies between us. Friends we are not; enemies we must be.

'Mr Blister,' Rebekah begins archly, 'this is my dear cousin, Miss . . . Miss Estelle Frost, visiting us from her home in Cornwall.'

'Enchanted, I'm sure, Miss Frost. And they say that Cornwall is the best county for honest minds and active men, do they not?' He makes to drop my hand, yet lingers. I pull my arm to my side, relieved to be released, and offer up a reluctant smile. 'I hope we shall meet again, Miss Frost, before you return to the West Country. In fact, I shall be quite out of spirits if we do not.'

Before I can reply, Rebekah says waspishly, 'We can't have you out of spirits, Mr Blister, now can we? We can't have you labouring beyond comforts and prayers, suffering a sore that cannot be healed, compressed by your unyielding desire to eat opium as though it were ambrosia from the gods. Oh, my pardon, Mr Blister. I confuse you with my brother. Please do excuse me.' I wonder if Rebekah means to deliver her words with a greater degree of innocence to disguise the disdain beneath, but they are spoken with such levity of tone that the cutting sarcasm is at once manifest and Blister clearly receives it with her implied intent. Her words end, but her stare is fixed directly on Blister's face.

'I sympathise profoundly with your concerns, dear lady,' he parries, the glib attitude now abandoned. 'But how could I possibly be responsible in any way? Does your brother not feed himself? Do you not also administer the remedy to him with your own hands? With your teardrops and admonitions, do you not go to him, knowing you collaborate in his demise? Come now, Miss Brock.'

'I suspected you might be ophidian in composition, Mr Blister, but I had no idea you could crawl so low.'

'Such eloquent insults, Miss Brock. Yet sadly unfounded. Such a waste of a woman you are, Miss Brock.'

'I do not still refer to Calder, sir. I refer to my journal. The same diary you stole, sir, yes; stole, from my own rooms on the ninth day of this month.'

I did not foresee Rebekah issuing this accusation, and inside, my heart turns in on itself, hot with the sting of deceit. But I cannot confess here and now, I can only stand, with blood pulsing thick in my veins, and await Blister's reaction. With a shake of his head, in apparent disbelief and in obvious innocence, he half closes his eyes and says through a simper, 'Miss Brock. I believe it is true what your uncle says about you. I am only saddened the symptoms appear to be worsening.'

He is about to take leave of us, when she says, 'And what do you suppose my uncle said about you, Mr Blister, when he discovered you fraternise with the likes of Jack Morton and Bill Corby at the Fortune of War public?'

This time, Blister is visibly affected by the words. He stops, turns and, with a creeping flush to his face, he leans in to Rebekah and says, 'Your threats are an idle wind, Rebekah. But be careful how they blow.'

'What is more, Septimus has notified the New Police and—'

Blister stares at Rebekah, the full force of his loathing radiating from his eyes. I am certain that we are in grave peril and that he purposes to harm us right here at this spot. His gaze penetrates me to the core and is enough to curtail Rebekah's sentence. Then, to my relief, Blister turns about and is at once absorbed by the blizzard.

The bones that join at my kneecap are strangely soft and a feeling of nausea rises in my throat. I have watched a hundred times as Uncle Jacob vented his wrath on Aunt Meg, but his anger, although blunt and physical, was always narrow and superficial; the ignorant ferment of a man-child. This repugnance from Blister is new to me, and a bruise is already beginning to contuse in the eye of my mind. I turn to Rebekah, expecting to see a similar reaction of discomfort. But she is composed – no, more than that, there is a vital glow about her.

'See what a ready tongue suspicion has?' Rebekah declares. 'He suspects we know all. He is shaken. Come, Hester. We must follow him.'

'Perhaps it is better if we wait,' I begin, dismayed that Rebekah appears to esteem recklessness above safety. 'Wait until we can—' I suspend my opinion; my words severed at the sharpness of Rebekah's expression.

'You must have faith, Hester,' she snaps. It is an order, not a recommendation, of that I am clear. 'Our lives are imperilled,' she adds more softly. 'Calder's life is threatened. We cannot wait.'

She inhales, tightening her cloak and forcing her bonnet lower on her head.

'He's heading north, on foot, away from his carriage,' she calls to me through the wind, and jabs her right forefinger downwards at Blister's footprints. 'It's the road to the heath.'

After Rebekah has sent Bostock to take our carriage and horse to the inn's covered courtyard and wait for us, Blister is no more than a bloated silhouette some forty yards ahead of us. He walks with intent but his pace is hindered by the falling snow. It is the heavy tread of his footprints stretched out before us upon which we focus our eyes and set our steps; two depressions from his boots and a hollow shaft from the puncturing of his walking cane. Whether it is the style of heel the cobbler has nailed to Blister's footwear, or my feelings towards the man, but to me his tracks are of cloven hooves and a forked tail, and I wonder if we are following the devil himself.

Brisk and solemn we stalk in his wake, the street cloaked in eerie quietude, save for a distant clock telling the hour with blunt chimes. The loudest noise is the rasp of our tread as the snow yields beneath our feet. Flakes dash against our faces, and on each occasion I inhale a lungful of brittle wind; it sends chill breaths to the base of my belly. Yet Rebekah presses on in a mortal hurry, directing her steps along an uncertain path beside the margin of the heath. At length, she slackens her pace and, on the right, some few yards on, there is an isolated cottage, barely visible through the snow.

It is one of those houses best seen in the dappled sun of a golden summer's day; when the fragrance of lilac and apple blossom perfumes the breeze; when hollyhocks and roses send up such colours as an artist might never find in his palette. But today is not such a moment and the winter light does nothing but expose the drabness and decay of the place in all its sadness. Desiccated shrubs arch their backs and sapless brambles reach out; there is no foliage, no birdsong, no life.

Rebekah manoeuvres us so that although we can see the cottage, we are obscured by the tangled branches of a thicket.

'Do you suppose he's asking for directions?' I ask.

'I shouldn't think so. His footprints suggest he didn't prevaricate. Look, there's no disorder of snow at the wicket, no trampled arc where he paced and pondered. No, I think he marched straight down the path to the door. Perhaps he's taking shelter?'

We wait. The cottage is dark inside, but there is candlelight behind what perhaps is the parlour window. A few moments elapse and the glow is extinguished, but reappears in an upstairs room, where a shape moves from one side of the window to the other and back again. Eventually, the upstairs light fades and reappears on the lower storey, where it lingers and flickers.

As the minutes advance the storm abates, leaving only a flurry of flakes, a quaking pulse of snow as the air holds its breath. All sound is muted, rendering thoughts all the louder in my head. I can only speculate that too much time is passing for Blister to be taking shelter. I am tormented that he may be harming the inhabitant of the cottage; that cries of anguish might come at any moment. I am in a high state of vexation when Rebekah nudges my arm. I follow the direction of her gaze and Blister is silhouetted in the doorframe. He steps outside and closes the door with such force that a splintering sound rents the air. The noise must startle a bird in the trees above us and there is a whistling of feathers as it takes flight. I duck my head and take a sudden step to the left, but Rebekah takes my arm, steadies me, and Blister must be insensible to us as he continues striding along the path towards the gate.

At the wicket he pauses and, instead of loosening the latch, he kicks out with his right leg and sends the gate swinging on its hinges. Although now unimpeded, he still seems dissatisfied and he turns and lunges again with his foot, this time breaking the gate clean away from its post. At last, he leaves, retracing the path back to his carriage, striding through the snow that by mercy of the wind has covered his tracks and ours.

'Surely, we can't go in,' I say. 'Blister may come back and—'

'That is precisely why we must go in. We must discover why he was here. We must be brave if we are to bring all this to an end.'

She offers up her hand and I take it. We tread the path that moments before quaked at the step of Blister and we approach the street door. Rebekah removes her glove and raps her knuckle against the wood. There is an uncertain noise from inside, perhaps the scraping of a chair leg against stone flags, perhaps the taking up of a poker. Rebekah knocks again and this time we are met with silence. She replaces her glove and pushes against the door, twists the doorknob, but it is barred against us.

'Your last visitor is a rogue,' Rebekah begins, her face close against the door, her tone forthright. 'I cannot presume to know his business with you, but my guess is he did not act as a gentleman. I have knowledge that suggests he is a villain, and perhaps you may share intelligence with me that ensures he no longer evades justice.' Here Rebekah pauses and we listen. There is a muffled tread, but no more. Rebekah sighs and adds, 'I reside in the city; the red-brick house on the corner of Arlington Street. I implore you to reveal to me whatever you know. People's lives depend upon you.'

Still nothing.

'I shall press you no more. If you have a change of heart, come to Arlington Street, I beg of you.'

Silence.

'My name is Miss Rebekah Brock.'

We turn about and walk three paces, when a latch is pulled back and a key is turned. We stop and hurriedly turn around, just as the door opens; cautiously at first, then smoothly on its hinges. A woman, perhaps aged five-and-sixty, stands in the doorway. Remarkably small in stature, she is fairly swamped by her black stuff gown and holland apron. Her cap is as white as her own hair; making it impossible to see where the lace frills end and the tresses begin.

'Perhaps I am being hasty,' the woman says, with a voice as aged as her frame. She looks about, perhaps looking for Blister, before saying, 'Well come in then, and take a warm by the fire.'

We are led into a parlour and are shown to a bench by the fireside. There are two wax-lights burned half down and their long wicks bend as we enter, throwing shadows about the room, revealing a dresser racked with plates one moment, and a table with a tangle of knitting on its surface the next. Each time the flame dips, I wonder whether the room will give up another secret and another, until they are all told.

The mistress of the house pulls a wooden chair to the hearthrug, sits herself on it and folds her hands on her lap. Her whole person is still, but her fingers remain active; twitching and flexing as though she knits with invisible needles. Casting and looping, purling and turning, her busy fingers appear so accustomed to the occupation that instinct prevails over politeness. The woman seems unaware of her nervous habit and looks shyly at Rebekah and then at me. She turns back to Rebekah and says, 'I believe you must be Miss Brock. I knew you'd grow to be a handsome woman; it seems like yesterday that your mother was just such another.'

'But . . . how . . .?' It is the first time I have witnessed Rebekah confounded by words that will not come. She blanches and her eyes grow wide.

The old woman notices her difficulty and says, 'Oh, it's been a long time since. Many a year. And as much as the deeds of yesteryear have gone to their grave, so their ghosts haunt me yet. And your father, Mr St John, such a fine young man. Never tempted by sin like his brother Septimus.'

'You have it wrong, Madam,' Rebekah says, sudden and defensive. 'It was my father who fell in with the rogues, not my uncle.'

'Ah, yes,' the woman says, nodding slowly. She examines Rebekah and, even in the scant light, it is obvious the woman's face colours.

Rebekah eyes the woman and I believe she might challenge her further, but she seems to regress and says, with coldness, 'Who exactly are you?'

'My name is Prudence Tyler, wife to Gabriel Tyler, parish clerk.'

'Have we met before?'

'Oh, you won't have recollection of me, my dear. You were just a poppet when I last cast eyes on you. You sat on my knee, lisping and prattling . . .' The distracted smile and mellow eyes of the old woman that have accompanied her rhetoric thus far are suddenly gone, as though a cloud of ill omen passes over the sunshine of happier remembrances, and darkness prevails. Mrs Tyler stares blankly and then lifts her eyes to meet Rebekah's. There is pity behind the old woman's gaze. She blinks, places the flattened fingers of each hand gently on the sides of her face, closes her eyes and inhales.

'I'm supposing you have come this way,' she begins wearily, 'on the same errand as my last caller.'

'Not at all, Mrs Tyler. I have no direct association with Frederick Blister beyond his friendship with my brother, which I believe to be highly undesirable.'

'Then why did you come here?'

'Blister is a dangerous fellow, Mrs Tyler. At great risk, my companion and I covertly followed him here. I have to know, Mrs Tyler, what was his errand?'

'For many years, Miss Brock, my husband, Gabriel, was clerk to this parish. Meticulous, he was, in his record-keeping. The fairest hand of any man I know. And the most honest of men, I can assure you.' Mrs Tyler stops at this point and draws her fingers to her lips and closes her eyes momentarily, before continuing.

'But, there are times when . . . when folks can suffer misfortune and sickness, when money is hard got and soon gone. I wish he'd never agreed to such a thing.'

'Agreed to what, Mrs Tyler?' Rebekah demands.

'He was paid, by a gentleman, to remove a page from the register and re-write the original with an omission. He was meant to burn the original page, but, oh—'

'Come now, Mrs Tyler,' Rebekah says. 'You have come thus far. You must finish your tale.'

'Oh, there's such shame in it.' Mrs Tyler draws the corner of her apron to her eye and sniffs. 'He hid the original and demanded payment to stay his tongue.'

'And how is Frederick Blister involved in such a scheme?'

'I don't know. He just said he was sent by someone; someone who wouldn't pay a penny more, he said. He'd come for the original page, or proof it was destroyed.'

'And what did you tell him?'

'The truth, Miss Brock. I don't know where it is.'

Mrs Tyler weeps tears, large and profuse. Rebekah looks at me, unsure as to how to continue, and I shrug and glance upwards, as though appealing for Providence to intervene. No sooner have I done so, than knocking comes from the room above. We crane our necks simultaneously and stare at the low, beamed ceiling.

'It's Gabriel,' Mrs Tyler whispers, and I am convinced she is referring to her husband's ghost. But Rebekah's thoughts differ and she says, 'Is your husband very ill, Mrs Tyler?'

'Yes,' the old woman breathes, her hand partially covering her mouth. 'He's been taken badly for nigh a twelvemonth.'

'Will his fortitude withstand a visit from two young ladies?'

'Oh, I don't know. Mr Blister was so rude, so angry. I can't say if it's all too much for my poor Gabriel.'

But Rebekah will not be refused and she rises, goes to a

curtained doorway to the left of the fireplace and says, 'Is it through here?'

Mrs Tyler nods and pulls the drapery aside, revealing a narrow stairway. She takes up a candlestick and Rebekah stands aside. We follow the uncertain flame as it ascends to the upper storey and leads us to a small bedchamber. The room is chill; unsavoury with the odour of sweat and bile, and lying in the bed is a man ravaged by disease. His hair is grey, and his skin too; the amber hue of the candle flame does nothing to soften the starkness of either his pigmentation or his emaciation.

'It's Prue, my dear. And two ladies come to visit you.' Mrs Tyler leans over the drawn skin of the man's skull and strokes his sunken cheekbone, but there is no response and his eyes remain closed. 'They come about . . . the entry, in the register. I told it all, Gabe, for she has a right to know. It is she, Gabe. It's Miss Rebekah. Miss Rebekah Brock.'

At the mention of Rebekah's name, the man's eyelids quiver. He blinks and stares, as though lately returned from a far-off land. Mrs Tyler speaks something in his ear, then turns and lifts the candle towards Rebekah, saying, 'Come, Miss Brock. Please step into the light, that he may see you.'

I am not certain if Gabriel's eyes can see anything in this mortal domain, so dark and vacant appear his pupils. But he seems satisfied with Rebekah and issues a dry, rasping series of words, which are incomprehensible to me. He raises his hooked finger-bone and steers it towards the window, his black eyes following the same direction.

'What is it, dear?' his wife asks. 'Do you hear something?'

Gabriel pokes his finger three times towards the windowsill before he lets his hand drop limply at his side, and I believe his reserves of vitality must be spent. But he is not finished. He reaches down, retrieves a walking stick and strikes at the stones beneath the window recess. His determination and strength are incongruous with his feeble frame, and yet he persists, until the stone he targets is loosened.

Rebekah takes up the wax-light and, having pulled back the blind, places it on the sill. She kneels, gives a tug at the stone and the mortar crumbles. Once removed, the brick reveals a pocket beneath, inside which is a folded paper. Rebekah retrieves the page, unfolds it and, with the paper in one hand and the candle in the other, she scans her eyes over the script. Repeatedly, her eyes move from side to side, devouring every word, until finally they stop. She sighs and passes the page to me, pointing to a line of text towards the bottom of the sheet: *'This thirteenth day of August, in the year of our Lord Eighteen Hundred and Seven, Septimus Algernon Brock, Gentleman of this parish, joined in holy matrimony to Elizabeth Cohen, Needlewoman'.*

The revelation quite winds me, and all I can do is stare at the script; so innocuous in its neatness and flat dimension, yet potent enough to unleash chaos. Rebekah is motionless, except for her chest rising and falling in alarming shortness of speed. Eventually, she says, 'We must take this, Mr Tyler. It is an attestation to a truth which has been concealed and it may have far-reaching consequences.'

What happens next is a mystery to me. I return the paper to Rebekah, for her safe-keeping. Her hand is inches from mine and the transition should be simple and quick. But the passage is never completed, for a skeletal hand lunges through the half-light and, in a moment, the page is grasped in the palm of Gabriel Tyler. He screws his fist so tight, I wonder that his fingers don't snap. They say the tongues of dying men enforce attention, but it is Gabriel Tyler's clasping hand that demands all the faculty of my observance. Rebekah appeals to the man, and his wife also beseeches him to release the document; but he will not be countermanded. Eventually, Mrs Tyler suggests we return to the parlour and Rebekah accedes.

'The only measure I can think to take,' Mrs Tyler begins, as we return to the downstairs room, 'is to wait until he sleeps, then I might liberate the paper from him. But some nights, he lies awake until dawn. Perhaps you might allow me to bring the paper to you at your home tomorrow?'

'The document is too important for me to leave without it,' Rebekah says. Her eyes are restless and I wonder if she is examining the implications of the discovery, studying not only the image of Septimus as the man she believed she knew, but also the man she now knows him to be. I, too, find myself considering Septimus and Mrs Cohen, wondering what circumstances prevailed to bring two such disparate people together. I must hit upon an idea at the precise moment Rebekah arrives at the same prospect, for she turns to Mrs Tyler and says, 'There must have been a child. Was there a child?'

Mrs Tyler looks at her feet and covers her face with her hands. She steadies herself, sits and says meekly, 'Yes.' Then the tears begin to flow again, so I approach her and lay my hand on her shoulders. She looks up at me, her face wet and her cheeks flushed up. I glance with concern at Rebekah, hoping she will leave off the poor woman. I can only wish that we had never happened upon the cottage and that we might leave this woman and her dying husband in peace. But Rebekah is not done. She has that look about her which suggests she is on to something and will not be distracted until she discovers a solution.

'Was it a girl?' Rebekah demands. Mrs Tyler, apparently paralysed by fear, says nothing. 'Was the child a girl?' Rebekah repeats, her lips compressed, her eyes narrow. 'If you will not speak, then I must answer for you,' she says. 'There was a child. She was a girl. And her name is Rosina.'

The mention of this name releases Mrs Tyler from her apoplexy and she gives a low moan, as though the sting of suppressing the secret causes her physical pain. I am grateful the inquisition is over. But I am mistaken. Rebekah moves closer to Mrs Tyler until she is standing over her.

'You see, Mrs Tyler,' Rebekah says, her voice artificially low and measured, 'I have met Rosina. A strange, sad girl. Haunted by the death of a forgotten soul. But the soul didn't die, did it? The soul she mourns was a twin, wasn't it? An infant that was taken from her and from her mother. A boy, perhaps, Mrs Tyler?'

Mrs Tyler begins to rock backwards and forwards, evading Rebekah's stare by every possible device: blinking; rubbing her eyes, her breath coming in heaves and sobs. 'Stop it! Stop it, I tell you,' she whimpers. 'It serves no good to dredge up ghosts from the past. Leave it be, I beg you. You have outstayed your welcome in this house, Miss Brock. Please leave. I will bring you the paper at first light, as I promised to. But pray leave, for all our sakes.'

'Rebekah,' I say, hoping she will repent under my appeal. 'Mrs Tyler is right. We have learned much today. We have enough to take to the constable. Let us take our leave, before—'

'And what,' Rebekah spits, ignoring my plea as though I have not spoken, 'was the name of that boy, Mrs Tyler?'

'I . . . I cannot recall.'

'Oh, I think you can.'

'No.'

'Does the man that grew from that boy now call himself Frederick Blister?' Rebekah's voice is now hoarse and she is shouting. She stamps her foot so violently that the poker dances and rings in its rack. 'Is my uncle's son Frederick Blister?'

'Yes,' Mrs Tyler concedes. 'Yes, now go!'

CHAPTER FOURTEEN

Momentarily I believe Rebekah, with her livid expression and wild eyes, might employ the poker and strike Mrs Tyler. Instead, she is motionless and mute. At this point, panic is my master – a convincing substitute for courage – and I am able to marshal Rebekah from the cottage.

The wind has blown itself out and it is through sombre stillness that we begin the journey back to our carriage. Beneath the compassionless skies, everywhere looks different; bare hedgerows tricked with snow, the world stiff with ice. We pace along the lonely way that bisects a sweep of wilderness, and our conversation is as barren as the landscape. I glance at Rebekah every so often and, although she has the same physical attributes as before, she seems different to me in other ways. I worry she might struggle to withstand the consequences of today's revelation; after all, she has so much to lose. Not least the question of safety that now centres upon Calder and herself, and it is Calder's name I offer by way of solace.

'All is not lost, Rebekah,' I say, my tone sanguine. 'Is it not now clear why Blister is so obliging in the provision of opium for Calder? Is a man subjugated by such a habit not easier to usurp? Once Calder knows how and why he is manipulated, will he not purge himself of the substance and become his own man again?

A man who will provide for you, protect you, as any brother would.'

When Rebekah fails to reply, I assume she is deep in private thought, rearranging facts and planning accordingly, as she always does. But the moments pass in taut silence, until I sense her hand catching hold of me, feel her leaning against me as I slip my arm about her waist to steady myself against the weight of her. I inspect beneath her bonnet and her eyes are open, but they are fixed and vacant. Tearing the glove from my hand, I touch my fingers to her face and it is hot on both cheeks. I can bear her heaviness no longer and she crumples, melts through my arms and slides down until she is prostrate upon a pillow of snow. I stoop to rouse her but she is insensible to me. I cry out for someone to help us; and each time I shout, the ghost of my breath lingers in the air.

Eventually, a man appears from one of the workshops, his hands and bare forearms black with industry and his leather apron flapping from knee to knee as he approaches us. I send him to the inn to call forth our carriage. I rage against time's ceaseless passage for an age before the carriage finally comes careering along, impeded by snowdrifts which were bright white not two hours since, and are now tinctured grey with soot.

When the carriage reaches us, Bostock jumps down from his box as the horse whickers and nods its head. The cobbler lifts Rebekah and places her in the carriage, and all I can do is draw the rug over her and hold her hand as I speak words of comfort.

'I'm here, Rebekah,' I whisper. 'We're going back to Arlington Street, where you shall be looked after.'

We creak and slide our way back to town, but Rebekah shows no signs of response. Her eyes are closed now and the snow-infused daylight flashing past shows clearly how pale her complexion has become.

When we arrive at Arlington Street, I extricate myself from Rebekah, and where before the warmth of her body has pressed against me, the chill now bleeds through the material of my outerwear and touches its clammy fingers against my skin. I shiver, my teeth knock together, and I feel the cold as I have never felt it before. I quit the carriage, my knees and ankle bones soft and uncooperative as I dash over the doorstep into the house and fetch Ned and Peggy to help bring Rebekah from the carriage.

It is almost too painful to witness her being brought so low, and I pray she has the strength to endure. I recall the Rebekah I first met at Waterford, and the one I have seen so overcome today: the contrast is powerful. Although staggered at our discovery, I believe I am more shocked at the impact on Rebekah that the disclosure has brought. But I suppose over the last few months, sorrows have indeed rushed upon her. Suddenly she has succumbed and become what all her yesterdays have made her.

Once in the hallway, I close the door behind me. My clothes are heavy, my gloves are a moist and adhesive skin bound tight around my fingers. My bonnet is low and limp about my ears and all the time I drip water over the tiles.

'Ned,' I say, 'and you, Bostock,' as I point at the coachman, 'please carry Miss Brock to her room. And Peggy, help Miss Rebekah out of her wet clothes, we must get her warm and dry. Ah, Tilly. We'll need your help, too; take a bale of towelling and a pitcher of hot water up to Miss Rebekah's room. Then prepare a cup of hot milk for her, with a little brandy mixed in to revive her. We may need to summon a doctor if she does not improve. Do you know the nearest and best, Peggy?'

'That'd be Dr Quince; two streets away, Miss.'

'Thank you, all of you.'

Ned and Bostock convey Rebekah upstairs as Tilly runs to the kitchen and Peggy makes her way to Rebekah's room. Soon after,

I hear Peggy's solid tread on the boards above and her muffled voice fussing and fretting. Bostock, still in his oilskin cape and cap, returns soon after with Ned, and I suggest the men both wait in the kitchen, take a warm by the fire and wait to see if we need to send out for the doctor.

I climb the stairs and gently knock at Rebekah's bedroom door. It opens and Peggy steps out, obscuring Rebekah from my view.

'I don't know what you young ladies are thinking sometimes,' she whispers, her tone pitched somewhere between worried affection and reproach.

'Is Rebekah all right?'

'Miss Brock is well enough. But she must rest. And you must take yourself out of those sodden garments: you'll catch your death, Miss White! I have looked after plenty of sick mistresses in my time, so you are not to worry.'

In the frantic moments since Rebekah took ill, I have quite forgotten the snowdrifts we walked through and the blizzard that blew around us. I look down at my saturated clothes, and begin to peel away my bonnet, gloves and coat.

'Not here, Miss. Best go to your room; I shall send Tilly to assist you and you shall come and sit with Miss Brock in good time.'

I submit to Peggy's will and retire to my room next door. True to Peggy's word, Tilly arrives soon after and, once clothed in dry apparel and with hands that are now less numb, I go to Rebekah.

She is lying on her back, the bedcovers pulled over her chest, her arms on top of the counterpane. At first, she appears to be subsumed by sleep, but as I approach, she must sense the movement of air and she rolls her head along the pillow, her eyelids quivering before opening. I seat myself on the edge of the bed as Peggy moves and stands a few feet away. And Rebekah locks her eyes on me and smiles.

'I must have given you a fright, Hester,' she says, her voice laboured.

'Not at all,' I lie. 'It was only for a moment and then—'

'I cannot recall our walk back from the Tylers' cottage. How strange. I remember a sensation of giddiness then nothing.'

'You must try to sleep, Rebekah. There's no need to remember for now. You must rest and I shall stay, here.' I point to the chair on the opposite side of the bed, but Rebekah's eyes are already closing.

As soon as Tilly has fed the fire with fresh fuel, and when Peggy has gathered an armful of wet clothes, they leave me to watch sentinel over Rebekah. As Peggy begins to close the door behind her, I call her back.

'Peggy?'

'Yes, Miss White?'

'Thank you for your diligence. You have cared for Miss Rebekah very considerately today.'

'Thank you, Miss.'

'Also, Peggy, I wonder if you might find time to dry my outerwear and boots overnight. I shall require them at first light for an errand I must undertake.'

'I shall have them hung before the kitchen fire, Miss, and then I shall return to sit with Miss Brock.'

'Oh, no, Peggy. That's not necessary, I shall stay with her.'

'What, all night?'

'Yes, Peggy. In part I feel responsible; we should never have walked so far in the snow. And, as Rebekah's friend, I should have counselled her better. It is my duty to stay with her.'

'Well . . . if you're sure. I shall bring you some victuals, of course. And I'll look in on you from time to time. Sure you've recovered enough, Miss?'

'Yes, thank you.'

Peggy steps back inside the room, lowers her gaze to Rebekah and straightens a crease in the bedding, glances at the fire and then leaves. True to her word, she returns within the hour, delivering a decanter and wineglass, a selection of cold meats, pickles and a hunk of cheese. Later on she brings oyster patties with bread and butter, and at nine o'clock makes her final visit, leaving a plate of gingerbread and a cup of coffee. All this time Rebekah's only appetite is for slumber.

The night begins to pass in a disjointed and confusing fashion. Rebekah sleeps almost noiselessly, her soft breathing the only proof she is alive. She never stirs, nor changes position, and I wonder if time is not advancing at all, whether we might be forced to remain in this quiet moment for eternity. Perhaps when the struggle is over and death finds me out, this will be my heaven: the warmth of a sleepy fire and Rebekah's presence; for what else is there, and for what reason would I ever tire of such a place?

Then, through the quiet and the peace, fragments of fear fall hard and chill against the window of my mind, leaving snaking trails of distorted visions. Aunt Meg tearing the clothes from my corpse; Blister pressing the life out of Calder; Septimus expelling Rebekah, without a farthing to her name. The blizzard of images whirls pitilessly until there are too many for me to differentiate. It is from these nightmarish visions that I awake to discover several hours have passed and it is half past three.

I rise and try to revive the glowing coals with the poker, gently so as not to wake Rebekah. Two wax-lights have burned out, but four sconces remain alight and ought to last until morning. I pad over to the window and pull back a handful of drapery; just enough to see that snow still blankets the ground. I return to my chair. But before I reach it, Rebekah fetches up a sigh and, with her eyes wide and alert, she says, 'Hester, the ache in my head is receding.' She pushes herself up as she speaks.

'The shock must have been very great for you,' I say. 'I'm glad you are feeling better, but further rest is surely imperative.'

'Hester, listen.' Her tone, although compromised by her infirmity, is no less imperious than ever before. 'I've had terrible nightmares. Not just last night, but before. They're disconcerting in their degree of reality. They centre on a common theme; they involve deep, black water. I can't account for it. It isn't a place I know and it is more of a sensation than a sight, but the thought of it grieves me. I overheard you talking to Peggy, asking for your boots and coat and—'

'I know the importance,' I say, for once heedless of interrupting, 'the importance of retrieving the page of that register. I intend to take a carriage to Haverstock Hill at daybreak then walk out to the Tyler cottage. I don't believe we can fully trust Mrs Tyler and—'

Rebekah smiles. 'I know what you intend to do and I am grateful to you. Don't think me alarmist, but pray, do have a care for streams and ponds. I know it must sound melodramatic, but I can't bear the thought of—'

She slips down again into a prostrate position and her words drift away from her, away from me.

'Hush now,' I say, as I indulge myself in brushing a lock of shiny dark hair from her brow.

She half wakes twice more, but seems to forget the thread of ideas she must have been attempting to pursue and, finally, the duress of exhaustion and the draw of sleep consume her.

By the time dawn's nervous light begins to break, I am dressed for outdoors and have surrendered my role as nurse to Peggy, who brings coals, candles and a tray of nourishing food to revive Rebekah, at the striking of six.

I enter the hired carriage, called from the stand by Ned, just after eight o'clock. The ride is uneventful, the carriage trundling on efficiently in yesterday's ruts made rigid overnight, and soon I am setting out on foot, passing the patch of ground where Rebekah's strength deserted her. I am keen to approach the cottage by stealth; by walking I make little noise and, if Blister is there, I am at liberty to run and hide on the heath.

The air might be thin and cold, but it is revitalising, and birds fly through it, plunging between branches and spilling sugary cascades with their wings. However malevolent the heath appeared yesterday, it is welcoming this morning with its mellowing sunrise and I make good ground. With each step, I have no reason to doubt that Mrs Tyler will also be stimulated by the virtue of the day and, true to her word, be approaching me at the same rate as I am nearing her.

But I meet no other soul until at last I draw near the cottage in the distance, its chimneys smokeless and its windows dark. An icy wind blows across this last quarter-mile, carried fast and hard over the barren heathland.

As I approach the low wall that encloses the garden, I am arrested by the sight of a man with his back to me. He appears to be a packman, his clothes, bag and boots carrying tales of the streets. He turns about, rubs his hands and stamps his feet, creating a drab-coloured semi-circle in the snow. He must catch sight of me, for he strides in my direction, his cap clutched in his hands.

'You all right there, Miss? Didn't see yer comin',' he says apologetically, now standing before me, his wiry frame slightly crooked. 'Billy Jobber, that's me, Miss.' He bows his head.

'And, Mr Jobber, what is your business here?'

'Well, Miss, I am what you might call a "connysir" of fine linens and muslins to the ladies of this and many a parish.'

'Am I to understand that you are in this present vicinity in order to sell your wares to Mrs Tyler?'

'Well, that's a good question, but I'm not certain I know how to explain the answer to your satisfaction, Miss, as I don't fully understand what's occurred since I last set eyes on Mrs Tyler.'

'And when was that?'

'I should think a three-month. She asked me to bring her a bolt of dimity and a length of lace next time I was passing.'

'Is there no answer at the cottage?'

'Well, see, that's the thing.' He pauses, scratches behind his ear. 'She ain't 'ere.'

'Has she been taken ill?'

'I don't know. See, I came 'ere at first light, just like I always do. I knocked at the door, just like I always do. But the door swung open, see. There was a fire going, and candles lighted and two muffins beside the griddle ready to be warmed, but there wasn't no Mrs Tyler. Then I hears a voice from upstairs. A man's voice – Mr Tyler's, or so I thought, perhaps recovered from his disease.

'But, blow me down, a gentleman comes striding down them narrow stairs, his girth only just able to squeeze through. His jaw drops to his boots as soon as he claps eyes on old Billy Jobber, so I says, "Everything all right, sir?" and he says, "I'm afraid Mr Tyler is dead." He asks me if I'm a son or cousin and I tell him I'm a connysir of textiles, come to sell lace to the Missus. And he says that she's gone. He says he was passing and saw the door swinging open, says he's an old acquaintance of the Tylers and felt obliged to stop and look in. He counts that Mrs Tyler must have had a . . . a seizure, yes; that's what he called it. She must have had a turn when the old man died and up and ran out into the snow. The gentleman said he'd sort all the arrangements; you know, for the burial and such like, and send for a search party to look for Mrs Tyler out on the heath. He gave me this shilling if I might stay until he returned, with the promise of a guinea if I'm here when he comes back.'

'Did the gentleman give you his name, Mr Jobber?'

'Come to think of it, no, he didn't. I suppose I might have asked, but—'

'And how would you describe his appearance?'

'Let's see now. Not so very tall. But . . . well fed, if you catch my meaning. Portly; that's how my old mother would have described him.'

'Was he on foot?'

'No, Miss. He had one of those old carriages where there's only just room for one.'

'A sulky?'

'Yes, Miss. Green it was.'

'I see. Well . . .'

The intelligence delivered by the packman causes my heart to expand violently beneath my ribs, stealing my breath, draining the blood from my head. The image of Blister looms large in my mind, but I have come too far to be thwarted and I will no longer be frightened of fear itself. I order my thoughts, before saying:

'I'm not as well acquainted with Mr and Mrs Tyler as you might suppose, but I have previously visited and . . .' I hear the words issuing from my lips, but my thoughts are directed solely to the prospect that Frederick Blister has no doubt, once again, hurried death's arrival to poor Mr Tyler and perhaps to Mrs Tyler also. The thought of his dark deeds is only superseded by the probability of his return, and it is this sense of mortal urgency that impels me into action.

'As I say, Mr Jobber,' I begin again, undisguised tension in the pitch of my voice. 'I am not profoundly associated with the Tyler family, but I would very much like to pay my last respects to Mr Tyler, if you have no objection?'

'Objection? Me, Miss? Oh, no. I applaud you for it, Miss. I shall wait here and let the gentleman know of your kindness when he returns.'

If I were able to abandon the strictures of propriety, I would run to the cottage, retrieve what I must, and hasten back to the carriage faster than a hare from a hound. But instead I walk with decorum, slowly and respectfully, until I am inside the parlour.

Just as Billy Jobber described, the room is not carefully tidied and packed away as one would do before leaving; the key to the wall clock is on the mantelshelf as though the springs have just been wound; the muffins are beside the griddle, just as Billy said; the cushion on Mrs Tyler's fireside chair is flat as though she has just risen from it; and her ball of green wool, the needles pushed through its centre, is on the table.

All these observations I make in the blink of an eye; all these signs of life I pass by in my hurry towards the dead man's chamber. I press on up the stairway, in virtual darkness despite the sunlight outside. The bedchamber itself is oddly lit by a square of red material hung at the window by way of a blind. The daylight is filtered and only a dim, bloody hue is splashed across the room. Mr Tyler is lying on his back, his lips dark and his eyes shut. The counterpane, which should be reverentially draped over his head, is in disarray, and the brick which hid the page has been extracted, perhaps its location given away by a pile of powdered mortar, perhaps surrendered by Mrs Tyler under Blister's duress, and is lying discarded at the foot of the bed.

I hold my breath and compress my lips, but a sense of rising bile persists as I move the folds of fabric away from Mr Tyler's arm. My fingers brush against his skin and it is colder than granite and has a moist sheen. I snatch away my hand and close my eyes for a moment, before daring to begin again. This time I am obliged to raise his arm to free the counterpane and his skin slips over his bones as though all the flesh has wasted away. I raise his wrist, expecting to find the page still in his grasp, that I may gently remove it, but instead his hand does not resemble a hand at all.

It is grossly misshapen, the thumb and forefinger snapped at the joints, black with bruising and swollen with internal blood. The other fingers hang loose now, the bones at their root pushed through his palm, a veneer of congealed blood coating the skin. I drop his arm and step backwards, neither able to blink, nor stop looking at that awful hand.

I wipe my palms against my side and then against each other and, looking down at my own hands, I imagine the pain inflicted on poor Mr Tyler. I begin to comprehend how merciless Blister really is. Such a sense of revulsion consumes me that I almost vomit.

The air in the room is so rarefied that I can barely draw a lungful. It is this sense of suffocation which forces me to abandon all dignity and run downstairs, through the parlour and out into the sunshine. Despite the polite intervention of Billy Jobber, I will not be prevented from returning to Arlington Street and, with his voice still calling after me, I ignore him and continue onward, moving as briskly as my body will allow, until at last I arrive at the carriage.

Back at Arlington Street, in contrast to the Tylers' bedchamber, the room in which Rebekah resides is warm and inviting, cheered by the open curtains and the firelight. Seated in a chair at the bottom of the bed, in the centre of this gentle light, clothed in a day-dress and with an open book in her hands, is Rebekah.

She rises to greet me as I enter. The effects of her illness are evident in the grey crescents beneath her eyes, but the old vitality is there in her smile.

Yet, as much as I am both pleased and relieved to see her recovered, the haunting image of Mr Tyler's violated bones still has mastery of my emotions and I feel sobs rising in my chest. Before I am sensible to my actions, I am kneeling on the carpet, my face covered by my upturned hands and all I can say is, 'I'm so sorry, Rebekah. But Mr Tyler's hand. What sort of man could do such a thing?'

It is some moments before I am able to speak again, and even longer before I allow Rebekah to help me into a chair. She rings for Peggy and has me drink a glass of brandy and water and, with her seat drawn close to mine and her hand on my knee, she waits until I am ready to talk. Eventually I describe what I have witnessed that morning. Rebekah listens, sitting perfectly still. At the end of my sorry tale her face is more pinched than before and her eyes are dispirited.

'I have given my mind over to thinking,' she eventually begins. 'This fit of the vapours has lent me time to study recent events in more detail.'

'Rebekah, you mustn't spend your energies on such a thing. Not until you feel well again.'

'It is so obvious, that I wonder I missed it,' she continues, intent on discharging the substance of her deliberations. 'It was the note that passed beneath your door, the night you fled. I was distracted by the handwriting and didn't pay sufficient attention to the words. Of course, it wouldn't have been proof positive, yet it would have turned up the suggestion. "Get out before you hear the fatal bellman give the sternest goodnight". That is what was written. What a strange choice of words, especially for a plain and simple needlewoman. Don't you wonder where she learned such a phrase?'

'Well, I suppose—'

'The words are inspired by Shakespeare, paraphrased from *Macbeth*, Act Two. I know this, because I have been surrounded by his works for as long as I can recall. Uncle Septimus, you see, is the most ardent scholar of the texts and cannot resist quoting them as frequently as possible. If I had expanded my mind, and not relied so much on reports and essays . . .

'So, there was a connection, you see. Not a definite one, but nevertheless . . . and I should have seen it. And . . . I . . . suddenly feel less invincible than—'

'Rebekah, you mustn't be so hard on yourself. You couldn't have known.' I speak from my heart, trying to distract her from the blow that has befallen her. But she just stares blankly, her features loose, her breath slow.

'I have written,' she eventually says, a forced positivity to her tone, 'to Calder. Three letters, to be exact. Well, one letter three times over: one copy to the villa, one to his surgery and one to The Oriental. If Blister intercepts one, he'll think himself clever; I'm sure he won't have the capacity to imagine there are two others, so surely at least one will reach Calder. I've explained to him what we have discovered and, as you suggest, drawn his notice to Blister's motives. I only hope we are in time to save him, in time to save us all.'

I believe the realisation of Blister's intentions, together with the limitless depths to which he might go in order to satisfy them, inflicts the same sense of oppression on Rebekah as I experienced all those years ago at the death of my parents. As misfortune and malevolence swept me into the gutter and to the yard at the end of the lane, this time it has returned with enough potency to claim Rebekah as well as me.

There is a sense of foundering which attaches itself to me from here on; that no matter what decisions we make, or turns we take, dark forces are leading us to a point which cannot be avoided or changed. I wonder if this is the source of Rebekah's dreams of black water? As we sit in silence, sometimes glancing at each other, sometimes staring mutely out of the window, it appears neither of us has the desire to comment that the skies are suddenly thick with snow again and that the flakes are already three inches deep on the ground; as though to acknowledge the onset of another storm might be to admit the inevitability of our defeat.

Eventually, it is Peggy who calls our attention to the weather and insists we do not stir from the house. Although I don't mention it, I wonder if, like me, Rebekah is also contemplating a means of self-preservation. What if we continue to stay here and do nothing at all? Would it be such a selfish action? Would inertia harm anyone? But, of course, it would; not least Calder. It is in an attitude of mutual depression that we sit by the fire in the drawing room after lunch until, with an air of resignation, Rebekah says:

'Perhaps it is best if we both retire earlier today, Hester. For unless we receive word from Calder, we shall have no choice but to take what documents and information we have to the Metropolitan Police tomorrow.'

Her look is distant and, when she next speaks, I am not entirely certain if she is addressing me or thinking out loud.

'This will be the end. The end of everything.' Her voice is low. 'But it must be so. I am reconciled to that; there is merit in knowing when to seek help and accepting all consequences: if we are proved right, the scandal will destroy the name of Brock. If we are disbelieved, then Calder and I are in mortal danger.'

I shuffle to the edge of my chair until our knees almost touch. I realise the dark waters are indeed gathering about us. But then Rebekah turns to me and smiles with her eyes, looking at me as though she has seen a garden of flowers, and I know she is glad we are in this together.

The following day, after an early lunch, Rebekah gathers up all the letters, reports and newspaper articles from her bureau, and packs them into a leather satchel, which she then hands to me. We take up our seats in the carriage and on we roll to the offices of the New Metropolitan Police.

We quit the carriage a little way from the building's entrance and walk back along the street. Once inside the office, the lack of light is oppressive, the odour bitter and stale, and I wonder if we have made the wrong decision.

We are ignored at first by the constable, until he looks up from his ledger and realises we are not vagrants and therefore worthy of his time. Rebekah gives her name and asks for an audience with a senior officer. She does not disclose the nature of our business and the constable does not ask. We are told to take a seat on a bench and, although Rebekah turns to view it, she chooses to stand with her hands on her hips in an attitude of impatience.

The corridors are busy and it is some moments before we are received by a Mr Truman, of Covent Garden's 'F' Division of the New Police. He wears an abbreviated expression. Perhaps on longer acquaintance his lips might lengthen and his eyes might crease at the corners, but not at present. He holds out a coarse, broad hand and platitudes are exchanged before he leads us to a room. He walks briskly, his right arm sawing the air, and by the time we reach the door to his office, I am several paces behind and must trot to catch up. He waits at the threshold and says, 'Please come in.'

The room is small and cramped, lit only by a window set high on the wall. Mr Truman drags two wooden seats over the tiled floor to the front of his desk and then squeezes behind and lowers himself into a heavy chair.

'Excuse the mess, ladies,' he says, his eyes on his papers, 'and please do take a seat. I must confess I am surprised at your visit. Is there no benefactor or relation you could appeal to? Of course I proffer any assistance I can, but it is unusual to see ladies of your standing in a place such as this.'

Rebekah seems unafraid to inspect both the office and Mr Truman in equal detail. She sighs, unfolds her arms, leans closer to the desk, and begins her exposition of our case. As ever, her words are delivered with clinical attention to every concern, and every piece of intelligence we have discovered is explained with confidence.

Periodically, she takes a paper from the satchel and presents it to Mr Truman to support her assertions. In turn, Mr Truman pays us the respect of listening, yet his eyes remain inattentive. After some half of an hour, Rebekah sits back and awaits Truman's response. He shuffles in his chair, thumbs through some of Rebekah's papers and twists the ends of his moustaches between his finger and thumb.

I am unsure what reaction I might be expecting. Perhaps Mr Truman is out of his depth and will need to refer to a more senior official? Perhaps the facts Rebekah has presented are sufficient to send men to apprehend Blister immediately. There is a certain excitement in my belly together with relief that, at last, we are able to lay down the burden of our suspicions and expose the villains to the justice of the law.

'I believe,' he begins, his voice deliberate. 'I believe you have gone to a great deal of trouble to record your thoughts. If some of my men could order their notes so well, I'd be a contented man indeed.' He pauses and wipes his tongue over the face of his front teeth. 'As it so happens, I'm involved with the ongoing case of Matthew Tulley; sorry business indeed, I should say, but as ever we lack hard evidence. I am also familiar with the names of Jack Morton and Bill Corby.'

'So, you believe we are telling the truth, Mr Truman?' Rebekah asks, a flicker of hope resurfacing.

'I don't doubt you for a minute, Miss.'

At this, I know Heaven's hand must be upon us, for where before my mind was filled with anxiety, now I am at ease; replete with relief.

But something is wrong.

'The thing is, Miss.' Mr Truman fronts Rebekah. 'I started in this line of work a long time ago. I was a Charley, then I was a Runner, and now I'm here. My first gaffer said to me that the law is like a cobweb: small flies get caught, but the big ones break through. What I'm trying to say is that it's not straightforward to catch a man and send him to Newgate.'

'But what about the defilement of the dead?' Rebekah asks with an air of pique, her eyes narrow. 'Do I understand from your allusion, Mr Truman, that respect for the human form is temporal? Are the deceased human forms which Corby and Morton appear to treat as currency simply forgotten vessels of the soul, oblivious hosts which elicit no concern in the eyes of the law?'

'In the eyes of the law, Miss, the acquisition of a corpse is a misdemeanour and not a felony.'

'So it is not worth your while to pursue such a crime?'

'I didn't exactly say that.'

'But you do not think it pertinent to question Morton or Corby, or even Frederick Blister?'

'Morton and Corby have been brought before the beak a dozen times before, but there's always a gentleman to speak up for them, see.'

'I assume the gentleman to whom you refer is Blister?' Rebekah spits, her contempt undisguised.

'Perhaps that may be so, I'd have to check the—'

'And what is stopping you from interviewing Frederick Blister? Asking him how he can account for his dealings with Morton and Corby?'

'You can't ask a gentleman to express opinions about such villains, Miss.' These words are delivered flatly and with disdain. 'And how,' he continues, 'am I to look narrowly on a man's business without proper justification? You believe there is something against him, but you give me nothing I might act upon. As far as

Mr Blister's association with Morton goes, believe you me, one business transaction with a rogue don't mean a man's gone native.

'Look, from my viewpoint, it seems to me your uncle must have had clear and plain knowledge of his legitimate-born son for all these past years, but considered him to be of so little threat, he didn't see the need to raise the subject with either you or your brother. And credit due to your uncle; he has, by your own testament, brought you up in the manner your own father would have wanted. He acted as a gentleman of honour at the time and has continued to do so, from what I understand.

'What you have here, Miss, amidst what in my design is a family squabble, is a lot of theories, some imagination and a great deal of second-hand information. In my opinion, that separate matter, about netting the likes of Morton and Corby, comes down to more than credentials. What I need, and the law needs, are eye-witnesses. If you don't have no eye-witnesses, then I can't proceed with further enquiries. I thank you, ladies, and don't be too put out by my thoughts, but I believe you might do worse than appeal to your uncle and—'

These final words of advice from Mr Truman are a spark to tinder, and Rebekah rises with such force that her chair first screeches against the tiles and then topples with a smack.

'I shall not visit you again without urgent occasion, Mr Truman. I am sorry to have taken up your time. Come now, Hester. Good day.' Rebekah throws these words over her shoulder as she stalks away and I trail in her wake.

CHAPTER FIFTEEN

My father once told me that the desolation of Babylon is a sight no worse than the defeat of human hope and, as I follow Rebekah, I realise this is true, for she appears as bruised as if she had received more blows than a dropped farthing. It seems to me that her cloak hangs looser about her neck, as though her whole frame is contracting before me.

It is almost four o'clock when we arrive at the Brocks' villa and dusk is already falling. The lamplighter is working his way down the street, igniting blue flames that flare until a continuous mantle of light is draped above the paving setts.

Rebekah, instead of descending the carriage steps and striding through the front doors, sends Bostock to summon George Rudd. When the coachman has left us, Rebekah turns to me and says, 'I cannot bear the possibility of rushing to Calder's rooms either to find them devoid of his presence or strewn with the articles of his habit. In my current frame of mind, it is too much for me to suffer, Hester.'

When George Rudd eventually arrives, his expression is a mixture of gravity and apology, and I don't believe it is necessary for him to say anything that Rebekah does not already guess. He confirms Calder has been absent for the last two days and, although it is supposed he is at his club, missives directed to him there remain unanswered. He pauses at this point and I almost think he might place his hand on Rebekah's in a comforting gesture. But he is unable to offer more than: 'I'm so sorry, Miss. I'm sure he'll be back soon.'

Rebekah nods her thanks to him, receiving this latest news of Calder without further visible effect. She then enquires about Septimus and Blister. Once he has confirmed the former is 'somewhere out of town on business' and the latter 'would do well to keep his distance', Rebekah orders our return to Arlington Street.

As we take dinner that evening, Rebekah nods as I am seated, but silence prevails. I am not offended at the quietness as there is so much to comprehend and consider. Her fingers curl around the hilts of her knife and fork and push a slice of goose around, ploughing a furrow through the uneaten potatoes and cabbage on her plate. I cannot help but recall the vigorous Amazon who tames horses and heals animals; that beating heart that pulses life into Waterford. With her dinner untouched and her wineglass still full, she finally sighs and says, 'Tomorrow is Friday, Hester. If we haven't made contact with Calder by tomorrow, we must keep our arrangement with Morton and employ our time night-sitting with his sister Bessie. We will, to borrow the phrase from Mr Truman, find it necessary to become eye-witnesses.'

'But what if he still doesn't believe us?'

'By our observations and descriptions, we must persuade him. It won't be easy. We may even be forced to observe the attempted destruction of an innocent; so, pray our constancy be braced by an honest cause, and that we may report first-hand to Mr Truman all we witness and that it is convincing enough to put an end to this once and for all.'

She heaves another sigh, as though the thought causes her as much suffering as the prospect of the deed. She reaches for her glass, plays her fingers around the stem, then draws her hand away and says, 'I am greatly fatigued. I find I must retire early. Goodnight, Hester.'

She stands, turns to leave, then seems to hesitate before giving me that kind, gentle look I have come to adore. She departs and her step is light on the stairs, but I still find myself straining to hear the faint creak of the landing floorboards. I sit in the dining room for some time after Rebekah has left, still charged with the echoes of her. Through the silence of the evening, Peggy's voice rises from the kitchen, then fades, and Tilly rattles the fire in the drawing room. Two men walking the streets outside laugh loudly enough for me to hear, the click-clack of their discourse waxing and waning as carriages rumble by. The conversation of life is never still; and time itself is always pushing forward intractably.

Eventually, I too retire. I catch sight of my reflection in the cheval-glass as I enter my bedchamber. Generally I avoid the image of my own reflection, but today I examine the image and note the marked change in my appearance. The hair I have worn short for so many years has now grown and regained some of its sheen. My hips have a greater curve to them and my breasts are fuller; more like a woman, less like a girl from Virginia Row.

But the most noticeable alteration is to my face. Where before my skin was as drab and spare as the food I ate, my cheeks now are rounder, my lips tinted with a warm, ruddy hue. And I cannot recall the last time I had chilblains or catarrhs. I suppose the obvious explanation is that a three-month of good food, dry clothes and warming fires has expanded the flesh on my bones. But I know the light in my eyes is ignited by something more than home comforts. I have been recharged by one thing and one thing alone: Rebekah.

It is, of course, Rebekah on whom I begin to meditate in that ethereal time between wakefulness and slumber, and so potent is its force that it repels the fear of returning to Morton's house and it repulses the twin demons of Danger and Uncertainty as though such sentiments are unknown to humankind. With the talismanic Rebekah in my dreams, I sleep long, full and at peace.

It is not until half past nine o'clock on Friday morning that I wake to discover Peggy has made the decision to allow Rebekah and me to sleep undisturbed to the fullness of our requirements. The house is tranquil and I am grateful for the rest that will help me get through the day.

I rise, dress and take breakfast, but sit alone at the table and remain in solitude for luncheon and on until the afternoon. Despite Peggy's reassurances to me that Rebekah has asked to repose undisturbed in bed today, and has reaffirmed this to Peggy each of the four times the housekeeper has gently asked if all is well, I rest uneasy as the day passes and am fearful of a relapse in Rebekah's constitution. But at twenty minutes past three o'clock, Rebekah stirs. As her footsteps sound on the boards above, I return to my own room and change into the linsey-wolsey frock, wrapper, cap and clogs that we acquired from Mrs Cohen's shop.

By half past four we leave Arlington Street through the back door and, no word or note from Calder having been received to reprieve us from the bent of our task, we are compelled to force events. Peggy closes the door behind us and, although she has undoubtedly been schooled in discretion and tutored in forbearance, her expression this time is one of dismay and outright disapproval. Part of me wishes to turn about and walk back through the door, tell Peggy that she, of course, is right; we must come to our senses and stay in a place of safety. Part of me wills Calder to be rushing through the eventide on his way to stop us, to protect us. But instead, Rebekah and I walk in silent unison, our footsteps striking a rhythm as we tread over paving stones, which soon become uneven and greasy, then cracked, then simply cobblestones clumsily set and spread with a layer of filth. The closer we draw to Old Street Road and Shoreditch, the denser the mesh of fog becomes, smothering and blunting all it cloaks.

By the time we reach Midden Street Cottages, heavy moisture

plasters our hair and clothes to our skin, drawing winter to our bones once again. Rebekah is trembling beside me and I press my arm gently against hers in a gesture of reassurance.

Although there is an orange light flickering at the window of number three, we both stand motionless at the picket fence. However much the air nips us, there is something preventing us from entering, as though this might be the final threshold, the last border between civilisation and chaos.

So we stand, in silence, and stare at the three cottages: numbers one and two just distant shapes, their shutters closed against the night; number three with its broken gutter pipes and dampness besmearing its walls. With her shawl wrapped close about her, Rebekah walks up the narrow limb of pathway which amputates the buildings from the main thoroughfare and approaches the low street door. I draw level with her just as she raises her hand, about to knock. She hesitates, sighs and looks at me, seeking assurance that I am here, that I am ready to slip into my London vowels and my aping of poor Annie. I bite my lower lip, then nod, quick and reluctant.

The knock of knuckle against wood should be a sharp noise, yet tonight it is muffled, the sound softened by the rotting door. Rebekah waits and then taps again, and again the noise is dispersed and silenced before it has time to exist. She casts a glance at me and then thumps the door with the heel of her hand. This time, the sound surges forward and quakes the door against its hinges.

From inside the cottage, there is the piercing wail of an infant, then the shrill of breaking glass followed by hollow tin against stone. Eventually the door latch is lifted and a woman, spare and aproned, appears in the passage. She is slouching, one hip higher than the other. Her hair is in disarray and her clothes are patched and stained. An unappealing odour rises from her, as though her menses are inadequately attended to and her armpits are unwashed.

She lifts the lantern she is holding in her right hand and tries to hook it on a nail. She misses twice and then catches the string and the lantern swings for a moment, then stills. The infant in her left arm squirms, stretching out a hand, its grubby fingers reaching out for the beam projected from the lantern. It plays its arm through the arc of light, and shadows flash across the woman's face as she eyes us. I wonder whether her summers are any greater in number than Rebekah's, yet the woman's features are slack, rather like Aunt Meg's, and there is suffering behind the grime. Her skin is tawny with dirt, rather like the skin of a pear that is bruised and rotting from the inside; skin which grows tough by dint of holding the badness in. She taps the infant on the back and rubs its legs, before she says, 'Well? What d'you want?'

Her breath is thick with gin, her teeth brown and uneven. She leaves her mouth partially open even after speaking, as though the sore on her lower lip causes her pain.

'It's Hester White. You'll be expecting me,' I say, attacking each word to give it a hard edge and show I am not an interloper. 'Me and my cousin, here, we've come . . . to work with Bessie, on account of Mr Morton's invitation. Like what my Aunt Meg used to and—'

'The devil you have.' The woman snatches a glance at the cooing infant and continues in a lower tone, 'I ain't seen that slack-Harry in three days. No more than I've seen his sister, Bessie. I don't know nothing about you coming here. For all I know, he's tired of that whore at The Birdcage and you're his next trollop. Don't think you're special, my girl. He'll tire of you, just like all the rest; and then you shall get it ladled at you, strong and hot you hear! No, I don't know nothing about you—'

Her words sheer off and she ends with a little grunt; a series of grumblings and mutterings replacing any coherent language until, the baby beginning to show signs of distress, she begins again, 'I don't wonder he's got himself into a fix or summat.' This is with the onset of tears. 'I shouldn't trouble about that Jack-Sneak, I know, but what about my rent money? And who's to provide for the baby?'

'Don't fret, Mrs Morton,' I say, trying to mollify, but instead nettling her.

'Fret! Fret!' she cries bitterly, eyes flaring with contempt. 'But I do fret, for what else am I to do? Three years since, why I – Daisy Morton – looked as fresh and round as you, now look at me! So if you sees him, you tell him from me that he can . . . go . . . back . . . to . . . his whore.' She cuts the sentence into four parts by reaching down, retrieving and then throwing out into the darkness in turn a man's boot, an empty bottle, a hat and a rag. She glances at the infant again, as though its innocence might moderate the volume of her voice, but proceeds anyway to shout: 'Clear off then, both of you. And tell him to clear off, or I shall do for him, damn my eyes if I don't.'

At this, she wipes her nose on her sleeve and a single sob escapes her lips before she takes up the lantern, brandishes it and dashes it to the ground in one last act of rancour. It rolls at my feet, coming to rest in the soft soil, with its wick still emitting a weak light. Morton's wife steps back into the shadows before the door is snapped shut and the bolt is drawn.

This interview with her and the unexpected absence of both Bessie and the man himself throws up feelings of panic and confusion. Rebekah also seems stunned by the turn of events, for she stares at the door with a look of incomprehension, as though no door might ever be opened again to us and, to whichever point of the compass we turn, the same closed door will face us.

I retrieve the lantern and raise it to shoulder height so the light penetrates the night as far as the cottage boundary. The sudden repulsion of night seems to have an effect on Rebekah and she moves forward with active eyes.

'Look,' she whispers, again stepping forward.

Nothing appears out of the ordinary. The rough-hewn palings, sparse shrubs and scattered ashes might belong to any number of plots this side of the Thames. Rebekah takes up a stick of wood and pokes at a heap of cinders. I follow her and lower the lantern. She jabs her stick deep into the topsoil and fishes out a length of rag. She disinters a petticoat, two woollen stockings, a shawl, a hat and a necklace of wooden beads. She then kneels, scrapes the earth aside and pulls out what appears to be a pair of boys' corduroy breeches and a jacket. I know such clothing is not unique, but I recall the description in Lady Appleton's letter to Rebekah and wonder if these last items once belonged to Edward. Rebekah tucks the soiled breeches and jacket under her arm. As she does so, I squat down, re-bury the other items and flatten the soil to disguise our excavation, and there in the powdered earth is a pewter pincushion in the shape of a pig and a bobbin of scarlet thread.

'Why would he bury clothes and trinkets that are to be sold?' I whisper. 'Why let them become soiled and degraded?'

Rebekah says nothing and we stand mute, deep in thought, our conjecture only ended by a man's voice, distant yet growing louder, some yards away towards Crabtree Row. A flush of heat radiates from within me but is gone in an instant and leaves a clammy coldness against my skin, colder and damper even than the thinning fog. Rebekah draws her fingers to her lips, as though she cannot be certain a sound might not escape by accident and expose our position. She draws me close and whispers, 'It may be Morton. We cannot let him catch us with these garments. Come, we might run to the privy and hide until he is inside the cottage.'

Rebekah takes the lantern and holds it close to her body, her left arm raising her shawl to shield the light. Hunched, we scurry down to the brick building at the bottom of the garden. The privy door is no more than a half-dozen weather-beaten timbers lashed together with rope and nails. With the lower hinge seemingly rusted away, the door is pitched at an angle, the base scraping against the dirt floor as Rebekah pulls it open.

With the air so still, the stench withheld in that confined space is concentrated and, by opening the door, we decant the full force of its fetidness into our own lungs. I gag and hold my belly. Rebekah cups her mouth and issues an empty retch. Without conferring, we both draw the corners of our shawls over our mouths in an attempt to dilute the potency of the rancid air.

Rebekah places the lamp on the floor and the source of the noxious air is revealed: the brick and timber latrine set in the back of the building is filled to the very throat with jute-wrapped parcels of varying sizes, each bundle stained with patches of a black resinous substance redolent of a cat-and-rabbit-fur dresser's manufactory.

Rebekah touches her forefinger to the uppermost package and, by doing so, she unfurls a fold of fabric, revealing a crescent of pitch-stained wood into which a row of ivory pegs has been drilled. The action also releases another wave of acrid air, so thick with putrefaction that this time I retch and dispel a mouthful of bile which spills down my skirts. Then a strange event happens. As I wipe the bitter-tasting evacuation from my chin, I cannot remove my eyes from the wood and the pegs, and as I stare at the odd contraption, I remember the shape of the crescent and the order of the plugs. Some are larger than others and the irregular pattern in which they are placed is as familiar to me as the twists of rag with which I used to tie my boots. Yet it is the present context which prevents my mind from knowing the object immediately. Then, gradually, my mind clears and I recall our last meeting. I remember the light that shone in her dull eyes, the joy which coloured her words as she spoke of her new life, her new opportunity. In my mind's eye I see her throwing her head back and laughing. It is with this image playing behind my eyes that I realise the wooden crescent is not wooden at all; and the ivory pegs were not carelessly hammered in, for they are not pegs: they are Annie Allsop's teeth.

I stare at the curved jawbone, dark flesh and black blood still viscid upon it, ragged of edge as though torn away with great force, pegged with more teeth than she ever did need; and I wonder at Annie's suffering and I want to ask Rebekah if Annie was long dead before they hacked the bone away from her skull, if she was insensible to such a base deed; but the possibility of such brutality on a living and conscious soul is too much for me to consider, so I remain silent.

It is not until Morton's voice grows loud enough to discern his individual words that I am aware of his proximity. He must have entered the plot at the top gate and is now halfway down the garden, by the old well. The prospect of being discovered presses on my bladder and softens my knees to such an extent that I lurch to the left, dislodging another parcel. It unravels, revealing a flap of leathery skin sticky on the underside, the topside swart with long tresses of human hair, still plaited in the manner Annie favoured, the roots still congealed with flesh from her scalp. Then all becomes black. But my eyes are still open and, as they adapt to the darkness, it is apparent Rebekah has extinguished the lantern. In the darkness Morton's voice sounds closer than ever.

'Come on, Bill,' he says. 'I can't do it on my own.'

'Can't it wait till tomorrow, Jack?' It's Corby's voice. 'I ain't got the stomach for it tonight.'

'Eight guineas says you have.'

There is a pause as Corby considers the offer.

'Do we have to be handling a Thing tonight?'

'You ain't going soft on me now?'

'No. I'm just tired. I'm going into the cottage to have a kip, like you promised.' Corby's voice is fainter now.

'We've business to conclude tonight. You can have an hour but no more,' Morton calls after him.

'Whatever you please.' Corby must be entering the cottage door for his voice fades.

Morton mumbles to himself and at first I believe he is kicking the side of the well cover, but the noise is wood on wood and I suppose he must be working the lid of the well loose, banging it up and down out of anger. He seems to exhaust himself and there is a final thud, as though he throws his weight on its surface. There is a slurping noise followed by glass breaking against the privy wall, followed by Morton incongruously breaking out into a tuneless song. All this time, I breathe short and uneven, my heartbeat tasting heavy, sounding thick in my ears.

The caterwauling grows louder and there is a shadow discernible through the door slats, before the dark mass leans its weight against the door. He must be less than a foot from us. I breathe in, holding my breath, and this last inhalation pulls in the scent of him: the gin, the tobacco, the staleness from his groin. Then, through the gaps in the timber, a fine, warm spray wets the back of my hand and Morton sighs. He walks away, singing a verse of 'The Nut-Brown Maid', and the smell of his urine rises, yeasty and sour.

It must be a full five minutes before we move. Rebekah pushes at the door, inches it open, until a vague moonlight colours the black privy interior grey.

'Are you all right, Hester?' she asks, inclining her head towards me.

Unable to address, let alone express, my own feelings, my features remain set, my voice monotone as I say, 'Do you realise they are teeth, Rebekah? Human teeth?'

'Yes. Morton's baseness knows no depths. It's almost too awful to—'

'They're Annie Allsop's. I know them to be Annie's.'

'Dear God. What depravity has taken place here? I'm so sorry, Hester.'

She starts to draw me to her. But I don't want comfort, I don't want soft warmth. Deep inside, my intentions are savage. With a cold, wild feeling, all I want is revenge for Annie, for Edward, for Matthew; all of them. I want Morton to be accountable. Not only Morton, but his cronies too. I start to push past Rebekah, muttering, 'He shall answer for this!' My face is stony, my lips compressed, entirely convinced I might singlehandedly upbraid Morton. She must guess both my intent and the reckless stupidity of it, for she folds her fingers around the top of my arm like the tender stroke of a nettle, and I feel the sting of her rebuke, even before she speaks.

'Hester. We can't rage against men such as Morton. We cannot use force against force; a little fire is quickly trodden out. We must make a great blaze, one which will raze these people to the ground. We must return to Mr Truman at the New Police and present him with what we have witnessed.' She slackens her grip, drops her arm and says, 'Now, look away, Hester. For, with the utmost care and respect, I must retrieve a sample of . . . of what has been done to Miss Allsop, to present it to Mr Truman, to be certain he understands the gravity of the matter this time.'

I direct my gaze to the wall, whilst Rebekah takes up one of the packages and wraps it in the clothing she excavated.

'Do you suppose,' I whisper. 'Do you suppose they were limbs and hands we carried across town with Morton and Corby, not plate and linen after all?'

Rebekah stops, but neither raises her eyes nor answers my question, perhaps the subject matter being too unimaginable to allow for either acknowledgement or proffered solace.

She returns to her folding and wrapping and I think uneasily of the bandbox I carried that day, recall the weight of it; the dimensions just large enough to house two hands and two feet, or perhaps a quantity of muscle, or even a head. I sense bile rising in my throat again and find myself breathing through my mouth and not through my nostrils, in order to occlude the odour of Annie's rotting chin. But the stench still enters my nose; and the smell of death, together with the thought of flesh decomposing in that hat-box, quite slows my own heart to the point that I know I will faint. It is Rebekah's voice which calls me back to myself.

'Hester. Hester, stay with me. We cannot risk being found here. Are you back with me?'

I nod but cannot speak. Rebekah takes my arm and, with life still coursing strong in our veins, and our bodies still whole, we leave Annie's tomb behind us and with great haste we return to Arlington Street, breathless by the time we arrive.

We enter the garden door quietly, subdued, and press on into the house. It is Tilly, the housemaid, whom we encounter first. She appears thrown that we are dressed in servants' garb. She bobs her head and keeps her eyes on the floor, perhaps heeding advice that Peggy might have dispensed to accommodate such unusual circumstances.

'Tilly,' Rebekah says. 'I wish you to fetch my needlework box from my room. The one in tooled lavender leather. Are you familiar with it?'

'Yes, Miss.'

'We'll remain here until you've brought it to us.'

'Of course, Miss.'

She leaves, her eyes still cast downwards. After washing our hands, Rebekah draws a bowl of water from the pump, unwraps the bundle of clothing and peels back the layers until only the jawbone remains. She dips the cambered bone into the water, slow and respectful, as though it is a nursling being wetted in a font. Then she removes her cap and wraps the jaw in it. When Tilly delivers the box and is dismissed, Rebekah unclasps it, removes the contents of threads, pins, bobbins and scissors, until the silk lining is all that remains, then she lays the body part in its small casket and closes the lid.

Rebekah touches her fingers to the casket's dimpled surface, then brushes the back of her hand beneath her eyes, catching the teardrop which steals down her cheekbone. With her eyes fixed on the box, she says, 'Oh, Hester. I cannot conceive we have been brought to this. When I first witnessed the disappearance of Martha last April, and soon after began to pen those lists of missing people, of course I couldn't rule out foul play; but here we are in February, so few months since I was living in a world of ignorance and innocence, and we have stumbled upon a degree of wickedness that exceeds my wildest nightmares.' She pauses and, without moving her head, she lifts her eyes to meet mine. Her brows are raised in the centre, softening her countenance, lending her a look of childish simplicity. She moistens her lips and says, 'Yet, these past few months have also brought your . . . friendship into my life and I cannot regret that.' She speaks more slowly now, as though feeling her way with her language. 'You see, Hester . . .'

This second pause is unusual, augmenting the intensity of the already charged atmosphere. She blinks. Her eyes move and she watches my lips. My heart begins to pant and the words I have rehearsed so often in my mind crowd on my tongue and will not break forth. Such sweet thoughts hive in my mind, but none can I speak. Voices in my head tell me that this is the moment I have waited for all my life; that every wind, every tide has been drawing me to this point. As my heart pulses tender and hot, my mind is awash with sensibility, and from sensibility comes susceptibility, and from susceptibility comes self-doubt, until one by one my emotions conspire and take mastery of me; they force me to question that such a moment can ever be true: why, after all, would a woman as intelligent, as magnificent as Rebekah Brock, look twice at me? And in this awful, weak state of prevarication the opportunity is lost to me by a simple knock at the door.

'Enter,' she says, her eyes on me to the last, as though something late might still be settled. But the seconds bustle forward, and as Ned enters, the episode is over.

'Yes, Ned,' she says, turning to face him.

'Miss Brock, Mr Rudd from your uncle's town house is outside. He says he has a message from young Mr Calder, quite an urgent one I—'

Rebekah does not wait to hear the end of Ned's sentence. She steps nimbly past him and slips through the doorway, her shape lost to me in an instant. Ned furrows his brow, gives a half-smile and moves aside. By the time I arrive in the hallway, Rebekah is walking away from the closed front door with a note in her hand. She looks up for an instant, then with eyes still devouring the paper, she says, 'It's Calder, Hester. He's received my letter, at his club.' She stops, apparently short of breath, then re-reading it she says, 'He says his head is quite clear of opium and that he feels a fool to have been duped by Blister. He says none of us is safe until Blister is caught. I am to meet with Calder at his surgical practice and rooms. They're on Little Windmill Street. He's always talked about them but I've never been before.'

She speaks rapidly without pausing, so excited and relieved she is to read that Calder is well and can help us bring an end to these dark deeds. But I cannot ignore the twist of jealousy I experience at the brightness conjured in Rebekah at the prospect of seeing Calder.

'When do we have to be there?' I venture, unable to disguise my surliness.

Rebekah frowns and says, 'Why, Hester, you must stay here of course. I will go alone.' There is no sharpness to her tone, but nevertheless, in my sensitive state, I receive it fully barbed. 'Calder is sending a carriage for me and I am to meet him at his rooms at ten o'clock,' she continues. 'But before I leave, I shall send Ned with a note to the New Police,' she goes on, 'requesting Mr Truman to attend here as a matter of urgency. You must be here to receive him, present him with the contents of the casket, and explain exactly what it is we witnessed at Morton's homestead and where he will find the evidence he needs.'

Suddenly, panic renders me breathless. Daunted by the prospect of facing Mr Truman alone without Rebekah composed and articulate by my side, I cannot understand why we must divide at such a crucial moment. How simple life might be if we could shape time to our need, but instead its silent footsteps walk on, leaving me in their wake.

Rebekah turns and begins to ascend the stairs before stopping. Leaning slightly over the banister, she says, 'We should attend to our toilette, Hester.'

She turns, climbs one more step then stops again, her shadow long and dark.

'Perhaps,' she says carelessly, 'once you are ready, you might come to my bedroom and help me to finish dressing.'

So, is this what it amounts to? The comfortable order of the universe returns and the circle is closed to me: Rebekah is the mistress and I am the servant.

I respond with a curt, 'Yes, Miss,' and effect a prim curtsey. As soon as my fit of pique is spent, I regret my tone, but Rebekah only slows for the smallest moment before continuing across the landing to her room without acknowledging me further.

It is in a mood of peevishness that I wash my face, tidy my hair and change into a plain blue day-dress. The same feeling of discontentment haunts me as I sit on the edge of the counterpane and, as each minute passes, I become increasingly sullen and resentful. I should be grateful that the danger has passed, and that Calder is safe. But I find I have begun to see Calder as a rival for Rebekah's attentions. The often petulant and less mature part of my character begins to dominate my feelings and I give it liberty to do so. Why is he the piper calling Rebekah's tune when I long for her affection and trust to be directed primarily at me? How quickly he is recovered from his addictions, and how readily she goes to him.

My thoughts are clouded for some time and I rumble on with the threat of growing anger, then gradually a ray of sanity clears my head and I begin to feel shamed by my aspersions and jealousy. Could I ever have competed with a sibling's lifetime of affection? Moreover, the feelings I have for Rebekah have now gone beyond sisterly. Resentment and envy still colour my thoughts, but despite my frustration, hope still prevails within me.

At a quarter past nine, I rise and leave my room. I pause on Rebekah's threshold to give ear to the sounds within, but all is silent. As I move weight from one foot to the other, the floorboards give a creak. There is a rustle of material from inside her room, then Rebekah says, 'Come in.'

I enter the room and close the door gently behind me. Rebekah is standing at the foot of the bed. She takes a step towards me and our eyes meet for an instant, but I am forced to look away. I stand, mute and awkward. Rebekah, clasping her hands before her, says:

'Are you well, Hester?'

'Yes,' I say softly.

'Are you sure?' she persists.

'Yes. I am quite well.' This time my tone is irritable and, with unbidden tears standing in my eyes, I walk towards the dressing table and take up her hairbrush, just as a maid might do. Rebekah follows and, standing behind me, she places her hand on my shoulder. A sudden sigh escapes my lips and the skin beneath her hand glows white hot.

'Are you afraid?' she tries again, but I can't even look at her reflection in the mirror, let alone speak my reply.

She squeezes her fingers and the blood throbs in my veins. My heart feels full, too full, and I close my eyes against the sweet agony which courses through me. I drop the hairbrush and am forced to lean against the dresser to steady myself. Rebekah, with some urgency, places both her hands on my shoulders and begins to turn me around, to face her. Now unable to avoid her gaze, at last our eyes meet. She searches my face, as though trying to read me, trying to decipher a language she does not yet understand.

I tilt my head and my breath comes short and fast, and all I can do is look at her with pure adoration. Logic tells me to speak, to tell her all I feel; let her unravel what it all means. But the strength of my emotions quite overpowers me and I cannot frame my words into sentences. I can do no more than sigh my love out to her and think impossible thoughts.

Then Rebekah's eyes narrow and her lips relax into a smile, as though the puzzle is about to yield its solution. She appears to dismiss the shallowness of deduction, replacing it instead with an instinct that is sensual and deep.

With her eyes fixed on mine, her right hand drops and I feel her touch descending my arm until her hand slips under the cuff of my sleeve. Her thumb is hot on my wrist, a place no other touches. Then she brushes her fingertips against the back of my hand and holds them still, as though drawing me out. She searches for consent in my features. Then her face breaks out into a smile and her eyes ask, 'Do you?' And, standing in her steady beam, my eyes answer, 'Yes.'

She draws her arm about my waist and pulls me gently towards her and she speaks low, without hurry, in tones that satisfy my ear like no other sound: 'You love me,' she says. 'You love me,' she repeats. 'I knew it, but didn't understand it before; didn't understand my own feelings until now.' Her words feel their way into my mind, light a path towards a new future.

Her speech is soft and low; warmth radiates out from within her as though a lantern dwells deep inside her, throwing out fingers of light that reach beyond the confines of her frame. I can almost hear the swish of material as the veil that has always dwelled between us is suddenly pulled apart: I know I shall remember this moment for the rest of my days. And, at this time of the night, when noises are culled and lights are extinguished, my day is not ending; my life is just beginning.

Emboldened, I reach my hand to her face and gently trace the curve of her cheek until my hand pauses on her neck. I touch soft fingers to her breastbone, then move my hand over her yielding breast, her flesh warm beneath the fabric of her gown. At this the colour in her cheeks heightens and her eyes widen. Lost in each other's gaze, I feel her hand on my own breast, warm and sensual, her touch tender yet penetrating. She applies gentle pressure and I let out a little gasp as the movement of her hand calls up a frisson of delight in my belly, then a deeper and more demanding contraction further down. I begin to feel liquid and hot between my legs and my head is swimming as I slip my hand about her waist and pull her to me. The scent of gillyflower rises from the warmth of her skin, and our breathing is the only sound. She bends her head towards mine and I raise my arms to encircle her neck. The world disappears, and the only elements are our shared air and our lips drawing closer together.

At last they touch, compliant and resistant at the right times, in the right measure; and the moment is more beautiful than I could ever have conceived. She presses her body against me but I do not yield, and instead push my hips closer still. I am thrilled to sense the flesh of her belly through the weave of her dress and the fullness of her breasts, flame-hot against me. The unrelenting softness of the kiss sends a thrill to my heart, and the force of my heartbeat seems to pulse against the walls. Then Rebekah's thigh slips between mine and I feel as though a sun has risen inside me, the slow warmth ever rising. She moves against me, pressing then drawing away, pushing her thigh in a gentle agitation, over and again, eliciting a slick heat from deep inside me. And this rocking motion, this blissful, straining tension, fetches such ecstasy from within me. A new thrill comes in waves, pulsing, molten, and it spreads with a hot blush and a quiver, soft as syrup, gentle as the filaments of a feather, until an unknown happiness is awakened in me and, once liberated and unimpeded, it blushes within me, every nerve in my body trembling with the fullness of life.

Rebekah must experience the same, for I feel the motion of her hips against mine, then she issues a little moan, before the tautness of her muscles melts away and she is slack against me.

As the passion subsides, a pleasurable ease with one another replaces it and she draws me to the cleft of her bosom where her heart is loud and fast. I lean my head back and unashamedly look up at her face, for I am no longer a shy girl; I am a woman who knows reciprocated love.

Her expression is so intense and I command her unbroken attention, all of her, and this creates a sudden and delicious softness in my soul, a rounding of edges, a sense of fitting completely into life's shape. Such a smile shines out of her eyes, and they are more radiant than I've yet seen them; brighter even than sunlight on water.

I feel myself suddenly unique and scrutinised, and the pleasure of it warms me. I pull her towards me, squeeze my arms about her. Our faces brush and I lay my lips on her cheek, her complexion perfectly smooth, and I am awash with feelings as new and fresh as summer rain.

Rebekah inhales slow and deep, then whispers, 'Hester, I wish to walk with you all the days, till the darkness sends us home.'

Her voice is tender and I cannot believe life can be so joyous. I fairly turn in on myself with delight at the thought. For the first time I am truly happy, as happy as a church bell. I catch the moment and hold it and it is good.

The knock at the bedroom door gives me a start. At first I am so deeply inside myself that I cannot think what to do. Rebekah is also slow to respond, which invites a second, tentative knock.

'Yes?' she says, her voice distant, as though back in another world.

'The carriage is here, Miss,' Tilly says.

'Yes. Thank you, Tilly. I'll be down shortly.'

Rebekah releases her arms from about me and a rush of cold air replaces the shape of her body as she steps away. She busies herself, fetching her coat, collecting her bonnet and gloves. Then she faces me. And here we stand, invested in our own separate silences, until a look from Rebekah draws us together. Our lips meet once again, and as I drink in a further draught of her, our kiss holds the promise of passions yet to come.

'I shall tell Calder what you mean to me,' she says. 'I'm sure we'll be back within the hour. Take care while I am gone, Hester.'

'And you too, Rebekah. For life has nothing to show me without you.'

Her look alone gives me solace until she takes my hand in hers and at last I understand the depth of our connection; for anxieties are forgotten, trust has been established and those long-anticipated passionate nights will now become reality.

At last, she turns to leave, picking up an envelope, written in her hand and addressed to Mr Truman, and tucks it under her arm. We descend the stairs to the hallway, where she gives the letter to Ned and presses him to make haste in delivering it. While buttoning herself into her coat, she never takes her eyes from mine; as though, like me, she is wringing the moment for all its pleasure until the very last drop is spent. Finally she takes my hand, presses it to her lips then whispers, 'Till tonight, Hester.' Her arms encircle me and I am enveloped by her. They say that nothing in the world is single, that those who seek love also search for their missing half. Here in Rebekah's arms, I know that I am complete. Then she is gone away into the night.

I stand staring at the closed door, unwilling and unable to remove my eyes from the spot where she last stood. I touch my fingers to the coat-stand with a feeling of universal amity; Rebekah may have touched it yesterday or may brush past it tomorrow. I'm certain the clock in the corner has a mellower voice, and the umbrella stand is much more pleasing to the eye than it has been before. Why, the very house exudes a fragrance of life, of promise, which was absent just an hour since.

As I turn about, I notice Rebekah has left her gloves on the hallway table. I take them up, draw them to my face and inhale. Then there is a knock at the door. She must have realised she forgot them.

'I'll get it, Peggy,' I shout, the joy plain to hear in my voice.

Smiling, I run to the door, gloves in hand, slip the latch and throw the door open. But it is not Rebekah, which alone quite rubs the gilt off the moment. At once I recognise who the caller is, and the realisation puts all my feelings of contentment out with a single stroke.

CHAPTER SIXTEEN

'**M**rs Tyler,' I say. 'What brings you here at such a late hour? Come in and warm yourself by the fire.' Despite greeting Mrs Tyler with kind words, at once I sense foreboding at the arrival of this unexpected guest.

Her chin is trembling and her eyes are swimming. 'I must speak with Miss Brock,' she says, breathless and rasping.

'I'm afraid she's not here.'

At this her eyes grow wide. She snatches my hand, her fingers tight about my own. 'Where is she? Not come to any harm, has she?' Now the full spate of unshed tears comes, the woman inconsolable.

'She left but a moment ago and she is well, I can assure you.' My voice is certain but my heart beats faster in response to Mrs Tyler's questions. Doubts begin to race through my mind.

Mrs Tyler seems to take heart from my reply and I am able to release my hand from hers and take her arm instead, lead her into the hallway. Her coat is made of coarse woollen cloth; perhaps twenty years ago it would have fitted the fullness of her figure, but the wearer now being the far side of sixty, the coat hangs loose about her shoulders and long about the cuffs. Three days since, her cap was as white as her hair, but now it is tinged with the drabness of the streets, as though she has not known the comfort of her own home since last I cast eyes on her.

'There is a fire lit in the drawing room; you must warm your-self,' I say, leading her towards the door on the right. 'I shall ring for some food, you must be hungry . . .'

'Supper is not what I want,' she whispers. She takes her seat slowly, her eyes never leaving mine. 'I must see Miss Brock. When will she return?'

'Why, I'm certain she'll be back by eleven o'clock. Might I add that we were both very sorry to learn of your recent bereavement.'

This last sentence provokes a noticeable effect on the woman; at once her restless fingers stop. She draws both hands to her mouth and she begins to rock herself gently back and forth, her eyes darting, as though suddenly uncertain of her surroundings. A coal snaps on the fire and she jumps to her feet with a start and looks about the room.

'Mrs Tyler?' I say, casting my words gently, trying to draw her back to me. 'Mrs Tyler, you're quite safe here. We're in the drawing room of Miss Brock's house in Arlington Street. Do you recall?'

I don't believe she either sees or hears me, so far away in her mind she seems to be. But eventually she nods, seats herself again and simply says, 'I shall wait for Miss Brock.'

She sits in this same attitude for some half of an hour, her eyes never still and her hands ever restless on her lap, looping and casting those invisible stitches. She refuses any offers of refresh-ment by a shake of her head, and her only audible utterance is Rebekah's name. 'Miss Brock,' she says, as though her mind is foggy and the only means of conjuring an object to which she might moor herself is to form the shape of Rebekah's name. And each time she says the words, Rebekah somehow seems further away from me, and by the time the mantel clock strikes eleven, I am in a state of considerable alarm. Suddenly, the unimaginable threat of spent time is on me again and where an hour since Rebekah was quite safe and expected, now she is late and in danger.

'Mrs Tyler,' I begin. 'Miss Brock's engagement is taking a little longer than I first believed; so, if you please, I would have you tell your news to me, that I may impart it to Miss Brock tomorrow.'

'I must tell it to Miss Brock and no other,' the woman rejoinders.

'But Miss Brock is not here, Mrs Tyler,' I persist. 'And if, as you alluded to earlier, she is in danger of harm, then it is not aiding her to withhold what you know, is it?'

The woman frowns, looks me up and down, but says nothing.

'If you know something, Mrs Tyler, you must tell me. Rebekah was expected home this hour but is not yet here. I have no explanation. You must tell me what you know.'

Nothing.

'Then I must ask you to leave. And may God have mercy on your soul if you have kept back something when you should have spoken.'

This last threat seems to cut deeper than I might have hoped and finally provokes a response. She sighs then straightens her back and begins.

'I knew he'd come back, that awful man.'

'Blister?'

She nods. 'After you left, I went up to Gabe, tried to reason that page out of his hand, but he wouldn't give it up. I took another paper, see, to trick him, and when he nodded off, I swapped the page. He come to a bit, clenched his hand, then he seemed satisfied the original were still there.' At this point, she rummages around in the lining of her coat, retrieves a scrap of paper, the torn page from the register, and hands it to me. 'As soon as I heard them carriage wheels return, I knew it would be Blister. I ran out of the back door and out onto the heath. The wind was tricky, whistling like the devil's breath.

'I walked the heath, biding my time, and then crept home later when all was quiet. I went in to Gabe; but he'd gone and died. They never look the same when the ghost's left 'em. It was his body all right, with those poor broken fingers, savaged by that man, but it weren't him no more. I stroked his face one last time, but he weren't my Gabe any more, just a parcel of cold skin and a bunch of damp clothes; as chill as the fog on the heath.'

'I'm so sorry, Mrs Tyler.'

'Oh, don't give pity to me, Miss. I'm not worth a speck of it. I brung it all on myself. I've been forging the links on my chains for many a year, and now they're weighing me down something cruel; but they're all of my own making. Five-and-twenty years since; that was when I should have chosen better, should have been stronger.'

'But how could you have stopped your husband doing what he did? You did nothing, but be forced into complicity, be an obedient wife.'

She laughs at this. Not a merry laugh, but a bitter one.

'You think I'm talking about the register? You think it's all about the vulgar tale of the gentleman, Septimus Brock, being wed to that woman, then coming to realise he might have married to better advantage and cancelled his debts? You think it's all about rashness, regret and deceit? Oh, I wish that were all of it. But, that's only the beginning. I came here this night to reveal a truth to Rebekah Brock that has been hidden from her for nigh a quarter of a century; it concerns her mother, the birth of her brother and the part I played in it.

'No more than a week after Gabriel and Septimus Brock cooked up their scheme, Mr Brock came calling at our house in the dead of night. Fast asleep under the blankets I was, when the knock came upon the cottage door. It didn't wake Gabe, and for a time I thought it was in my head. Over the years, I've often wondered what our lives would have been like if we'd ignored that knock.

Perhaps he would have moved on, found someone else. But I shook Gabe out of his slumber and sent him down to answer it. Septimus Brock was surely the last person we expected to see, but there he was, standing in our parlour, that cold look on his face. I'd only ever seen him from afar, but where his older brother was rounded and gentle looking, Septimus was hard and pinched about the face.

'He said I was needed to help with a birthing – the lady was wanting a handywoman present with her doctor to preserve her decency. And Mr Brock had come for me, saying we were to meet the physician at the lady's house. Well, I told him straight that I'd barely any experience in such things; I'd nursed a sister through her first, and I'd lost three of my own, but I didn't think I was the right woman for this job. He wouldn't have none of it, though. He said there wasn't time to find another, so I must do. Gabe must've sensed I was troubled and said he would come with us; prove to me there was nought to be feared. Mr Brock was easy on the point, appeared to take neither threat nor offence from such a suggestion; it made no difference to him if Gabe went or not. So, off we set.

'Well, we were taken in his carriage on the road to Kenton and we galloped through the dark like demons doing the devil's work. Once, I asked Mr Brock how I may best work to aid the doctor when we arrived, and he replied, "In silence, woman. In silence." He never said another word for the duration of the journey. He set my hair on end, I can tell you. Gabe just kept whispering to me that the physician would direct me, but I was not keen, I should say.

'We arrived at the house, must have been two o'clock in the morning. A smart house, not a manor or nothing, but a rich man's house for sure. We swept in through a gate in the wrought-iron railings and pulled up outside the front of the house, made gay with white paint and a balcony.

'We was ushered in through the front door – the front door, mark you. Then we was sent to the kitchens, so I might find a pinny to wear. The house was all in slumber, or so we thought. But in the kitchen, there was a maid with a girl of two or three years; earnest little thing the child was, with black hair and inquisitive eyes. She came up to me and her little face was all serious, as though she were trying to make sense of it all. I took her on my lap for a moment and she were as good as gold. Then Septimus rang for me and the child returned to her nurse, back to her cup of warm milk, and up the stairs I went, up to the lady's lying-in room.

'Well, she was fit to burst, fat as a goose her belly was. When Mr Brock announced that the doctor could not come, well I nigh set to fainting. He told me I must be brave for the lady's sake, so I set about preparing her as best I could. The woman was calm, called him "Sep" like she knew him well. I was careful and gentle and the baby boy came quite easy after only a couple of hours. Little scrap of a thing it was, but it took suck right away. The woman hardly looked worse for wear, neither. She sat up, asking for the babe. But Mr Brock said she must rest, so she lay down, happy to do his bidding.

'He turned to me and, never saying thank you or nothing, he said I should go home. I stopped on the threshold, intent on demanding at least a shilling or two for my trouble, but Mr Brock was on my heels, like he knew what I was thinking. He stood over me, them hard eyes burning down into mine, and he says in a whisper so as the lady can't hear, "One more thing, Mrs Tyler. Remember what you have witnessed tonight. The baby is plump and strong, the mother is weak, spent; she might not last until sunrise." I says, "That's the wrong way round. You're mistaken, Mr Brock, the lady is—" But I never did finish my words, and the look on that man's face will haunt me till my dying day. Then he presses a purse of coins into my hand and says, "If you are asked, remember only the scene I have described. You are already in too deep, Mrs Tyler. You and your husband both. Just go, do not turn back, do not ask any questions." Well, I knows a threat when I hears one and I couldn't wait to get out of that house. I began to see just how wicked and clever Septimus was. He'd used me as a witness, see. He'd planned it from the first and knew he'd need someone to speak up for him. So off I went, and back to the woman's room went he. But when I got halfway down those stairs, I realised I'd not got my boots on; I took 'em off, see, when I was helping the woman, to keep my tread gentle.

'I turned back, but paused on the top step, wondering if I might do without them. But they'd only just been fixed up by the cobbler, and I can tell you new pegged soles don't come cheap. So, back I went. No sooner had I turned about than Mr Brock comes out of the birthing room. I was certain he'd see me, so I darted across the landing and into the shadows. But he wasn't going downstairs, after all; he just opened the door across the corridor. "Elizabeth, come now. Give me the boy," he said. I peeped out and there was a woman, dark haired, Jewish-looking. She was holding two babes in her arms. They weren't newborns; must've been at least three months old, I reckon, and the woman was crying. She said, "No, Sep. I know I said I could do it, but I can't." Well, this sent him into a rage. The light weren't bright, but by my eyes he was in a temper, for sure. "Give me my son," he says. "Or, by God, I'll be rid of you, and your precious Rosina."

'Well, there was a bit of to-ing and fro-ing and plenty of tears from the woman, then she yielded up the boy, took the girl back down the stairs, right past where I was standing. When she'd gone, I followed Mr Brock back to the birthing room. The door was almost closed but not quite. I put an ear to the crack and there was an odd, snuffling noise. I pushed the door a bit and peeped in.

'My eyes were set upon a scene of horror just inches from where I stood. Mr Brock was bending over the lady and his hands were smothering her mouth and nose, pressing down on her lips. Her arms and legs were thrashing about, pushing at his chest and face, then grasping at the air. Harsh sounds, wet sounds, came from her throat. Her breaths were tight and short, and all the time her eyes were wide with alarm and terror. I can't say how long it went on; I just know it stopped when no more air could be driven from her chest. The only noise in the room was Mr Brock's laboured breathing from the exertion of it all. He panted so heavy, it was like he'd sucked the air out of her and it was too much for his lungs to bear.'

From the beginning of Mrs Tyler's speech, I watch her eyes and listen to her words with growing horror and revulsion, but at the conclusion of this final revelation, I draw a sharp breath and say:

'Mrs Tyler, are you saying that Rebekah's mother was murdered at the hands of Septimus Brock?'

She nods, quick, eyes closed, cheeks damp, lips compressed. 'I didn't know it was her at the time,' she volunteers, her eyes blinking quickly. 'A week or so later, after church, we heard that Mr St John Brock, elder brother of Septimus, had been returning from his business trip and was set upon by a parcel of men and beaten to death; Septimus had witnessed it all, said it was over unpaid gambling debts, or some such nonsense. Everyone knew it weren't Mr St John what gambled and drank, but Septimus. But no one would speak up; and why would they? Same as me, we all feared the man's vengeance. When news got around that Mr St John's wife had died in childbirth just a week before her husband, we came to know just who the poor woman was that we visited that night and I came to understand it all better.'

'Stop, Mrs Tyler! Don't you see? If Septimus is capable of

murdering Rebekah's mother, then both Calder and Rebekah are in more danger than we ever suspected.'

I jump up from my seat as I speak, pace this way and that, with my hands clasped together.

'Rebekah is late; she's never late,' I mumble to myself. 'Something is wrong.' I turn to Mrs Tyler and say, 'You must stay here, Mrs Tyler. But I must go; I must warn Calder and Rebekah immediately.' I turn towards the door, but she rises and catches my sleeve.

'You can't go yet; there's more I must tell you. I have told lies in the past, God knows I regret it. But on my body I'm telling you the truth tonight.' She sobs now, but does not stop speaking. 'I should have told you everything back at the cottage.' She puts the back of her right hand to her mouth, then wipes tears and phlegm from beneath her nose. She swallows and breathes in, as though it might be her last breath, then says:

'I was just frightened of Septimus—'

'You should have trusted us,' I say.

'And I was a-feared of Miss Brock that night. Don't you recall? She had a fearsome temper on her.'

'You mustn't blame Rebekah!'

'I'm not blaming anyone, Miss. No one, save myself. I am grist to the Lord's mill and he waits to grind me down, his eternal judgement ever at my heels. I withheld the truth, Miss, because I am a coward. I was, and am still; but no more shall be.'

'Then tell me everything, Mrs Tyler. Tell me now!'

'On that awful night, as I watched that poor woman's final breath, I was rooted to the spot; I could neither breathe nor move. I turned my face away from that brutal act only to see that the little boy the Jewess had surrendered to Mr Brock was in a cradle, quite content, fidgeting his little arms and legs, just inches away from that hideous sight. I began to back away, but not before I noticed on the floor at the side of her bed, there was a bundle of rags. Except it wasn't rags, it was her baby, all blue and still, its little neck skewed in the middle, its little head bent back as though it were looking at its mother. But, of course, it weren't looking at no one.'

I cannot believe such words have been spoken, and with every fibre of my being I am willing this truth to be unsaid.

'Dear God,' I say. 'We got it wrong.' I press my fingers to my temples, but the blood still pounds in my ears. 'Blister isn't Septimus's son; it was Calder all along! But what about Rebekah?'

'I'm sorry I lied. God help me, I was false for the sake of Septimus Brock and now I'm doomed, for those who maketh a lie are cursed: that's what the Good Book says.'

Mrs Tyler lowers her head, her eyes contrite, but I have no time to console her. My only thought is to go to Rebekah.

I tell Mrs Tyler that she must wait in case Rebekah returns and I rush from the room. Seizing my cloak and bonnet, I run out of the house and into the cold night air. I hear only my footsteps and my heartbeat; other sounds of the city are lost to me.

I think only of pressing forward, one foot after another, until I reach Rebekah. The strategy I might apply to save her when I arrive is one thought too many for my mind, so on I push, for it is all I can do.

The further I travel towards Little Windmill Street, the more I am confounded by thoughts of Calder. I picture him in my mind, always a smile on his lips, ever mirth in his eyes, but is there a knife beneath his cloak? Or is he unaware that Septimus is his father? And surely his brotherly affection cannot be a lie?

On I roll alone with the fog, down broad stretches where street lamps are fewer, the gloom is denser, and not even the ghost of a footfall humanises the streets. My sense of unease increases and I begin to imagine movement in the shadows that instantly evokes an image of Rosina, drifting mysteriously through that curtain of drab garments, hovering silently in the shadows of Mrs Cohen's shop. The image persists, and recollection of her spectral appearance adds to my strained state of mind. I turn on my heels, and for a heartbeat I see her silhouette in the gloom behind me. I take a step forward, peer into the darkness.

'Who's there? Rosina?'

Of course there is no reply; there is no one there. Irritated by my own imagination and annoyed by the unnecessary delay, I turn about, and with renewed determination press on, until I eventually find myself on the corner of Little Windmill Street. The buildings are a mixture of shabby and smart and the haunt of the day's business has long since faded. With daylight road-traffic now absent and no townspeople astir, all is quiet.

The recollection that it was this part of town to which we carried the boxes for Morton and Corby does not escape me, and the puzzle of it all still confounds me. Where before Morton was fastened to Blister and Blister in turn was connected to Septimus, that no longer makes sense; and where does Calder fit in? Above all of this, I think of Rebekah and the sting of her uncle's plans and wicked deceit.

These thoughts deluge my mind as I shuttle my way down the street, criss-crossing from one side to the other to examine the numbers and the plaques, until, adjacent to a haberdashery, I notice a three-storey house, four windows wide.

I walk the length of the building, following the line of black palings that divides the edifice and the street. In the middle, the fencing curves alongside a path which leads to a black front door and there, to the left of the street door, is a plaque. 'School of Anatomy. Calder Brock, Doctor of Morbid Anatomy and Physiology'.

So, Calder is a very learned man and not simply a medical

physician after all. But the field of medicine he has chosen is not to soothe fevers or heal cuts and sprains; it is something quite different indeed.

As I stand in the shadows, prevaricating, I fret about Rebekah and the impending dangers which strew her path. But I see there is no sign of her carriage, and this gives me an earnest of hope. Perhaps Calder is detained or Rebekah never came here; perhaps she is waiting for me back at Arlington Street? It is through this medley of thoughts that my attention is drawn to the sound of a horse approaching.

Whether it is the lateness of the hour or the emptiness of the street, the noise of those clopping hooves galvanises me into action, and I am back in the present; the ignorance of future ills more useful to me now than the knowledge of them. I slip down into the shadows and crouch amongst the rats in the gutter as they nose for scraps.

The jingle of tack grows louder and a Berkshire waggon, with two silhouetted shapes behind the reins, begins to slow as it approaches the anatomy school. The driver pulls rein no more than ten paces from where I hide; the two men jump down and begin to loosen cables from the back of the waggon. With the night so quiet, I cannot risk running out into the street in hope of taking flight. But, certain to be discovered unless I move, I crawl on my hands and knees until I am obscured by the alleyway which runs between Calder's rooms and the haberdashery.

I stand and search with my hands through the darkness in hope of finding a place of refuge. I lay my palms over cold, clammy bricks, until I feel the raised framework of a doorway and my fingers catch a door handle, which I squeeze and gently turn. There is a squeak and a click, then I lean forward and the door opens, its hinges letting out the smallest of whimpers.

It is the smell which my senses note first: a peculiar odour, sickly and corrosive. I cannot place it. Wrinkling up my nose and breathing through my mouth, I cast my eyes about the room. It is small and sparsely furnished; just an old table in the centre with a solitary wax candle, and a charcoal stove on the chimney wall sweating out small vestiges of heat and light. Four wicker hampers are stacked, two over two, against a wall, and a passageway leads off to the right.

As I deliberate, considering whether to return to the alleyway or to press on through the corridor in hope of finding a different exit, footsteps and two men's voices sound from behind me. In the briefest of moments I drop to my knees and crawl behind the hampers, pulling my skirts about me and making myself as small as possible. Within a heartbeat, the door through which I entered is opened, and legs and boots draw closer as the two men from the waggon enter the room.

'Mr Paterson? You there?' The voice is Morton's and he projects it loud and coarse towards the inner door and the corridor.

From beyond the passageway, a man's voice answers, 'All right, all right. I'm coming.'

From my covert position, I raise my head, just enough to see between the two upper hampers. Morton is flattening his hair with the palm of his right hand, and his cohort, Corby, is sliding a wicker trunk from his shoulders. Corby ledges the box on the corner of the table and begins unthreading its straps. An arc of yellow light appears from the corridor and expands to fill the room, and following the light there is a man, smoothing the creases in his jacket and loosening his neckcloth.

'I was told to ask for you, Mr Paterson. So you're the new porter, then?' Morton asks, his voice ever blunt.

'I am, sir. Good evening to you, gentlemen.'

Corby frees the lid of the trunk, tips up the base and empties its cargo onto the table with a dull thump.

'What size today then?' Paterson enquires, sliding his spectacles along the bridge of his nose and inspecting the goods with a great deal of interest, his voice light and easy. But Morton and Corby are standing close together with their backs to me, so I cannot view the table top and see what Mr Paterson is scrutinising.

'We brung you a small,' says Corby, 'and a large small, too.'

'Not been in a box then?' Paterson asks, his tone accusatory now.

'How so?' replies Morton, testily.

'Well,' Paterson goes on, 'there's no sawdust in the hair, is there?'

'No, but—'

'I trust there are no marks on them? No sign of violent hands laid upon them?'

'Of course not.'

'Yet the subjects have no grave dirt about them. Am I to suppose they were stolen from a charnel-house?'

'Yes, that's it, Mr Paterson,' Morton says. 'They're lately come from a charnel-house,' he repeats.

Paterson seems satisfied and leans forward to study the wares. Morton moves to the right, thus creating a space through which I might look. But I wish I could not see, for the scene is unimaginable, beyond even the depravity I suspected of Morton and Corby.

I try to rationalise to the best of my capabilities. As unsavoury as some aspects are, I know that surgeons need to enhance their knowledge of the human form by examining what is left post-decease. Blister is perhaps some sort of broker for Calder, who I now know is such a physician. Morton and Corby are employed in meeting the demands of this vile market, and souls coming close to meeting their maker are 'helped' along their way by a night-sitter. So it never was a modest market in dead men's chattels; clothes and trinkets were just an inconvenience, some to be sold for small change and most to be buried or burned to disguise the greater crime. Then Morton and his cronies deliver an arm here and a leg there, for the surgeons to perform their studies.

As unpalatable as this is, body parts are indeed what I expect to see on the table top; parcels of varying sizes, such as we saw in Morton's privy, leaking fluids and putrefied. But in the yellow light of the ante-room, I behold a far more horrifying scene.

The 'small' Corby describes is an infant of not yet two summers. The fine, soft hair on his scalp, once kissed and smoothed by a mother, is plastered to his skin, as though it has lately been wetted. His skin is plumped with no visible injury or sign of disease to indicate why death has visited itself upon the child. For all the world he looks as though he sleeps and might yet wake to a sudden noise and the realisation his mother is not to hand.

The 'large small' lying at the infant's side perhaps owns some twelve years of age. She lies in the same peaceful attitude, as though she might have fatigued herself playing hopscotch and has found a bale of dry linen on which to rest. But she has been stripped of her clothes, and her hair is roughly shorn; I wonder if her tresses are already being sold at the wigmaker's. I have a sudden inclination to vomit, but swallow it back and try to breathe long and slow. Then Paterson says, 'I'll pay you sixteen guineas the pair.'

Morton hesitates, as though he might bargain for more. For more! Sixteen guineas would pay a weaver's wage for a year and better. So, limbs pay well, but it is fresh whole bodies supplied to order that is the lucrative business, the source of their filthy profits. Dear God, they're all in it together: supply governed by demand; servant by master; murderer by surgeon!

Paterson adds, 'Come now. Shake hands and let us take sup.'

Morton and Corby take turns to shake Paterson's outstretched hand, before the porter disappears into the shadows, returning with a bottle and three drinking vessels. Glasses are chinked, the contents drunk off, before being refilled and the process repeated. So the men toast their own health as the purse of monies is handed over, seemingly indifferent towards their items of trade. But there is more to come when Corby says glibly, 'I thought I might take the grinders from the older one, Mr Paterson. You know, to sell on separate, like.'

'Of course, go ahead,' Paterson says, ever the obliging gentleman.

Corby takes out a bradawl from his jacket, but I cannot watch. The operation is over swiftly, his quarry rubbed clean and wrapped in a length of cambric, the same as Annie's. Just as a deal is struck at the meat market, so this transaction is now complete, and the sides of meat on the table are packed in their hamper, which Corby fastens and then lifts.

'Over there, man. With the others,' Paterson says.

I shrink further down and take the shadows for my own, offering up a silent plea to God that I might remain undiscovered. The wicker casket creaks as Corby places it on top of the other hampers. The rear edge hangs over the lower hamper and affords me greater cover, for which I give thanks to Providence.

Morton and Corby take up their lantern, mumble some words of accord to the porter and take their leave. It is at this point I expect Mr Paterson also to leave the ante-chamber, return to the rooms he was previously occupying. But the porter tarries, softly humming to himself. He pours himself another gin and records an entry in a large register.

Eventually, some ten minutes after Morton and Corby leave, Mr Paterson fetches his coat and hat, extinguishes the candle on the table, takes up his lantern and departs. With only the glow from the stove giving any light, I crawl out from my refuge. When

I press the door handle, I imagine it is stiff with age. But as I push and rattle it in increasing alarm, I realise Mr Paterson must have locked it behind him as he left.

This sense of being trapped, of sharing the compact room with only cadavers and ghosts, sends my heartbeat into a frenzy. I am not alone: my fear becomes a creature in the room; I feel its cold breath on my skin and its obliqueness swallowing me.

It is with little thought for consequences that I snatch up the unlit wax-light, ignite its wick at the mouth of the stove, turn and enter the passageway. There are two doors, but both are locked against me and, just as a lost thing cannot be found till every cranny is searched, I am forced to move forward into thicker darkness until I find myself at the foot of a flight of steps. I ascend them, heedful of risk, but drawn by gain; breathing a sigh of relief at the promise of escape when I find a doorway at the top.

I twist the doorknob, my palm wet against the cold iron. I turn it with only a half-hope, yet it relents and the door swings open. As I enter, the smell finds my nose. It is a denser odour than that of the ante-room, but it has the same sour strains through it. I clap my hand to my mouth, but the aroma will not be stayed. It brings to mind fly-blown ham, mixed with urine and dog foulings. It is worsened by preserving chemicals bitter in the atmosphere. This must be where Calder does his work.

I follow the arc of light from my candle. The room is fourfold the size of the reception room and I move through it, coughing in response to the offensive air. On a table to the left, a large book of diagrams lies open. With the neatness of a methodical man, Calder's bottles and jars are arranged on a shelf, their labels turned forwards, written in a tidy hand: Nitrate of Silver, Spirit of Ammonia, Iodide of Potassium.

Eventually, I discover the source of the smell; on a low bench on the right, specimens of flesh have been left. As I navigate forward, I am obliged to walk alongside the table and, briefly, I glance at the remnants. From the mound of meat, I discover what must once have been an animal, a dog, its body stretched across the bench, a small pool of congealed blood beneath its nose.

Bound by a hideous fascination which stays my feet and chills my veins, I stand gaping. All four of its paws are nailed to the table on which it lies and it is greatly emaciated. The right flank is stripped of skin and hair, pelt and muscle peeled back, livid red flesh and white bones exposed to the air. I crane forward, both drawn and repulsed. One pendulous ear is cut away, the other matted with blackened deposits; perhaps the dog was once a setter or a pointer.

There is a swelling on the right foreleg, as though induced by a blow upon it, and I note a cut from where the skin is puckered as it has been folded back. The mouth is encrusted with dried sputum, the dry tongue pushed forward, and the eye; the clouded eyeball is sunken in its socket, surrounded by a great swelling on the side of the head. I stare into the dead eye and see it is not at peace.

Finally, I close my eyes against it and move on. But as I take up the wax-light, there is a whine, a faint whimper. I hold up the candle, searching the half-light with my eyes. The whine comes again, and this time is accompanied by a sudden movement from the muscle and flesh on the table. Fear breathes cold against the back of my neck as I watch the animal struggle convulsively. One spasm follows another until its whole frame is seized with violent tremors. Where before its mouth was mute, there is now sudden and shallow respiration. It attempts to draw its hind legs up towards its chest, as though trying to rise, to sit on its haunches. All the time its eye is upon me, appealing to me.

'Oh God. Oh Dear God Almighty in Heaven. What manner of . . .' I cannot finish my sentence with coherent words; I can only let out a series of moans, punctuated by the words Jesus

Christ and Lord. I turn about, my only thought to escape the sight, the smell and the noise. But I am drawn back. With hands damp and quivering, I place the candle down on the bench. With my eyes half closed, my teeth clenched, and with sobs and moans issuing from my lips, I try to free the beast. I pull at a rusted nail but it is driven in hard and my attempt only gives rise to more suffering. His glistening musculature tenses and he lets out a high-pitched squeal, which fades into a series of whimpers, and all the time I know his eye is on me, entreating me to stop the pain, begging me to end his distress.

Seeing a rack of surgical instruments, I reluctantly take up a chisel. I raise the blade. God knows how I sink it, but I do, for I know I must end his suffering. I plunge it down through his ribs, feel his flesh give way as the tip enters his heart. All the time I am wailing in an agony of sympathy, relieved to mask the dog's final mewls, for they tug at my heart so. Then he has no voice, all power of movement now lost, and the beast takes passage to a welcome grave.

Slackening my hands from around the chisel's hilt, I back away from the bench. My breathing is still uneven and there is a roaring in my ears. With black specks dancing before my eyes, I stagger and reach out for a place of anchor. I knock a jar of liquid, which topples and smashes to the floor, and as I turn to the left, I catch a hooped pail with my shins. It tips out its contents; glistening clumps of flesh. In the shadows to my right, a human cadaver lies asleep on a table, his chest and arms unpeeled, his face skinless.

Leaning my weight against a chair, I wonder if I am trapped in some sort of purgatory. I focus solely on my breathing. I fight to suck air into my chest and I battle to dispel it. Eventually, my senses begin to return. From the nape of my neck to the backs of my arms I am wetter than an eel, and as much as I fold my arms about myself and rub my skin, a profound shiver engulfs me.

My eyes dart this way and that, from the candle's swaying flame, to the dead dog, to the corpse, as I try to comprehend it all. Then I look beyond, to the doorway. Through the silence, my ears pick out a noise from downstairs. Doors are being opened, floorboards are being trod.

'Paterson?' A man's voice calls out. 'Paterson? Are you up there?'

There is a flash of orange light and the stairs groan beneath the weight of a footstep. A tap and a creak, over and again, ever louder, as the footsteps keep on coming, as the orange light grows brighter.

I search for a place to hide as I extinguish the candle. I drop to my knees, pulling myself through the darkness until I am beneath a table. I shuffle backwards until I am against the wall and can go no further. Here I wait, and with fearful, corroding dread my thoughts turn to Rebekah. I realise now that we have strayed far beyond the realms of purgatory and, with our unity divided, we each stand alone at Hell's door, where demons dance around us with flaming tongues and knotted whips. I do not know how Rebekah fares and I cannot imagine how each of us will survive. I have nothing left but prayer and hope.

Keys jingle and locks click, the noises growing louder. I hold my breath and close my eyes, feeling faint with fear, willing that this room will not be visited. But life does not always deal a fair hand: the door opens and the darkness pales; a wave of brightness washes over the floor, splashing amber puddles where before there were shadows. Drowning in this sudden sea of light, I can only look up at the man holding the lantern, and I know he will not save me. So I sit and await the inevitable.

I suppose he must see me the moment he enters the room but, as a cat takes pleasure in watching a mouse, so Frederick Blister throws a viperish look at me. His waistcoat has ridden up and he tugs at it, trying to stretch it over his heaving paunch. He casually lights the candle from his lantern, doubles the light, and studies me with the eyes of a man who never forgets. He draws his lips into a curl and creases his eyes, but a smile does not come through, and in this moment I truly fear for my life.

'What do you do here, Miss Frost?' he asks, his voice sardonic, 'on such a night, and in such a place? How strange that Calder has no recollection of his dear cousin Estelle from Cornwall! You and the superior Miss Brock must imagine that Calder and I are quite the imbeciles. When I described you to him, he knew exactly who you were . . . Hester.'

There is a pause and, seeing I will not respond, he continues with, 'I don't suppose a girl such as you could ever understand the greatness of a man like Calder Brock. He is a God, Hester. Do you know, he can make a dead man smile by orchestrating the sinews and muscles of the cadaver's face? As amusing as that is to witness, it has led him to unravel the mysteries of facial palsy. He understands what only God has understood before. Why, he is certain to publish his papers before either Sir Charles Bell or Herbert Mayo. Can you imagine surgeons referring to "Mayo's Palsy" or even "Bell's Palsy"? No, of course they won't; it will be known as "Brock's Palsy". Calder will be hailed as a hero of this modern era of discovery, and no one will be concerned by his methods. Does your own contribution to such a wondrous achievement not fill you with a sense of fulfilment, Hester?'

Believing he will be too slow and distracted by his own self-importance, I dart towards the door. But I underestimate the speed and litheness of his substantial frame. He is on top of me in an instant, his weight bearing down, his breath and spittle against my cheek.

'No you don't,' he laughs, a grin hanging at the corner of his lips. But his mirth is empty. He presses his knee into my back, dispelling air from my lungs. He ties a cable around my wrists, my arms pulled awkwardly behind my back, before he stands and lifts me up. He pushes me against the wall, pinning me with his full body weight, his stout chest heaving. With his cheeks round and ruddy, only inches from my own face, and sweat breaking forth from the bridge of his nose, he reaches into his coat, fumbling as I squirm. He uses his teeth to pull the cork stopper from a flask, then secures my chin in his left hand as his right hand tips the liquid into my mouth.

I spit and gnash, swallowing no more than a salt-spoon full, yet it is enough, it is enough. The liquid burns my throat; my muscles and mind become weak in only a few heartbeats. I don't believe I can stand without Blister propping me up and I feel myself slipping. With hardly an ounce of air left inside me and unconsciousness falling fast, I shape my quivering lips to speak words which may be my last: 'Rebekah,' I whisper. 'Rebekah knows; she will find me.'

This seems to vex Blister and he raises his right fist, bringing his knuckles down upon my face with a sharp crack, and I know nothing more.

CHAPTER SEVENTEEN

S mell is the first faculty to return to me. The scent is half-familiar, a rotten and hateful stench; a composite of earth and meat with a bitter substance I cannot account for. My thoughts incongruously turn to food and I feel hunger pangs, thinking irrationally of ham hock and piccalilli.

Next, as though standing by a water-mill, there is a rushing sound in my ears; a rhythmic throb as the waterwheel turns, its paddles forcing cogs to twist, shafts to spin. The noise conjures a vision of broad lowlands with a river. I long to hear the lapwings' call and the purl of the stream, but the waterwheel's grinding is too dominant. My thoughts are content to dally in this idyll, until I realise that both the rushing and the throbbing are wrought by my own heartbeat. Then the smell becomes stronger as I begin to regain consciousness.

I am now aware of being imprisoned in a confined space, my knees pressed up against my chest, my ankles sore and my wrists smarting. I am not in comfort. My face is both numb and tingling.

The more I dwell on the constraints I am subjected to, the faster my heart beats. Inside my head, I believe I cry out. But I know nothing is issuing from my lips and, after a period of time which could be a minute, a day or an hour, I stay my efforts and slip back inside my thoughts. Either in blindness or subjected to total darkness, in my mind I retrace my steps.

At an achingly slow pace, I begin to remember, and fragments re-form in my thoughts. The smell, I know, is from Calder's dissections, from his bottles of preserving chemicals; the numbness around my left eye and across the bridge of my nose is courtesy of Frederick Blister's fist; my hands and feet are bound; I must be in a trunk or hamper. Perhaps they think me dead; perhaps I am dead?

From time to time, I make an attempt to move, to open my eyes. But either the elixir from Blister's flask, or the blow from his fist, has made this impossible. Yet my mind is still awake, and eventually the panic subsides enough for me to catch hold of a noise; a man's voice: Calder's voice. It is both near and distant, muffled, as though Aunt Meg is tipping a jug of water over my head as I sit in the tin bath, and I cannot be certain if it is even real.

'Are you certain she can't have seen you, Freddie?' Calder asks, his voice sounding narrow and dull to me, as though he pinches his nose whilst he speaks.

'Am I not always discreet, Calder?'

'The devil you are. You're clumsy and careless. But I haven't the time to discuss that now. Just stay out of sight. But if I can't handle her, well – you know what to do.'

Such is the level of my delirium that I cannot tell whether I imagine their voices, or truly hear them; whether the sum of my fears is conspiring against me, or my senses are reporting a true representation of reality. The relentless desire to sleep is gathering fast about me, pulling me under, dark and dangerous as black water. All I can do is submit to it.

Eventually, from somewhere outside this deep and unhappy slumber, a word is spoken and I find myself swimming towards it, and with flailing arms I catch it and hold it. The word is not important, but the speaker is vital to me. It is Rebekah; I knew she would come for me! To know that she is safe and well satisfies all my senses, all my thoughts and feelings. I redouble my efforts and struggle against my paralysis; to push through it and make an audible sound to alert her. In my mind, I am thrashing about, shouting, bellowing. But I cannot rouse myself and I know I can only listen.

'I've been so worried about you, Calder,' Rebekah says. 'I thought something terrible had happened to you tonight. What was so important that you had me driven about in a carriage for over an hour?'

'Oh, just business, Becky. A last-minute delivery. You wouldn't understand.' Surely Rebekah can hear the sourness behind his words, and sense his intent?

'Calder, you really must learn to trust me. With enemies all about us, we surely have greater need than ever to rely on each other.'

There is a silence, then a chair-spring creaks.

'So, these are your rooms?' she asks, her voice brighter, but in a controlled, empty sort of way. 'Does the taint of the drains not disturb your faculties?'

'I . . . I suppose at first it did. But . . . I find it necessary to work amongst the people.'

'Ah yes: *noblesse oblige.*'

'Becky, is there something wrong? You seem changed.'

'I'm as well as I have ever been, dear brother. Perhaps just fatigued. As I wrote in my letter to you, these last few days have been an intense period of discovery. Are you not shocked by what we have unearthed?'

'Well, by the deuce, of course I am! I trusted the fellows, both of them. Sep's done so much for both of us; and Blister, well, I thought he was a capital chap. A bore at times, but nevertheless a decent sort of fellow.'

'So, if I show you all the evidence I have gathered, demonstrate to you the proven connections between a gang of body snatchers who have turned to indiscriminate murder and the involvement of Blister and the motivation of Septimus, then you are willing to support me in making a statement to Mr Truman of the New Police?'

'I thought,' Calder says, 'your greatest concern was for my safety, for our preservation. Yet you seem to dwell on Blister and his business transactions.'

'And what think you of them, Calder?'

I suppose he must roll his eyes or shrug his shoulders, deposing he has no knowledge of such a thing, for there is a period of silence, before he says, 'If you have something to say, Becky, out with it.'

'I have nothing to say. I am simply interested in your opinion, as I have ever been. I am curious to know if any of your medical brethren have ever witnessed the post-mortem examination of a human form.'

'Don't be such a spoon, Becky. Of course they have. As have I. And there's nothing wrong with it. In point of fact, it's a most necessary part of our education and our investigations into disease.'

'And how many dissections must a medical student undertake each year to pass his tutor's scrutiny?'

'I don't know . . . two, perhaps three.'

'And how many medical students are there in London, do you suppose?'

'How should I know of such a thing?' Calder is testy now, his voice less composed.

'Well, I shall tell you,' Rebekah counters, calm, controlled, her tone now carefully weighed. 'It is some five hundred.'

'What is your point? Or is this just about your manly mathematical brain?'

'The point,' Rebekah continues, ignoring his derision, 'is that to supply the London medical fraternity with sufficient corpses for dissection, then upwards of fifteen hundred bodies would be required.'

There is a period of silence, then a scratching noise and a puff, and the smell of tobacco enters my dream, as Calder gratifies his lungs with cigar smoke before answering, 'Are you so very naïve, Rebekah? Have you never heard the stories about snatchers, of resurrection men? Perhaps the appellation "*resurgam homos*" is more fitting for your educated brain. Men have been taking buried corpses out of the ground for longer than you or I have lived. And in the eyes of the law, a human corpse belongs to no one.'

This time it is Rebekah's turn to sit in silence. Perhaps she is hoping her hypothesis is wrong, and that Calder is not involved. Yet, like me, she can surely hear no betrayal of emotion in Calder's voice, no empathy or remorse.

'But does it not surely breach common decency?' she entreats. Her voice is tired now, a sudden weariness behind the contralto tones.

'Be that as it may, a corpse does not constitute legal property and is therefore not subject to legal judgement.'

'And what,' she counters with new emphasis, her voice jagged and penetrating, 'what if the graveyards are filled with putrefied flesh too rancid to touch? What if the resurrection men cannot bring up the bodies you want? What then, Calder? Is that when you send Blister out to release your brutes?'

Rebekah peels back the facade of politeness and there is nothing left but the bitter pith of truth. It is an outright accusation and there is no turning back.

'There is no case to answer!' he cries out, but he does not deny

Rebekah's censure. 'Such accusations can answer no good purpose without evidence. Show me the bodies! Show me the proof! There's none to be had after dissection. What shall you do next, dredge the belly of the Thames and piece the fragments of flesh together? You cannot stop this, Becky. You must understand that it is for the greater good. Innocents must fall in the war against man's ignorance. Without such knowledge, how is a man supposed to mend the leg of a pauper girl who falls beneath the wheels of his carriage? How is he to save her life?'

Rebekah is contemplative for longer than a moment, thrown by a perspective she may not have thought of before. Eventually, she says anxiously, 'Calder. Calder, the opiate substance you take is changing you, altering your perspectives. Perhaps it transforms respect into antipathy . . . you know this cannot be right. That you have committed deep and unforgivable sin.'

'I am not the monster you believe me to be, Rebekah. I am a scientist, a discoverer, a—'

'A being with no reverence for life.'

'Our profession is driven by necessity and—'

'What do you mean by *our* profession? How many anatomy schools are there in London?'

'Sixteen or seventeen, I believe. Does it matter?'

'Do you all use the same methods?'

'I don't know. I suppose so.'

'How on earth can such a business exist?'

I believe this last question from Rebekah is rhetorical, an internal thought exposed by dint of careless speech. But Calder chooses to reply, in a cold manner.

'I can't speak for the others, but on my part Uncle Sep sits on the council at several of the city's colleges and the fellows of those institutions grant me the sums I require every few weeks.'

'Do you mean to say they all know where the money goes?'

'Of course, because without it we will not make scientific advances, we will never understand the mysteries of the human form. I am so close to making a great discovery. I will go down in history as a great man.'

'And how many—'

'How many subjects will those grants buy me? I don't know – ten, perhaps twenty, depending on the level of . . . freshness.'

This last word even Calder speaks with repugnance, and it lingers in the air as pungently as his preserving chemicals. When Rebekah next speaks, her throat is tight and I suspect she is crying.

'You are deluded. Success and fame seem to have become your new opiate. But Calder, if you would only take a step back and view your business as I do. You derive your livelihood by sending your men out to prowl the streets and murder innocent men, women and children. They kill to order, Calder. To your order, heartless and indiscriminate, without even having a grudge against their victim! Can you not see how base such an action is?'

'I don't press these men into service. I pay them handsomely and allow them to give vent to their brutal natures.'

'How do you suppose God views your hypocritical seat on The London Society for the Suppression of Mendicity?'

'What better way to select subjects?' he mutters.

My mind recoils, horrified at the scale of his depravity. He is inhuman.

Rebekah pauses too, before continuing:

'You must think yourself greatly favoured that you are answerable to no one. You are an aberration, Calder. They are just specimens to you, aren't they? Just beetles and emmets. But what of your altruism in wishing for an education for Hester?'

'I never wanted to prove her capable, you goose,' he laughs. 'I wanted to prove that the likes of her are incapable of bettering themselves and should therefore be used as subjects. This will give their life and death meaning. The city is teeming with poverty; an excess of society's dregs. But our knowledge of anatomy is insufficient. Why not give the underclass a purpose for the greater good?'

'You vile, vile—'

'Oh, spare me the diatribe, Becky. I'm tired of you, your face, your voice, whining on and on. Just explain to me, with all your intellect: why did you come here tonight, if you suspected all that you do?'

'I wish I could tell you it was because I couldn't believe all I suspected of you. That I wanted to give you the opportunity to disprove my doubts; to assist me in bringing an end to it all. But the truth is, Calder, perhaps I did lately suspect your involvement. You paid your cabman to delay my arrival by instructing him to run contrived errands. The longer he took, the more suspicious I grew. So, I paid him more, Calder. As time passed and the dawning realisation of your guilt was nigh, I paid him to take me back to Arlington Street, where I expected to find Mr Truman from the New Police. But he had called and left, owing to the absence of Hester, with whom he was scheduled to meet. An old woman was there in her place, and she told me stories, Calder, of Septimus, of my father and mother, and of you. How interesting those stories were. How does it feel, Calder, to be the son of a man who murdered his own kith and kin?'

'You can't hurt me, Rebekah. Do you know, I respected Sep even more when he told me that he was my real father, when he explained what he had done for my sake. The man is my hero, he has sacrificed everything to give me the place in society I deserve, and the resources I need. And I protected you from him, didn't I? How I adored you as a child, my fondest playmate and my dearest companion. My affections have never waned, but you make it increasingly difficult for me to safeguard you now. You are no fool; you must know how our finances are these days.'

'And now I realise why you always turn a blind eye to his profligacy.'

'Of course I do; he's my father. But, one day, I shall make my own way in life. I shall publish my papers and become a great man of our age. And what of you? You continue to remain unwed and persist in this pointless inquisition into business affairs you can never understand. You are trying my patience, Becky. Most of those who dare to challenge me only ever live to regret it.'

Rebekah sighs. 'Idle threats and tales of your dubious lineage are the least of my worries, Calder. What concerns me now is that the old woman at Arlington Street had already disclosed her facts to Hester and I presume the only reason Hester would leave the house in such a hurry would be to come here and warn me of what she had learned. It doesn't take such an inordinate amount of intellect to realise you are no ordinary physician. But I believe I am a step or two ahead of Superintendent Truman, which gives you time, Calder.'

'You wish to help me?'

'I cannot stop the net closing, but I wish to bargain with you. The people of this city will not tolerate this slaughter. The city walls are littered with police handbills on every edifice, bearing endless appeals for missing children, absent husbands and wives. The matter will come to a head, Calder, for the numbers are too great to disguise any longer. Tonight, even the cabman did nothing but talk ceaselessly of the Tulley murder. Rumours abound that the boy's body was presented to the dissecting-room porter at a college, who then, thank God, alerted the authorities and cried murder. Even your own myrmidons have no loyalty to you. Morton must have thought, no doubt, that he'd obtain a better price for his merchandise elsewhere and so you were forgotten in an instant. You are all monstrous men without honour and none will come forward to speak for you. They will not support you,

Calder. Your sponsors will desert you. But there is time; I am offering to withhold my evidence against you.'

'Why? Why would you wish to help me? You called me an aberration a moment ago.'

'Because I want something from you, Calder. I know that Hester came here this night. I wish you to give her up to me.'

'Is that all?'

'Yes.'

'But you must tell me why.'

'You are incapable of understanding.'

'But I thought you said we must trust each other.'

'Will you surrender her to me?'

'Not unless you tell me why.'

'So she is here?'

'Tell me why, Rebekah.'

'Because I care deeply for her.'

'What an absurd one you are, Becky. And such a ridiculous notion.'

'I have no shame in calling it out to you. I love her. Let her come with me now and we will both disappear; you will hear of us no more.'

With senses benumbed and flesh inert, there is still a flutter through my soul at hearing Rebekah's words spoken so fearlessly. At last, all doubts are banished. 'I love her.' Such simple words, and how sincerely spoken; she adds no clause of condition.

With new urgency, I try to move again. I attempt to force a cry from my throat, but nothing responds to the force of my will, and the utmost I can wish for is to instruct Rebekah's soul to listen for mine and to pray the kick of my heart will tell her that I am here. But it is no good; Calder is hot on her heels and, as soon as her pledge is voiced, he tramples the words down with malice and deceit.

'Oh, how I wish I could help you, Rebekah, but I cannot do as you ask.'

'Don't play games. You say you have tired of me; well, I am weary of you and your world. Just let her come to me now and I will leave.'

'I'm afraid she's already gone.'

'Gone? Where?'

'Blister has taken her to be dealt with by Jack Morton. By now, they'll be at Midden Street Cottages and, well, I am sorry, Becky. It's too late to save her. There's nothing to be done.'

He has learned deceit at the devil's own school and his words are as sharp as his scalpel. There is the sound of pacing footsteps and Rebekah's voice hails from a different position in the room: 'How long since?'

'Oh, I don't know.' Calder's tone is distracted. I can hear mirth behind his words. I attempt to move my head, thrash my legs about, but I am still trapped inside myself. I try to call out, but nothing comes. 'And you say you love her, Becky?' Calder pursues. 'You have feelings for that urchin from the rag and tag? What a scandal you would bring upon yourself!' This is followed by a sort of deranged laughter.

'You unspeakable brute,' Rebekah cries, her words delivered short and fierce, accompanied by muffled gasps from Calder, and I wonder if Rebekah is attacking him. 'If you've hurt a hair on her head I swear—'

The consequence is not named; instead there is laboured breathing and something falls to the floor and breaks. There must be a physical struggle between the two of them and I am helpless to offer any influence. There are gasps of exertion, then a blow is effected; perhaps with a bottle or decanter, for there is a shattering sound followed by silence, then a slammed door.

In the following stillness, I am insensate. There are no further noises to stimulate my mind, but instead I feel the blood pumping in my heart. In turn, a tingling sensation begins in my fingers and slowly spreads upwards. There is no definite transition from slumber to wakefulness, just a gradual sharpening of senses. I am aware of my own breathing and able to move my head. My next conscious perception is a voice, reedy, weak.

'Hallo?' it calls, barely above a whisper. 'Is anyone there?'

I cannot recognise the tones, so low and feeble the owner must be. But this time it is closer than the voices before. I expel a deep breath and this time sense a vibration in my throat; I hear the noise as it leaves my mouth. The other voice, perhaps encouraged by my sympathetic response, speaks again.

'Blister?' the voice asks, its tones deep again, its impatience obvious. 'Damn it, Blister,' Calder shouts again. 'Get in here! Now!'

Distant footfalls crescendo and heavy wheezing fills the room, before Blister says, 'Good God, man. What happened?'

'That vixen took a bottle and . . . never mind. Go after her, Freddie. You know what to do.'

'But what about your head?'

'Go now, by the deuce, or we'll lose her.'

Calder is quiet after Blister leaves. Occasionally, he grumbles under his breath, throws out vile execrations on Rebekah and her parentage, but in the main he is silent, and I wonder whether the blow Rebekah afforded him is more serious than he would acknowledge. Just once, the air moves and a cupboard door creaks. I hear him chewing ravenously, his lips and tongue smacking as the food is bitten off and swallowed. Then a stopper pops and he gulps, at once coughing, then gulping again. All this time, my senses are ordering themselves and sensations are returning to my limbs.

Gradually, I am able to move my arms. I work at the cables

knotted about my wrists, liberate my hands and remove the gag from my mouth. The freedom to breathe accelerates my recovery and I push my thighs down, sense the resistance of my boundary against the soles of my feet. As strength returns, I push harder, kick against the wall of the box which incarcerates me until there is the snap of wicker or wood, and my legs, instead of being bent and restricted, are now straight and unimpeded.

Where before there was blackness, now candlelight floods over me. I shuffle, wriggle, until I lie outside the hamper in which I have been kept. Winded by my efforts, I can only look about me. The room is silent and the books, papers and leather chairs fill the place to capacity, giving a sense of oppression.

I struggle to my knees, unbind the cable around my ankles and stand. The floor moves beneath me for a moment before I steady myself. With my head pounding, I advance, squinting against the air which stings my eyes so. Still I am uncertain of what is reality, and doubts swarm about me, thick and black in their multitude, until at last I begin to doubt my doubts.

I look about me and note a broken bottle before the hearth, its neck still intact, its body jagged, edged with sticky blackness. And slumped in the fireside chair is Calder, in his lap an empty glass tipped on its side and a decanter without its stopper. Crumbs of opium litter his knees and a patch of wet saliva bleeds dark and wide on his trousers, the source of which still drips down from his mouth.

I stand over him indecisively. Perhaps I should help him . . . but no. Whether he lives and breathes, or is lost to this world, I have no care. There is no more to be done for either the man or his soul. Still unsteady on my feet, I quit the room, leave the building and run to the only person I believe can help me.

I dash through the fog-dimmed streets and arrive at the police building. Decent folk are all a-bed, and it is vagrants and ne'er-do-wells with whom I share the streets at this hour. A cabman stands behind his hackney-chaise, talking to a uniformed constable, and a drunkard sits on the steps to the police office. Two streetwalkers sit in the gutter, their skirts drawn up to their shins, their grey petticoats mired in dirt, with stockings ripped and tattered. Each is distracted by their own troubles, so I enter the building unchallenged. I make my way to Mr Truman's office. The door is closed, but unlocked. I push my way in and Mr Truman, asleep in his chair with his booted feet crossed neatly on his desktop, wakes suddenly.

'What? Who?' he stutters.

'Mr Truman,' I blurt, still breathless. 'My name is Hester White. I came to see you, with Miss Brock.'

'Steady on now. Calm yourself, Miss,' he says gently. 'I can well mind the occasion. I called to see you at the request of Miss Brock's man this very evening, at Arlington Street, but I was told you had both left.' He brushes the palm of his hand over his hair, buttons his collar and offers up a smile.

Perhaps if he had been abrupt, as he was during our last meeting, then I might hold myself together. But the kindness in his voice weakens me and all I can do is weep. I raise my hands to brush aside the tears, and Mr Truman must notice the striated marks on my wrists and the swelling above my cheekbone, for he jumps to his feet and says, 'What's all this about then?'

'The surgeons, Mr Truman; they're sending men such as Morton to kill for them; to provide corpses for dissection when there are no cadavers available. They take them to Midden Street Cottages and once there, they . . . dispatch them and—'

'There, there. Calm yourself. Who has taken a hand to you?'

I snatch my fingers up to my face and cover the swelling inflicted by Blister. But I say nothing. I just watch as Mr Truman takes up a lantern, holds it above his desk drawer with one hand and rootles around with the other, eventually producing what appears to be a calling card.

'There's a woman I know. She runs a very reputable set of lodging rooms—'

'No, no, Mr Truman. You are not listening to me. It is not me needing your help, it is Miss Brock. They took her from her brother's rooms on Little Windmill Street and must now be transporting her to Midden Street Cottages with the intent of . . . They are holding her against her will and mean to—'

There must be moments when honesty and fear are so plainly recognisable that no oath of sanction is required to support them. Something changes in Mr Truman's expression; perhaps he has a daughter of his own, or a wife whom he loves more than life itself. Or perhaps the cold logic of a superintendent's mind is gently put aside and replaced with emotion. Whatever thoughts run through his head, he takes up his hat and coat, and seizes upon my wish without me having to articulate it.

'Jack Morton's place?' he asks, ushering me out of his office. I nod my reply and say, 'You see, Mr Truman, as you advised, Miss Brock and I went there to serve as eye-witnesses, to Midden Street Cottages.' My voice falters, and tears come now at full spate. 'We found . . . the remains of an acquaintance of mine called Annie Allsop. We have her jawbone back at Miss Brock's house.'

My final words are delivered through heavy sobs and the news I impart stops Mr Truman in his tracks.

'Fowler?' he shouts over my head, his voice vaguely directed to a room off the corridor.

'Guv'nor?' a man replies, appearing from one of the rooms, fastening the last of the silver buttons on his jacket as he approaches us. He disappears briefly back into the room and reappears clutching a tall hat in his hands. 'Sorry, Mr Truman. What move are we on tonight, sir?'

Mr Truman steps away from me and the two men take counsel together out of earshot, the younger man bending his eyes towards me as he listens to his superior. They finish their deliberations and Mr Truman strides back towards me, his boots heavy against the boards.

'You certain you're up to it, Miss? I shall send an officer to Little Windmill Street forthwith to search for Miss Brock in case she's being held there. But it would help if you could show us exactly where you and Miss Brock made your discoveries.'

'Yes, of course. I don't know exactly what time she was taken. I don't even know if they caught up with her. You see, they forced me to drink laudanum, Mr Truman, imprisoned me in a casket—'

Mr Truman studies me and then says, 'Right then.'

He cups his hand beneath my elbow and presses me forward to take our departure, down the steps and into a carriage. As he climbs in, he calls to the driver to get us to Midden Street Cottages at all hazards, and then he takes his seat beside me, and Constable Fowler sits opposite.

The horses are urged into a gallop, the carriage tipping to the full extent of its springs. We rush along at great speed and I am forced to reach for the carriage strap to steady myself. As the streets of London fly past outside, all three of us look for signs of Rebekah. Eventually, through the sound of clattering hooves and the swing and creak of the carriage, Constable Fowler says, 'Do you suppose it'll stick this time with Morton, sir?'

'The facts are thickening upon him,' Truman says. Then he is silent, before he says, 'It's Smedley's patch up there; we'll call at Worship Street, send for more men.' The tone in which he speaks now is slow, troubled, and has a quietening effect on Constable Fowler. The stop at Worship Street is brief and we resume our journey.

In the last quarter-mile there is not even a single street lamp, and the road is unpaved and undrained. The carriage slows, its wheels sinking into deep ruts every few paces. Fowler lays his hat on the seat, leans his head briefly out of the window and says, 'Mortal dark up this way, Mr Truman.' And, dark as it was before, his words seem to deepen the blackness, and we arrive at our destination with the two carriage lamps casting rods of light forward, but showing nothing but the darkness itself.

Before the driver pulls the brake, Constable Fowler leaps out of the carriage and sets about striking a match to light two more lanterns; one of which he hands to Mr Truman, the other he pushes out into the shadows, drawing trees and shrubs out of the darkness and lighting them for a moment before they slip back into their recesses and the light moves on. Mr Truman makes a round of the garden, apparently noting its features, and I am left alone inside the carriage, relieved at the absence of both Rebekah and the Mortons; for the cottage is in darkness and no one answers Mr Truman's knock.

'Not a soul about, Miss,' Mr Truman says, as both he and Fowler return to the carriage.

'We must have arrived here quicker than they,' I say. 'We must return to Mr Brock's rooms on Little Windmill Street; Miss Brock must still be there after all.'

'And well we might when Mr Smedley's men arrive; but for now, if you would be kind enough to show me exactly where you found the evidence of Miss Allsop?' His voice is measured and calm.

He takes my hand and draws me from the safety of the carriage. A sudden wind blows, worrying the tree limbs, and the atmosphere gathers heavy about us. I walk with Mr Truman up to the privy and wait as he searches inside. He eventually turns, but says nothing, then to Fowler he shouts, 'What about the wash-house?'

'Nothing, guv.'

'And no one next door?'

'No, guv.'

At this point, keen to resume the search at Little Windmill Street, I make to return to the carriage.

'Sure and certain you are at ease, Miss?' Mr Truman says. But before I can answer, and before the order to depart from this awful place can be given, Constable Fowler shouts:

'Guv! There's something here!'

The words, once thrown to the breeze, linger painfully. Then Mr Truman lifts his lantern and the shadows sever and part, to reveal Constable Fowler standing at the old well, brushing away a layer of grass cuttings and vegetation to reveal a wooden lid, which he raises. Mr Truman advances and I follow; but, before we reach the well, Constable Fowler jumps, sudden and quick.

He is squatting on his hunkers now, pointing to a wooden plank lying horizontally across the top of the well, attached to which is a knotted rope. His face is white and contorted, as though he has swallowed something sour. Mr Truman steps forward; I try to follow, but my sleeve is ensnared by a shrub and I am glad of a momentary excuse not to proceed, so fearful am I of what we may be about to find.

I approach them and, despite the poor light, I see that something is beneath the water's surface, suspended on the rope. I gaze down into the well and the black water reflects my own image. There is a silence to match the question I dare not ask, then Mr Truman dips his hand through the mirror and a small tremor wrinkles the surface. He clears his throat, not out of necessity, I'm certain, but to stay the progress of time, to delay his next words. But speak them he eventually does, a tone of hollowness in his voice.

'Please step back now, Miss. We must attempt to retrieve . . .'

My thoughts are scattered and I cannot reply, so I do as he bids and step back, and although my eyes remain centred on the well, my vision is distorted and the scene begins to quiver before me. I wait and I watch.

To my horror, when the two men unite their strength and pull at the rope, the water gives up two human feet, tied at the ankles. Then, as the men bring in their catch, it is clear the body, this time, is whole. First the legs, then the hips, the chest and shoulders. Most of the flesh is concealed with wet undergarments, but any outerwear must have been stripped away.

A film of water clings to the face that rises, and although the hair is limp and wet and the left cheekbone is marked with an abrasion, the sudden and unexpected familiarity stings my soul; for it is a face I love so well, a face that has won my heart and my mind. But she is so still, her profile white against the surrounding night. Deep inside I sense a shiver, small at first; the type of tremble a cobweb makes when a breath of air is blown through it; then it grows, it expands, until it is venom rushing through my veins. Inside me there is such heart-piercing sorrow as I cannot withstand. I watch transfixed as she is gently laid down onto the broken earth that surrounds the well and the night air wraps around my neck, scarf-tight and choking.

'Rebekah,' I sob. 'Rebekah. It cannot be. No, no . . .'

I throw myself on the ground at her side and hold on to her with the strength of a drowning man. I take her fingers in mine and rub them, but she won't be kindled up. I appeal to her with hands and voice, still expecting that she will rise, bright and certain like the sun. I brush soil and dirt from her skin and try to bear the weight of her, lift her helpless arms about me.

'Is this the lady, sir? The one what visited you?' Constable Fowler asks.

'I fear it is,' Mr Truman says, his voice barely above a whisper.

'They've killed her, guv'nor.' The constable adds, his voice low, 'They've gone and drowned her. How is anyone capable of such a murder?'

'Such is the temper of the times, I'm afraid,' Mr Truman says.

Constable Fowler's words don't reach me immediately, for I am lost in my own sorrow, but then the full shadow of realisation eclipses all other senses: 'murder'.

The word falls, continues falling through a deep shaft of darkness, down and down, until finally it breaks out with a splash in my ears. It drenches me, bloats and swells inside me, and I cannot breathe. Rebekah Brock, my Rebekah, my only Rebekah, is stifled, and all life spilled out of her heart.

'A mortal poor way to go, I count,' Mr Truman says quietly. 'Please take my arm, Miss.' His voice is fatherly and he treats me as though I were very young; but I have never been so old.

He presses my hand, but I snatch it away and I struggle for breath, a river of air around me, yet nothing to fill my lungs. A tide of noise rises within me, breaking as waves of whimpering which build in my throat until a flood of sound issues from my mouth. I must be sobbing, for I sense the convulsions in my breast, but my weeping is distant, choked, as though my heart is under water, as though I will always be immersed in grief. I am insensible until a hand falls on my shoulder and Mr Truman is obliged to break the hex of my reverie.

'Many a sad eye has come from hard sorrow,' he says. He slips his hand under my arm and adds, 'Come now. Up on your pins. There's nothing more you can do. She's gone,' he says.

I don't move, so he repeats himself, forcing the words into my ears. I don't want to understand him, but however much I try to evade the truth, I know it is here. I cannot escape it, I must go with him.

Beneath the trees, and despite the lateness of the hour, a crowd collects. Men fall in talk with one another, women huddle together, all pointing, all murmuring. Then a carriage arrives and more shapes, this time uniformed men, begin to flow into the garden. One man runs to the cottage and returns with a winding sheet in which to wrap Rebekah, and another man blows a toot on an old whale-bone whistle.

Mr Truman, perhaps believing my grief might yet be mended with kind words, says, 'You must bear this heavy blow, my dear. Hurt soon forgets what the eye sees not. Why, a pretty young girl like you; well, you'll be wed within a twelvemonth, I'm certain of it. You'll soon forget about all of this.'

I don't know what to say.

Before she is shrouded, I can only stare through my tears as her body is covered, a screed of packthread to hold it fast. Despite the storm-waves of grief all around me, I can do nothing but linger, hope I too will drop out and away to death. Mr Truman senses nothing of my thoughts. For how could he? How could anyone ever understand the depth of our love, and what we have endured together? He simply says, 'You'll be well in a couple of days, my dear.'

But I no longer see the world that others view. Rebekah and I will always be preserved in this awful moment, in this hopeless circumstance: the parallel wheel-tracks of a carriage, travelling on together, yet never to meet. Death has been and gone, noiseless, colourless, little evidence of its steal save the one now lost. The black water, which Rebekah so feared in her dreams, is all around me. Rebekah is gone, the world is darker, and everywhere and everything might as well be mantled in thick, sticky coal tar, for I have neither the energy nor the inclination to push through it.

CHAPTER EIGHTEEN

M r Truman drives me back to Arlington Street, though I have no memory of the journey and, as soon as we arrive, Peggy tries to revive me with tea and toast before putting me to bed. She weeps for Rebekah as she fusses over me, saying that while I must grieve, in time I will grow strong, start to recover, and the sorrows will fade. But I don't want the past to grow dim; I never want to forget; I never want to recover from Rebekah.

Six days I labour under the toil of it and I am left unable to close my heart to the thing which most pains it. The two most powerful influences in human existence, Love and Death, are now forced to live in my heart, side by side, two strings to the same harp; and as one is plucked, so the other vibrates in response, and all my memories of Rebekah are equally mourned and cherished, are both whole, yet bruised.

On the seventh day, at last I am aware of my surroundings. Peggy says that I must begin to eat more substantial food than the broth I have been taking, or she fears I may be lost. She tells me that Doctor Quince has been called and that I must be ready to receive him. But all I wish for is to sleep, and in my dreams I am back at Waterford, for those times remain the most vivid to me: almost real; an oil painting with colours that are true. But they are, after all, just dreams, and with springtime soon to be upon us, I cannot imagine how the seasons will move on from that fateful winter's day, or how the bluebells might ever be in bloom again.

My only solace comes from Rebekah's diary. Whenever I am alone I slide it out from beneath the mattress, take it gently in my hands and, through cold tears, I turn the pages. With gillyflowers rising then fading from each sheet, and my fingers caressing the loops of her script, I imagine her watching me from afar. I dream her eyes are exuding that familiar tenderness; the slanting light that falls from sun-drenched clouds. For a moment, the agony eases, but it is only ever a brief respite in the onward march of pain.

Mr Truman, though busy with the court case against Morton and Corby, visits me occasionally to ask after my recovery and tell me how the prosecution is proceeding. I accept that I may be called as a witness, but am truly fearful of revisiting those dreadful events. In time, Mr Truman explains to me that the case is being brought against the two men, who will be charged with 'wilfully and, of their malice aforethought, unlawfully killing Matthew Tulley'. Mr Truman says it will only confuse matters if the men are charged with any of the others, given the lack of evidence, and that the certainty of one conviction is better than the uncertainty of more. 'And, after all,' he says, 'a man can only be hanged once.'

The case drags on, and in spite of my ambivalence both towards it and the world in general, Mr Truman keeps visiting me with his updates and delivering copies of the newspapers, as though exposure to the details might somehow aid in my recuperation.

In the end, I am not called to the courthouse and only my statement of account is read out. The trial concludes and both men are found guilty. Mr Truman makes one last visit to me, on the afternoon of the Monday, when Morton and Corby are hanged. He takes great pride and relish in describing the scene to me.

'Such a clamour the crowd made this morning, Miss White,' he says, as he sits in the drawing room. 'They'd kept good order since sunrise, but when Mr Vardy, the hangman, appeared on the scaffold just after eight o'clock, they became troubled with unrest and gave voice. "Hats off" they all cried, encouraging every last man Jack of them to take off their hats so they could get a better view. And what a roar, Miss White, when Morton was paraded beneath the beam; such hollers as I can't repeat! Then Corby appeared, weeping and trembling as they hooded and noosed him.

'The Reverend Taylor stood by their sides and I think he was asking them to pray for their salvation, but Mr Vardy took the signal for the drop and the men was both turned off, as you might say.

'They had to take them up to Hosier Street, number thirty-three,' he goes on. 'It belongs to the Royal College of Surgeons. Quite the ceremonial parade it was, I can tell you; driven by the city marshal, mark you! My lads had the deuce of a job trying to keep the crowd from getting their hands on the corpses.'

'But why,' I ask, 'would they need to take the bodies to the Royal College of Surgeons?'

'Well, to complete the ceremony.'

'What ceremony?'

'Why, the cruciform cutting, of course. The president, and the court of the college must be present when the bodies are ceremonially opened across the chest and the stomach, before being stitched up again and presented.'

'Presented to whom?'

'Well, the anatomy schools, of course, Miss White. Any man found guilty of murder and hanged for it, they are legally available to be used as specimens for the anatomists.'

So the circle is closed; the merchants have become the goods. How extraordinary that Morton and Corby are now, of a fashion, victims themselves. Throughout the court case and, in turn, within the newspapers and shilling shockers that are hawked around the city, there is not one mention of any individual anatomist, surgeon, or gentleman. No blame is ever attributed to Septimus, Calder or Blister. The anatomical theatres of London, it would appear, are indeed impenetrable, even to Justice.

In my final conversation with Mr Truman, I quiz him on this point.

'What about Septimus Brock?' I ask.

'No case to answer, Miss. Rumours there might have been, but evidence we had not. They say the gentleman's gone abroad now, for the sake of his health.'

'And Blister?'

'An opportunist hired hand, last seen taking passage for India, Miss.'

'And do you believe the rule of right has been well served, Mr Truman?'

'See here, Miss. When one man stabs another, all guilt is carried by the one holding the knife. We don't arrest the murderer's father because he took a hand to his son and turned him violent. We don't go after the man's mother because she took to drink and neglected her son's needs. It's about direct responsibility. Morton and Corby knew what they was doing; they was caught fair and square and they have paid the price. Case closed. The public are satisfied and justice has been seen to be done. It's hard, I know. But that's the way it works, Miss. And they say that Parliament's discussing a new law: the Anatomy Bill. They reckon it will be approved within weeks. It will mean that the bodies of paupers unclaimed by family or friends will be made available to surgeons and anatomists. It will arrest the inducement of murder for dissection, and we're hoping the whole murky business of resurrection will stop, once and for all.'

Day by day, nursed by Peggy, I begin to regain my physical strength. I discover that when I first fell ill, the dear housekeeper wrote to her mistress, Lady Appleton, and appealed to allow my convalescence to continue at Arlington Street. The kind lady was quick to reply, insisting that I stay on until at least the beginning of summer, and longer if need be.

As soon as I am well enough, I send a letter to Lady Appleton expressing my sincere gratitude for her generosity and she replies with kind words and a list of three names and addresses: friends and acquaintances of hers, with homes where I might seek work as a maid. All are located in the finer districts of the city, and each would be willing to provide me with a situation when my health permits.

So, the days begin to pass and my former health gradually returns. Peggy is pleased with the quantity I eat and the pounds I gain. I sometimes catch her softly weeping as she passes Rebekah's room, but she has begun to mask her sadness by outwardly being brisk and cheerful and, in common with Mr Truman, she believes that confronting the source of melancholia is the key to its defeat.

She says we must try to move away from the past, see a brighter future. She tells me how different the streets seem since the hangings; how fear has been cast out for the present and replaced with cautious relief. She has noticed that no new handbills are being pasted to the walls, and that the stories of men more brutal even than the devil himself are no longer reproduced in the daily journals.

Peggy's hopefulness and refusal to dwell on the past is also reflected in the newspapers she encourages me to read, for they never allude to the numbers Rebekah and I suspected. Perhaps they will never be spoken of, the prospect of such a vast crime too unpalatable for even the people of London. I think of Edward and Annie; the family and friends they left behind. For each soul lost, there must be many left grieving and no answers to be had.

Not long after the hangings, I come across Calder's obituary in a copy of *The Times*. There is no mention of the tortured dogs, the butchered corpses that littered his rooms, or the copious quantities of opium he ingested. Instead, he is honoured as a young man of great potential who worked himself to death in his endeavours.

As pleased as Peggy may be about my bodily well-being, she is less satisfied with my low spirits. I try hard to chide my heart for its aching, make great efforts to overcome my despondency and bear the cross of Rebekah's death as well as I can. But sometimes the pain bites as keenly as it did on that long, awful night when I was forced to abandon her poor, broken body to the shivering winds.

I stay at Arlington Street until the change of the season, but I know I cannot exploit the generosity of Lady Appleton for much longer. Determined to support myself I apply to, and am accepted by, the first of Lady Appleton's recommended employers: a Mr and Mrs Gordon of Kensington. I am to be lady's maid to their adolescent daughter, Lavinia, who is an invalid.

So, on Tuesday, 12 June I gather my belongings, pack up Rebekah's diary and I prepare to start my new life. With tears and unsteady voices, Peggy, Ned and Tilly exchange fond farewells with me and I leave Arlington Street for the last time.

I soon settle into the routine of my new employment and, desirous of fulfilling Lady Appleton's confidence in me, am diligent in my duties, and seldom have occasion to leave the set of rooms in which I live and work. At first this new life suits me; it is quiet, we go out very little, and it is just as I would have it, for on the night Rebekah Brock died, my own heart burst inside me and I do not believe I will ever truly recover.

A month later, I receive a letter from Peggy explaining that the house on Arlington Street has been sold and that she and Ned have taken up domestic roles at Lord and Lady Appleton's country seat: Fenbridge Manor. I feel sadness at their departure from London; another door to my past is closed against me, and my happy times with Rebekah are one step further away.

As the seasons come and go, I experience increasing dissatisfaction with my life. I brood on an intangible past and set store on an opaque future and, in that crevice in-between, I search blindly for some sort of contentment. It is with this feeling of seeking, of reaching out, that in September I write to Mary at the Brocks' villa.

Initially, I receive no reply and then, at the end of October, she writes a charming missive back to me, the letter I sent having taken a circuitous route to find her at her new abode. I discover that after Calder and Rebekah died, and Septimus left for the continent, the villa was sold and Mary was sent to work at Waterford, which was soon after closed up for good. Now engaged to be married to George Rudd, Mary and her husband-to-be are back in London; George is a clerk to a shipping merchant, and Mary will take in laundry until she and George are wed. I find great cheer in news of her engagement and am fortified by her invitation for us to meet up, which I readily accept.

Through Mary and George I find not only solid friendship, but also a means of connecting myself with memories of Waterford and the villa; they somehow bridge the chasm of my two worlds.

The time glides by: their wedding; the christening. These moments I witness with a fullness of pride, but when I'm alone, a certain emptiness prevails that can only be tempered with Rebekah's diary; that token of hope, that enduring emblem of love. The page corners are a little creased now, the cover somewhat paler and the scent of gillyflower is all but faded. But it still gives me solace to hold it in my hands and know that in a place back in time I was truly loved.

The unforgiving winter of 1834 has a stark effect on Lavinia Gordon, and her fragile health begins to decline. The family therefore makes plans to move to continental Europe, to warmer climes, where her symptoms will be appeased. With a nurse now required instead of a lady's maid, it is with sadness that I prepare to relinquish my role and search for a new position. But equally I'm aware of a feeling of new beginnings. I recall the sensation from all those years ago when I directed my feet to Smithfield market, searching for hope, wanting change, seeking some sort of escape.

My employment with the Gordons finally ends, and to bridge the gap between that and my new situation, I take temporary lodging rooms. They are clean, spacious enough for my needs and are on a quiet street. At first, I am content for my daily walks to be contained in the south and centre of London: tea with Mary; a stroll through an arcade of shops; a visit to the chandler's. But one May morning I wake with a feeling of clarity; more than that, it is an overwhelming impetus to regain the sense of possibility that I felt so strongly four years ago. I rise, dress and resist the draw no longer.

I head towards the east of the city, back to the part of town I know so well, where earthy damps rise and gables sag, where ceilings bow and hinges rust. Back to the courtyards and cracked paving stones; the mud-coloured streets. As the hawkmoth is attracted to the flame of a lantern, so I am drawn to the place where it all began, the west side of Smithfield market.

Each stride I take gives strength to my limbs and dispels doubt from my soul. By the time I gain the main thoroughfare at High Holborn, sheets of pale sunlight reach down from behind the rooftops, a cloth of primrose light wiping away the shadows, drying the tear-shed of last night's dew.

I approach the market from Snow Hill, past the barber's and the fried fish shop. Great flocks of sheep are driven past The Bear and Ragged Staff. Everywhere is in motion, alive. I turn about, full circle, and on it goes, a river of movement. People and dogs, horses and sheep: all swimming with and against the current of life. I am back in a place that is so familiar to me and the sunlit noises rise and fall, harmonious in my ears.

I suddenly feel as though I am being observed – not casually, but with a degree of intensity. Occasionally over the years, I have experienced similar feelings; the sensation of being watched from afar. Perhaps when I have been walking to the butcher's, or the cobbler's, a shape in the shadows will move or a face in the crowd will be still, too still. Always the shape of a woman, dressed in black, veiled and shawled, will suggest itself to me, and I cannot help but think of Rosina. But before the ghost of her image might be laid to rest, the vision in my mind always transforms into Rebekah. Such a sight always invites my steps to follow, but by the time I blink, it has disappeared, and I curse the fallibility of my imagination.

Today, however, through the crowds and cattle, I fix my gaze on the spectre dressed in black, standing at the top end of Giltspur Street. The assemblage of sheep and drovers is in constant motion, but the enigmatic shape remains still. Without blinking, I step forward, jostling men's elbows and treading in horse dung, but still the figure across the way does not move as I approach.

I am only twenty paces away when I sense the faintest ripple of agitation from my target. Although veiled and shawled, the woman is clearly uncomfortable, and moves her head first one way and then the other, searching for an exit route, before briskly striking into Giltspur Street, only once glancing over her shoulder in my direction before quickening her pace. I pursue her, and somehow this time I know this is no indulgent fantasy invoked by my own grief. No, this chase is pressing and real, and it feels as though my own life depends on it.

I have not frequented these streets for over three years, but the old familiarity is marked inside my mind. Much has changed. Several of the old covered alleyways have perished, and new buildings have been erected where before it was scrub. But beneath all this, the region is still as known to me as the back of my own hand.

Tantalisingly, I gain on the woman twice, only to watch her slip out of sight. But my agility begins to return, along with the cunning learned at Uncle Jacob's knee, and I let my quarry scuttle away down a covered yard, knowing full well that if I take the next byway, I will eventually meet her head-on.

Breathless, I wait. As I hear her approach, I step out to hinder her path. She is forced to stop in front of me and my heart trips over itself: does she match Rebekah's height, her build? Is she real? As these thoughts chase around my head, she loosens her veil and peels away her bonnet.

Her hair white where once it was grey, I stand face to face with Mrs Cohen. The contrived hopes I have set my heart on are turned to ashes, and a new and heavier sense of futility begins to take mastery of me.

'Well, Hester. The time has come at last.' Her voice is narrow, supressed into a whisper by wheezing. 'The time has come at last,' she repeats, as though testing the power of the phrase.

I say I am glad to see her, but my speech is clipped and my tone reproachful. I stare at her, devoid of any real emotion. My disappointment is obvious, and I am overwhelmed with regret at discovering my enigmatic observer is nothing but an old woman from the past with whom I no longer have any reason to acquaint myself. I have no care to be in her presence, no desire to hear her speak. In view of her son, and her estranged husband, I am obliged to be set against her. Yet, is there some information to be had from her? Are there still secrets held behind those eyes?

'What can you mean by "the time has come at last"?' I say. 'What business is there between us?' I speak faster than I intend, crowding my questions together.

'I had my doubts this morning, Hester. You had a bit more of a spring in your step today than I've seen for a while. That's why I tried to make my escape; I wondered if I should let sleeping dogs lie. And I wasn't sure you was ready,' she says. She speaks with as much haste as I do, and takes great pains to seek out my eyes, as though she might only discharge her speech once, so hot seem the words on her tongue, so certain she must be that I am paying her full attention.

'Ready for what?' I ask.

She knows I have taken her bait, that I am hooked by her words, for she turns in silence and, as though we are attached by rod and line, I am obliged to follow her. She leads the way and I follow a yard or two behind, until we arrive at a soot-coated house with a black street door, one amongst a cluster of six. She produces a large key, wriggles it beneath the doorknob, and pushes open the door.

I follow her into a neat room fitted up as a parlour-cum-kitchen, and she closes the door behind me. She takes a poker to the fire-grate and rattles the coals into life, then swings a kettle over the flame. Although the sun shines through the windowpane, the small frame allows only a limited part of the room to be lit up. The rest of the room is in half-light, obscured, rather like Mrs Cohen herself.

She draws two wooden chairs into the centre of the room, saying: 'Well, don't just stand there like a finch on birdlime. Sit your body down, child.' She pats the seat of one of the chairs as you might do to encourage an infant or a cat to climb upon it. I sit; she moves her chair closer and begins to talk.

'I have a story to tell, Hester. There ain't any fancy words at the end of my tongue, and for that I ask your forgiveness. I'll tell it plain, for that is the woman I am. And remember,' she adds after a period of reflection, 'good wombs have borne bad sons. You remember that, my love.' She pauses, her eyes looking down at the fire-grate.

'They all thought me quite the belle when I was younger. These locks,' she touches her brittle, white hair, 'were as black as a daw's wing. Granted, I wasn't your English maid, with golden tresses and apple cheeks, but you'd be surprised how many gentlemen prefer to choose what is not expected of them. Give a man sweet-meats for a month and all he wants is a beefsteak.

'I was fifteen, and I fell in love with the son of a merchant; a fine match, or so I thought. I trusted him.' She scratches her head, as though the solution to some conundrum still eludes her after all those years. 'Of course I learned a few months later that it is better not to promise at all, than to vow then never pay. Once he learned I was with child, he broke all ties with me. I was ruined, cast off. Set adrift by my lover and my family. The fact the child was stillborn appeased neither my father nor my mother. They said I must bear my own sin and that, having wrought my evil deed, I must suffer the shame of it.

'I took a rented room, paid for by selling a pearl ring; a gift from him. I found work as a needlewoman at a milliner's. I was soon to discover that the dark and sultry looks of a Jewess garner no favours; for the women reviled me, jealous of the attention I received from their menfolk, and the men – well, they saw me as a conquest to be won and nothing more.

'I was dismissed by the milliner and his wife after only a month, at the wife's insistence, and was forced to move from workplace to workplace, only for the same pretty kettle of fish to present itself every time. In the end, through lack of lucre, I was obliged to do what countless others like me have done since the beginning of time. I surrendered to the demands my looks excited and I took money for it. There, I've said it to you. I told you I'd talk plain, and so I have.

'Wouldn't think it to look at me now, would you? I set men's hearts a-flutter all right. Especially when they knew I was a woman with a promise. A promise I'd keep for them. I earned ten times the money the old milliner paid me, for half the effort and twice the fun. You blushing yet?'

I cannot deny the heat is rising, creeping up to my neck. But my face is unchanged and, with a coolness born out of a simple desire to hear her tale to the very end, I turn and in an encouraging tone say, 'Go on.'

'I finished up working at a certain . . . establishment,' she says, any raillery quite faded from her voice. 'A bordello, that's the word Mrs Birch liked to use. I think she thought it sounded continental. I'd only been under her protection for two days when a regular young blade saw my face and seemed smitten. He came every day, just for me, no one else. After a month, he paid Mrs Birch enough to secure my attentions for him alone; I didn't have to see none of the other clients. But it made all the other girls jealous, see. Bunch of feral cats they was towards me, and I hated them all except for one: Meg. Your Aunt Meg. Sore and sorry I was when she left. Of course, I was pleased that one of her regulars saw fit to make an honest woman of her, but still I was upset to see her leave. So, off she went with him, to be the wife of a gardener far away at a parsonage in Lincolnshire. "Be sure to come and see me if you're ever in need," she said on that last Saturday.

'So I lived at Mrs Birch's and met the needs of my young buck. Charles Foxton, he called himself. He brought me presents and he made me promises. But I sold his gifts and I told him so, for I needed the coins. I laughed at his promises and told him it suited me to use him just as much as it pleased him to use me. He said he admired me more for those aspects of my character than any other. Over time, he came to trust me. And he discharged his real name to me: Septimus Brock.'

At this point Mrs Cohen pauses, then starts again; but her voice is quieter now, and in this strained atmosphere I become frustrated at the endless regaling of her own long history. She'd known of Septimus's plan to have his older brother St John murdered, in order to inherit the family fortune. Yes, she says, she'd been a party to its planning, for at least a year before the scheme was carried out. She had given the names of ne'er-do-wells to Septimus; old clients of hers who would get the job done and keep their tongues quiet. What a deal she'd struck, oh yes, my love!

The promise of a shop of her own, no less. But the fatal key of fate turned against her, and she found herself with child again; abandoned once more. Septimus sent her no money and stopped visiting. With no money, no protection, and unable to work, of course Mrs Birch turned her out.

She mumbles a few more words but my mind is tiring of her. I shuffle in my seat and find myself distractedly reviewing the cracked teacups on her cluttered shelves. Whether she notices my inattention, or whether her story has reached this point regardless, I know not. It is her description of a house which is the hook for me.

'. . . on the edge of a Lincolnshire village, bound by a low wall. A chimney at each end, and a tree by the gate. I walked past the parson's house and on to the gardener's cottage just down the lane. I'm not certain if Meg was surprised or dismayed to see me on the doorstep, what with me being so clearly in the family way. But, true to her word, she and Jacob took me in and she helped me through the birthing. More than that, though. It was your dear father what saved me. Despite him being so busy with his own parishioners, he still found time for me. Ain't it funny? Me a Jewess with children out of wedlock and him a parson. But it weren't God what made me listen to him, and I'm certain it weren't just God what made him talk to me; no, it were the goodness of his heart. After a lifetime of false and empty promises that I heard the rabbi preach and my own father speak, it were your father's noble words what stuck with me; the confidence he placed in me made me confident about myself in return. He made no promises and he judged me not, only listened to me and carried all my pain away. And, in time, I told him about Septimus: not from the bitterness and scorn of it, but for the pity that Septimus would not own me as a wife and, moreover, would not own the son and daughter I had borne him.

'Well, I never thought anything would come of it. I was settled, taking washing in and being a wet nurse while ever I didn't run dry, and for as long as Meg and Jacob would have me. Then, out of nowhere, Septimus called for me. He must have acquired the address from Mrs Birch; at least, that's what I supposed. But I always did wonder if your dear father played a part in it. Anyway, Septimus sent a man with a carriage; right up to the street door it came. Off I bowled in it, with my two dear infants, his dear twins. And we was married, Hester. Proper and right, signed into the book and everything! I thought all would be well. I truly did.

'I'd only been at Septimus's house for four or five weeks when he started talking about schooling for the boy, Calder. He wanted him brought up as a gentleman, he said. I agreed, of course, for what mother would not want the very best for her child? But, I hadn't realised Septimus was intending to exclude me. The son of a woman like me would never truly be respected by his peers; Sep only married me to keep me sweet until he had Calder. And what better plan? Disguised as the Brock orphan, the boy would be accepted by society and the uncle would be lauded as a fine guardian. How Septimus must have laughed to know that the boy the world thought to be his nephew was in fact his own son. Yes, I finally got my shop, but I lost my son: what a price to pay. And what a fool I was! I shan't tell you how it came about, Hester, for it grieves me to this day. Septimus went too far the night he took my son from my arms. Under threat of my death and Rosina's, I never did meet the lad again. I've so many regrets and there's such effort in striving to forget.'

Mrs Cohen breaks down at this. She lets her weathered face drop into the palms of her upturned hands and she weeps. Not a discreet release of gentle tears, but a torrent. Then, as though time itself were calling an end to her confessional, the clock on her sideboard sounds the hour.

'I'm very grateful, Mrs Cohen,' I say, standing. 'Grateful that you have felt able to trust your story to my ear, and gratified to hear you speak so fondly of my father.' I turn towards the door, preparing to leave.

'But Hester!' she calls out. 'You can't go! I ain't told you yet. I can repay the kindness, I can! I know I'm a bad woman, always have been. I done it all to myself, I know that. I let them all take what they wanted. I knew what I was doing. But your father and mother, they was different. They was so kind to me. They never once judged me and they restored my self-respect. I have to repay that kindness before it's too late. You see I'm dying, Hester. I have a swelling, just here.' She points just below her left armpit. 'It'll do for me. And soon, so it will.'

I take her elbow and lower her back into her chair. There is contrition in her eyes and I find myself beginning to forgive her, recalling a phrase my father once used: he who with repentance is not satisfied, is not of Heaven nor Earth.

'I'm sure you take comfort from having Rosina at your side,' I say, grasping at words of solace.

'Ahh, my Rosina,' she says, her eyes misting. 'She was treated cruelly by Septimus. He cast us both out of his life the night he took my son from me. True, he did set me up with a shop. But he didn't send money as regular as he promised. And he never troubled himself to visit Rosina, never saw her again.

'Eventually, we was forced to move to a different pitch, and then on again, till we took the shop in Thieving Lane. On the day we moved in, a funeral cortege went past; Rosina was only five or six years old. The widow was in black, with a veil covering her face. Rosina asked me what it was all about and I told her, "Why, the woman has lost someone dear to her heart and she's wearing the veil to show respect, and to ease her suffering." Rosina did no more than find an old offcut and cover her own sweet face.

I told her it weren't necessary, that we didn't know the man or his wife. But she said, in her piping voice, that it was the one she'd lost when she was a babe. Well, I was struck dumb. I'd never spoken a word of Calder, no one ever had. As you know, Hester, she never more took that veil away from her face.

'They were hard years, Hester. Time passing makes a woman think back on her life, her choices, the people she has met. I kept coming back to your parents, them letting me lodge with Jacob and Meg, and showing me such kindness. So, when I heard from Meg that they'd gone and died and that you was an orphan, well, it grieved me. I encouraged Meg to take you in. I'd send her shillings every once in a while if I could spare it, see, to help pay for your keep.

'And I always made it my business, Hester, to find out what was happening with the Brocks. You'd be surprised how loose a servant's tongue can be when guineas and gin is on offer. Over the years, I've greased the palms of a fair few maids and footmen at the villa and Waterford. So when I learned you'd been taken in under Septimus's roof, I wrote you a note, tried to warn you. I sent it with a young stable boy, but he said he couldn't be sure you'd got it before you left. Imagine my shock when you turned up right outside my shop, like a light among shadows. It was like a talisman returning to me; evidence of the goodness that had once touched me. I could see your father's eyes in yours and your mother's smile on your lips. Oh, how I ramble on. It's the nearness of death, my love. It makes a woman want to talk about things in the tiniest of details; but there ain't the time to do it, that's the rub!

'I have a gift for you, Hester,' she says, but she doesn't produce a box with ribbons around it or indeed an object of any sort. She simply takes my hands in hers. 'I've watched you, these past few years, Hester. I've taken the trouble to keep my eye on you. I've seen how you grieve for her, how your heart's broke up about it. The wound might close, but the scar don't ever heal. Am I right?'

'Yes,' I whisper. 'Yes, I cared for Rebekah so very deeply.' At that, tears well once again in my eyes, fresh and full at the chance to speak my love for Rebekah to another.

'I can well mark it, for I have felt it just as keenly. It's a dark weed what turns inside and twists about you, tightening every day. You can scarce endure to draw breath, so painful the world has become without them. You see, Hester, I've felt it too. That night, three years since, I heard what had served out at Morton's house. So I went to the morgue, paid my shilling and looked upon the dear girl's face. It was a face I knew; and why should I not? With those beautiful dark tresses, and that fair face that only a Brock could carry. It was my own Rosina.'

At this, Mrs Cohen's face contorts and a series of sobs are released from her narrow lips.

'No, Mrs Cohen,' I cry. 'It was not. I was there. It was Rebekah.'

'Dear child. Does not a mother know her own daughter? It was only I what ever saw Rosina's face. To all others, she was just the girl in the veil. It wasn't until you came to my shop with Miss Rebekah Brock that even I realised the likeness; that same indefinable look that the Brocks all carry. Of course, differences there were though, not least the little birthmark beneath where they'd scratched her dear face. I knew in an instant it was my Rosina lying there on that cold slab, stifled by those animals. She'd started to wander at night, see. The day after you and Rebekah came to our shop; yes, that was when her wandering began.'

'I think I saw her in the shadows one night, Mrs Cohen. I thought it was a figment of my imagination.'

'It might well have been her. Perhaps it was looking upon Rebekah's face what made her start doing it, noticing the likeness to her own. Perhaps she thought Rebekah was the one she'd lost or, if not, might lead her to the answers she craved. Jack Morton must have seen her, must have thought her such a soft target—'

'But Mrs Cohen,' I protest. 'Is what you're saying true?' As I speak, I search my mind for images and memories. Yes, the moonlight was sparse, the lanterns dim; but could my tortured mind have tricked me?

All the certainties of before become doubts and the truth begins to appear. A fresh flood of tears comes, but this time takes the edge off my sorrow. And the exquisite thread which once bound Rebekah and I together, but has grown slack by dint of grief, at once grows taut again.

'But . . . where . . .' I stutter.

'Where is Rebekah?' Mrs Cohen says. 'Well, that was the mystery of it all. Perhaps I should have spoken up. Should have told the world they was burying my girl and not Rebekah Brock. But why shouldn't my Rosina have a velvet-lined casket and a marble vault in which to lie in peace for eternity? After all, she was a Brock, however much Septimus denied it. It served his purposes too. Made the world stop looking for Rebekah. Of course, on the streets, some folks had questions; but no one could produce evidence to gainsay me. No one knew her whereabouts. Not any of the narks and the snouts what know all the business of London and beyond. Not one of them could say where she was. Then three months ago, a seafaring man what I'd kept company with many years since came visiting. He knew I'd had my dealings with the Brocks and he came to tell me old Septimus had died, in Italy, a town called Bologna; the place where he'd run to as soon as he'd got wind of the Morton and Corby affair. My friend thought it might be worth my while to go there, plead my case to the lawyers before his last remaining assets was bequeathed away. But it weren't money I was after. I just wanted the peace of knowing for certain he was finally dead. The comfort of seeing his tombstone.

'So I booked my passage to the continent. Paid my way from the proceeds of the shop sale. For what else was I to spend it on? Childless widows soon for the grave have no need for gold, Hester, that's for sure and certain. Anyway, I asked about a bit, when I was there, you know, among the English maids what go with their mistresses. There was nothing at first, then a girl from Bethnal what had worked her way up and was with a family as nursemaid, told me of a woman she'd heard about. There was a convent near a town called Ferrara. She called it Saint Anthony's, but said the locals referred to it as Sant'Antonio's, or something like that. She said she'd overheard her mistress talking to another lady about an English woman, who'd gone to live with the nuns. The woman would be about thirty years of age, they said; educated, but quite austere. They thought she might have been placed there by her uncle. That's all the girl knew.

'So I wrote to her, Hester: the woman in the convent. I took a chance and addressed it to Rebekah Brock.'

'What did she say? Is it Rebekah?'

'She didn't reply, my love. Nothing came back. So, I sent another note saying how you was still grieving over the loss of her. Whatever she'd been told was a lie, I wrote.'

'And?'

'And she agreed to see me. Oh, Hester. It shook me up, I can tell you, when I first saw her. Paler than marble she was. But it weren't no pedlar's trumpery; there's no mistaking it. Rebekah Brock is alive. It's a pearl of truth, I swear. Calder must not have been able to bring himself to have her killed. Perhaps there was one last grain of mercy in my lad after all.'

All at once, I am living in a better world, in the brightness of an endless day, where sorrows do not exist, as though an aching sore has been healed.

'She took a time to be convinced, though. Septimus and Calder had used Frederick Blister to go after her, see. He used brute force to subdue her, knocked her about most cruelly. Said she awoke on board ship. Then Septimus worked on her mind for weeks and weeks, convincing her it was you what those beasts killed. Like you she must have been quite undone by the grief of it all, and she submitted to their will and went quietly into the convent.'

'But what then? Where is she now? Is she—'

'Now then, dear child. Miss Brock needs time to recover.'

'She's ill? How ill?'

'I suppose same as you; the heart controls a woman's consti-tution. Miss Brock didn't even know her uncle had died. She still feared his wrath, just like the rest of us what knows the things he's capable of doing. But in spite of her health, she was determined to take the voyage. Her ship's due to berth tomorrow.'

'What did she say about me? Am I to meet her?'

'Well, you see, I wasn't sure where you'd be. I knew you had a place but wasn't sure of the address, hadn't seen you about town since I uncovered it all.'

'I must go to Waterford then. She'll surely go there first?'

'Not so, Hester. Septimus sold Waterford more than a twelve-month since, to service his gambling debts on the continent.'

'Then where?'

'Well, Rebekah was quite particular on that point. She said she'd go to the site where it all began, where your destinies collided. She wished she could have answered your prayers, she said. She'll be there at eight o'clock, on the morning of 12 May: at Smithfield market; the place of your accident with Calder.'

I close my eyes and steer my mind back through time. Back and back I go, from Arlington Street, to Waterford, to the villa, until there I am back at Smithfield. There I stood in the eventide of the day, the gas-lamps cloaked in choking mist, the costermongers packing away their wares.

As though I am viewing my life from the pages of a picture book, I watch, page by page, as I turn my head to the right and study my surroundings. In the distance, a team of horses clatters over the cobbles, a carriage swaying behind. Just as before, I see the image through the mist of my own breath. Rooted and immobile, I wait for the impact. That was the very beginning, I'm certain. I hadn't met Rebekah, but my need for her was so strong, I believe God answered my prayers at that place and at that time, and delivered me to her. Perhaps at that moment, sitting in the library at Waterford, the sconces just lit and the fire throwing light across the bookshelves, she sensed my plea; heard my prayer.

'She's right; it all started on that day at Smithfield, Mrs Cohen,' I say. 'But what if something happens to me before I get there? What if her ship is delayed and we miss each other? There's so much I need to tell her.'

'Steady now, Hester. She'll be there. Nothing will happen between now and tomorrow. But if it helps, then why not write a letter to her!'

'Yes. I could write to Lady Appleton with the wonderful news and enclose a letter for Rebekah.'

'Well? What are you waiting for?'

At that, Mrs Cohen rummages in a drawer and provides me with ink, pen and paper. She clears space on a table and invites me to draw a chair up to it and light a candle. She looks tired now, and takes up her seat with a heavy sigh. She closes her eyes and somehow she is different. Where before, she was always on the alert, she now seems disburdened and free, as though the sins she has carried have now been laid down, leaving the peace of contrition soft on her features. I take up the pen and begin to write.

Miss Rebekah Brock   11th May 1835

c/o Lady Appleton

Fenbridge Manor

Louth

Lincolnshire

My Dearest Rebekah,

My fingers tremble as I write your name and tears fall fast,
obscuring the page before me. In the years of our separation, I have
wished for this moment with such yearning that it has become my
only prayer. Without you, I have existed as though a part of me were
living outside time itself. I sleep ill at ease and force myself to wake
before the nightmares come.

As time has passed, so the images in my mind have become
foggier; the more I focus on them, the more insubstantial they
become. All except the image of your face, which grows clearer and
more precious to me as each second passes. And I still hear your
voice to this day, as melodious as ever it was. Not with my ears, but
in the bruised chambers of my heart: a soft, low whisper beneath my
ribs.

I am sitting in Mrs Cohen's parlour, as it is she who has brought
me the glorious news of your homecoming. I cannot help but write
freely; if some misfortune should befall me before we meet again, I
cannot risk you not knowing the words held inside my heart for so
long; words which so often dammed upon my lips.

First, I must ask your forgiveness for a treacherous act I once
perpetrated against you. For it was I who took your diary. And the
truth is, presented with the same circumstances, I would do it again,
albeit for different motives. To read your private thoughts and to
begin to know you better than any other, has been the greatest
privilege the mortal world did ever show me.

So, pray forgive me for my deceit, but you must also forgive me for falling in love with a blazing comet that illumines my world, with a light that can never be extinguished.

You are as dear to me now as any time before, even more so. Each morning as I wake and each night as I lay my head on the pillow, it is your face, only yours, that I fasten upon my fancy, and to learn you are alive; well, it is a joy that outweighs the misery of all that has gone before, and in this present moment, I have never felt so happy.

My pleasure is so great, it is an agony, a wonderful agony. Dearest Rebekah, you are my saviour; you are my church. I loved you from the very beginning and time has neither blunted nor trimmed it. And when we meet again, I will give you all my love, for I have saved it only for you.

So, as I draw this letter to a close, the candle burning low and Mrs Cohen asleep in her chair before the embers of the fire, know that my love shines steady for you and that I will return to Smithfield at first light. If an incident arises to delay our meeting, I shall return to the market each day until at last we are reunited. I will await the arrival of my fate, just as I did four years ago. With ill memories now stifled, I shall watch for your carriage door to open, and inside I shall see Hope and Love, and you will look out and see Love and Hope.

Ever yours,
Hester White

I stay with Mrs Cohen until early evening and, after Rebekah's letter has been sent to Lady Appleton, return to my lodging rooms. I stand at my window and watch night slip over the rooftops till all the houses are blotted. I try to sleep but the night passes slowly and I cannot settle; I endlessly beguile myself with thoughts of what tomorrow might bring.

At last, sleep draws over me and, when I wake, it is to the trembles and sighs of a fine spring morning. I wash and dress as quick as ever I have and, by the time I pull up the blind, a tender stream of sunlight has expanded over the horizon, brimming the day with yellow.

I set my steps towards Smithfield, the sun now fully risen, bright and clear in the honest blue air above me. The streets are thin of townsfolk at this hour of the day, but as I near the market I pass a girl carrying a milk pail, and she gives me good morning. I wonder if she can see beyond my eyes, into the centre of my being. I wonder if she can sense the amity, love and excitement that I harbour in the chambers of my heart.

Finally, I reach the spot: the scene of my collision with Calder's carriage. I am early, but there is nowhere else I would rather be. I simply stand and wait as the sun drinks up the silver cloud of early morning mist that shifts noiselessly about me.

Then, as the bells chime eight, I feel the rumble of carriage wheels through the soles of my feet and the clattering of hooves. A coach arrives and the driver pulls rein a few feet from me. Rebekah is out of the carriage doors in an instant, and for a heartbeat I embrace her image with my eyes; her beauty grown richer for the passing of time. Then she runs to me. My heart stops a moment as she nears me, and I call out to her; the sweetness of her name on my lips.

There is a flash of blue velvet and then her arms are about me. I set mine about her and pull her closer to me. Tears of joy swell my eyes and I weep with the bliss of it. There we stand, robed in folds of sunlight, heady with the fragrance of gillyflower and I know, at last, that I am home.

EPILOGUE

15th August 1835

It has been a full three years since I have kept a journal and I believe it will be cathartic to discharge my thoughts with pen and ink.

Hester and I awoke early this morning, just as dawn was breaking with its cordial light. So kind of Great-Aunt Eleanor to rent the old dowager house to us; the most comfortable and snug dwelling we could ever have wished for. The residual monies from the villa and Calder's rooms should give us a comfortable living for some time to come.

This morning we walked past the far meadow and on to the river beyond. It was one of those perfect summer days when the sky is pale blue and the sun simply falls through the air. The meadow was foaming with flowers, all in full blow and all in their finest glory. We strolled past hedgerows pink with foxgloves, the grass beneath our feet gilt with the summer sun. The air throbbed with birdcalls. We paused and watched the swallows looping their dance over wheat that gently rocked, and tassels of barley that shimmered on their stalks.

The sun was high, no remembrance of dawn, no thought of dusk yet to come. And that is exactly how Hester and I live our lives. Through a living death we waded and are now more alive than we've ever been. Now we are together, it makes amends for all our sorrowful yesterdays. With our time of darkness put out of mind, we find ourselves simply living in the present; our only hope for tomorrow is to dream of looks as yet uncast, and of conversations as yet unspoken.

The sun has now set and it is growing late. We are in the parlour, seated close together, with a warm breeze drifting through the open window. As I write in this journal Hester rests her head on my shoulder, her arms encircling my waist, and I invite her to read as my pen scratches its path along the page. It is not lost on either of us that in a time long ago, a journal such as this served to whisper hidden feelings and draw two souls together, guide us both to this happy moment. And the precious letter Hester wrote to me three months since is tucked carefully between the pages of this diary, its edges a little frayed and its creases soft with the repetition of reading. Hester now looks up at me, with a smile and a blush; for she knows at last I am about to record my thoughts on her.

I have no need to delineate her virtues, because I know them instinctively. I cannot write the intricacies of her mind or the beauty of her eyes; but I can love them. Of late I have reduced the complexity of my life, pared it down to its simplest factors: Hester is alive and I love her in a way that can never be diminished by time or discovery. I love her purely, honestly, and not for reason, but for the sake of love itself, just as she loves me.

So, a new life has come in the old one's stead and not a single day passes when I don't rejoice in my gladness at Hester's presence. Our time apart has served to edify our constancy and we will pass our life's remainder content in the liberality of our love; a burning flame of the purest light. As a prism reveals the secret of a sunbeam, so our love will light the path of future days.

Rebekah Brock

AUTHOR'S NOTE

While *The Wicked Cometh* is a work of fiction, some of the characters, places and events are inspired by real historical figures, locations and incidents. I am greatly indebted to Sarah Wise for her meticulously researched and brilliantly presented books: *The Italian Boy: Murder and Grave-Robbery in 1830s London* (2004) and *The Blackest Streets: The Life and Death of a Victorian Slum* (2009).

There are many sources from which I have drawn inspiration for this story and some of the other books that have helped me along the way include: *A History of Everyday Things in England 1733-1851*, by Marjorie and CHB Quennell (1945), *English Fashion*, by Alison Settle (1948), and my careworn and cherished copies of the periodicals: *Cassell's Household Guide* and *Virtue's Household Physician*.

ACKNOWLEDGEMENTS

For their unstinting patience, love and support; profound thanks to my partner, Shirl, and my daughter, Tiff.

I am truly grateful to my editor, the inspirational Melissa Cox, for her astute editorial advice, sharp eye and even sharper sense of humour.

Deepest gratitude to my wonderful agent, Laura Macdougall, for her unfailing wisdom, support and encouragement.

Special thanks to Abby Parsons, Veronique Norton, Will Speed, Aimee Oliver, Fleur Clarke, Anna Alexander, Nathaniel Alcaraz-Stapleton and everybody at Hodder & Stoughton who has worked on 'Team Wicked'; it feels great to be part of such a strong unit.

Finally, generous and heartfelt thanks to Janet Carlin, Mike Underhill, Caroline Lee, Brian Lee, Graham and Ann Richards and the many others whose benevolence and enthusiasm has enabled me to reach this point.

A NOTE ON THE TYPE

The text of this book is set in Fournier MT, a typeface designed by Monotype in 1924 based on types cut by Pierre Simon Fournier circa 1742, and called 'St Augustin Ordinaire' in Fournier's *Manuel Typographique*. These types were some of the most influential designs of the eighteenth century, being among the earliest of the transitional style of typeface. Transitional type is so-called because of its intermediate position between old-style and modern.

The distinguishing features of transitional typefaces include vertical stress and slightly higher contrast than old-style typefaces, combined with horizontal serifs. Some of the most influential examples are Pierre Simon Fournier's work circa 1750, and John Baskerville's work from 1757 onwards.

The chapter headings etc. are set in 1785 GLC Baskerville – a distressed version of Baskerville.